FIGHTING CONVICTION

Conviction Series Book Two

GREER RIVERS

Cover Design: Cover Me Darling

Editing and Proofreading: My Brother's Editor

ASIN: B08TQQX3Z2 / ISBN: 9798510224498

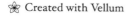 Created with Vellum

CONTENTS

A NOTE FROM THE AUTHOR

Fighting Conviction is a best friend's sister, age gap romantic suspense with legal, military, and mature themes. It is the second in the Conviction series of interconnected standalones, all of which contribute to an overarching plot. The series is best enjoyed in order, but not required. Don't worry, there's no cliffhanger for the couple in their respective story. HEA guaranteed.

This series takes place in Ashland County, a small, fictional, southern county somewhere in the mountains of the Carolinas. Ashland County is full of steam and legal intrigue, so some characters may appear in other stories written in the same universe.

The Conviction series should only be read by mature readers (18+) and contains sexually explicit scenes, along with descriptions of human trafficking, drugs, strong language, suicide, and physical and sexual violence.

Reader discretion is advised.

For information on human trafficking, go to humantraffickinghotline.org.

If you or a loved one needs help, there is hope. Call the National Suicide Prevention Lifeline: 800-273-8255, or go to suicidepreventionlifeline.org and save a life, maybe even your own.

Never, ever forget: You are loved. You are wanted. You matter.

For those who are fighting their minds
just to stay alive.
It's worth it.

PROLOGUE

One year ago

"Go, go, go."

Hawk's command echoed against the shipping containers, shattering the silence.

Devil broke the line and emerged from their hiding spot. A dark figure appeared at his three o'clock. All it took was one shot from his Glock. A thump of a body hitting the ground, followed by a moment of silence, confirmed the threat was eliminated. The dead don't scream.

A sudden onslaught of gunshots drummed a staccato beat against Devil's senses. Cries of pain called to the medic in him, but he forced himself to concentrate on one woman's safety. Adrenaline twisted his chest but steadied his aim as he picked off the enemy, one by one. Blood rushed in his ears, muffling all distractions from his objective.

Devil reached the van, giving a wide berth to the first casualty of the night. A man sprawled out in the dim light, shot down by Jaybird's bullet. Judging from the odd angle of the man's legs and the dark stain creeping across the concrete, he wasn't getting up.

Nora, the woman with purple hair who'd made the shot

possible, was pushing herself up onto the bumper of the van, attempting to get back in its open doors. She'd flung herself out to attack one of her captors, but the vehicle was the only safe haven among the chaos.

Gun ready to fire, Devil defended them as they climbed inside, turning halfway to scoop her up with his free hand. Still aiming while he hefted her into the van, he grunted from the effort of doing both at once. She was a tiny thing, but dead weight in the heat of battle only made more dead weight.

When Nora was tucked inside, he chanced taking his eye off the enemy and crawled in behind her, pushing body-sized duffel bags aside so he could shut the van doors.

Slamming the doors closed muffled the gunshots outside, but the van's thin metal walls only provided a false sense of security. He widened his eyes to see in the dark and realized how many heavyweight canvas bags there were. How many *victims* there were. The panic he'd always held at bay during a mission wrapped cold fingers around his heart.

"Where is she?" His hands skittered over zippers, afraid to open one and find something he couldn't unsee. Or worse. Someone he couldn't help.

"Here," Nora rasped. Her pale hand patted the lump next to her and Devil's heart stalled. Nora's head lolled to the side as she closed her eyes, her lethargy and labored breathing all signs of the drugs those bastards poisoned them with.

Devil latched on to the bag she'd indicated and unzipped, revealing blonde hair in the dark. He grabbed his flashlight from his tactical belt and shined it above the occupant's head to avoid beaming it straight at the woman inside.

Bleary caramel eyes fluttered open in the light. He couldn't resist brushing his fingertips against her warm cheek.

Even though she'd been kidnapped—and God-knows-what-else—a soft smile spread on her face and the stone barrier he'd erected years ago cracked. Tightness formed around his mouth and he felt the foreign sensation of his lips widening into a smile of his own.

"You're safe, Ellie. I'm with your brother. We're gonna get you out of here."

Ellie blinked and a tear escaped, crumbling his defenses further.

"You found me." Her soft whisper battered into his soul. The words splintered fissures in the barricades surrounding it.

Surrendering to his emotions, he bent to brush his lips over her forehead and smoothed her tangled hair away from her face.

"That's right," he answered.

Silky golden tendrils surrounded her, forming a halo. The air he sucked in couldn't make up for the breath she'd taken away. Devil rested his forehead on hers and he closed his eyes reverently, knowing he only had a moment before he had to aid his men outside.

"I found you, angel."

CHAPTER ONE

Present day

We've got another survivor. Get here when you can.

Ellie tucked her phone into a backpack side pocket and glanced around the half-empty classroom. Everyone was facing forward, listening to their professor drone on, so she slid her Russian textbook off the desk before stuffing it into her bag.

"What're you doin'?" Virginia hissed, making her platinum curls shake around her furrowed brow.

Ellie caught herself before she rolled her eyes. Barely. On move-in day, Ellie had been gifted a life-sized Barbie, Platinum Busybody Roommate edition. Ever since, Virginia Lowell had been butting her nose into Ellie's business. For some reason the peppy socialite never realized Ellie had neither the time, energy, nor desire to become friends.

"Gotta go to work," Ellie whispered before checking to make sure she'd gathered everything.

Satisfied, she silently stood and crept up the steps to the exit. Shuffling movements behind her and the feeling she was being watched made her turn around. All eyes were fixed on her. Turns out, every student was paying as much attention to the Russian 102 lecture as usual. Meaning *nyet* at all.

Language credits were a requirement at Ashland State University, but because it was a small, local college, the other more popular language options filled within the first hour registration was open. Ellie was probably the only student who'd voluntarily signed up for the dang class.

Despite the fact Ellie was the most interesting thing in the room, Professor Novikov droned on about determining Russian grammatical gender. Why a bed is considered "female" wasn't ever something she wanted to analyze too deeply. Her prior interaction with Russians made her shudder to imagine that particular word's origins.

She turned back around and continued her trek up the stairs until she heard a throat clear.

"Miss Stone, do you have somewhere else you'd rather be?"

As usual, the harsh consonants grated on Ellie's nerves. At least hearing the language didn't give her panic attacks anymore.

She slowly pivoted, her hand still on her backpack strap. While studying Russian as a form of immersion therapy eventually took, anxiety still flooded through her under the heat of Professor Novikov's scowl.

Ellie tried to ignore the stress sweat already prickling at her forehead and avoided the blatant stares from her fellow classmates. The classroom had stadium seating, and with Ellie at the top of the room, inches away from the exit, Professor Novikov had the ability to glare up while simultaneously looking down on her.

"Erm... no, ma'am," Ellie began in English. While the class had taught her how to handle certain triggers, she still hadn't learned the language well enough to comfortably speak it, especially not on the fly or in front of an audience. "I-I have to go. I have a family emer—"

"—Emergency," Professor Novikov interrupted in English, also evidently lacking confidence in Ellie's grasp of Russian. "Yes, yes, I know, Miss Stone. You have explained this to me before, but I have to point out this is the fourth family 'emergency' in as many weeks." Professor Novikov peered over her rectangular glasses and frowned.

Ellie sagged in relief. Good. Professor Novikov hadn't noticed the many other times she'd snuck out, even though Ellie had never suffered through a class in its entirety. She must've gotten lax after the first few times, and the woman had finally caught on.

"The word 'emergency' is beginning to lose its meaning where your excuses are concerned, but putting that fact aside, this is a college lecture. You can't keep interrupting those of your peers who are interested in learning. I think your classmates and I need some sort of explanation."

"Um... I-I'm sorry, I don't have time to explain. I really gotta go." Ellie hedged her way toward the door as she spoke, but never let her eyes stray from the older woman pursing her lips and tapping her foot at the front of the tiered classroom. As Ellie's heel breached the exit threshold, Professor Novikov sighed and threw up her hands.

"Alright, but when midterms come, don't blame the mirror for your face, Miss Stone. It will not be my fault if you fail. Then again, maybe you are more punctual than I give you credit for. Maybe you are planning ahead to make up your absences in this course next semester."

Heat rose from Ellie's chest into her cheeks and she tried not to notice the depth of the silence around her as humiliation weighed her down. She nodded but Professor Novikov had already turned her attention back to her lecture. Ellie turned on her heel to leave and power walked, zigzagging around students moseying through the halls.

Bursting through the double doors, she was slapped in the face by unseasonably warm winter air, making her skin, already hot with embarrassment, feel cool in comparison.

She hopped down the stone steps of the Humanities Building two at a time and jogged to unlock her bike from the rack. When her foot met the pedal, Ellie tightened her grip on the handlebars and cycled hard to relieve her frustration. She tried to forget the guilt pricking at her conscience for disappointing Professor Novikov, and focused on riding through the campus pathways to get onto the street.

Why she cared so much, she didn't know. The few classes she actually gave a flip about were for her psychology major. And nothing else was a higher priority than her job. But if Professor Novikov had finally noticed that Ellie had been leaving early, then her other professors were likely noticing as well. *That* was definitely not good.

It would be such a hassle if she was placed on academic probation for skipping class. Not to mention the fact her brother, Jason, would rip her a new one if she failed out of college in her first year. She'd survived her first semester. Second semester wasn't looking as good, grade-wise at least.

Shaking her head to get free of the negativity, Ellie brought her concentration back to her destination. It wouldn't do anyone any good if she walked into work tense and aggravated. The least she could do was have a level head and sympathetic heart. Lord knows the survivor had suffered through a nightmare way more traumatic than a freaking classroom scolding.

It was almost a shame her teachers couldn't know about her job. If they did, maybe they would understand how hard it is to be concerned about conjugating verbs or memorizing music history in a required elective course when there were much bigger problems in the world.

How could she care about anything else aside from the nation's 20,000 daily domestic violence hotline callers? Or the 1.2 million children who were predicted to be trafficked in the next year, joining the six million who were already suffering? Or the ten million men and women who will endure intimate partner violence?

The numbers were staggering and some days she felt crushed by the weight of responsibility for the missing and broken people in the world. It was only eleven months ago Ellie had been one of them.

At her last turn, a white Corolla passed her. Ellie kept her eyes on the road while confirming the tag with her periphery: ERT 675. Raised spoiler on the back. Ellie couldn't see it from the corner of her eye, but she'd bet a week's worth of iced Frappuccinos the driver's side had a medium-sized dent in it.

She sped up and her heart began to race, but it had nothing to do with her bike ride. The past few days, Ellie had hoped she'd imagined seeing the car around town. But despite the fact she'd changed up her bike route and her schedule was never the same, she'd still noticed it every day on her way to work.

Maybe she was losing it. In this small college town, if the Corolla driver was also a student at ASU, of course she'd see it everywhere.

Ellie groaned at the thought of having to tell her brother. Jason had calmed down with the seen-but-not-heard bodyguard crap in the past few weeks and Ellie had thrived with the breathing room. It was probably nothing but her paranoia, but telling him was part of the deal she'd cut for her freedom.

For almost a year, he'd insisted on one member from the BlackStone Security team watching her at all hours. It was freaking creepy. When she'd accomplished a whole semester of college and eleven extremely uneventful months while a watchdog hid in the shadows, she'd put her foot down. She'd even enlisted Jason's fiancée, Jules, to help convince him to let her live a normal life without a babysitter, and that was only after Ellie had promised to inform him any time she felt nervous.

A pale brick building on the edge of the block came into view and the familiar plain black lettering of Sasha's Thrift and Save Store sign set her at ease. She hoped other people who came to the store felt the same, since it was a front for Sasha Saves, a nonprofit crisis center for survivors of abuse and human trafficking.

Ellie and the other founders quickly discovered that some

survivors who entered the building were stalked and monitored by their abusers. That's why Sasha Saves was a secret to *everyone* until it was needed. Word of the clinic was passed on from survivor to survivor, through their hotline, or from vaguely worded flyers they'd strategically posted in local bar bathrooms, and baby and intimate aisles of stores.

Hidden in plain sight.

And by turning the entrance to the clinic into a storefront, it prevented abusers from finding out their victims were getting help. Victims would call the survivor hotline, be given the address, and be instructed to say they were going to the store. Jason's private security firm even installed strong safety measures to further protect survivors, helping them seek relief and escape without getting damned for being their own hero.

Ellie hopped her bike up the sidewalk and skidded to a halt in front of the looping bike rack. Her fine, sun-bleached blonde hair tickled her cheek in the wind and she tossed her ponytail back over her shoulder as she locked her bike up to the metal. She glanced around, not surprised to find the Corolla had disappeared.

Yep. Losing it.

Still, it was better to be safe than sorry. Ellie pulled her phone from her backpack side pocket and sent off a quick text to Jason. He was probably getting as sick of her anxiety as she was.

Jason: I'll get Snake on it. Be safe. Stay near Devil. Text me if anything changes.

Ellie rolled her eyes. Jason was always trying to persuade her to agree to bodyguards again, but she was ready to move on. Sure, she might have to deal with her lingering PTSD, but she'd never shake her jitters until she started to live life like a normal college student.

After reading Jason's text, Ellie turned back to the nondescript, pale building. She rolled her shoulders back to gear up for what she was about to walk into. How bad would it be this time?

Would she be able to help save this one? Would this one even want to be saved?

Ellie closed her eyes and lifted her face to the sun. The heat from its rays warmed her skin and a cool breeze soothed her nerves. A slow, deep inhale of the fresh air calmed her, thanks to the faint scent of the lavender she'd planted in the store window boxes. She whispered into the wind, knowing without a doubt her best friend was listening somewhere up there.

"It's all for you, Sash. All for you."

CHAPTER TWO

Ellie shouldered open the heavy-duty metal clinic door. Wails coming from the medical room immediately bombarded her senses. She fought the panicked instinct to flee and instead ran toward the screeching.

The sight of the handsome, brooding redhead in a black T-shirt and jeans made her knees wobbly with relief. Whatever she'd barged in on was under control if Dev was there.

Ellie pressed a hand to her heart and willed it to slow as Dev methodically dabbed a patient's cheek with gauze.

The woman looked exhausted, slumped over crosswise on the examination table with an ice pack against the other cheek. She seemed half awake, despite having a little girl in a green dress clutching her legs and screaming her lungs out.

Dev glanced up from his ministrations before gathering supplies from the counter. Raising his voice over the girl's bawling, he introduced his patient. "This is Naomi." He paused and indicated the child with a slight wave of his hand. "And this is Thea. Can you get her? I think she's upset."

Ellie held back a snort and relaxed at Dev's unemotional delivery. It always set her at ease despite the circumstances. If he was freaking out then she'd have broken down right along with the child.

"Hi, Naomi." Ellie lifted her hand in greeting and gestured to Thea. "Can I?" Ellie waited for the frazzled woman to give permission before approaching.

This was always a sensitive situation. Women who'd just escaped an abusive situation were still on high alert and extremely protective of their children, more so than usual. Putting the children first, even as their own wounds were being tended to, was their main priority. It was likely what drove them to the clinic in the first place.

At Naomi's nod, Ellie tossed her backpack to the side of the room. She returned and bent low to gently peel Thea away from her mother.

"Shh, shh, shh... Thea? That's your name, right? Thea... Can you look at me?"

Thea screeched louder and clung to Naomi's jeans until Ellie kneeled to the ground and rubbed the girl's back in small circles.

"Thee-aahh... what a pretty name you've got there." After a few more off-key notes, Thea's cries lowered to whimpers. She stopped climbing the examination table and slid to the floor before sagging against her mother's legs. "There ya go. Do you want to turn around and say 'hi' to me? My name's Ellie."

She finally turned and Ellie sucked in a breath at the girl's round face and the dimple in one of her cheeks. Her heart flipped in her stomach, as if she was falling into the dark pools of the girl's eyes.

"Found you, Sasha!" Ellie whispered as she climbed farther up the gnarled tree. "You always hide up here."

High in the branches, Sasha giggled before slapping a hand over her mouth to silence herself. "That's because no one but you ever finds me."

To give Ellie room to join her hiding spot, Sasha scooted across the treehouse planks. They settled in to wait for the other seekers in their manhunt. She and Sasha always won the game. No one ever bothered to look up.

Ellie pressed her closed mouth against her knee, still wanting to be quiet. Just in case. Sasha did the same and grinned at her. Ellie smiled back. They were safe.

"Ellie!"

Something shook her out of her flashback and Ellie blinked back into the present. She'd fallen on her butt with her hands bracing her. Dev kneeled beside her with a ginger grip on her shoulder while his brow furrowed in concern.

"You're okay, angel. You are safe. You are in control. You are here, in this moment. You are at the Sasha Saves clinic."

"I am safe," Ellie mumbled. "I am in control. I am here, in this moment." The robotic words left her lips automatically, as if each phrase were a button activating the next. Almost a year of therapy and the meditation was reflexive. It should've been. She'd sure as heck done it enough times.

"That's right, and where is here, Ellie?"

"Sasha Saves clinic."

The little girl with wild red curls and hazel green eyes watched her, curious underneath her long, spiky wet lashes. Except for the dimple in her left cheek, Thea actually looked *nothing* like her childhood friend.

Ellie swallowed back the reality that her flashbacks came without rhyme or reason. Whatever had sparked this one, she had no idea. All she knew was she had to bury that crap deep and get herself under control.

"What's wrong with her, Mommy?" Thea whispered loudly. Her red curls bounced against her shoulder as she tilted her head to the side. Ellie didn't like being the center of attention, but at least the girl's tears had stopped.

"Nothing, she's fine," Dev answered for her, his thumb smoothing small circles over the T-shirt sleeve on her shoulder.

Thea's mother frowned from behind the ice pack on her cheek. Ellie felt heat rise in her chest and brushed imaginary dirt from her hands.

"Sorry." Ellie cleared her throat. "I..."

"Got caught up in a memory." Dev's soft monotone was jarring in the quiet room. Ellie lifted her gaze to his sad smile and her heart stuttered as he squeezed her shoulder one final time.

"God, he's pretty."

She'd thought the words, but they giggled across her mind in Sasha's voice. Ellie nodded to both Sasha and Dev, hoping no one *in* the room could tell she was losing it. Her therapist explained that Ellie talking to herself in Sasha's voice was a natural, healthy way to understand her grief. It would go away eventually when she no longer needed the coping mechanism.

"Copin' mechanism, my ass."

"Exactly." Ellie blew out a breath and pasted on a smile. "Thanks Dev, uh, Thea do you wanna go check out our toys—"

"No! I wanna stay with my mommy."

"It's alright. They're over here in this corner. See?" Ellie waved Dev's hand away as she gathered herself up from the floor. "And look, you can watch a show on this cool bean bag." Ellie took Thea by the hand again and led her to the toy box in the corner, along with the beanbag and tablet. "You can still see your mommy, but now you don't have to hear the grownups talk about boring stuff."

Thea scrunched her nose and lifted her chin in her mother's direction.

"It's okay, baby. I'll be right here." The woman's raspy voice broke on the last word. Knowing what usually caused vocal cord injuries made Ellie want to scream on her behalf. But she bit her tongue. She'd have to run her frustration out later.

At the time Sasha Saves opened, Ellie had totally sucked at keeping her emotions to herself. Since then, she'd gotten so adept at hiding her feelings, even she was hard-pressed to know what they were anymore.

But she could always identify rage.

Naomi's little protector nodded slowly and chose the tablet. Ellie inhaled a slow breath before gathering her courage up again. Unfortunately, fighting past a child's reluctance to be helped was the easy part. Sometimes the adults fought back.

After a few moments of listening to make sure Thea was enthralled with the Pixar movie, Ellie braced herself and faced Naomi. The eye she wasn't icing was nearly swollen shut, leaving Ellie worried about how much worse the side that needed icing was.

"El, like I said, this is Naomi. She came for our assistance." Dev scrubbed his beard before calmly leaning against the counter and crossing his thick arms. His bedside manner was straightforward and had the air of a regular doctor's checkup, which seemed to put survivors at ease. There's no judgment in facts.

Giving a slow nod to Dev, Ellie stepped in closer and gave Naomi her full attention. "You met Nora when you came in, right?" At Naomi's nod, Ellie continued. "She's our manager and lets me know when someone wants to chat here at the clinic. I'm Ellie Stone. I'm the Survivor Services Director and Advocate. We can help you."

"Survivor services?" the woman mumbled with a lilt on the end.

Ellie nodded and smiled. "We don't say victim around here. If you're seeking help, you're a survivor." She watched as a spark of hope lit Naomi's brown eyes before Ellie continued. "Can you tell me what happened? Who did this to you?"

As soon as it lit, the flame extinguished. Naomi's face hardened as her lips formed a thin line. But while she could snuff out her words, the pain in her eyes couldn't be dampened. Like recognized like, and Ellie recognized that anger. The kind that burned inside until it either consumed or was extinguished. This woman may have been beaten back, but she'd never be beaten.

Naomi swallowed and grimaced at the effort. "Nothin' happened."

The lie grated against Ellie's skin, compounded by Naomi's

gravelly voice. Dev's lips tightened while he retrieved his notes and marked something on the paperwork.

"I understand," Ellie began. "But your injuries... something happened... I'd love for you to tell me, rather than come to my own conclusions."

Naomi narrowed her uncovered eye in warning. "I came here to get checked out. I didn't come for anything else."

Naomi's insistence on silence weighed on Ellie, and she leaned on the nearby counter for support. "Please, Naomi? I think I can help you, but we need to know which direction to take."

There was only so much they could do if a survivor refused to disclose anything. There were ways to still support them, but handing out pamphlets was much less effective than filing a police report.

"Bike accident," Naomi muttered.

Ellie leaned closer and tilted her ear. "I'm sorry, what's that?"

Naomi opened her mouth, only for her lips to tighten shut again. Dev cleared his throat.

"Ma'am, you've suffered numerous contusions, including petechial hemorrhaging in and around your eyes, and lacerations to your upper body and facial region. Those are most consistent with strikes with a closed fist, likely right-handed given the swelling and discoloration concentrated on your left temple and orbital area."

"It was an *accident*." Naomi's light olive skin blushed even under the bruises, and her voice lilted up on the end, as if she was asking a question instead of trying to convince them.

"I'm sorry, Naomi..." Ellie began in a gentle voice, trying not to cause the woman more stress. But it was important she knew that *they* knew her story wasn't plausible. "Your hoarse voice and the fingerprint bruising on your neck aren't typically caused by—"

"It was a bike accident!" Naomi's whispered shout cracked painfully and Thea's attention swiveled toward them, her nose scrunched as she assessed the situation. Naomi, Ellie, and Dev remained silent, and Thea huffed before turning back to the tablet.

"Thea and I were ridin' our bikes and... uh... hers swerved into mine. I crashed onto the ground."

Dev's schooled expression dropped enough to expose his concern.

"You have the opportunity to get help for you and your daughter... Don't you want to take it?" He delivered the question in his cool monotone, despite the worry rolling off of him, but Naomi's swollen eye narrowed a fraction as she hissed.

"Are you sayin' I'm a bad mother?"

"No, but—"

"Absolutely not, Naomi. We don't think that," Ellie answered. "If your injuries need to come from a bike accident, then that's where they're from."

Ellie scowled at Dev and his light cheeks reddened. He nodded at her silent reprimand before sagging against the counter. They'd been doing this long enough he should've known from Naomi's mannerisms she'd shut down at a pointed question like that. But some cases—like ones involving strangulation—were too daunting to keep silent.

She returned her attention to Naomi, hoping they could move forward. "Do you think you need to go to the hospital?"

Naomi's subtle shake "no" led Ellie to her next routine question, although she knew what the answer would be.

"Would you like to report this... bike accident? We can protect you—"

"No! No. I-I can't."

"Okay." Ellie nodded once and retrieved a pen and paper from her backpack.

"Okay?" Naomi asked in her rough voice. "That's it? You're not gonna make me report it?"

Ellie raised an eyebrow. "Do you *want* me to report it?"

"Oh, God, no. I-I can't come back if you do."

Ellie bit her lip. The fear they wouldn't come back the next time they needed help was why she never pushed too hard. "Do you believe there's any way Thea would get hurt? Does she get in... accidents, too?"

Naomi's exposed eye widened. "No. Of course not... it's just, um, me."

Ellie shrugged. "Well, I guess we can't report a bike accident."

There was a heavy pause, one with the weight of decisions hanging in the balance.

"You're really not gonna report it?" Naomi asked again, the relief in her sigh made Ellie wonder for the hundredth time whether the decision to trust the survivor was a good one.

"No, I'm not gonna report it. We'll keep documentation for our office, just in case you ever need it, but we've designed the fine print for our shelter so our staff aren't considered mandatory reporters in this state. We'll give you a phone number you can call anytime and someone will help you with whatever you need. I wish *you* would report it. But I can't make you and I won't take that choice away from you."

Naomi might have scrunched her nose up like her daughter, but her face was too swollen for it to accomplish the same effect. Her chest puffed out on a deep inhale. After a long moment, Naomi finally shook her head. "It was just a bike accident."

Ellie rubbed the fiery ache in her chest, yet another survivor refusing to bring her abuser to justice. It'd hit hard the first few survivors who'd refused to prosecute and receive all the help Sasha Saves could provide. But they had a saying around the clinic: 'Help doesn't always mean justice. Sometimes it means escape.' If they scared survivors away then they wouldn't even be able to provide that.

"Alright, I understand." Ellie reached out and placed her hand over Naomi's resting on the examination table.

Naomi's breath hitched before quiet rivulets trailed down her cheek. "Thank you. Just... thank you."

Her shoulders slumped and she suddenly looked much older than she was, which was twenty-five, according to her chart. The poor woman had been carrying so much for so long. Ellie gingerly patted her shoulder and squeezed.

Naomi carefully dried her tears with gauze. "Can I take this off?" she asked Dev before indicating the ice pack she'd pulled from her cheek. Ellie couldn't help her eyes widening. The iced side of Naomi's face was mottled with purple bruises and the thin skin of and around her eyelid was swollen shut to the size of a golf ball.

Dev checked his watch. "In a few minutes."

Ellie averted her stare from Naomi's injuries and brought her hand up to massage her forehead.

"Well, our attorney should be here soon—"

The door behind them crashed open and everyone's eyes snapped to the noise. Naomi clutched her chest and threw one leg over the side of her seat while the other was poised on the floor, ready for escape. Dev's back was suddenly in Ellie's view as he shielded her with his body, so she peeked around him to see who it was.

Blue hair was the first thing Ellie noticed as Snake stood in front of the doorway. He lifted an awkward hand in greeting despite the fact both hands were holding boxes of wires. His pale cheeks flushed to a bright crimson.

"Oh... um. Hi."

CHAPTER THREE

Ellie couldn't help but grimace in secondhand embarrassment at the less than graceful entry. BlackStone Security's intelligence commander and former Night Stalker in the Army, Wesley "Snake" James, laughed nervously as every eye watched him close the door with his foot.

If Clark Kent had navy blue streaks in his hair, he and Snake could be twins, especially with Snake's glasses accentuating his piercing blue eyes. And if Superman had a full sleeve of tattoos and talked a mile a minute, they'd be identical. He was tall and fit, but much leaner than Dev, and would've totally been Ellie's type if her eye wasn't already on the quiet, muscular redhead in front of her.

Not that the feeling's mutual. Ellie swallowed back the disappointment that had become a constant bad taste in her mouth ever since she realized Dev was out of her league. The clinic was no place for her to throw a pity party.

Snake cleared his throat. "H-hello," he stuttered, his baby blues concentrating solely in Ellie and Dev's direction. Naomi lifted her chin, almost in defiance, but sucked in a short breath as the ice pack shifted on her cheek.

"Snake." Dev shook his head as he spoke low. "I know you're

not used to coming to Sasha Saves but you can't barge in like that."

"I, uh, I know. I'm sorry." Snake waved his hand to the corners of the room. "I'm here to upgrade the security for the pla—*shit*."

Snake's face contorted with his lip curled and his black brows pinched together, almost as if in pain. Ellie shifted to follow his gaze until she realized it was laser focused on Naomi's injuries. Her mind raced to find ways to protect Naomi from the horror written all over Snake's reaction, but it was too late. Naomi flinched before averting her head in shame to the black-and-white tiled floor, hiding her wounds.

Ellie's heart jolted in empathy and she whipped her head up to glare at Snake. At least he had the decency to look contrite, but his response was inexcusable. Sure, seeing a survivor injured as badly as Naomi was always hard, but Snake never handled it well. Unless he was absolutely needed for his security expertise, he was the only BlackStone agent who made it a point to steer clear of the clinic. Based on his reaction, apparently for good reason.

Dev cleared his throat. "Can you come by later? We're kinda in the middle of—"

"Hey, look what I got." Thea's sudden appearance made Snake jump, before she jabbed a corner of the tablet into his stomach, forcing him to catch the device and juggle the boxes at the same time. The tense furrows in his brow relaxed as he looked down at his tiny assailant.

"Oh wow." Snake smiled genuinely before setting his boxes aside and bending to her height. "What do you have there?"

"It's Merida, from Brave. You hafta come watch." Thea clutched his long sleeve and pulled him to the bean bag.

"Thea—" The girl paused to listen to her mother but didn't let go of Snake's shirt. "Baby, don't be rude. What if he doesn't wanna watch the show? He has things to do."

"Sorry," Thea mumbled and toed the ground with a green slipper. "You hafta come watch... if you wanna."

Snake's smile lifted at the corners. "I think I have some time. As long as it's okay with your mom." He glanced at Naomi and gestured with the tablet. "Um, is this... is this alright?"

Naomi's mouth opened and shut before she nodded her head once and winced.

Thea beamed at her momma and tugged Snake to the beanbag, instructing him to sit on the floor beside her. His smile widened as he followed her directions and Thea giggled when he asked her questions about her favorite shows.

"That's so strange," Naomi whispered. "She's never taken to anyone like that. Not even her—" She cut herself off and coughed before placing the ice pack back onto her cheek.

"You can take that off now. It's been enough time for you to take a break from the icing." Dev offered.

Naomi grimaced and alternated a panic-stricken glance between Dev and Snake. "Can I... can I keep it on? For a little while longer?" she whispered.

Dev seemed to follow her hesitation and nodded before grabbing a towel from a drawer. "Here, you can use this instead if you want to keep your injuries... discreet."

Naomi nodded and a shaky breath escaped her as she exchanged the ice pack for the towel.

"Okay, next steps," Ellie said, aiming to steer the conversation. "The attorney for the clinic, Jules, and our manager, Nora—the one you met when you came in—will be in soon." As if on cue, there was a quick knock before the door cracked open.

"It's Nora! And I brought backup." Nora's voice called out into the room.

"Come on in," Ellie answered.

"We having a party?" Nora joked, relieving tension in the room Ellie hadn't realized was there. Nora stomped in with her combat boot heels in a whirlwind, and Jules click-clacked right behind her in her signature red stilettos, blazer, and dress. Ready for court as always, despite her noticeable baby bump.

Nora was obviously making a joke about the number of people in the room, and she had a point. The medical room wasn't small by any means. It was more of a multi-purpose room and big enough for multiple kids to play around, officers to question survivors, or for prosecutors to prepare, but not all at once. It was getting crowded.

"We finally lost Jason, so I have about an hour of freedom," Jules mumbled. When Ellie snickered, Jules narrowed her brows and placed her hands on her hips. "Think it's funny, huh? Ever since I *helped* you kick him off your security detail, I haven't been able to so much as pee without company, and I don't even have a kid yet! I mean, for the love of God, I already have a whole human attached to my uterus. I don't need one attached to my hip, too."

Dev scoffed and shook his head as he scrubbed his beard. "I'm sure you didn't *lose* a BlackStone Securities agent."

Nora only smirked. "You'd be simply *astounded* at the things I can do, Devil, my dear." She turned and clapped before waving Vanna White-style in Jules's direction. "'Kay Naomi, doll. I brought our lawyer. Are you feelin' up for a chitchat about boring legal-Sméagol stuff?"

"I wanna go home now." Naomi sighed. "There's nothin' to talk about—"

"Yeah, yeah. I hear ya." Nora interrupted before peering over Dev's shoulder to see the notes he'd placed on the counter. She looked back up at Naomi and twirled a fingerless gloved hand in the air. "Bike accident, hm? Well, just hear her out. You bought a ticket by coming here, so now you get a free show. We do this with every survivor who's had 'bike accidents,' 'fallen down stairs,' 'fallen up stairs,' 'landed face-first into doorknobs,' yada yada. You have no idea how many clumsy people we get in here." Nora smirked, undeterred by the scowl forming on Naomi's face.

"Anywho, like I said this morning, we've got suitcases,

clothes, toys, whatever you need from the thrift store, if you decide you need somewhere else to go. Even if you decide to stay, it'll be good to have as a cover if anyone questions where you went. It's totes free and you can pretend like it's a shopping spree for Lil' T over there."

"Thank you," Naomi rasped out before a small smile lifted the corner of her lip. Nora had that effect on people. Even though she was blunt, people loved her for it because her delivery was so dang disarming.

"Hi, Naomi. I'm Jules, I'd like to go over some—"

"You're an attorney, right?"

Jules frowned before nodding warily. "Yes, I'm a victim's rights attorney."

"And attorney-client privilege..." She darted an eye toward Ellie. "Whatever I say, you can't repeat as long as it's in confidence between you and me?"

Jules's brow raised, and Ellie had to imagine it was from the grasp of the legal concept. Most people didn't know that particular loophole, that if someone was in the room between you and your attorney, the right for your words to be kept a secret didn't apply to the others in the room.

"That's right... would you prefer we speak more privately?" Jules gestured to Ellie, Dev, and Nora. "If you'd like, these three and Snake can step out in the office right there until we're finished." Jules pointed to the adjoining room.

Naomi's head dipped in agreement. "I'd appreciate that, thank you..." She peered over Jules's shoulder before bending her head closer. "But, um... Snake, right? He can stay. So long as we whisper... Thea looks so... carefree, right now. I want her to keep that feelin' for a little while longer."

"Sure thing, babe," Nora replied and turned on her heel to the office. "Let's go kids."

The poor woman looked a little guilty for asking them to leave and she had no reason to. Ellie gave Naomi what she hoped was an encouraging smile, to let her know it was okay she'd asked for privacy.

Nora settled in behind the computer and Dev leaned up against the opposite wall as Ellie shut the door to the small office. Before it was closed, Ellie heard Jules begin to murmur, and Ellie didn't need to hear to know it was her usual spiel about legalities. She'd heard it so many times, she could give it herself if she had a legal degree to her name.

Ellie's stomach twisted at the reminder of how far away she was from getting a degree. She'd just started Ashland State University to become a therapist and was already bristling at how much time college life wasted.

According to brochures and everyone's two cents, there were lessons college could teach her that on-the-job training couldn't. Although the more she worked at Sasha Saves, the more she questioned what lessons she'd learn from mandatory electives, like the history of the dang flute.

Dev lightly tapped her shoulder with a pen, gently bringing her back to the moment. "You okay?"

She hadn't realized how close she'd gotten leaning next to him, but she had no complaints when his warm breath tickled her ear as he leaned into her space, making her shiver.

"Yeah, I'm fine. Just thinking."

"Damn, Ellie, you cold?" His brow furrowed in concern before he pulled his jacket from the coat rack in the corner of the office to give to her. "I keep telling you, you don't wear enough clothes."

"I'm *fine*." Ellie rolled her eyes. While he might chastise her for not keeping herself warm, wearing more clothes around Devil Ray Vos was the last thing she wanted to do. But she took the offering, forcing herself not to burrow her nose into the fabric for the whiff of cinnamon she knew she'd find there. "It might be winter, but it feels like summer outside so I thought I'd be okay." She laughed and elbowed him. "And, I've already got one big brother, ya know. I don't need another one."

Dev grumbled something and Ellie tilted her head. "What's that?"

He leaned into her ear again. Even though he wasn't touching her, his words puffed against the loose hair from her ponytail, sending tingles along the back of her neck. "I *said*, I sure as hell am not your brother."

Ellie whipped her gaze up to see his facial expression, but he was already looking away. Dev confused the heck outta her. Whether he knowingly toyed with the line between friendship and flirtation, she wasn't sure.

And that was the problem.

They'd known each other for almost a year and she still couldn't tell if the spark she felt when he touched her was something she imagined or if he felt the same way. Or if the attraction was one-sided entirely. Oh God, now *that* would be embarrassing.

The comment he'd made about her clothes, for example, sounded like he only saw her as his friend's kid sister. But the way he whispered in her ear afterward felt like anything but.

However he talked to her, she'd take it. It was better than how everyone else spoke to her. Like a victim.

Dev saved her back then. He was the first sign of hope she'd seen when she was kidnapped. For a while, she'd chalked her feelings up to a harmless hero crush. The more she was around him, though, the less innocent it felt. She huddled farther into his jacket, imprinting his scent on her skin. Maybe they wouldn't be innocent, but in her fantasies, the sinful things Dev did to her felt absolutely heavenly.

"Hey... I thought you had class right now?" Nora asked Ellie before lifting a dyed gray brow and glanced up from the computer screen, only to do a double take. "Damn, girl, now that I look at ya, you kinda look like shidoobie. When was the last time you slept? Or ate? You look like you're about to fall over from lack of one or the other." She paused and looked her up and down. "Or, Hades, maybe both." She sobered a little and spoke more softly. "I'm glad you're outta hidin' babe, but are you takin' care of yourself?"

Ellie's cheeks heated at the truth. She'd shut herself off emotionally from everyone for nearly a year after her kidnapping. It was only this semester she'd forced herself to interact with the world. Before then, she'd hardly gone anywhere but Sasha Saves and the library. Besides sleeping, she rarely even stayed in that tiny cell of a dorm room. It felt too much like a prison.

"I'm fine," Ellie mumbled, but Nora's gray brow lifted higher. Nora couldn't be more than a few years older than Ellie, but she treated her hair and eyebrows like a mood ring. Lately, she'd only chosen gray or black.

Ellie got Nora's need for self-expression. Sasha, Ellie, Nora, and several other women were kidnapped as bids for an auction in a sex trafficking ring almost a year ago. What had happened to Sasha... Ellie closed her eyes to concentrate on blocking out another flashback. Ellie was with her captors for three days, suffering her own hell. Meanwhile, Nora witnessed one of the BlackStone men, Draco, almost die trying to save her from being kidnapped. He was shot twice and had been in a coma ever since.

The men who were behind it all were still at large, and that fact drove Ellie, and everyone around her, crazy. Jason, Dev, and the rest of the men at BlackStone Securities were attempting to solve the puzzle. But whatever they knew, they weren't sharing any of the pieces with Ellie.

She was drugged for most of her abduction and whether it was from the drugs or trauma, Ellie could only recount what happened in hazy, disjointed fragments. She'd tried for months to unlock those memories, but it was no use. They only barged in on their terms.

Besides, even if she did remember everything, she'd never be invited to help with the investigation. Dev didn't see her as a victim, but she knew he was overprotective of her. And Jason?

Jason would never stop seeing her as the baby sister he almost lost.

"Look alive, El," Dev grumbled and prodded her arm gently. "You're doing it again."

"What?" Ellie blinked away the light-headedness brought on by her daydream, recognizing from Dev's prompt and hours of therapy that she'd taken another "mental vacation from the present." That's what her therapist called dissociating, when Ellie retreated from conversations and blanked out, taking up residence in her mind instead. She came back to see Jules had stepped into the office, probably to leave Naomi to think things over.

"Are you supposed to be in class right now?" Jules whispered before closing the door behind her and perching her hands on her hips. Jason thought her lawyer voice was cute, but he was insane. Even whispered, it was still scary as all get out.

"Um... yes, but Nora texted me," Ellie hedged. "If she didn't want me to come then she shouldn't have messaged me."

Nora snorted. "Don't blame this on me. You know the drill. 'Get here when you can' means after class, baby doll."

Ellie huffed and crossed her arms. "Fine, but I have absences left. And—"

"Yeah right, girl. I call bull hockey," Nora interrupted and rolled her eyes. "You've been here more days than you've been in class."

Ellie stuck her tongue out at Nora, and Nora stuck hers out right back. Dev grunted and the grim line of his mouth thinned even more. Ellie felt heat rise up her chest and into her cheeks. She'd acted like the child they all thought she was.

"Seriously, El, what's going on? Going to college has always been your dream," Jules's eyebrows drew together with concern as she spoke.

"Not by myself," Ellie muttered. Behind her crossed arms, she clenched her fists. Going to college without her best friend had never been the plan.

Silence crushed their objections. Jules and Nora's eyes shot to the ground and Ellie could feel them searching for the right thing to say. But they'd never find it. What would make any of this better was scattered in ashes.

A throat cleared in the other room, and Jules opened the door wide. Naomi waved the pamphlets at them after steering her eyes away from Snake and Thea. "I-uh. I'm finished. Y'all can come out now..."

Jules nodded and they all filed out of the office to give the woman their full attention again. "Good, I'll take those so you don't have to keep them, or take them home." She took the pamphlets and handed them to Ellie. "I know I threw a lot at you, but do you have any questions?"

Naomi hesitated before shaking her head and Ellie stepped forward to speak. "It's okay if you don't have all the answers now, or ever. We're here if you need us. No judgment."

Naomi gave a dazed nod and Ellie followed Naomi's gaze to where Thea and Snake were giggling at something on the screen. When Thea squealed with happiness, Snake's grin widened, his blue eyes shining.

"I think," Naomi whispered before clearing her throat with a wince. "I think we'll be fine. Thank you for all your help. Do you, um, have a card for that number I could maybe call?"

Ellie shook her head. "Nope. All sevens. That's our number. It's easy to remember and you don't have a trace of us to get you in trouble."

"All sevens," Naomi whispered as she slid off the patient bed to leave.

As Ellie and Dev went to help her, Nora spoke in an even higher pitch than usual. "Hey, kiddo, come with me and your mommy and we can go shopping in the store. You can get anything you want."

Naomi's unbruised light olive skin paled before she objected. "No, Nora, we can't possibly—"

"It's on the house," Ellie interrupted with what she hoped was an encouraging smile, but Naomi shook her head.

"No, Ellie, that's not the issue—"

Thea squealed, cutting off Naomi's objection before jumping off the beanbag and landing on Snake's unmentionables. His grunt made Thea gasp and crawl back. A look of utter terror on her face made Ellie's heart crack.

"Sorry," Thea squeaked with a cringe on her face.

A laugh rumbled through him. "Oof, you got me good, kid."

Thea glanced at her momma and after seeing whatever she needed to see, the little girl broke out into nervous giggles before leaping toward Snake.

"Okay, but Wes has to come!" She grabbed his hand and rattled off about shopping and dress-up even before he agreed. Ellie glanced at Naomi to see a ghost of a smile before it disappeared.

"All right, let's go, Babs. I gotta get my favorite boss ass bitch back to the office before your fiancé decides to unalive me for keeping you from him." Nora waved Snake, Naomi, Jules, and Thea out the door. "Go to class, Ellie!" she yelled before closing the medical room door, leaving Dev and Ellie in the room.

Alone.

The hair on the back of Ellie's neck stood on end as she realized how close they were again. The air thickened around them and Ellie stepped away to give herself room to breathe.

"I should, um, go study or something. See ya." She turned to retrieve her backpack, but every step away from Dev felt like she was trudging against the inescapable undercurrent between them. She swallowed around the denial she'd been cultivating for months, refusing to explore her feelings further.

What the heck is wrong with me?

Dev was twenty-seven years old, and her *brother's* friend and teammate. That was all he'd been to Ellie, too. Just a friend.

But still, she couldn't shake the overwhelming instinct he was more than that. They'd seen each other nearly every day since he'd rescued her. And nearly every day, she had to remind herself to forget the first thought she had when his flashlight revealed his small smile. That he was her savior. Her hero.

She didn't want to be the damsel in distress anymore. If Sasha Saves had taught her anything, it was the importance of learning to save herself. It was something she tried to empower survivors with every day. Those women who depended on Sasha Saves needed her full attention, and on top of that, Nora had a point. Ellie didn't even know how many absences she had left.

Bottom line? There was more at stake than a little hero crush, and Ellie needed to grow up and accept that.

"Hey, do you want a ride?"

Ellie tugged her backpack on slowly as she searched for an excuse. "Oh no, that's okay. I rode my bike here. It's hooked up to the rack. Oh... and—" She shrugged off his jacket. "Outside is hot as blue blazes today so I won't need your jacket out there." She tossed it to him, afraid of what she would do if their fingers touched and sparks flew everywhere like in one of Virginia's romance novels. "Um, thanks though."

He nodded and flipped the jacket over his shoulder. "I can still take you back to your dorm, if you'd like. I'll put your bike in the bed of my truck, like usual." Dev's lips angled up in one corner and Ellie averted her eyes to focus on smoothing down her T-shirt, as if the task was impossible without intense concentration.

"I, um. I think I'll ride home." The room was quiet and she dared a glance back to see the raised side of his mouth had flattened into a hard line and he'd stuffed the hand not holding his jacket into his pockets.

Is he... disappointed?

"But, could you walk me out?" Ellie quickly followed up. The compromise was worth it when his mouth curved up again. It wasn't even a real smile by normal standards, but it still had the power to tie Ellie's stomach into hopeful knots.

"Love to, angel." This time he said the endearment like a

brother to a sister, and Ellie bristled at the tone. So dang confusing.

Dev tugged a pack of gum from his pocket. Big Red, like always. He popped a piece into his mouth before offering her one.

"No thanks." She shook her head. Her mouth was already watering enough.

He nodded and stuffed both the pack and his hands back in his pockets before leading them out, both of them making sure to wave bye to everyone in the store before leaving.

Nora was talking to Naomi near the check-out counter, no doubt trying to enlist another volunteer. If a survivor helped around the thrift store under the guise of a volunteer opportunity, they were able to keep Sasha Saves close in case they needed help. The thrift store was advertised as a non-profit for kids with cancer. No one questioned or fought against helping kids with cancer. Some of the proceeds did actually go toward them, so it wasn't even a lie. Hopefully, Naomi agreed and the two would come up with a plan to convince whoever caused her injuries.

Ellie weaved behind Devil through clothing racks and tried not to be frustrated that even as he held the door open for her, he seemed to carefully avoid touching her.

They hardly ever did, she'd noticed, as if their bodies had conspired to leave a buffer as an attempt to never give in to the tension swirling between them. But the constant focus on *not* touching had the opposite effect on curing the charged energy that zipped over Ellie's skin whenever Dev was only inches away. Instead, any time their fingers brushed, a delicious shock traveled up her arm and down to the bundle of nerves that craved his attention.

What would happen if she gave in to the urge to pounce on him? Just once? If he pressed his body up against hers, would it finally relieve the ache inside? Or would it make it more unbearable?

Ellie suppressed a shiver at the same time her stomach

lurched. Not even her body could decide whether being brave enough to act on her needs was arousing or terrifying.

Moving on from her past was the equivalent of standing on the edge of a cliff. She'd managed to avoid looking down until that point, but would taking the leap with someone like Dev feel like flying or a total crash and burn?

Things had gotten hot and heavy with a few guys before she was kidnapped, but she'd never had sex. After months of therapy, she was trying to regain some semblance of a normal life as a college student. That included a relationship, right? Maybe Virginia could fix her up with some guy. Not that he'd ever compare to Dev.

Ellie tripped over the welcome mat outside the doorway. One second, she was falling to the ground, the next, strong hands whisked her up, gripping her around her waist.

"Careful, angel."

It was back. His tone a soft caress against her skin. She looked down at Dev's hands, spanning her waistline as he held her tightly with her back flush to his chest. Ellie leaned sideways to meet those big forest green eyes and gulped back the butterflies threatening to escape. The heat in his gaze lit her up inside. It was the first time they'd *ever* been that close.

Relief? Or unbearable?

His fingers twitched on her lower belly, sending the flutters there straight down to her core and making her throb with need.

Guess I have my answer.

CHAPTER FOUR

"Investigator Burgess, I'm not sure these meetings are as productive as we'd hoped," Hawkins Black, the BlackStone Securities leader, growled across the Ashland County Sheriff's Office conference room.

Devil raised an eyebrow at Hawk's show of emotion. Their team lead was usually methodical, like Devil. It was the Jaybird between them, Jason Stone, who had the temper. He was barely keeping it in check, bouncing his leg so hard he shook the table.

But Devil couldn't blame Hawk for the slip in character. They'd all been pushed to the limit, and this case was a sore spot for each of them for different reasons. It was high-time Burgess was called out on his bullshit.

Over the past several months, the BlackStone Securities Crew had hit a dead end in their search for answers about the county's human trafficking. The Crew had been able to stop the operation, and even eradicate some of the assholes, before they could take off with Ellie and the other women.

But now the fuckers had gone radio silent and the Crew had no other choice but to work with the man none of them trusted. Investigator Burgess of the Ashland County Sheriff's Office had tried to pin Ellie's kidnapping and Sasha's murder on Jaybird, for

Christ's sake. Not to mention the fact the only sources of scientific identification of the subject were missing in action. Sasha's DNA samples "somehow" got lost and her body was "accidentally" cremated. Even after Sasha's parents sued the county for emotional distress, the apologies from the sheriff's office were weak at best. The whole situation was fucked and Burgess was the shitty ass dildo.

Devil's hands tightened around the chair rests, teasing the skin on an exposed nail he'd found at the beginning of the meeting. He leaned back, schooling his face as he pressed harder into the sharp point. It was past the point of soothing pain, but not close enough to break skin. He didn't have time for another tetanus shot.

Investigator Burgess squirmed in his leather seat. How the overweight man sat comfortably in his already bulky police-issued uniform was a mystery. "Now fellas, this has been a big case. Lots of movin' parts—"

"It's been months," Hawk interrupted through gritted teeth. "I think it's time to say the trail has gone stale, and all these so-called leads you've been sending us on have been nothing but one long wild-goose chase." Hawk's quiet accusation rang out despite the poor acoustics of the wood-paneled walls. Jaybird nodded silently, every muscle tensed, on the verge of exploding.

As their leader, Hawk took on more than his share of guilt when jobs went south. He'd been that way even before Devil served with him in MF7, their paramilitary group where Hawk had been second-in-command.

After Eagle.

Devil shook his head and focused back on the argument at hand.

Investigator Burgess crossed his arms and shook his head with an exaggerated exhale. His theatrics and idiosyncrasies always tripped a wire in Devil's brain, putting him on alert for the older man's reactions. Burgess had crazy-ass moods. At least he seemed more subdued this time. Still not a damn bit useful, though.

"I know, gentlemen. I'm as angry as you are. I want to get these bastards even more than you do." Investigator Burgess raised his voice at the end and pounded his fist on the table for emphasis. Devil scoffed. Men like him always use volume to try to prove a point.

"I highly doubt that," Jaybird muttered under his breath.

Burgess's scowl made his graying eighties pornstache dip down at the corners of his frown. "Haven't you figured anything else out? Anything we can go off of? You're the professional security agents." He paused and narrowed his eyes. "Maybe the question is whether y'all've been holdin' up your end of the deal?"

Ah, there it is.

"Is that what you really believe, Investigator?" Hawk asked, positioning his body to face Burgess head-on.

The goal was to share information and swap what they knew, but it hadn't panned out that way. According to Jules's friend, an assistant district attorney, they'd kept the details of the case between two officers to make sure no one was compromised. Investigator Burgess and—after some of Jules's wheeling and dealing with the sheriff—Officer Henry Brown. Thank God, too. Jules trusted him and it was good to have a man on the inside. Especially when the alternative was a trigger-happy, slimy fuck.

If Devil had his way, they would've kept the shithead out of it altogether. But Hawk, Snake, and Phoenix, their wheelman, had won out against Jay and Devil in a vote as to whether they should involve the authorities.

So there they were, Hawk, Jaybird, and Devil playing the luck of the draw with Burgess, wondering who would fold first. Hawk and Burgess stared at each other for moments longer, both probably trying to determine if the other was bluffing.

"Well," Burgess started, trying to find his defenses. "I mean—"

"Come on, sir," Officer Henry Brown piped up from his corner behind Burgess. "If they knew somethin', don't you think they woulda told us?"

Burgess whipped his scowl back to Henry, his eyebrows pinching closely together to create a unibrow.

"I don't like what you're suggesting, Burgess," Hawk growled. "We know the Ascot, Rusnak, and Strickland law firm is involved in some capacity, since Andy Ascot was wrapped up in it and was murdered helping us save those girls. Plus, Ellie and Sasha were kidnapped from a party thrown by a multitude of firms, one of which was A.R.S.."

"We already know all that," Burgess grumbled.

Of course he did. Hawk wouldn't give real information. Like the fact Ellie and Sasha were recruited by someone who'd given a fake name. Whoever had lured them into the trap had planned ahead, thinking of every possibility the naïve girls hadn't.

They also didn't know how deep the root had rotted in Ashland County's elite, but they had a hunch Mitchell Strickland was involved based on a dying man's final words.

The stalemate went on for minutes. Officer Henry finally cleared his throat to get his superior's attention. "Um, sir?"

Wrenching his eyes away from the stare off with Hawk, Burgess shook his head and punctuated a heavy sigh with a coughing fit at the end. "Listen, boys, I know we got off on the wrong foot with all this shit..."

Jay scoffed at the understatement and Burgess sent him a cutting glance before powering through.

"But I came to see the error in my ways. If we could get our resources together, I'm sure y'all know more than what you're tellin' me. You have to. You were the best of the best, after all, weren't you?" He smiled stiffly.

Unease slithered in Devil's veins and he rolled his shoulders to lean forward, out of the relaxed pose he'd feigned for the past half hour. He glared at Burgess's ruddy face, now growing pale, and spoke low. "And what do you mean by that... exactly?"

There was no way he should know about MF7, and any record that the BlackStone agents had been members was redacted, sealed, and burned. The government washed their hands of the clandestine military group and purged MF7 from history as quickly as fucking possible after their last mission.

All anyone knew was that each member of MF7 had been a soldier in one of the military branches and they'd all been medically discharged from their posts for psych reasons. With some government-led clerical magic, their records had been made to say they were discharged around the time they were each initially recruited, backdated after their disaster of a final mission in Yemen where the men had walked into a trap while trying to save a group of women from being trafficked.

Only Nora, a computer nerd as brilliant as Snake, had ever found out the group's name. They still weren't sure how she'd been able to finagle that information. The woman was a vault.

"Oh, um... you boys were military, right? The best of the best? Better'n a little ol' Podunk local sheriff's department, amiright?" He laughed harshly until he coughed himself into a fit. Amidst the hacking, he reached for his water bottle and patted his police-issued uniform until his coughing ebbed and his shoulders relaxed. He pulled out a lighter from another square in his vest and flicked it on and off in his fingers.

"Right." Devil nodded and leaned back in his chair, taking note of the investigator's hand beginning to tremor while he fidgeted.

"With that party... You know, the one where you're-uh" —he pointed to Jason— "sister and her-uh-friend were kidnapped? What do y'all think about them throwin' another shindig? Think they'll be bold enough to try again?"

The three BlackStone men stilled. Devil forced himself to make at least some small movements to avoid drawing attention to the concern stiffening his muscles.

They'd never talked about the party with Burgess, afraid they'd give too much away. They did think the traffickers would be dumb enough to try the same crime in the same party. They had no concrete evidence yet, but it was their theory the traffickers hid their evil under the cloak of the party, helped by some of Ashland County's finest. But no way in hell were they going to tell Investigator Burgess.

"We haven't thought too much about it." Hawk hedged.

"No way they'd be that stupid though, ya know?" Jaybird offered.

Burgess nodded and grunted. "Might be somethin' worth lookin' into."

Hawk tilted his head at Burgess before nodding to himself. "We'll do that." He templed his fingers and tapped against his lips. "We might have some leads."

Burgess grunted his assent and the BlackStone men waited for the inevitable question of who their leads were. But each passing tick of the dated clock above the door echoed in the silent room, reverberating inside Devil's head and bringing on a painful tension headache.

If only he could see Ellie after the meeting. Her gentle spirit was always the warmth he needed to melt the icy stress accumulating in his veins.

When Jason had shown the Crew her picture for reference to save her last year, Ellie's soft face and effortless smile lit a fire inside him. His hardened heart had been cracking ever since.

And he hated it.

Everything about Devil was logical, methodical, planned. And for good reason. He'd come face-to-face with what emotions could do to a man.

Six years ago, he was burned by a light that was snuffed out too soon. He learned then that when his control faltered, someone got hurt. Ever since, he'd honed the skill of cold detachment.

Until Ellie.

She was becoming a distraction, and the only way he could think to get Ellie out of his head was by getting inside someone else. It'd been months since he'd gone to Original Sin and gotten an easy lay from one of the dancers at the strip club. He and Phoenix would've left right after the meeting, but the lucky bastard got out of going to the sheriff's office at the last second with another client meeting. Devil would have to keep both heads in check until he had the chance to blow off some steam.

"Welp boys..." Burgess slapped the table with a pasted smile on his face, bringing Devil back to the moment. "I appreciate your time. Whatever you're lookin' into, keep me in the loop."

"Sir? Are you, uh, sure you want to end the meeting so soon? They just got here," Officer Brown asked from behind the investigator, obviously as confused as they were that the meeting was being cut off half an hour early.

"I think we've covered everything, haven't we gentlemen?"

Hawk narrowed his eyes at both officers and glanced back at Jaybird and Devil. "If you think so, sir. We'll follow up with what we find out."

Burgess nodded and they all shifted to get up.

"One more thing." Jaybird lifted his chin at Burgess.

Burgess's eyebrows raised and Devil resisted the impulse to do the same. Unable to hide his hatred for Burgess, Jaybird never piped in with his two cents. He'd already met his word quota for that meeting.

"Now, son, I'm on a tight schedule. I-uh, I think we can wait until next time, don't you agree?"

Jaybird shook his head. "Unbelievable, man. This is important." He gave Burgess a pointed look.

"If it's so damn important, why'dya wait 'til the end to talk about it?"

"Maybe because I don't trust you farther than I can throw you assho—"

"Enough." Hawk's lips tightened in a thin line before nodding at Jaybird to continue.

Jaybird huffed and seemed to mentally collect himself as the investigator idly flicked his lighter, like he had nothing better to do.

"I've had one of our guys look into this, but we've come to a dead end. My sister told me yesterday she's seeing the same car following her around town—"

"What the fuck?" Devil growled and his whole body swiveled to glare at his teammate. "How could you not tell me about this?" He thought back to the last time he'd seen her. It must've been around the same time she told Jaybird, but she'd still chosen not to tell him. She'd even turned down a ride home.

What the fuck is she thinking?

Jaybird's eyebrow lifted and he frowned as he turned back to the investigator. He seemed to keep his eye on Devil in his periphery for a second longer before giving the description of a Corolla down to the dent on the driver's side and some of the locations Ellie remembered seeing it, all near the clinic.

Spots appeared in Devil's vision and he gripped his chair as he concentrated on deeper breaths. He swallowed back the nerves and sat up straighter to listen.

Why didn't she tell me?

He had no right to be kept in the loop revolving around Ellie's life. Although Devil's world was revolving more and more around Ellie—no matter how hard he tried to fight it—the bottom line was he was nothing to her. Just her brother's friend. A coworker. Her not confiding in him proved it.

"You coming, man?" Jaybird swatted Devil's shoulder, bringing him out of his thoughts to realize his teammates were ready to leave. Burgess and Henry were already shaking hands with Hawk.

He stood to do the same and shook Burgess's clammy grip. It took all of his control not to immediately dry his hand on his pants. Officer Henry tilted his head up as a goodbye before heading down the hallway back to the pit, where all the beat cops had their cubicles and desks. Burgess walked them out of the conference room while fishing in a side pocket on his vest with one hand and digging his phone out of his pants with the other. He dialed quickly and shoved the phone up against his ear, speaking rapidly before charging into his office.

Devil shook his head and followed behind Jaybird and Hawk down the hallway. He wasn't sure if it was because of his distrust of the investigator, but his intuition was telling him the man's idiosyncrasies were odd as fuck. Devil didn't know what to do with that information except watch him closely.

"Hey, man." Jaybird paused for Devil to catch up. "Mind doing me a favor?"

"Mind telling me what the favor is before I agree to it?"

Jaybird cocked a smile. "That's probably wise." He chuckled and swiped his hand through his hair. "I've gotten to the point in Jules's pregnancy where I can't stand to have her out of my sight. Nora fucking figured out how to hide Jules's location on her phone and it drove me crazy. I get she doesn't like to drive alone anymore, but I sure as fuck wish Nora would stop taking off the damn GPS I keep putting on her car. I searched all around town for Nora's damn Chevy Spark until Jules finally called to tell me she was on her way home."

"She probably wants you to leave her the fuck alone."

He barked out a laugh. "Well, joke's on her, that ain't happening. I love her and she's carrying around my baby, Jules is gonna have to suck it up that I'm gonna keep being a psycho until she gives birth. Probably after that too, if I'm honest."

Devil grunted in response. "And? What's this gotta do with me?"

Jaybird shook his head. "Damn, man, lighten up a little. I can't ever read you. It's unnerving as fuck." Despite the words, Jaybird chuckled. "Anyway, I've been giving Ellie self-defense lessons the past few months—"

"Shit, really?" Devil interrupted. He'd had no idea.

Fuck, I need to stop losing my mind over this girl and start paying attention.

A creaking sound played in his memory and he clenched his

fists until all he could focus on was the pain in his fingertips. Never again.

"Yeah... but Hawk agreed to let me be Jules's bodyguard until the baby comes. I can't be in two places at once. Do you think you could take over lessons?"

Devil blanched as he fished through his brain for any excuse to keep his distance from the woman who already lived rent-free in his head.

"Well, damn, there's a reaction." Jaybird laughed as he opened the door out of the precinct.

Hawk waited outside, rubbing his nape as he talked on the phone. When he saw them, he jutted his chin up in acknowledgement as they stepped outside and the three of them made the trek to his sedan. They usually parked as close as possible and backed into a spot so they could haul ass if necessary. But with it being a police precinct, the first several rows were taken up by cop cars.

Devil shoved his hands into his pockets against the brisk fall wind, and sucked air between his teeth. "Can't someone else do it?"

"You're the best hand-to-hand after Draco... And well, Draco's in a fucking coma. Hawk has a business to run. Snake is great with a keyboard and a weapon, not so great with his hands—"

"Phoenix?"

"Fuck, dude," Jaybird scoffed. "Do you really wanna sic that hound dog on her?"

A surprising flash of anger flooded his body and he clenched his jaw. *Nope. Definitely do not want that.*

Jaybird rubbed his hand through his hair again. "Anyways, I didn't ask him. Hawk's got him on client intake meetings lately. Besides, Ellie likes you. And don't you think she deserves the best?"

Devil scowled. "Of course I fucking do."

Jaybird smirked. "Alright then. It's settled. We were supposed to have a lesson next week bright and early before her classes, but Jules's doctor scheduled an appointment last minute. That work for you? We can switch off with you as her trainer after that."

Devil's lips tightened into a thin line and he bit his tongue. He was out of options and couldn't help feeling cornered into what felt very much like a trap.

But Jaybird had a point. He was the best at hand-to-hand, even better than Jaybird. Besides, the girl needed someone to make sure she took care of herself, what with skipping class, forgetting to eat, letting some creep follow her around for God knows how long. She was dragging ass the last time he'd seen her at Sasha Saves.

"Fine," he grumbled.

"Excellent. I'll tell her to be ready at BlackStone's gym then —" A faint buzzing sound interrupted them. "Hold on." Jay pulled his phone from his pocket and held his finger up. "Sorry man, it's Jules." Jay patted Devil on the back and jogged to the passenger side of Hawk's sedan. "Hey, baby girl. Everything okay?"

Devil shook his head. People talked about "pregnancy brain" making soon-to-be mothers scatterbrained, but Jules was still sharp as a blade. Now, her fiancé on the other hand...

It was probably why Hawk was letting Jaybird devote most of his time to her instead of BlackStone. Distractions were unacceptable, especially in their line of work and Jaybird was a liability at this point.

Hopefully Jaybird wouldn't have to learn the hard way how dangerous emotional ties could become. Devil had let his feelings cloud his judgment too many times. He wasn't going to let anything—or *anyone*—distract him again.

CHAPTER FIVE

"It's Burgess."

"Yes?" The gruff male voice on the other end wasn't angry enough for Neal Burgess to detect the accent, but he knew it was only a matter of seconds before the inevitable. No conversation with the Russian ended well.

Neal rounded the hallway corner before immediately entering his office and shutting the door behind him. He leaned against it to relieve his tired bones before answering. "Black-Stone Securities was here again..."

"... And?"

"And I-uh, I'm reportin' it, like you asked?"

The long, insufferable sigh on the other end grated at Neal's nerves. "I told you to report to me if they know anything. Do they?"

Neal tugged at his mustache. It needed a trim. "No," he finally answered.

The boss wasn't going to be happy Neal had nothing to share. Again. But if the men of BlackStone Securities insisted on being tight-lipped about what they knew, then what was he supposed to do about it?

"Do they suspect anything about the party?"

Neal thought back to the conversation before answering. "No, sir."

His fingertips grazed down his uniform, remembering late to press the button on his chest before searching the lower pockets. The loud beep of the body worn camera was muffled by all the stacks of paperwork in his office. Although he was an investigator, Neal still wore the duty-issued vest. Bulky as hell, but it was more convenient for his needs than the tweed blazer and ironed button-down Hollywood portrayals.

Still waiting for a reply on the phone, Neal made his way around the cluttered room, dodging the files haphazardly stacked on the floor in chaotic heaps. He glanced through the indoor windows that gave him a view of the officers milling around in the precinct. When he was sure no one was watching, he carefully pulled the drawstrings so the brittle and yellowed slats wouldn't break on the blinds.

When he had his thoughts to himself, protected by the flimsy barrier between him and his nosy colleagues, Neal plopped on his threadbare desk chair. With the force of his collapse, he rolled back against the wall and groaned at the worsening of the whooshing pulse in his skull. The annoying buzzing in his right ear wasn't helping, either.

Wait, not buzzing.

"Sorry, could you repeat that?"

"No, Burgess. I do not fucking repeat myself. Pay attention you worthless piece of shit."

Neal winced as the Russian accent came out and patted the pill bottle in his pocket. The motion calmed his pulse to a steady beat rather than his usual staccato that threatened a heart attack at any moment. It was amazing how the simple gesture created a façade of relaxation, even if only for a moment.

It was nothing like the pills though.

Eleven.

That's all he had left in this particular bottle. He kept track of the number and never forgot, always knowing when he'd have to refill from the dwindling stash at home. He pulled the orange cylinder out of its pocket and stroked his thumb over the worn label.

Cicilia Burgess.

It was a miracle there was any sticker still stuck to the bottle, considering how long he'd been shoving it in and out of his pockets.

Neal swiped aside paperwork to reveal his coffee-stained, empty desk calendar. It'd been too long since he last took his medicine, but he wanted to make sure he had enough. He moved the phone to hold it between his shoulder and ear as he twisted open the bottle with one hand—a reflex at this point. He shuffled out the tablets, one by one, to make sure he'd remembered correctly.

One-two-three-four-five-six-seven-eight-nine-ten-eleven...

"That should do," Neal whispered into the void.

"Burgess!" The screaming in his ear made Neal jump. The *pitter-patter* of pills scattering across his desk sent a shock of panic down Neal's spine that rivaled the anxiety he felt when the Russian yelled at him.

"What is that sound?"

"Shit, sorry. Hold on." Neal cursed and dropped his cell phone onto a stack of papers and scurried his fingertips over the desk, searching for each tablet.

One... two-three-four... five... six... seven-eight-nine... ten...

"Where's eleven?" he mumbled before repeating the question to himself over and over again. He dropped below his desk, ignoring the crack of arthritic pain in his knees at his poor landing, instead feeling along the patchy green carpet for any sign of the missing tablet.

A fuzzy noise from above vibrated the wooden walls around him and Neal crawled backward, using the desk for assistance to stagger up to his seat.

"*Damnit*," he muttered. Worrying over his missing pill had made him completely forget he'd been on the phone with the Russian. He had to get his shit together. All his focus had been zapped away by the BlackStone meeting, and now all he could think about was whether he had enough pills to take one immediately.

"Investigator Burgess." He braced himself for what was going to come next.

The male's voice on the other line was too loud and angry to understand and parse out each word, but his accent was unmistakable.

"Will you stop yellin'... please?" Neal wished he could give the asshole a taste of his own medicine, but the man made good on his threats. That alone was enough to keep Neal's damn mouth shut. And sweat for another bar.

And one of them's missin'.

"We were on the phone you incompetent *mudak* and you disappeared! What could possibly be so fucking important you would interrupt our conversation?"

"I-uh, I dropped somethin'. I apologize—"

A groan on the other end scratched at Neal's eardrums. "Let me guess. A small rec-*fucking*-tangular pill?"

Neal tugged at his collar and loosened the vest now restricting his breath. "No. Of course not. I'm at work."

"Fuck! That is it. I am cutting you off."

An anvil of dread dropped into Neal's stomach and he reached for one of the pills, rolling it between his fingertips for comfort.

"What're you talkin' about? There's no need for that. It was a file. I dropped a file. That's all."

"Right." The man cursed. "What do you think? That I am the fucking *durak*? I am cutting you off. Whatever you have left is all you have until you clean yourself up. You are no use to me high and I do not need my contact being a liability."

Neal swore and ripped his phone from his ear to wind it back and throw—

"All you have to do is clean yourself up. You can do that. You've been doin' this for years. No need to worry about it now. Just dial it back, one step at a time. We'll do it together."

The gentle, feminine voice flowing in his mind made him long to remember what peace felt like. At one point, he'd found solace in her encouragement. But it'd been years since he'd believed the words she'd never said.

"We can do this," Neal whispered, fighting for conviction, and brought the phone back to his ear. He pasted on a confident smile, as if the person on the other end of the line was in the room. "No problem. Just one last buy to... um... safely cut myself off. I hardly even need them anymore."

While tugging at his collar again, he looked around for his water bottle. Unable to find it, he rolled his chair to his mini fridge and bent to retrieve one.

"No. I am cutting you off... for good," the caller spat out. "We need to move on. I do not have all day to console a junkie. Is that all you called me for? To tell me BlackStone knows nothing?"

Burgess nodded and cleared his throat. "Y-yes, sir. Nothin' to report."

A huff of breath into the receiver filled the phone line again. "You realize this has been a goddamn waste of time. I do not believe for one second BlackStone is clueless. They must be bluffing. Or maybe you have lost your touch, detective."

Neal's silent curse and accompanying gesture made him fumble with the phone. Once he brought it back up to his good ear, he remembered there had been something they needed to talk about. "There was somethin' they said. The little blonde who went missin'—you know she's one of them's sister—"

"Of course we know that *now*. We never would have chosen her if we had known *then*. Fear of reprisal is the only reason why we are no longer interested in her. It would have been helpful of you to give us that information last year before this whole fiasco went sideways."

"I went off the tips I received, damnit. The one's *y'all* gave me. I didn't know who all was involved—"

"Fucking idiot," the man muttered.

"Well, you say you ain't interested in *her*, but are you gonna try to pull the same stunt at the party again this year?"

"That is none of your concern. We ask the questions, you tell us the answers. That is the deal."

"That's how we got in trouble last time. I'm doin' things different now." The man on the other line started to grumble, but Neal wasn't finished. "I thought all that was over with. That you'd moved on from Ashland County with that shit. Just gone back to the drugs."

"Naivety is only attractive in females, Neal." A low huff of laughter resounded over the phone, making Neal shiver.

He should've kept his mouth shut, but his need to know outweighed his self-preservation. "Her brother said she thinks she's bein' followed. Is that true? If it is, maybe y'all oughta stop."

Neal sat up in his chair and sorted out the pills again. He tried to listen. The answer was important. But he still needed to find that last one. Now that he had a limit, none of them could go unaccounted for.

"... we have lost interest in her but we keep tabs on people who know our business. From what you have said BlackStone knows, she does not remember anything of value and we want to keep it that way. Keeping our distance and a low profile ensures our privacy."

"So... you'll leave her alone?"

"Are you fucking deaf too? I am not having her stalked! She is a liability unless she falls into our laps. We might be able to make her useful but only if she were to stick her nose where it does not belong. At that point we would be cutting loose ends. Even then there is the possibility of exposure we cannot afford."

That was good. One less thing Neal had to worry about. There was already too much on his plate.

Neal mopped the sweat accumulating on his forehead with the back of his sleeve. Fingers shaking, he carefully put one pill in his hand and swallowed it down with the water. The small lump accompanying the cool gulp down his throat lifted the anvil on his chest so he could breathe again. He sighed as heavily as his ol' smoker's lungs would allow, leaning all the way back in his chair until his head rested against the wall.

"Alright, well I think that's everything."

"Fucking imbecile."

The call disconnected and Neal stared at the phone in his hand as he wondered how his life had gotten to the point where he had to depend on that Russian bastard.

Maybe the Russian was right. Maybe he should be cut off.

Despite his thoughts, he tapped each pill, slowly putting each one back in Cici's old medicine bottle. He counted them back into the bottle.

One-two-three-four-five-six-seven-eight-nine...

He'd have to figure out where the missing pill was ASAP. He had a limit now... But one more couldn't hurt.

Rather than deposit it into the medicine bottle, Neal popped the last tablet into his mouth. He'd earned it. Talking to the Russian always took him to his wit's end.

He bent his head back and embraced the calm flowing down his throat and rooting into his blood. The promise of peace and quiet would soon rush through his veins. In the meantime, he pulled out his lighter and flicked it on and off. It was a habit he'd developed years ago as a smoker and it'd become a mindless thing for his hands to do to pass the time. Resting his eyes, his head at an awkward angle at the back of his chair, he tried not to think about the one pill he hadn't found yet.

Eight left. We'll find the other one later, won't we, Cici?

The fog of his memory revealed Cici's sad brown eyes and he ached to see her smile one more time. He hadn't deserved one in a long time. Too long. Even before the world became too much for her to endure.

It was one of the reasons why she'd left it in the first place.

Neal squinched his eyes closed against the burn inside until finally, cooling euphoria washed over him, and he did his best to forget the woman he'd damned with his love.

CHAPTER SIX

Harsh, rhythmic slapping of shoes against asphalt grew louder and louder, making Ellie's heart race. She tried to anticipate what direction they were coming from, but they sounded like they were already on top of her.

"Behind! Left!"

Ellie scooted to the right and let the sprinter pass her, trying not to be annoyed her pulse shot up twenty beats every time someone approached. It was a lined recreational track, for God's sake, with plenty of room in every lane. But for some reason these runners insisted on getting *right behind* her before they passed.

Jerks.

She would've been running her usual route around campus, but Jason was even more paranoid than she was and insisted she ran inside the Ashland State University gym. But half her love for running was being in the fresh air. Plus, she hadn't even seen the Corolla since Naomi came into Sasha Saves five days ago, so the outdoor track was her secret compromise. Jason would probably still rip her a new one if he found out.

Running was part of her therapy "homework" so the track was better than nothing at all. Completing her therapeutic to-do

list every day was the only way her therapist agreed to appointments over the phone "as needed" rather than in-person every
other week. It'd been a hard-won fight, but it was worth it not
having to waste all that time talking.

"This track is nice, but when can we run our route again? It's
crowded in the mornin'."

Unfortunately, Ellie's roommate hadn't gotten the "no talking" memo. Ellie's campus runs had been soothing the first
couple of weeks. But when Virginia found out her exercise
routine, she insisted they run together at the butt crack of dawn
this semester. Feeling guilty for declining every other invitation
Virginia extended, Ellie figured she had to run anyway, might as
well make Virginia happy, too. Couldn't hurt, right?

Wrong.

Every morning, Virginia blasted "Oh Happy Day" by The
Edwin Hawkins Singers in the dorm, and sang loud as heck
until Ellie was forced to go running with her to shut her up.
Rain or shine, sleet or snow, every day, Ellie suffered in silence
with someone who insisted on not listening to music so they
could *talk* and 'get to know each other' for 3.1 miles. What used
to be meditative was now one scream away from feeling like
torture.

Ellie's side seized and she nearly tripped from the pain.
Slowing down, she breathed deeply through the stitch, ending
the breath on a frustrated groan. She was dragging from staying
up to study for her midterms. What sucked the most was her
exhaustion might not even have been worth it. She had no
memory of what she'd studied for and she'd woken up with a
crick in her neck from her cheek being plastered to a pool of
drool in her textbook.

"...Then I think I'll go into the history surroundin' Ashland
State U. Oh, hey, you okay?" Virginia slowed and circled back to
Ellie, her eyes narrowed in concern.

Ellie nodded before putting her hands on her head and
dodging runners to step off the track to stretch out the cramp.

"Yeah, yeah. I'm fine. What were you sayin'? About your university tours?"

She didn't particularly want to hear more about Virginia's ASU job, but she also didn't want another nursing student examination. The girl was smart, but Ellie couldn't take another worst-case scenario diagnosis. If Virginia told her one more time that an injury was a sign of impending death, Ellie was going to have to follow through just to put herself out of her misery.

"Well, if you're sure..." She watched Ellie for a second longer. After seeing whatever she needed to ensure Ellie wasn't gonna die there on the spot, she nodded. "Right, where was I? Oh, maybe I should tell them about how delusional our professors are. Like Novikov last time you jetted from class?" Virginia's back straightened and she pretended to look down invisible glasses. "Miss Stooooone, your peers are interested in *learning*." She laughed at her own terrible impression and Ellie couldn't help but grin. "Like any of us ever want to be there, amiright?"

"I don't think you'll persuade too many students to apply with that story." Ellie huffed. "But your southern-Russian accent combo kinda sounds like you've had too many vodka crans, sooo that's fun."

Virginia rolled her eyes. "Yeah, yeah, yeah. Those kids aren't listenin' anyway. It's all about gettin' the parents." She snapped. "Maybe I'll get the parents with the story, and the kids soundin' at nine a.m. on a Tuesday."

Ellie outright laughed and immediately felt a stab of guilt in her chest. Virginia reminded her so much of Sasha. It felt like betrayal to enjoy her company.

Virginia didn't seem to notice. "I'm thinkin' of usin' one of my class assignments as a history lesson. My University 101 seminar is doin' a project on Ashland County and my topic is Hatcher Gardens. You're from here, right? Ya know it? Maybe I'll put you in my bibliography."

Virginia laughed at her joke, but Ellie's heart clenched worse than the slight stitch in her side. "The neighborhood? Uh... yeah.

I think it's mostly abandoned houses and addicts now, but my, uh, friend used to live there when we were kids." She swallowed and tried to control the shake in her voice.

It felt wrong to bring up her best friend to Sasha's personality clone. But Ellie was turning over a new leaf and trying to pretend she wasn't dead inside. Talking about Sasha was a good step. Right? Gritting her teeth, she pushed past the ache.

"For real? You think she could give me a tour?"

"She, um... doesn't live in Ashland anymore. Her family left a few months back." Ellie would've done the same thing if she hadn't missed her chance. The plan had always been to become roommates and live it up in college. After she'd been rescued and Sasha hadn't, Ellie refused to open any college letters. Losing that future was too much to face.

"Damn, it's a shame your friend doesn't live there still. The neighborhood's been 'round forever. All that history... the old architecture with the root cellars and vaulted ceilings, the centuries-old trees, how it was a neighborhood before ASU was even established. Parents eat that shit up on tours. And hell, if there are ghosts, the prospects'll eat that up, too." A perfectly arched blonde brow raised at Ellie. "Are there ghosts?"

"This bitch is a little cray. I like her."

Ellie tucked her chin to hide her smile at Sasha's declaration. *Of course you do.*

She lifted her chin to answer Virginia. "If there are, we never saw 'em." She didn't know about ghosts. The only thing the neighborhood held for Ellie now was bittersweet memories.

Her stitch was gone, so she began jogging again. Virginia joined in, keeping pace but never slowing her verbal stream of consciousness. If Ellie had to admit it, Virginia wasn't *so* bad. It was actually kind of nice to have something else to focus on.

If it hadn't been for therapy, Ellie would've never met Virginia, or even gone to college. With every session, Ellie realized she wanted to provide survivors with the same healing she'd received, and to do that, she needed a license to practice. If a license was what was best for survivors, then a license was what she was gonna get.

Unfortunately, life doesn't pause for grief. When Ellie was finally ready to accept an offer, she'd already missed other college decision deadlines and Ashland State University was the only school that would take her.

Ellie's brain stopped going a million miles a second when she realized there was a lull in the conversation.

Shoot.

Ellie glanced over at Virginia to find her perfect smile was waning as she obviously waited for a response.

"Fascinating," Ellie muttered.

Virginia brightened with the meager encouragement. "Right? Blizzards this far down south are crazy and a couple of times every year way back then. Insane. That's what I was talkin' about with the cellars underneath the houses. Did your friend have one of those?"

Ellie swallowed past the metallic tang of regret and icy air on her tongue. "Oh, um, yeah." She had to start saying her name aloud. It'd be good, right? Like ripping off a Band-Aid. Maybe.

No. Losing Sasha was nothing short of an amputation.

"My friend... Sasha... her family had one of those. We used to hide there and in our treehouse in the park when we played manhunt with the neighborhood kids."

The cramp Ellie thought had gone away came back as a steady throb. Okay, she was officially overdoing it. She slowed her pace and staggered off the track again to put her hands over her head and breathe through the pain.

"Manhunt?" Virginia slowed to stop with her, and her voice hit a funny pitch as she stretched her arms over her head.

"It's where one person goes to hide and everyone else tries to find her. When they find her, they hide with her until there's one person left. Like reverse hide-and-seek."

"Oh my God! How fun! I woulda loved playin' that as a kid!" Virginia clapped her hands rapidly.

Ellie blinked at Virginia's enthusiasm, trying not to see Sasha in her place. When she opened her eyes again she only saw her roommate.

Right after she'd been rescued, Ellie could've sworn she saw Sasha everywhere. It was unnerving. Now Sasha's voice was the only thing that stuck around. But seeing her friend was a natural association for her mind when Virginia was around. She was so like Sasha it was painful.

The two looked nothing alike, but their mannerisms were identical and it was hard not to compare them. The southern belle had big bottle-blonde hair Sasha would've totally sneered at growing up. That hair was a mean girl trademark at their high school. Thankfully, Ellie's experience with Virginia had been the opposite, although Ellie hadn't allowed herself to get too close. The idea of opening up to someone else scratched her insides raw.

"I was thinkin'..."

Oh boy.

Virginia always took on the light, airy lilt in her voice whenever she tried to convince Ellie to participate in some semblance of friendship. Ellie hated to keep her roommate at arm's length, but she couldn't help it. She wasn't ready to make new friends. Sometimes she wondered if she'd ever be.

"I'm gonna go shoppin' this weekend. I'd love for you to come with me." There was a note of vulnerability in Virginia's voice as she slowly asked her question.

Ellie winced. "I'm sorry, Virginia. I can't. I have to... work. And I should probably study."

Virginia groaned. "You never come out with me! Girl, ya need to live your college life or it's gonna blow right past ya. Please, please, please come with." Virginia's bright blue eyes stared Ellie down, and her hands were up in a prayer stance. "I'll get on my knees if I have to."

Ellie rolled her eyes and snorted. "Good Lord, please don't

do that. Why do you want me to come with you so bad anyway? We barely even know each other."

Virginia's smile wiped from her face, like one of those Greek theater masks. "Ouch."

Ellie's cheeks grew hot and she shifted on her feet. "I mean... I don't know. It's... I mean it's true, ya know?"

Virginia bit her lip before muttering, "Not for lack of tryin'." Ellie opened her mouth to explain, but Virginia continued. "I know you don't have any friends, unless they're all at that secret job you're failin' out of school for." She gave Ellie a pointed look and Ellie toed the ground. "I know you're from here and you went through somethin' real bad. I don't know the deets 'cause I want you to share with me when you're ready. But, I've... heard rumors. And I know you lost your best friend."

Tears pricked behind Ellie's eyes and she breathed through her nose slowly in and out to clear the pain.

Virginia sighed. "Look, Ellie. I'm not tryna do anything but be friends with my roommate. Go shoppin' with me, or don't. I don't wanna force someone to hang out with me." She straightened her posture and turned to leave the track.

Ellie took a deep breath, raised her face to the chilly wind and closed her eyes. Virginia was right. All Ellie's roommate had ever done was try to be friends with her, but wasn't it still too soon? She couldn't open up like that again. Not yet. Besides, she had so much on her plate, what with the survivors at Sasha Saves, school, therapy, and defense lessons with Jason. She barely had enough time to herself as it was.

Ellie watched Virginia's back as she walked away, her shoulders slumping with each step away. Sasha's voice rang in her mind.

"Go after her, dummy. She's good for you."

"Virginia, wait up!" Ellie called and jogged to catch her. "I'm sorry. It's... complicated. I- I'm having trouble lately—"

Ellie's phone vibrated in her leggings and she mumbled for

Virginia to hold on before pulling it from her pocket and opening

Dev: Where are you and why are you not at Black-Stone Securities yet?

A flash of panic shocked through her. She had no idea why he'd be demanding her to be at BlackStone, but it couldn't be good. Normally she'd be there for self-defense training, but Jason canceled their lesson a couple of weeks ago due to Jules's doctor appointment. A thought sent an icy burn down the sweat on her spine.

Is everything ok with Jules and the baby?

Virginia must've sensed the situation and waited in silence with Ellie. After a minute of no response, Ellie shoved her phone in her pocket and called over her shoulder as she ran toward the parking lot and Virginia's pink Jeep Wrangler.

"Can you take me to BlackStone Securities? Something's wrong."

CHAPTER SEVEN

Offbeat thumping echoed outside the gym, calling to Ellie like a beacon as she rushed through the BlackStone Securities complex to find Dev. The facility was completely soundproof, so she'd already explored the garage, shooting range, and medical room before finally hearing the faint beat. The fact the whole first floor had been empty didn't help her anxiety.

Dev wasn't answering his phone, and the wild-goose chase was making Ellie light-headed with worry. She'd let Virginia leave as soon as she'd been dropped off, believing she'd find Dev right away. Worst-case scenarios were flitting through Ellie's mind, and the fear something was wrong with Jules and the baby was enough to make Ellie feel on the verge of passing out.

As she made her way through the halls, heavy metal blared through the speakers ahead of her and still the thumps grew louder and faster over the beat. When she rounded the last corner before the gym and entered the propped open door, she realized the source of the arrhythmic thudding noises.

In the corner of the gym, Dev was hitting a punching bag with enough force that Ellie was surprised it was still hanging from the walls. His bare back was to her, and the muscles in his rounded shoulders flexed with each hit. For the first time, Ellie finally saw the beautiful, tattooed, skeletal wings spanning his entire back and arms.

She'd seen the feathers lining the backs of his arms, but she'd never seen him shirtless. A closer look at the artwork showed the wings she'd always imagined on the rest of his body were broken and torn. Feathers hung from inked bone and sinew, and there were rips in the design's exposed membrane. The ink work was so vivid, it was easy to imagine the rest of the wings spread out and wide around him in tattered shreds. Like a fallen angel.

Or a demon.

A lump formed in Ellie's throat, making it hard to swallow. Whatever tragedy had inspired that tattoo was embedded much deeper than the skin it covered.

The divots outlining Dev's back muscles contracted and bulged as he boxed, and Ellie couldn't help but stare at his strong arms as he punched the bag. She'd seen those hands heal and she'd ached for their soft touch over her skin. For his fingertips to graze over her, move her body where he needed her right before they fell apart in each other's arms.

Great. First flashbacks, then nightmares. Why not add delusions in the mix?

But as she observed his strength in such a violent display of power, Ellie found herself gravitating to him while an entirely different fantasy flashed in her head. Instead of gentle caresses making her tingle, she imagined his fingers gripping into her hips as he held her from behind, shoving her up against the mirrored wall right behind him.

Ellie rubbed the goose bumps on her skin, already growing sensitive just from her imagination. If she didn't stop daydreaming, she was going to do something stupid and desperate, like fall and crawl at his feet. She locked her knees to keep from embarrassing herself.

After a cleansing exhale, frustration filtered in. She was being ridiculous, salivating over some boy even though she had no clue why she was there or if there was an emergency. And here Dev was, working out.

Sasha's laughter barked in Ellie's thoughts. *"'Some boy'. Shyeah, right. That right there's a man. One you should let bend you over and—"*

The slaps against the punching bag stilled, and Ellie shifted her gaze to find Dev's steady on her in the mirror.

For the love of God, please don't be a mind reader.

The corner of his lips twitched, sending her hopes spiraling. Of course he knew what she was thinking. He always did.

She braced herself against being teased, but Dev only shook his head, like he was trying to get her thoughts out of his own mind. Adopting a sour expression, he crossed his arms before yelling over the music. "You're late."

"Late? What the—" She scoffed and mirrored his posture. "What's going on, Dev? Is it Jules? Are she and the baby okay?"

Dev frowned before walking over to his phone and pausing the music. The silence pulsed through her in several staccato beats before she realized it was her heartbeat.

"They're fine as far as I know. But I've been here an hour." He narrowed his eyes and looked her up and down. "You training in that?"

At the hint of disappointment lacing his question, Ellie looked down even though she knew she wore leggings and a long-sleeved T-shirt with tennis shoes. "Um... yeah? What's wrong with—Wait, what do you mean 'training?' Was that what your text was about? My self-defense training?" She flopped onto a weight-lifting bench and slapped her hand against her chest in relief. "I thought it was about something serious, dang."

"Self-defense *is* serious," Dev grumbled under his breath before drinking from his water bottle.

Ellie tilted her head. "But, wait... Jason's been teaching me—"

"And with the baby he's asked me to help. He also said he'd tell you. But he didn't, I take it?" Ellie shook her head. Dev's frown deepened before he muttered, "His distractions are getting dangerous."

Ellie's mouth fell open. "Are you *seriously* calling Jules and their baby a distraction? What the heck is wrong with you?"

Dev rolled his eyes. "In our line of work, hell yeah they're distractions."

"I ask again, 'What the heck is wrong with you?'" Ellie scoffed only for Dev to shrug.

"I said it. I meant it. Now step up to the mat. We don't need to waste any more time."

"Someone's feeling sassy. Sheesh. Where is everybody, by the way? I searched everywhere for you and it was a ghost town."

"Your brother's with Jules. The rest of them are on assignment or out. We have lives outside of this place, you know. Come on," he huffed before tugging her by the forearm to the mat.

She shouldn't have felt anything. He was being a total butthead. So why did his gentle grip around her arm set her nerves on fire?

When they reached the middle of the mat, he let go and Ellie rubbed her arm to get rid of the tingles his fingertips left in their wake. He crossed his arms, making his chest muscles harden under the pose.

"Look alive, El. Eyes up."

"Hm?" Her stare whipped up to his forest green gaze. Heat flushed over her skin at the smile in his eyes. Yep, she'd totally been caught. "Sorry. Training... yeah. I can do that."

Dev smirked. "Something on your mind, Ellie?"

She scowled and scrambled for something to say before finally returning his smirk with one of her own. "Careful, Dev. You keep smiling and your face might get stuck like that."

His cocky grin evaporated before he bent to get something from his bag. "Fine. I'll be serious."

The blank look that replaced it made her chest tighten with guilt. "So, uh, what's on the agend—oof." Ellie caught the item Dev tossed at her and examined what looked like a roll of some kind of tape. "What's this?"

One of Dev's strawberry blond brows raised as he spoke to her like she was an idiot. "It's wrapping tape."

"Okay..." Ellie gestured with the roll. "I don't know why I'm supposed to know that."

Dev cocked his head to the side as he scrubbed his short beard. "It's for your hands." He held up his, covered in the same red material. "Does Jason not make you protect your hands and wrists?" When Ellie shook her head, Dev whistled. "Damn. That's tougher than I thought he'd be."

She shrugged, not really sure what that meant. "Guess so." She flicked the edges of the cloth wrap and pulled it awkwardly around her knuckles.

"Here let me do it." Taking Ellie's hand in his, he dressed her knuckles with quick efficiency before moving to the other to do the same. "There's no reason for you not to wrap it, except to feel the real impact of skin on skin." Dev paused and dropped her hand like it was on fire before clearing his throat. "Which, I mean, has its merit." He tossed the roll into his open duffel bag and picked up his phone. "Let's get started. How long have you been taking lessons from Jason?"

"A couple of months, or so." Ellie flexed her hands, testing out their mobility.

"Excellent. That's good to hear." Heavy metal resumed playing at a lower volume over the speakers before Dev tossed his phone back onto his duffel. He retrieved curved punching pads hanging from the wall and approached her. "Let's see what you got then."

Ellie's heart flipped up into her throat, anxious to show off all her hard work, especially to Dev.

"Let's do this." Ellie bit her lip and got into the fighting stance Jason had taught her, with her legs shoulder-width apart and her right foot slightly in front of her left. She brought her right fist to eye level and her left beside her chin, tucking her elbow near her body.

Dev furrowed his brows. "Huh, you're a southpaw?"

"A what?" Her nose scrunched, but she never got out of stance, worried she was doing it wrong.

"You're left handed?"

"Oh... yeah." Ellie stood up a little straighter and analyzed her offending left hand. "Is that bad?"

Dev shook his head. "No that's great. I don't know why I didn't notice it before. Lefties are better at surprising an enemy." The reference to an enemy made the flutters in her stomach leaden with panic. "We have to make sure you're ready for jabs coming at you from straight on. Now, fists up. Everything looks great but make sure your wrists are slightly bent and your chin is tucked so I can't hit you there... Oh, and—" He reached out with his thumb and pulled at her bottom lip from between her teeth. "Don't do that. You might bite that pretty lip off."

Ellie's eyes widened at the caress, but Dev only coughed and continued to speak, moving on as if her insides hadn't just melted at the touch of his finger.

"You know... for good form." He pushed his hands into the padding before hitting the long rectangular mitts together. "Okay, yep, that's better. Now, lay it on me."

She didn't want to dwell on the fact he'd adopted yet another perfectly blank expression. His hot and cold routine was giving her whiplash, but at least her irritation made it easier to want to hit him.

She pulled back her left fist and struck the mitt with all her strength and frustration.

Synthetic leather immediately smacked her in the face, making her head fly back. The rest of her body went with it, and even on the padded wrestling mats, she landed on her butt with a resounding thud. But the sound was a whisper compared to the deafening roar from the giant towering over her.

"*What the fuck* was *that?*"

CHAPTER EIGHT

"What the fuck was that?"

The exclamation slipped out of him before he could rein it in. Devil hated cursing in front of Ellie, but the damn waif of a girl was laid out on the mat like he'd gone full throttle with the punching mitt. Which he hadn't. He'd made sure of that, actually.

He kneeled on the ground beside her and tossed the mitts to the side. "You okay, baby? Shi-*oot*." He brushed his hands over her face and cradled her cheeks, careful not to move her too much in case she'd hit her head too hard or suffered whiplash.

Ellie groaned and those caramel eyes peeked out between half closed eyelids. "What the heck did you do that for?" She grunted as she sat up on her elbows. "You tryna kill me?"

When she sat up without any sign of injury, Devil released the breath he'd been holding. It wasn't until he sat back on his heels and relaxed her words finally registered.

"Kill you? I barely touched you! And what was that? You didn't even try to block my strike!" He pulled his hair at its ends trying to figure out what the fuck she was thinking not protecting herself.

"What do you mean, 'block your strike?' You weren't supposed to hit me. I was the one doing the hitting!"

Devil paused, first to assess her already reddening left cheek —damn the girl had sensitive skin—then to see if she was joking. But no, she was dead serious.

"Hold on... you didn't expect your attacker to strike back? Do you honestly think they'll sit there and take getting beat up by a girl?"

She covered her face and groaned. "Ugh, no. Of course not. It's just... Jason doesn't ever hit me back. I wasn't expecting you to do it."

Devil's mouth opened and shut a few times before he finally figured out what to say.

"How the hell are you supposed to be prepared for a fight if you don't practice the other half of it? Fighting isn't just about offense. Especially not in your case. A girl your size needs to figure out how to outsmart, outmaneuver, and outrun her attacker."

He held three fingers up for emphasis. "Your priorities are to run, hide, fight. In that order." Unable to help himself, he reached out and brushed her now bright red cheek. "Not to mention, it's absolutely vital to know what a hit is gonna feel like so you can react through the pain during the real thing." He reluctantly brought his hand back and shook his head. "Shi-*oot*, Jason wasn't teaching you how to save yourself. He was killing you slowly with misguided confidence."

Ellie's otherwise tan cheeks paled, making the mark from his strike more pronounced. "You mean, I can't defend myself? Even after all this practicing?"

Devil cursed inwardly at the defeat laced in her words. He didn't want to scare her, but coddling her could prove deadly in the real world.

"No, I mean... you gave a pretty killer punch. I had to put some resistance behind the mitt. But without knowing defensive moves too, you may as well be fighting with your hands tied behind your back. Literally." He scrubbed his beard. "Actually, that might be a good exercise..."

A thumping sound brought his attention back to the woman in front of him, now collapsed on the floor and groaning in frustration. "This is hopeless. I can't even take a hit by a padded pillow without falling to the ground." She rubbed her cheek with the hand that wasn't flung over her eyes. "That kinda hurt by the way."

"Get over it. Physical pain is easy. Mind over matter." Devil leaned forward and pulled Ellie's hand away from her face to make sure she was paying attention. "It's not hopeless. You've got a good foundation. We'll work with what you already know." He stood up from the mat and held out his hand. She gave an adorable grunt before grabbing his offering.

The touch shouldn't have been anything but platonic. It always had been whenever he'd assisted his teammates in getting back to their feet after a fight. But Ellie's hand in his made his fingers ache to feel every inch of her skin. He dropped it and backed away as soon as she'd steadied.

"Let's try again. Get back into your stance, but this time— wait, what're you doing?" She was pulling her goddamn long-sleeved T-shirt off. How was he supposed to teach her like a regular trainee if she was half naked? "Ellie..." He gritted out each word through tight lips as she tossed her shirt near his duffel bag. "What are you doing?"

"Hold your horses, okay? If we're gonna do some serious fighting, I'm taking this thing off. I'm so sweaty the sleeves are sticking to me."

He massaged his eyes and turned away, praying he wouldn't get hard just from her stripping a sweaty shirt off. Why he was being so fucking insane, he had no idea. Already, he'd made an ass of himself by flirting with her. She was his buddy's sister and now he was charged with training her to protect herself. If he didn't get his shit together he'd be no good to her and if anything happened to her on his watch it'd be just like—

No. It'd be worse. There'd be no coming back from that.

He inhaled a deep, centering breath through his nose before forcing a hard exhale out of his mouth.

"What do you think?"

Devil blinked and realized she'd been talking to him. "'What do I think' about what?"

Ellie perched her hands on her hips and tapped her foot, obviously annoyed he hadn't been paying attention. "Well... If you train me and I learn how to kick some butt, could I join the BlackStone team? You know, to help figure out who was behind taking me and Sash—"

"No."

The word came out harsher than he'd intended and she clamped her lips closed. There was no way in fucking hell he was letting Ellie anywhere near their plans to take down the bastards who kidnapped her. He'd never forgive himself if she got hurt again.

"Welp, that's that, I guess." She studied the ground as she mumbled, compelling him to explain, but she spoke before he had a chance.

"I'm ready." She rolled back her slumped shoulders, seemingly shedding her disappointment for the sake of the exercise.

Devil paused mid-nod and his eyes widened. Ellie's new posture highlighted her breasts, two perfect handfuls trapped inside her tight black sports bra that zipped in the fucking front. He didn't even know they made those, but now that he did, his fingers ached to draw down the short zipper and free them right into his eager hands. It didn't help her black leggings were just as tight. There was nothing to hide her trim hourglass figure, and he desperately wanted to get lost in time.

He closed his eyes and rubbed the back of his neck as he turned away to hide the evidence of his arousal. They weren't there to fuck around, especially not literally. He was teaching her to defend herself if she was ever attacked. Again. That sobering thought was enough to calm his dick back down.

"Right. This time, look forward and keep your rear fist up to block while you punch with your lead fist."

She got into her stance again before nodding. "I need to look at your shoulders, right?"

Devil shook his head and put the padded mitts back on. "Nope. Just forward. It's best if you don't look at anything specific. Watch my upper body and look for openings to get a good punch in. You'll more naturally defend yourself if you're focusing on where you can hit next."

"Got it. Oh wait! First..." She ran to his phone and paused "Shout at the Devil" by Motley Crue.

"Hey, that's a good—" Low piano keys came over the speaker until a woman asked lyrically, "Why a man great, 'til he gotta be great?"

Devil groaned louder than the music. "Come on, El. Lizzo again? You have her on fu-*reaking* repeat at the clinic."

Ellie burst into laughter. "Hey, if you get to beat me up, I get to listen to what I want while you do it. We can turn it back to that old depressing crap when your mitts are off and I'm the only one doing the hitting."

"Watch it," Devil shouted over the music, unable to hold back a grin. "Just because the lyrics actually mean something doesn't mean it's depressing. And don't knock it just because it was before your time. You should respect your elders." Devil made sure to give her a pointed look as she returned to the center of the mat.

"Elders?" she scoffed. "You're twenty-seven, hardly a senior citizen."

"Well, in this gym, I'm the professor and you're the student, so you get one Lizzo song and then it's back to my 'old depressing crap'."

Ellie rolled her eyes and resumed her stance. "Whatever you say, *sir*."

All sensation from his extremities shot to his groin. He

watched helplessly as Ellie giggled, still totally unaware of the effect that word had on him.

That's what he should remember. She was too innocent to even know what she was saying. Too naïve to know the power she could have over a man like him.

Instead of aiming what he knew would be a lust-filled gaze at Ellie, he turned to study his mitts, adjusting himself behind one of them. He couldn't resist watching her in the mirror, though, even as he clenched and unclenched his hands around the straps.

"Is something wrong with the pillow thing?" she asked before her golden eyes met his in the mirror. Her sharp inhale made his cock twitch against the tie of his gym shorts and he brought his stare back to his own green eyes. His hunger for her showed plainly on his face, and he was looking at her like a fucking dessert.

She shifted on her feet, squeezing her legs together, and he ground his teeth to the point of pain to try to regain control. If he didn't act quickly, he'd have his cake and eat it too. Right on the gym floor.

"Stance," he barked, keeping one mitt low in front of the tent in his shorts.

"What?" she asked, her brow raised in confusion.

He drew his arm back in an exaggerated motion to hit her with the mitt. Reading him properly, she brought her right fist up, barely in time to block her face.

"What the heck, Dev—"

"Stance, Ellie. Always be in a fighting position and ready for strikes."

She narrowed her eyes at him for a moment before she shook her head slightly and followed his command. Getting back into training mode was helping. Concentrating on making sure Ellie was able to fight for herself should the moment arise was the cold shower he needed.

"It sounds counterintuitive but if you don't have time to block, lean into the punch. The attacker will likely miss and scrape the side of your head or you could absorb it with your forehead, which knowing your hard head, would do more damage to the other guy."

"Hey!" Ellie yelled and delivered a good hook.

"Nice." Dev caught it with the mitt. "Keep going."

They began to spar and Devil made sure to use exaggerated movements to help Ellie learn where to block. Her strikes and blocks were already efficient, but after just a few sets they became fluid, only needing a couple adjustments.

"Tighten your neck muscles. Clench your jaw, and if you anticipate any hits to your stomach, tighten those muscles, too. Try to shift so the punch lands to your sides rather than some-where vital." She got too close again and Devil feinted to hit her with the mitt.

She growled and backed away, finally out of the danger zone —the area where Devil could hit her with his long arms, but she couldn't reach him.

"Yes, exactly. Keep backing up when you can. You need to stay in the safe zone." Ellie raised her eyebrow. "Where neither of us can strike the other."

"Sounds familiar," Ellie muttered.

Devil ignored whatever that meant. "Remember to strike when necessary, but every fighting strategy you have should center on escape. Let's keep going. Just one more set."

Her movements were growing slow, like she was tired already. Ellie nodded and blew blonde wisps out of her face while she tracked his body language.

"Do you have a bobby pin?"

"What?" She paused in her movements and looked up, still looking back and forth to his mitts.

"A bobby pin. Those little things for your hair?"

"Oh, um, not on me but I own them."

"Start wearing them."

"Excuse me?" Her face scrunched up cute and Dev resisted the urge to grin like a fool at her.

"They're good for making sure your hair stays back. That way, when you kick someone's ass, they can see your pretty face while you do it." He dared a wink at her, knowing he was flirting with danger, and when she laughed it off, he continued. "Plus, it can help you unlock doors, break out of handcuffs, they're really probably the best covert weapon a woman has at her fingertips."

"Good to know," Ellie muttered, getting back into stance.

Goddamn, her focus is hot.

They continued to go back and forth, this time with her actually managing to get some jabs at the mitts on his hands.

He hadn't lied before. For how little she was, she packed some power, even when her stamina was waning. He'd always been impressed with her inner strength. Witnessing her physical strength was a new pleasure.

Emotions Devil had locked down were threatening to break free. He didn't need to question why they were battling against their cage. He knew why.

It was the first time they'd had time alone together without the threat of people coming in and out. No BlackStone agent was at the facility. It was just them.

Him and Ellie.

The devil and his angel.

And damn, was that tempting.

Devil pushed the thought away when he noticed her posture slacking past the point of fatigue and her strikes slowing. After she missed a few attacks from the mitt to her face and body without any attempt of blocking, Devil called a break.

He tossed her a water bottle and watched as she swallowed, mesmerized by a single glistening bead of moisture on her neck as it dripped down to the valley between her breasts. It was that drop that made him realize her chest was heaving with each panting breath. A crinkle of the plastic water bottle drew his attention to her shaking hands and he registered, not for the first time, the prominent bags under her eyes.

"You okay, angel?"

She paused in her sips. "Uh, aside from the fact I'm getting beat up? Yeah, I'm okay."

"Har har, very funny."

Ellie curtsied a fake skirt and Devil smirked.

"Okay, cut the sass. When was the last time you slept? Or ate? You should be tired after a hard workout, but" —he gestured in her direction— "not this tired."

Ellie scoffed before tossing the now empty bottle near his duffel bag. "Wow, thanks jerk." She rolled her eyes and Devil felt a pang of guilt at the hurt she was trying to hide with her flippant hair flick.

The gesture was out of character for her, almost a shadow of someone else. From everything Jaybird said, Ellie's friend, the one who'd been murdered when they were kidnapped, was bold and full of life. Devil knew from experience the imprint a childhood friend had on your personality. Especially one you lose.

"I'll have you know, I already ran a 5K today and I had no plans this morning of getting my *sass* kicked." Her arm moved across her chest as she stretched it out with the other. "What's next, *sir?*"

Devil gritted his teeth, refusing to acknowledge that word. It went straight to his cock every time and she wasn't going to get to deflect this conversation again. She'd already sidestepped it at Sasha Saves with Jules and Nora the week before. He didn't know if anyone else had called her out on it since, but he didn't need SOCM training to know something was up. Her health was more important than hurting her feelings.

"Here." He bent for his duffel bag and tossed her a small towel along with her shirt as he grabbed his. "Let's call it for the day. I'll drive you home."

Ellie eyed him cautiously and her mischievous smile slipped. "But... I can get Virginia to take me—"

"Nope. If I drive you it'll be easier to see if someone's following you."

Her eyes widened. "You know about that?"

"Yep. And I'm not too happy I didn't hear it from you." She looked down and he lifted her chin to look at him. "Why didn't you tell me?"

She pinched her eyes closed and groaned before opening them again. "Ugh, I felt dumb because I'm afraid of my own shadow lately. I only told Jason because that was our deal." She withdrew her chin from his fingers and pulled her shirt on with frustrated, jerky movements. "And besides, ever since I told him, I haven't even seen it around anymore. I hadn't thought to say anything since."

He shook his head and pulled his shirt over his head. "I don't like it, El. Your brother is preoccupied lately. If you notice anything else odd or making you feel uncomfortable, let me know, got it?"

A spark of defiance flitted across her face before she nodded. He would've harped on it more, but something about her submission made his chest puff out in satisfaction. Instead, Devil wiped his face and led Ellie toward the garage in weighted silence.

When they reached his truck, Devil opened the door for her before she got a chance to do it herself. The lift kit Phoenix installed on Devil's old Ford was too high for her to climb in gracefully, so he appreciated the opportunity to admire her sexy ass in tight leggings as he boosted her into the cab.

He adjusted himself while he rounded the hood to the driver's side and hopped behind the steering wheel.

"I could've done more, you know." Ellie's voice was soft, like she didn't quite believe herself. "I wasn't tired or anything."

Devil entered the keycode on his phone that Snake had set up to open the garage, and drove out of the gated complex toward Ellie's dorm. BlackStone Securities was on the outskirts of town, which only gave him around twenty minutes to get something off his chest before they reached the ASU campus.

"I've been meaning to talk to you, actually." He watched from his peripheral as Ellie sat up.

"So talk," Ellie replied, adding a false airiness to her tone.

He inhaled a deep breath, reminding himself that making them both uncomfortable was going to do her some good. "You seem awfully... busy, lately."

Ellie lifted her shoulder and fidgeted with her hands in her lap. "I've had a lot on my plate. With Sasha Saves, school, dealing with... things."

He waited for her to continue but she didn't pick up after her words drifted off. At a stop sign, he reached to squeeze her leg, only to return his hand to the steering wheel when Ellie lifted her foot up on the seat and rested her chin on her knee.

"How's that going? Those... things?"

Ellie shrugged again. After a few more moments of silence, Devil's hands tightened on the steering wheel. Black feather tips outlining his forearms rolled with the veins in his clenched hands.

Getting the tattoo had been a twisted welcome home present after his massive failure in MF7. After Eagle died in his arms, wounds Devil thought had scarred long ago, threatened to bleed out through the new cut. The ink ensured he never forgot the deaths haunting him the most. The ones he could've prevented if he hadn't let distractions get in the way. In his mind, losing focus brought on the demon whose tattered wings were tattooed on his back.

The angel of death.

The devil.

He didn't want that guilt for Ellie, though he had a feeling the angel beside him agonized over her past as much as he did. Maybe more. But unlike him, Ellie didn't deserve the shame. Knowing she suffered in silence sliced at his wounds all over again.

"You know, if you ever wanna talk..." As he spoke, Ellie refused to look at him and she started picking at long strands of gold from her ponytail. "I'm no conversationalist, El, but I'm a listener..."

She nodded slightly. Silence passed between them before she slowly unbuckled herself.

"Ellie, what are you—"

She scooted closer to him and locked herself in the middle seat. Grief radiated from her, seeping through the space left between them.

Devil blinked back the sting her gesture brought to his eyes. She hadn't verbalized anything, but his body replied. He wondered for a split second whether returning her touch would be the right move when she leaned against him. He shifted to drive with his left hand and hovered over hers on her thigh before he held it in a loose grip.

On an inhale, Devil savored her faint flowery scent. After what she'd been through, to reach out with touch was the ultimate sign of faith. The weight of her trust in him grew in his chest, making it difficult to speak. He swallowed past the emotion gripping his throat.

"I've lost people, too, angel. I don't know everything you're going through. But I might know some of it."

Ellie rested her head on his shoulder and nodded against his arm.

Making sure he could still see to drive, he whispered a kiss against her hair before laying his head against hers. The pain she hid under her responsibilities and determination shed from her in shudders as she cried softly. He'd do everything in his power to heal her.

Devil may have been haunted by his own ghosts, but he'd be damned if he couldn't bring his angel back to life.

CHAPTER NINE

Neal Burgess tapped the file against his thigh as he paced back and forth in his office. He had three minutes and thirty-nine seconds before Officer Willis went on break, leaving the evidence room open for business. It was time. A slow walk and mind-numbing chitchat was all that stood between him and another fix.

He slipped his hands underneath his desk and slid them along the surface to make sure there weren't any cameras or listening devices. One part of him knew the gesture was paranoid, but the other part knew he could never be too sure. The sheriff had been acting off lately and Neal wouldn't have been surprised if the bastard had enlisted one of the rooks to spy on him. Officer Brown was definitely one of his little bitches. He was always way too interested in everything.

Satisfied he was alone, Neal shuffled to a pile of files in the corner, a large stack of cold cases that'd been open for nearly a decade. It'd taken nearly a year to compile, but the investigatory work for the file in his hand hadn't been nearly as difficult. Crimes are easy to solve if you've already found the criminal.

Neal bent to shove the dense file underneath the rest and brushed his hands on his pants as he stood back up. When he returned to his desk, he found the drug trafficking case he'd depend on for his next task. It'd been a good haul and it was too bad he hadn't been in on the raid. He'd gotten good at slipping a few baggies into his pocket before they'd all been accounted for.

Thankfully, the Russians didn't like competition, and the tip from the boss had made the case open and shut. The defendants probably wouldn't even request a trial so the evidence wouldn't be missed.

His head was killing him, but he resisted taking any more medicine until he had his next fix lined up. He pulled out Cici's prescription bottle and shook it in front of the dim light in his office.

One-two-three-four-five... it's a close one this time, Cici, but the last bust will do me good through the next few days. Just need enough to wean me off and then I'll be done for good. I'll go to that center we talked about.

Holding the file as a shield for his deception, Neal made his way down the halls to the basement evidence room. It was nearly the middle of the night, a pretty slow one, too. Officers had been cutting up since the beginning of the shift. Must be a damn full moon.

The lights in the hallway were brighter than a motherfucker, but when he passed an officer he tried his best to meet their eyes and mimic their greeting, hoping they'd move on without question. He didn't need witnesses and the fewer people who remembered seeing him go down to the evidence room, the better.

Neal navigated the stairs before he pushed open the door to the office preceding the evidence room and noted there was no one at the messy check-in desk. He grinned at his fortune. While there were a few evidence custodians designated to maintain evidence, Willis was the lazy SOB he'd been waiting for and it looked like he'd even left his post.

As soon as the thought crossed his mind, footsteps shuffling over cement echoed from the evidence room and Neal bent his head to flick through the papers in the file. Hopefully the chatterbox would get the hint Neal was too busy to shoot the shit. He'd go on his break and leave Neal to his own devices.

The heavyset officer in question poked his head out of the double doors of the evidence room and waved. "Thought I heard someone else down here. Heya, sir." He ducked back into the evidence room but continued to shout through the propped open doors. "I was about to go on break, but what can I do ya for?"

"No need to worry 'bout me, Willis. Just came by to check on a few things for a big case a prosecutor asked me to check out."

"Oh?" A deep male voice entered the office before the man it belonged to exited the evidence room. "Which one? I can tell them what you find."

Neal's mouth fell open. "ADA Aguilar? W-what are you doing here?"

The assistant district attorney stuffed his hands into his pockets, a habit Neal suspected Marco Aguilar believed made him look more approachable. But the man was well over six feet and built like a bodybuilder. Add a suit on top of that, and he was damn formidable.

"Here to check on a case for one of my new prosecutors. ADA Thoms has an evidentiary hearing tomorrow and the defense is putting up a fight." He cracked a smile and chuckled. "She's fucking great at her job, but Judge Powell's also fucking great at hers. I wanted to quadruple check without Thoms thinking I was overstepping. Mum's the word, gentlemen, if you don't mind."

Willis laughed but Neal frowned at the answer, biting his tongue to keep from interrogating the lawyer.

Why would a prosecutor be working so late? Why didn't the new prosecutor come on her own? Wasn't it awful convenient Aguilar had stopped by right before Willis went on break?

Something was up.

Should I come back another time? No. I'm down to five. He mentally counted again after envisioning the bottle. A baggie of small white rocks flashed into his mind. The one he kept under his bathroom counter for emergencies. He physically shook his head against the thought. *No, we're not there yet. But there was that one pill I never found in my office...*

He huffed out a sigh. One would never be enough to help him get clean. He needed at least a week's worth and then he'd be golden. The baggie at home had to be a last resort.

Neal felt the weight of the men's stares on him as he searched for something to say. He was torn between slinging accusations at Aguilar or going back to his office empty-handed.

One-two-three-four-five.

The reminder made his mouth dry and he swallowed to moisten the anxiety parching his throat. There was no other choice, he had to get his medicine right then. Or he'd miss his chance to get better altogether.

Damn Russians. It was all their fault.

He lifted his head to find the men chatting, as if they hadn't just stared him down like a fucking criminal. They could pretend all they wanted but he knew they'd been eyeing him. He coughed for attention, but ended up submitting to the hacks he'd cultivated from smoking multiple packs a day for over a decade. "I'm, uh, down here for ADA Garcia. We've got that case comin' up."

"What's that now?" Aguilar paused from pretending to act preoccupied with Willis. "Oh, right... sure I'll tell—" Aguilar paused to rub his goatee and shook his head. "Wait, Garcia doesn't have a case coming up. The drug team's not on the docket again for a few months. It's all violent and general crimes up for trial right now."

Neal's face grew hot and he tightened his hand into a fist. *How—the fuck—dare he question me?*

"Calm down, baby. He's doin' his job."

His wife's voice, the one she'd always used to soothe him while he ranted about work, cooled his burning nerves to a sizzle.

"But you know what?" Aguilar chuckled and pointed at Neal

in what might've been a playful gesture if Neal hadn't been watching so closely. "The bastard's pretty damn thorough. I'm not surprised he's planning ahead." He went to sign out on Willis's evidence room sheet. "He'd also shoot me dead if I tried to handle his case in any way, so I'll leave you to deal with him."

Neal nodded and tore a handkerchief from one of his pockets to wipe the sweat he knew was already beading up on his forehead. "Yeah... right. You know how he gets. Y-you have a good night then."

A pause in the air set Neal's nerves on fire as Aguilar insisted on staring at him.

"You alright, Burgess? You look a little..." Aguilar waved his hand around his own face for emphasis.

"I'm fine," Neal blurted out.

The stairwell door behind them all opened and cool air coated Neal's feverish skin. Willis peered behind Neal and smiled.

"'Sup, Brown?"

Neal turned to see Officer Henry Brown give an easy grin. "Not much, Willis. Not much at all. What're y'all up to?"

Brown IS fuckin' spyin' on me. I knew it. Sheriff's one damn sonofabitch.

Neal grunted and nodded, deciding the best course of action was to move on. "I don't have time for y'all's gossipin' like ladies." He bent to the sign-up sheet but Willis snatched it away farther from Neal's reach.

"What the hell, Willis? Lemme sign in and do my job."

"I-I'm sorry, sir. I can't let you do that. It's past time for my break now." The kid made odd jerking movements with his head, but Neal narrowed his eyes, unsure of what the kid was trying to tell him.

"S'alright. I don't need ya, son. I'll sign out when I leave." He reached for the notebook sign-in again but Willis brought it to his chest. "Willis, goddamnit what the fuck?"

"Uh, I-I'm sorry, sir." Willis's eyes darted to Aguilar, whose frown had deepened. They returned to Neal, seemingly begging him for something. "I think you might've forgotten Sheriff's policy that an evidence custodian be present with whoever enters the evidence room..." He widened his eyes and flicked his head slightly in the ADA's direction.

Neal felt his face grow flush again. He hadn't been prepared to come up with another strategy on the fly. Getting through Willis was supposed to be a breeze. Normally, the man didn't give two shits about policy, but apparently having a tattle-tale in a suit present was enough to discourage him from swaying away from precinct orders.

"I'll be back in an hour after my break. Y'all wanna come by then?" Willis was still watching him out the side of his eye as he locked up the evidence room. The officer turned to grab the log and filed it in the cabinet behind the desk, locking it too with another key before tucking the key ring back into his pocket. Paranoid asshole.

Now that he knew the sheriff had Brown spying on him, Neal had to come up with a different way to get his medicine. The station was compromised and he couldn't be under a microscope while he was detoxing. Maybe it was high time for him to actually take a vacation.

But no, the party was coming up soon. He didn't know the exact date. No one did until only a few weeks before. Sneaky highfalutin bastards always tried to do their evil in secret. He only knew it was around the same time every year, so he needed to be sharp for it. The more he thought about it, the more he realized he'd need his medication now more than ever. Maybe quitting wasn't a wise choice at the moment.

If Neal demanded to see the drugs now, the ADA would still be there, sticking his nose where it didn't belong. It'd force Willis to follow damn policy for once in his pathetic career and chaperone Neal like a goddamn child. Besides all that, insisting Willis wait to go on his break would be an asshole move, especially since, like Aguilar so helpfully pointed out, the case Neal was using as his ruse wasn't urgent.

"Sir? Erm, I-I'm gonna go on my break?"

Neal snapped out of the tug-of-war in his mind. After a swift nod, he tightened his lips to hold back his rage against the lazy officer. There was no other choice.

"Th-that's fine, son. I-I'll come back later."

He wouldn't though. They were already onto this plan. He'd have to come up with a new one.

The relief on Officer Willis's face was obvious, spineless fuck was probably thankful he didn't have to do his job. "Great! See y'all, then." He turned to head in the opposite direction to the basement break room.

Neal did an about face to the stairwell, bumping into Brown's shoulder before marching his way back to his office.

"Burgess, hold up." Aguilar slapped him on the shoulder to stop him right before he reached the stairway door. Brown was close behind.

"What is it, Aguilar? I'm busy."

Aguilar cleared his throat and held the door open, allowing Neal to ascend the stairs first. "It's just... well, I know the past year has been hard for us all. What with our..." Aguilar looked up the stairwell and lowered his voice. "Special case we're working on with BlackStone... and of course losing that girl..."

A pin needle poked Neal's heart. That's all the pain he ever allowed himself to feel over that situation. The smallest prick so the dam holding back all his regret wouldn't burst. It was easier to patch over with his medicine in his system.

The kidnappings had caught him off guard. Neal had always known he'd made a deal with the devil when he signed on with the Russians to be his own personal supplier. But when he decided to give up the rest of his life for the sake of moments of guaranteed peace, he'd only known about the drug pushing, not the human trafficking.

His dependency on the Russians dug that girl's grave. He'd

missed blatant signs that could've stopped her murder. Maybe if he'd been clean, or maybe if he hadn't latched on to the first tip they'd tricked him with—the one about Jason Stone being the kidnapper and murderer—maybe the girl would still be alive.

Afterward, he'd been forced to do a sloppy cleanup, burning the girl's body before the autopsy, and losing the little evidence he'd had his team collect. Under the Russian's direction, he'd washed the dirt off all their hands, making sure no one ever found out who held the shovel.

He still had to play by their rules for as long as he could and not only to keep his fix. If Neal was ever found out, he wasn't sure there'd be anything left to bury.

"It's been a rough year. What's your point, Aguilar?" Even though it'd only been one floor, the steps were testing his failing heart. Not for the first time, he wondered why the county never fixed the goddamn elevator when the police station had three stories.

"This is my stop," Aguilar said, poised to go through the exit leading to the parking lot. "I don't know Burgess. You seem like you might need a break. Take care of yourself, alright? You've been doin' this job a while. But it still takes a toll on us all." Aguilar waved before exiting outside. His dark eyes had seemed sympathetic, but why would the ADA care?

"Excuse me, sir." Brown pushed past him to continue up the stairs two at a time as the door closed behind Aguilar. "You comin' up?"

Neal's gaze shot up to Brown, already on the next landing. "Huh? Oh, yeah, yeah. I'll be up in a sec. These stairs weren't meant to be run up, boy."

Officer Brown shifted his feet. "Aguilar's right, sir. This job can make us go crazy... Maybe even make us do crazy things." The rookie's eyes widened on the last point.

Neal glared up at him and waved Brown off. "Keep your damn nose in your own business, boy. And stay the hell away from mine."

Neal bent over to catch his breath. The throb of his heart-beat pounded in his chest, up through his neck and head, making his migraine even worse. He had to get in better fucking shape.

Brown's feet were still at the top of the second landing, shuffling back and forth, as if deciding whether to go up or down. Finally, they chose up and Neal waited until he heard the top floor door slam shut. He inhaled three deep breaths before leaning his back against the cement block wall, barely keeping himself from sliding down.

"What am I gonna do, Cici?" He brought his fingers up to his eyes and massaged them, pushing until the pressure in his head was less than the pain against his eyeballs. The slight shift in discomfort was actually a relief in a way.

The truth made him swallow back the lump of anxiety in his throat that was big enough to choke on. He'd resisted his only other option for as long as he could.

"It'll be hard to come back from this one, Cees. Once I go over the deep end, I'm not sure how much longer I'll last." Neal whispered the words to the ghost that carried him through life.

"I understand more than you know. I love you."

He blinked back the sting in his tired eyes. Hearing those last three words one more time aloud was something he'd craved for years. Maybe if she were still alive, that would be all he would need. He wouldn't have to resort to his medicine, the crystal he'd hidden from himself for emergencies, or the Russians. He could be his own man again. Maybe if he'd just listened—

"Neal, don't blame yourself. I did this. And if I hadn't, the cancer would have. I was unhappy before you even knew."

"But what if I'd been a better—"

"I was sick, Neal. It was only a matter of time before it got to be too much."

She was right. She hadn't wanted to live, long before the doctors told her she'd have to fight for her life. He had many regrets, but his biggest was that he hadn't fought hard enough to make her try.

CHAPTER TEN

Ellie kept up pace as she followed Dev past the BlackStone's shooting range viewing gallery and into the indoor firing range. It'd been only two weeks since he began training her, but already she was getting more confident with her fighting and self-defense skills.

They'd even moved on to weapons training, hence the reason they were entering the nearly empty, cavernous room. Along one side was a window for people to view shooters without having to put on ear protection or watch out for flying casings. On the other side were six spaces, with walls separating each shooter. Each stall ensured every shooter had enough room to focus on their own training, without having to worry about a casing flying at them from someone else's gun.

They'd only been there one other time, but Ellie was pretty good at hitting a target thanks to shooting with her brother. Too bad when it came to Dev, her aim was crap.

Who knew two hour training sessions with Dev three times a week would bring out the flirt in her? Unfortunately for her, apparently Dev still didn't know.

She'd tried everything Sasha had taught her: jokes, innuendos, flirtatious giggling that made her feel like a complete bimbo. She'd attempted to touch him more, let her hands linger, and even taken to wearing only a sports bra and small loose shorts, hoping showing more skin would do the trick. No reaction.

Nope. Nada. Nothing.

Keeping her mind out of the gutter was nearly impossible and it hadn't helped he was often shirtless whenever they were training. Was he deliberately ignoring her, or was she that awful at coming on to a guy? Then again, pursuing her brother's friend was a bad idea in the first place. Maybe Dev just had the good sense not to encourage her.

Despite the fact she constantly embarrassed herself in the face of his unyielding disinterest, she still looked forward to their lessons. Maybe it was the exercise, or maybe it was knowing she was *doing* something about her helplessness, but training with Dev gave her a sense of confidence and freedom nothing else could.

Learning how to hold a gun or a knife was freaking empowering. She was taking her life into her own hands and just the idea she could be safer on her own merit made her feel like anything was possible.

Plus, she could forget her exhaustion, school, survivors, and even about her past. It felt good to just be *Ellie* again. Be in the moment and not worry about anyone else.

Dev's deep voice brought her out of her musings. "Get a nine mil from the wall and grab your holster." He pointed to the wall of weapons before indicating the stall directly in front of them.

Ellie followed his direction and grabbed her favorite Glock. Dev had bought it for her, saying she needed one she was comfortable with. Once she was old enough to get her concealed weapons permit, he was going to let her keep it as her own. She turned to her favorite stall and took a deep breath before entering, wishing, for what felt like the hundredth time, the walls around her didn't automatically feel like they were closing in.

He turned to the other wall where a stack of posters and

other supplies were kept. When he reached across the table, Ellie watched taut muscles roll his tattooed wings as they curved to accommodate the stretch.

She'd been striking, blocking, and kicking him for two weeks. Not normally very sexy. But she couldn't get her mind off of what it would feel like to be able to caress the smooth marble of his back. How powerful would she feel if she left her mark on such a strong surface? Her skin flushed at the thought, and she almost didn't catch him speaking.

"Which target do you want to do today?"

"Hmm. The devil."

A small, sinful smile twitched at the corner of his lips and she crossed her arms in case her nipples were pebbling in the cold.

Yeah... the cold.

"Again, Ellie? I'm gonna get a complex if you keep trying to kill my namesake."

"Well, maybe I've got some pent-up aggression toward you." *Or something else.* When he shook his head with a dry laugh, Ellie didn't hold back the giggles bubbling from her chest. Teasing Dev was one of her favorite hobbies.

"Alright, let's get serious." He slipped a sheet from the pile and brought the poster of a black-horned figure with him to the stall.

Ellie sobered as her heart started to beat in her ears. She tried not to think of how much smaller the closet-sized space felt after he joined her inside. But then her only other thing to focus on was how Dev's skin radiated heat, warming her down to her lower belly where it twisted with desire. So yeah, that wasn't helping either.

She busied herself with her magnetic leather holster, snapping the magnets together on to either side of the elastic waistband in her leggings. Most normal holsters weren't made for Ellie's favorite apparel, so it'd made her all warm and fuzzy inside when Dev got it custom made for her.

"Hey, what *is* your real name?" It was a feeble attempt to keep thinking about anything else besides the fact the metal wall kept touching her skin because there wasn't much room. She had to get past the initial onset of panic first, then she'd be fine. "I feel like I should already know by now, but—"

"You do know it. It's Ray." Dev grunted and drew the clothesline pulley, bringing the clip at the end of the track forward.

He hung the poster and cranked the pulley, flying the poster to an abrupt stop nine feet away, or the 'length of the average self-defense encounter,' according to Dev.

"*Ray*? That's actually your name?" His reply took her mind off the narrowing walls completely, and she couldn't help the incredulous tone in her voice. "I thought that was part of your nickname, 'Devil Ray' Vos. You don't look like a 'Ray.'"

He shrugged and chuckled. "Nope, it's my name. That's why I like the shortened nickname."

"Huh." Ellie analyzed his red hair and beard, six-foot-four muscular physique, and harsh jaw line, trying her best not to get sidetracked. "Yeah, Devil suits you much better."

"I think so too." He laughed and faced the shooting range again. "Check to make sure there aren't any bullets in the gun before we practice form."

Ellie turned her attention to his instruction and pressed the button to pop out the magazine before laying the cartridge on the metal table in front of her. She slid back the rack and double-checked the chamber before holstering the empty pistol.

"Clear."

"Good. We'll do some stance work before our target practice so no earplugs yet. Even though we've only done hand-to-hand combat for thirty minutes so far today, I can tell by your posture you're already tired, but you shouldn't be after all the training we've been doing the past couple of weeks... Are you getting enough sleep?"

"Um, yeah—" Ellie turned around and eyed him. "I wouldn't be this tired if I didn't have to do the same move a thousand times in a row. If you'd told me 'just one more', one more time I would've stomped your big toe."

Dev raised his eyebrows and crossed his corded forearms over his rock-hard chest as he smirked. "You should've done that. It's a pretty effective move, especially if you're wearing heels."

"I'll keep that in mind." Ellie gave him a pointed look and brushed back an invisible piece of hair. It was second-nature still, even though her hair didn't bother her anymore now that she wore bobby pins all the time.

"We'll have to work on your stamina. But now's the time we need to train you to push through that fatigue. Fights aren't like the movies. They're fu-*reaking* exhausting and muscle memory can save your life."

She tilted her head at him. "Why do you do that?"

He paused to consider her question. "Do what?"

"You don't curse in front of me. Unless something bad happens and it slips out..." She watched as his face grew a healthy shade of pink. "You know you can curse in front of me, right? I'm a *fu*-reaking adult, in case you hadn't noticed." She winked at him, enjoying the way his light skin reddened more by each word.

"Oh, I've noticed," he grumbled and Ellie felt a flush burn her own cheeks. "But, I don't want to make you uncomfortable."

Unsure what to say to the first comment, Ellie lifted her shoulder and decided to breeze past it. "Well, Jason does it. Jules does it. Heck, literally everyone around me curses like a sailor. I don't like to because Aunt Rachel would've tanned my hide growing up if she'd heard me swear. Even now, curse words taste soapy in my mouth." She stuck her tongue out for emphasis. "But that doesn't mean you should censor yourself around me. I can handle whatever you've got, Devil Vos."

The impact of her words hit her as soon as they left her lips. Even though she knew she was blushing from her cheeks down, she held her head high, challenging him.

Dev's eyes widened before a dark chuckle rumbled out of

him and went straight to her pussy. "I guess, I'll have to do my worst, then, angel."

His gaze traveled down to her lips, lingering there, and she squeezed her legs together to keep from dampening her panties. The space between her and Dev was a magnetic field, and she gave in to the need to lean into him. His head lowered toward hers and she bit her lip, heart pounding in her chest at their closeness.

"Dev... I—"

Dev lurched back and faced forward like he'd snapped himself out of the moment. Ellie mimicked his movements and rubbed the ache in her chest, feeling like she'd suffered another bout of emotional whiplash. She opened her mouth and closed it, fighting with herself on whether she should say anything, but Dev cleared his throat and picked up the pistol.

"We'll run through some speed exercises. It only takes a second for a pro to take his gun out of his holster. You need to be ready with your own draw should you have to. But remember—"

"I know, I know. Run or hide before I fight."

He nodded once and squeezed her shoulder. "Yep, you got it. Now let's go, I'll stop you when I want you to pause and check out your own body posture. That way you can figure out where you need to fix your grip on the gun to make sure you can reach it quickly and hit the target accurately."

He stood behind her with his hands on his hips. "Stance."

She immediately pulled the 9mm from the holster and went into a shooting stance he'd drilled into her.

"Good. I like what I see. Oh, wait." His hand came into her field of vision and she jerked her head back before his thumb pulled her bottom lip from between her teeth. "Can't do that, baby, you'll bite your pretty lip off."

The gentle brush of his finger and the low murmur of his voice sent a shocking quiver straight to her sex and her panties dampened with need. It was the second time he'd touched her like that, but good God did it make her swoon each time.

Before training, her crush on Devil had been easy to manage. She rarely saw him outside of Sasha Saves. But now that they were around each other all the time, one-on-one, she didn't know what to do with him.

Should she come clean and get all her feelings out on the table? How would he react? Could he feel the same way? She was still too nervous to find out. It was better to find comfort in the dream and keep her dignity than confess her feelings and lose both.

He stepped behind her, the heat from his hard chest seeped through his thin tank top and warmed her bare back. He manipulated her body into what she assumed was a more natural position, setting her nerves on fire and making her skin tingle. Despite her aching muscles, she tensed at his touch.

"Try to relax where you can."

As he leaned away, cool air flowed between them, a quick reprieve on her burning skin. His strong hands kneaded her shoulders, but it had the opposite effect of loosening her up. When he ran his fingertips along her arms to guide her on how to aim the gun correctly, wrapping her in his strong embrace, her self-restraint went up in smoke. A moan escaped her, and every one of her muscles froze in embarrassment as she silently pleaded with the universe that Dev hadn't heard it.

But all hope was lost when she realized the hard body covering hers was still as a statue. The air in the room stilled, so thick with her desire Ellie felt like her lungs were fighting against a wall to inhale. Dev's chest rose and fell in deep breaths behind her, as if he was struggling against the weight of his need, too.

She wasn't sure what he felt, and her stomach twisted at the thought she might act on a wrong assumption.

"I'm sorry, El—" He dropped his arms to release her, but in a snap decision, Ellie snatched one of his hands in hers and with the other, gently laid the gun down on the metal.

"Don't." She wasn't entirely sure what she was begging for. All she wanted was to go back to the moment before she'd screwed everything up and mewled like a cat in heat. If she hadn't stopped him just then, he would've rejected her. The thought leadened her stomach and she blinked back the sting in her eyes. His apology for making her need him was too much to bear.

Eyes blurry with tears, she stared hard at the shadowed devil on the paper target nine feet in front of her, too afraid to look at the one flush against her and face the look of pity that was likely there.

Dev swallowed roughly against the crown of her head. Letting go of his hand, Ellie picked up the gun before raising both arms to aim.

"Relax?" she asked, licking her lips while concentrating hard on the paper figure in front of her.

He nodded against the side of her head. "It's normal, uh, to be tense during a fight, especially when you're about to shoot someone. And I can tell from your shoulders how tired you are. They're overcompensating by remaining tight. You have to loosen that tension..."

I have to loosen the tension? No freaking kidding.

"...But if your posture is relaxed—" His hard chest encompassed her entire body as he molded around her. "—and comfortable..."

God he felt so good. Since that first training day, he'd gone back to avoiding touching her as much as possible.

His rough calluses stroked up her arms until he gently raised them to see the target in her sights. Shivers followed the trail of his warm hands. "Keeping your emotions in check will make it easier for you to aim true." His fingertips continued their pursuit up her arm and glided down her sides, leaving goose bumps as heat moved on to settle on her hips. "Or escape. You never know what kind of danger you could be facing."

His low whisper against her ear was finally too much and she turned halfway to search his face.

"What if... what if I don't want to escape?"

Dev leaned his forehead against the side of hers and closed his eyes. She was at an awkward angle, but when he squeezed her hips to pull her butt tight against his hard length, she didn't dare move. Air escaped her lungs and he opened his eyes again. She swallowed in his cinnamon scent and their breaths flowed in tandem.

He stared down at her before dipping to whisper in her ear. His lips brushed the shell and her clit throbbed with each word from his deep voice.

"That would be dangerous, Ellie."

She laid the gun down on the small table in front of her and ground her hips into his hardness. Her damp panties clung to her center and Dev's curse covered up her moan. Pulses through her core were almost painful as it clenched at nothing, begging to be filled.

"What if I want your type of danger, Dev..." She desperately hoped those were the right words to convince him to relieve the ache between her thighs.

"Ellie, stop." But his grip never loosened. "You don't know what you're saying—"

"You're the only one who's ever made me feel safe," she whispered, pleading for him to hear the truth in her voice. He'd been her savior when she needed him. And good God, did she need her demon with broken wings right then.

"I'm the type of man who needs control." He shook his head and tightened his lips. "But with you? I don't know if I can keep it."

She tried to turn around completely but he wrapped her in his embrace. One hand spread the width of her stomach, the other in the middle of her breasts. He bit her ear and she cried out in a mix of pleasure and pain.

"But if you want me to lose control, know this—" He ground his cock against her, pinning her hips to the metal ledge in front of her. "There will be no one to save you."

"I don't want to be saved from you." She used a defense maneuver he taught her to whip around in his hold. Their chests heaved against each other and she met his deep forest green eyes.

"After a night with me, angel, I'm not sure you'll have a choice."

Dev's lips crashed into hers and he shoved her up onto the small table. His kiss set fire to her need, flooding her body with heat down to her core. When his tongue teased the seam of her mouth, her own lips parted on a gasp and he thrust inside. One hand cupped her butt and the other delved into her hair, pulling her ponytail from its tie.

Ellie held tight to his bare shoulders. They were hot and sweaty from working out, even after being in the cold room, but she didn't care. It only made his cinnamon scent stronger and she could've sworn she was getting intoxicated from it.

He turned her head slightly, finding a better angle for their kiss. His tongue took lead in the dance with hers and the rhythm pounded through their bodies.

Dev lifted one of her legs and raised it around his hip. She was on the very tip of the small ledge and he ground his shaft into her core, with only the thin fabric of their workout clothes between them. When he hit just the right spot, Ellie shuddered. He grinned against her lips and repeated the motion, forcing Ellie to moan into his mouth.

"Fuck, Ellie. I need to be inside you."

The words sent a frisson of anxious excitement down her spine and her hands began to tremble on his shoulders. On instinct, she bit his bottom lip as it brushed against hers. He groaned into her mouth and ripped away before traveling down her jawline. Open-mouthed kisses to the base of her neck turned into small bites that made her jump farther against his shaft.

He scooped her raised leg over his forearm, lifting her butt from the metal table ledge. The angle made it impossible for her to stand on her own, forcing her to lie back on the cold steel.

The *really* cold steel.

A shiver wracked through her until his other hand stroked up her bare stomach. Fingers grazing the bottom of her bra made her squirm before they pulled down the zipper in the front. She yelped when her unzipped bra popped open, exposing her.

A breath took too much of her concentration to inhale, taking her out of the moment. She reached her hands to the side but felt hard, cold wall against her fingertips. She was completely caged in.

Her panties and loose shorts were pushed to the side. Cold air burned her entrance, drawing Ellie's attention to the fact she was completely vulnerable in front of a man for the first time.

Not the first time.

The threat of a memory caught in Ellie's brain. She shook her head, desperate to flee from the fog in her mind, only to be surrounded.

Please. Not now. I want this.

There's an aura to the worst flashbacks. They roll in like the trembling breath just before a confession, promising to reveal a moment the subconscious tried to shelter you from. Every time, the memory tasted like a lie as it came to the forefront of her mind, making it almost impossible to believe that something so horrible had happened in her life. Even faced with the truth, most of the time she still questioned if she'd even lived through it at all.

I am safe. I am in control. I am here in this moment.

Ellie had refused to delve deeper into her memories of what had happened to her, hoping that healing the surface would be enough. But over time, she'd come to realize the undercurrent of her past was always there, swirling around, biding its time before it could drag her under the surface.

"Ellie?"

I want this. I want this. I want this.

Her name was a muffled plea, barely registering in her mind. Tingles that had felt so good before, sparked along her skin like electric shocks, making her jump against strong arms. Her breathing, once bated with anticipation, increased to forced rasps and she clawed at whatever was binding her chest, trying to free her lungs to get air inside. Trying to see past the man on top of her, Ellie could tell the walls were stretching to tower over them in the small space. Snapping her legs closed, Ellie kicked at the man holding her, even as a part of her deep down wanted to tug him close to stay in the moment.

I want this.

I want... this.

I... want... this.

I... I... don't...

I don't want this.

She succumbed to the fog and everything around her flashed white.

The sound of ripping fabric invaded Ellie's eardrums. Hands grabbed at her chest, tearing into the dress Sasha had painstakingly made for the party. Her body jolted as her back hit the cold floor.

Sweaty fingers painfully groped down her breasts and torso before pushing aside the only cloth she had left to protect her.

NO.

She screamed in silence.

Dirty fingers. Scratching. Digging. Pressure. She burned until she was empty again.

On fire, inside and out.

"Ellie!"

She shook on the floor, attacking the monster in front of her. It couldn't happen again.

Not again. Not again. Nononono.

"No!"

"Angel! Baby, it's me. It's Dev. You are safe... in control, you're here, with *me*. You're here. At BlackStone. You're safe." Strong arms wrapped around her so tightly she couldn't fight anymore. "Breathe, angel. Breathe with me. God, please, baby, just breathe."

Deep inhales and exhales breezed cool air over her forehead and—unable to move anything else—she fell into the pattern. Slowly, too, too slowly, the room came back into focus. She was surrounded in a tiny closet-sized space by warmth and inked black feathers. Dev was clutching her against his chest. The reflection from the large viewing window showed broken wings cocooning a woman with haunted eyes.

"Dev?" she asked, her voice monotone from shock.

"God, Ellie. I'm so sorry. I wasn't thinking..." Dev broke off into mumbling about innocence and his grip tightened.

"Dev, I-I can't breathe..." she rasped out.

"Fuck." His hands shot off her and they both fell backward. The abrupt change from safety and warmth to the hard and cold floor was jarring enough to bring her completely back to her senses.

"Ellie, shit. I'm sorry, angel. I didn't mean to drop you. You said you couldn't breathe. I'm sorry, I wasn't thinking. I fucked up. About all of it. I should've—goddamnit I wasn't *thinking*."

Ellie's cheeks heated. She didn't want Dev to have to think about what she'd been through, or for him to feel like he had to hold himself back.

He reached for her, but Ellie jerked back instinctively. She only knew she couldn't stand the thought of being touched while her skin was on fire from embarrassment.

She looked up to find Dev's face had turned a sickly pale. His hands trembled as they raked through his hair. He abruptly stood up and paced away from her mumbling about everything being his fault.

"Dev," Ellie called meekly. She tried to get up herself until she realized her bra was still unzipped. Her chest was clawed with bloodred scratches and she knew her face looked the same. She clutched the halves of her bra and tried to zip up the front zipper, but her fingers were shaking with adrenaline. She held the fabric together before following Dev's pacing.

"Dev, stop. Please." She attempted to pull at his arm but he avoided her touch, instead tearing his hair again. He only stopped to stare at her, wide-eyed and unseeing as he slowly backed away to the door.

"I did this to you. I can't... I can't hurt you, Ellie. I just..." He turned around and slammed his fist into the gallery window in front of them. "*Fuck.*" He turned around, his knuckles bloody as pieces of glass crashed to the ground. "I'm sorry, Ellie. I'm too fucked up for you. I'll fuck it all up."

"Please! Dev, it's okay!"

He whirled around again, every emotion etched in the look of pain on his face. "Don't you get it? *I* did this to you! I-I didn't even *notice* you were about to have a fucking panic attack. This is what happens when I lose control, when I let my emotions get in the way. Someone gets hurt every *fucking* time. I can't let that be you!"

"I had a little episode, alright?" Ellie choked as she tried to catch the breath that was still leaving her lungs too quickly. "I think I need for us to take it slow at first. Or, I don't know, like talk me through it? I-I'm sorry I freaked out..." He shook his head as she trailed off. All the heat left her body as she realized he'd already decided he was done with her.

"I-I can't, Ellie. I-I'm s-sorry. I can't be this guy for you. In my line of work, this need—" He slammed his fist against his chest. "The way I want you is a distraction that'll fuck everyone else up. Losing control like that—I can't hurt you and if we keep going that's what's going to happen." His lips tightened. "I'm sorry." He threw his hands up in surrender before turning to flee out the shooting range door.

Ellie leaned up against the wall of the small stall and tried not to think about the closet-sized space closing in on her like a trick in a funhouse. The viewing window reflected everything she felt in harsh focus. Ellie watched the broken woman in the reflection attempt to hold her pieces together as she slowly slid down to the floor.

Ellie always told Sasha Saves clients seeking help had the power to transform them from victims to survivors. They could take their lives into their own hands and work toward being free from their past.

Survivors took control of their lives and Ellie had always thought she'd done the same. That she could move on from what had happened and have a normal life, one without bodyguards or fear of being kidnapped and sold. That wasn't too much to ask, right? She'd gone to therapy, worked hard in school, devoted her life to helping others. She'd even tried to flirt with the guy she liked.

Ellie looked at what was left of her in the viewing window. Her past had swallowed her down and like the mirrored glass in front of her, it'd spat her back out in jagged, broken pieces. Their sharp edges cut away any future she would ever have.

For the first time, Ellie admitted to herself the truth that'd been swimming deep in the recesses of her darkest fear.

She was no survivor.

She was a victim.

And victims had no future at all.

CHAPTER ELEVEN

Ellie scanned the area around the bushes to make sure the coast was clear before stuffing her bike inside them. It was easier to hide it in the wild brush now than when she and Sasha first started coming to the park. When she finished fighting the brambles, Ellie took measure of the towering Eastern White Pine, somehow seeming both much smaller and much bigger than it once had.

She circled the tree, one hand following the divots of the bark, like trails to her memory, before she once again checked to make sure nobody was watching. It was still the middle of the school day and her shoulders relaxed when she realized no one but toddlers and their caretakers were there. She didn't have to worry about them because they were far off in the designated playground.

Satisfied she was sufficiently secluded, Ellie balanced the pink box she'd brought in one hand and climbed the tree with the other, using the gnarls in the trunk as footholds and trying to avoid getting too much sap on her hands until she reached the first wooden platform Jason had built.

Wobbly, long-forgotten tree climbing skills got her to the first nailed rung, but after that, it was a lot easier to reach each scaffold thanks to her height. Back when they were kids, it was one of the deterrents for other children to follow them up. Parents didn't like having their child suspended on shoddy craftsmanship twenty feet up in the air. Then again, not many kids had wild brothers as their chaperones.

"How the heck did Jason ever think this was safe," she muttered and kept climbing until she mounted the last floor, high in the tree. Ellie pushed the small box across the wooden slats and hoisted herself into a seated position against the tree.

Jason built them the treehouse when Ellie and Sasha first started going to the park. Although "treehouse" was a little generous. It was basically a bunch of two by fours haphazardly nailed in a semblance of a floor with ledges leading up to it that passed for a ladder. When she and Sasha would climb all the way up, it was a challenge to get back down. Not that they were ever eager to leave.

"It's been a while since we've been up here, huh? We practically lived up here when we were little." Ellie patted the landing and gazed up through the pine needles. "When did we stop coming up here all the time? Was it before high school? I guess we got to be too cool for treehouses." She smoothed her hand over the well-worn wood. "We always made it for birthdays, though. Didn't we, Sash?"

Ellie stretched her tired legs as far as they would go on the three-foot-wide platform before leaning against the trunk. "Geez, Louise, you'd think I wouldn't be out of shape with Dev running me ragged all the dang time."

The past week had been lonely, but unfortunately necessary. Part of her was disappointed and ashamed Dev had canceled two of their training sessions. The other part had been relieved.

They'd finally gotten back to it that morning, but Dev was more closed off than ever. To make matters worse, she'd been preoccupied thinking about the last time she'd seen him, when she'd been a pathetic ball of emotion and he'd—well, if the wide-eyed, tongue-tied look Dev wore was any indication—he'd been terrified.

She'd used the vacancy in her schedule to call her therapist and squeeze in a few therapy sessions over the phone. Discussing freak-out moments whenever Ellie needed to was one of the perks of appointments over the phone. They'd discussed how Ellie had gone nuts at the shooting range at the mere thought of being intimate. It'd helped. Sometimes talking through her issues was all she needed. Her therapist even said acknowledging both with herself and with Dev what happened—and that it could happen again—was a healthy first step to moving on.

It sounded easy enough. Just *talk* to Dev. She'd talked so many of her issues to death over the past year she should've been a pro. But every time she'd opened her mouth to open up to him about it, she'd snapped it shut again. Taking that 'first step' felt like gearing up to jump out of her treehouse.

After collecting her breath, Ellie opened the small "Go Nuts Donuts" box and pulled out her chocolate glazed, cream-filled donut. She then reached for the next one and pretended to gag.

"Here's your gross one, Sash. I can't believe you like freakin' sour cream, ya loon." Ellie placed it on the edge of the floor in front of her and sighed.

"Happy birthday to you," she sang softly under her breath, not caring she was a little off key. Sasha always sang the melody and had made Ellie find the harmony. Admittedly, Ellie was never any good at doing either. That was part of the fun, though.

"Cheers." she whispered, her voice cracking on the word as she brought her donut up to "clink" against what would've been Sasha's sour cream donut.

"So, um." Ellie cleared her throat. "My therapist said it'd be good to keep up tradition, if I was ready for it." She took a forti-fying breath. "And I-I think I am. I, um... We haven't been up here since your last birthday, ya know. We only would've had to wait a week to do mine too, but... You were gone." She swal-lowed. "I imagine you've seen it all. I hope you have anyway, since you're up there somewhere." Her gaze glossed over the carved letters in the trunk of the tree.

SS+ES=BFFs 4 ~~LIFE~~ EVER AND EVER AND EVER.

Ellie chuckled. "I remember when we did this." She traced the carving with her fingertips. "We were still in elementary school and you stole Jason's pocket knife, you rebel. After I carved it, you yelled, 'Besties for life' and nearly fell off the dang tree tryna hide from the kids who heard you." The lump in her throat grew until it was nearly impossible to talk. "Then... do you remember what you said?" Ellie smiled as the memory answered in her mind.

"You know what? Life isn't long enough, El." Sasha grabbed the pocket knife and flipped it open before bending to carve.

"What're you writing?" Ellie asked, trying her best to balance and see around Sasha's curly hair.

"There." Sasha leaned to the side and twirled her hand to reveal her masterpiece.

"You carved over 'life'?" Ellie tilted her head. "Why?"

"Who wants life when you can have forever? Best friends forever, and ever, and ever. And then, you know... beyond that." Sasha smiled through the teeth she'd lost. "You're stuck with me, bestie."

Ellie blinked back the sting in her eyes and leaned against the tree. "You were right," she choked. "Life wasn't long enough." She wiped away the moisture on her cheeks until she gave up the battle and let the tears flow, tired of fighting them back. If she couldn't be free to be emotional high up in their treehouse, she couldn't be free anywhere.

It'd been a long time since she'd let go. Mostly she welcomed the empty numbness clouding her daily life. But after spending so much time with Dev for the last month, her emotions were wrecked. Especially after losing her mind the week before. She needed to let it out. Besides, Sasha would've wanted to hear everything.

With that in mind, Ellie smiled softly and took a bite from her donut.

"Like I said, I don't know how much you've seen. But I kissed a boy... and then totally freaked out on him," she began around her mouthful. Her legs were much longer than they used to be and Ellie propped her feet on one of the branches to make sure she didn't slide off the small platform.

"Oof, how we stayed up here all the time when we were kids is a mystery to me and my butt right now." She rubbed at the sore spot quickly forming on her behind. "Doesn't help I've been getting beat up lately..." She waited with a grin, pretending she would get a response.

"Beat up? No shit, girl. Who do I need to kill?"

Ellie laughed and closed her eyes to better imagine her friend angry at the world on her behalf. It was one of the best things about her. Everyone needs a champion.

"The same boy who kissed me, if you'll believe it. He's my self-defense trainer you like so much. I believe you said I should let him bend me over..."

"Hm, I still don't know if he's delicious or dickish. Spill, girl. I need more deets."

"There's not much to tell." Ellie shrugged. "I don't know what to do with him. He's sweet... well, to me. He's kinda... I don't know... surly, maybe? He's hot as heck. I like him, ya know? I think he likes me, too. But I'm worried now he thinks I'm... broken..." She sighed, thinking about her reaction the week before. "Maybe I am... like I said, I lost it when we tried to go farther than a kiss. You would've thought I was a blushing virgin."

There was a snort in her mind. "Okay, I'm *technically* still a virgin, you're right. But I've done pretty much everything else... sorta." She rolled her eyes and chuckled to her friend. "Anyway, I've talked it over with my therapist, and I think I'll be ready next time. Because let me tell ya, if he isn't traumatized by my trauma then I wouldn't mind using him to get that technicality outta the way. I just hope I didn't screw it up or scare him away with my freak-out."

"If he's right for you, babe, he'll be back around. Give that shit up to the universe. Let fate decide."

"You always did believe in manifestation stuff." She tried to ignore the cynic inside her that seethed when she thought of how her friend had trusted the universe, only to have the universe betray her by taking her too soon.

"Trust the universe, babe. Set your intentions!"

"I don't want to fight with you, girl. Not on your birthday," she teased and smiled before sobering at the next thought. "He's the one... he's the one who—" She swallowed back the emotion that threatened to overwhelm her every time she remembered herself almost a year ago. The trauma she'd been through had created a different person. "He was the first one to reach me back then and the only one I remember during the rescue. He's the one who saved me."

More tears rolled down her cheeks. "I'm sorry he didn't save you, too." Her breath caught. "I-I'm sorry I didn't save you." Ellie brought her hand up to her aching chest, wishing her heart would go ahead and crack open the rest of the way to finally let her shame break free.

She'd never escape that darkness, though. Regret was a part of her now. When she saw her friend being beaten, raped, and *murdered*, pain had burrowed inside her. It was a parasite, sucking the life out of her every day, despite all the hard work she put into trying to just live at all.

For months, Ellie's therapist had tried to convince her that Ellie had been drugged and helpless to do anything for her friend or the rest of the women she was trapped with.

But there was a part of Ellie that knew the truth. That deep down, fear had ruled over her that night. Ellie had told everyone she couldn't do anything. But that night, Ellie's most terrible sin was she hadn't *wanted* to do anything.

It was a brief moment, all of it now seemed to have passed by in a hazy instant, but it'd felt like forever then. She'd been too afraid to move. Too afraid to cry out. Too afraid to have the same thing happening to Sasha, happen to her. But it was a damning conviction. Ellie hadn't been helpless. She'd been a coward.

It was that part of herself she hated.

"That's why I do what I do, ya know?" she explained, as if Sasha had been privy to her introspection. Heck, for all Ellie knew, she could be. "I help those victims who don't have anyone else. Who think there's no way out. I-I'm trying to be braver. Make up for my failure." She sighed and held herself in a hug. "But, to be honest, it's exhausting."

Tired muscles screamed out at her, confirming her confession. Ellie tugged her legs close to wrap her arms around herself and lay her head on her knees. The cold breeze lifted her hair and Ellie closed her eyes with both gratitude and guilt for the chilly whispers pricking the few inches of bare skin exposed to the elements. Gratitude that she was alive to feel the bite of cold air at all, and guilt that Sasha never would again.

CHAPTER TWELVE

The club's pounding bass vibrated the pleather chair up through Devil's arms and into his jaw. He scrubbed his beard hard, working his mouth open and shut to stop his teeth from grinding as he forced his eyes forward to watch the stage.

Anything to get his mind off the gorgeous blonde he'd traumatized the week before. He'd put off the two lessons they were supposed to have since then because he was too much of a coward to look into those innocent caramel eyes and see the hurt he'd caused. Because *he'd* let his need for her make him lose control. That's why when Phoenix had invited him to Original Sin, Devil jumped at the chance for a mind-numbing fuck.

He was waiting for just that while his usual request finished up her last set. His eyes wandered to the silver-haired vixen pushing her ass into his teammate's lap. Charity turned to straddle Phoenix, moaning obnoxiously, like she was coming solely from him stroking her spine. Devil hated that fake shit. He didn't need a woman to stroke his ego. Just his cock.

Phoenix winked at him and chuckled. "Wanna join, man? You look awful tense over there."

Charity's smile widened, her pointed teeth glinted in the

strobe light. A demon succubus measuring up her prey. "Y'all can share me, Devil baby."

Devil scowled before whipping his head back to the dancer on the stage. He'd shared with Phoenix once before but Devil had quickly realized threesomes with another alpha male weren't his thing. He needed control in the bedroom and when Phoenix had tried to take over, it'd only pissed him off.

But even without that hang-up, there was no way in hell he'd ever fuck Charity. The woman was a conniving bitch at the best of times and he didn't trust her not to brag about adding him to her client list. He didn't need word of his extracurricular activities to get back to Ellie.

His chest hollowed out with guilt and he rubbed his sternum through his thin, black Henley. Goddamn, it hurt to see her upset. That plump pink lip trembling the last time he saw her fucking destroyed him. He hadn't even been able to get a full sentence out. The onslaught of emotion he always kept tamped down and the overriding fear he'd fuck up his angel's life was more than he could handle at the time.

Punching the window had been totally uncalled for but fuck him if it hadn't felt good to fixate on the pain in his hand rather than the one in his chest.

Devil breathed in deeply despite the sickeningly overpowering scent of coconut, cocoa butter, and body odor. He relaxed knowing he didn't need to be afraid of ruining any angel's innocence at Original Sin.

Every dancer at the nicest strip club in Ashland County— whatever that meant—wore either white or black wings, calling themselves Sinners. Charity, Phoenix's soon-to-be good time, always wore white with a silver wig, making her easy to remember even in a building full of beautiful women. Smart business move if you thought about it. Easier to remember, easier to request.

But the woman on stage doing anti-gravity shit on a pole was the one Devil wanted. Jezebel was a bartender and despite dancing not being her usual gig, every time he came around she made sure to be available for him.

They'd go to a confessional, a small private room, so it could be just the two of them. She was one of the few at Original Sin who was good with her mouth and didn't run it. Devil wasn't secretive about his conquests, but he didn't like his business spread around town like Charity was liable to do. Good for her that Phoenix didn't mind. Hell, he seemed to encourage it.

Jezebel performed a split on the pole while also somehow shaking her ass to the music. He would've been impressed, if his mind wasn't on someone else entirely. Instead of the raven-haired temptress on chrome in front of him, his thoughts were still on the blonde, wingless angel he'd left in a broken heap the week before.

Devil closed his eyes against the bright lights and was thankful the music covered up his sigh. He'd let himself get carried away. Lost control. Ellie had been so tempting he'd given in to his desire to finally taste her. Getting so caught up he didn't even realize he was hurting her was a clear sign it could never happen again.

Loss of control was completely new to him. Since he was seventeen, Devil had worked to perfect his discipline and it'd always served him well. He'd devoted his life to his country, and after Draco recruited him, his team with MF7. His carefully chosen professions thrived on his ability to compartmentalize and disengage.

Knowing that about himself, he should've never agreed to train Ellie. It was fucking with his system. She made him feel, and feelings were distractions. Distractions were fucking dangerous.

Devil wasn't concerned about himself, but it wasn't the first time his losing focus and lack of control ultimately hurt someone he cared for. He'd be damned if he let his weaknesses affect Ellie.

The week before was the perfect example. He'd gotten lost in the feel of her tight, round ass against his cock and the promise of finally being with her, and he hadn't realized she was having a panic attack until she was already hyperventilating. Ellie hadn't had one of those in a long ass time, and that one had been his fault and he fucking knew it.

Since then, Devil had come up with a plan for how to prevent another mistake from happening. The team was focused on crashing the secret elite Ashland County scholarship function so he'd dive his focus headfirst into that. He'd keep training Ellie on a strictly professional basis. Not working with her simply wasn't an option. Jaybird had been right that Devil was the best, and he didn't trust anyone else for the job at this point, either.

Meanwhile, Devil would make sure he worked out with one of the other agents to get the sense beaten back into him and he'd go to Jezebel every time he needed to release the control valve on the need consuming him.

Every time he saw Ellie, his need flooded through him. If the other day at the shooting range was any indication, the dam holding back his control was on the verge of breaking. He was terrified of the devastation his emotions would leave in their wake.

Devil sipped his whiskey before he pulled out his switchblade and flicked it open. The music was so loud and Original Sin was so crowded no one paid attention to the guy with the knife, a thought which was in no way comforting except for the fact he'd be left alone. His fingertips ran down the smooth flat blade while his thumb glided below the sharp edge. Freedom from his guilt was just a cut away, attempting to seduce him. But he didn't deserve the absolution.

"Hey stranger. It's been some time since you came 'round." Jezebel's husky whisper heated his ear and his grip on the knife slipped, biting into him enough to break the skin. His breath released in a hiss and Jezebel smoothed her hands down his chest from behind him pulling his head against her large breasts, thinly veiled by black lace.

As he shoved his knife back into his pocket, he realized he

had no recollection of her finishing her set. He looked to his right to find Phoenix and Charity were gone, too. Goddamnit, even thinking about *not* thinking about Ellie made him fucking careless. Pathetic.

"I've been busy," Devil growled out. Jezebel's tongue swirled around the shell of his ear as she threaded her hands through his hair.

"Shame." She tightened her grip, tugging and causing a burn in his scalp. He had to hand it to her, she knew exactly what he liked. "I'm never too busy for what you can do to me."

He tried to lose himself in Jezebel's touch, but when he closed his eyes, images played unbidden across his mind, Ellie's smirk after she shot a bullseye for the first time. Ellie laughing even after she was knocked on her ass, smiling every time he teased her, or blushing when he flirted with her. Ellie trying to hide her soft gasp when his hard cock pressed against the curve of her ass.

Devil re-situated himself in the chair. His cock had twitched to life, but not for the woman pressed up against his back.

"Come on, Devil, baby. You know you want me."

The husky whisper in his ear was all wrong. The arousal that'd spiked for Ellie, flattened for Jezebel. He blinked his eyes closed for a moment and willed his cock back to at least half-mast, to get what he came for. But it was no use. It wouldn't work unless Ellie was in the picture. The idea to use her to get off with another woman flashed through his mind only to have his stomach twist in rebellion at the thought.

Devil slid his hands over Jezebel's and extricated himself. "This isn't a good idea."

Jezebel laughed over the beating bass and circled around his chair, her hand never leaving his body until she stopped to straddle his lap. Devil jerked his hands back and away from touching her, but Jezebel used the opportunity to shove her hands underneath his shirt. Her claws scratched at his chest and Devil tried to give himself over to the sting of pleasure and ignore the utter insanity telling him he was hurting Ellie by being at Original Sin at all.

Black wings enveloped him, blocking out the strobe lights and muffling the music to a thick thumping his pulse's cadence increased to match. Breasts pushed up against his chest and dark curls, thick with hairspray, crunched against the side of his face. Closing his eyes, he willed the whiskey to give him enough buzz to let loose. Gripping the shapely thighs on either side of him, he worked his way up to her hips and tried not to think about the lithe body he'd held on to the week before.

"I love the way you hold me down, Devil. Don't you want that?" Jezebel breathed hot air against his neck. "I know I do. You, fucking your Sinner from behind, like the devil you are." She pulled one of his hands from her hips and threaded it behind her neck. "You rip my hair in your hands, and I come on the spot."

Jezebel was right. She knew exactly what he wanted and he knew she could handle it. Hell, Devil had never had a relationship, but Jezebel was probably the closest he'd ever come. The first time he'd choked her, she'd let him until she'd nearly passed out. She would've, too, if he hadn't lost his shit and dropped her like a rucksack with a target on it. It'd been the first time he'd ever given into his urges during sex and it'd freaked him the fuck out. But when she'd rubbed her neck, smiled, and insisted he do it again, he thought he'd hit the jackpot of sexual partners. Since then, he'd fucked her too many times to count.

There was no way in hell Ellie could take that kind of abuse and he wasn't sure he could control himself to protect her from *him*. Ellie had been traumatized by evil men enough. She didn't need him to victimize her, too. Pain, inflicting, receiving. Fuck, she was too damn innocent for him. She was only eighteen to his twenty-seven for Christ's sake. She wasn't ready for what he needed to get off. Rough, unemotional sex was the only way he ever grew hard.

His eyes closed at the last thought. Because that wasn't true, was it? All Ellie had to do was fucking exist, and even in a sweaty sports bra and loose shorts, he was hard as steel at one touch.

Fingers entwined in the strands, Devil imagined it was Ellie's soft blonde hair tangled in his grip instead. He grew harder and lifted his hips up into the heat above him, groaning when he made contact.

Jezebel's knowing chuckle dimmed the haze. "There you are. I was beginning to worry I'd lost my touch."

Her voice was all wrong and Ellie faded from his imagination. If Jezebel kept talking, he'd never get it up. As it was, his dick was only hardening when it had other things to think about.

The deep charcoal orbs in front of him were empty black holes compared to the rich caramel he craved. Jezebel rested heavily on his softening cock and moved around with a slight frown, before forcing a smile. Every inch of her golden skin was covered in glitter that stuck to his hands as he tried to pull away. Devil squirmed into the plush pleather chair, not ready for her assault. The urge to push her off when she dove in to whisper against his lips was overwhelming.

"Want me to get us a confessional, baby? You know I have a few tricks to make sure you're ready for me. I'll get a room with the ropes."

"Enough," he growled in protest. It was no use. His cock was hiding at this point and it didn't feel like it was ready to come out to play anytime soon. His hands widened to grip her thighs and lift her off, but Jezebel grabbed his face and giggled.

"Hard to get, huh? Mmm, we haven't done this one before. You usually have a one-track mind." She kissed him, biting his bottom lip, reminding him of how he'd almost come on the spot when Ellie had done the same thing. This time he felt nothing but annoyance.

"The fuck are you doing, Jezebel?" He pushed her shoulders back with enough force that when she tore away from his lip, he tasted blood. "You know the rules." He swiped at his mouth with the back of his hand, confirming he was indeed bleeding. He'd fucked her plenty of times, but never had he allowed her to kiss him. Why she thought she could do it now, he didn't know, but it pissed him the fuck off.

"Get off. Now."

She ground into his soft cock and laughed. "I'm tryin' baby. You just gotta get with the program."

Devil pushed Jezebel to the end of his knees, giving her the opportunity to detach herself from him instead of shoving her away.

"I said, 'off.'"

Jezebel's plush lips stuck out in a pout and her dark eyes narrowed in the flashing lights.

"Oh, come on, why not?" She leaned forward to push her breasts into his chest. Sequins poked through the fine fiber of his shirt to irritate his skin. "It's been so long, fuckin' months. I've missed you."

Devil rolled his eyes, not caring whether it was too dark to see his expression. She'd only ever been good to him, but miss him? Yeah—the fuck—right. He knew the score. Jezebel had taken a liking to him, for why he didn't know, but she could be the best lay of his life and he'd still just be a client to her. If she missed him at all, it was for the same reason he missed her. The release.

"Come on, Devil. You came here for a reason. Don't let another angel have you when I'm right here."

And that did it.

"Off, Jezebel. Now." He growled and stood, giving her barely enough time to stand up straight. His delivery wasn't loud or disrespectful, but it was a tone that should have ensured silence in return. Jezebel had become too familiar though.

"Devil, what the fuck?" Jezebel huffed out, straightening her wings and checking around her to make sure no one had seen his clear dismissal. "What's goin' on? I can get someone else or you can fuckin' leave if you don't wanna do anything. Damn."

A crowd began to watch their standoff. Devil became acutely

aware of the linebacker bouncers taking their time to advance on him, as if they weren't ready to tackle as soon as Jezebel gave them the signal.

Another Sinner came to comfort Jezebel and Devil slowly raised his hands, trying not to cause more attention than his weak idiot ass had already garnered.

"I'm going, alright? Everyone, just relax."

He pulled out his phone to text Phoenix, and the light shined partially on the two Sinners in front of him. The one helping Jezebel had white wings and silver hair, and it took Devil a minute to realize who it was. Jezebel rolled her shoulders back, making her dark wings flutter before she sniffed and walked away. Charity scowled at him but Devil stopped her before she could follow her friend.

"Where the fuck's Phoenix?" The bouncers were still advancing on him and Devil gave them a pointed look before continuing to speak. "When I find him, I'll go."

"Phoenix?" Charity asked. "I have no idea. He said he'd meet me in a confessional and never showed. When you see him, tell that asshole he owes me fifty bucks for the time I lost waiting for him. Honestly, I should charge a hell of a lot more for some of the shit he's pulled."

Devil frowned before hammering out a text to tell Phoenix if he didn't show his ass in the next five minutes, Devil was out. They hadn't ridden together, so it wasn't like he'd be leaving him stranded. They'd realized early on riding together was weird as fuck after both of them got laid. The vibe in the truck was always off and it was best if they met up at Original Sin instead.

After exactly six minutes beside his two new best bouncer friends, nearly as big as he was, and no read receipt, Devil cut his losses and left. He looked around for Jezebel as he was all but escorted through the club, but couldn't find her.

He might've burned a bridge, but then again, maybe not. It wasn't like she could think he was a gentleman when he was the type of man who tied her up and fucked her while choking her from behind.

She was right about one thing, though. He'd come there for a reason, to fuck his need for Ellie out of his system. Even if it wasn't in the literal sense, it was clear *he* was fucked. One touch from a different angel shook him. It'd been months since he'd even gone to Original Sin and his sex-deprived cock had still decided to pussy out. At this point, there was no way he could be with another woman until he figured shit out with Ellie.

The thought pissed him off as much as it excited him, making his cock twitch back to life. He slammed the door to his truck as he got in and as he started it, his phone vibrated.

"Fucking Phoenix." Devil pulled it from his pocket, cursing as he thumbed the green button to answer without looking. "Hey, asshole, I'm leaving. Things went south with Jezebel—"

"Dev?" A harried whisper he could barely hear interrupted him. But he'd never mistake the voice.

"Angel?" After an infuriatingly long pause—his heart beating so loud he was afraid he missed her answer—he checked the phone and cursed, ready to hang up and call back until the voice whispered out again.

"Dev, please. I need you."

Devil thrust the gear into drive before whipping out of his safety park. "El, baby, where are you? I'm coming."

A beeping pounded into his ears, indicating the call had been dropped. He had one hand on the wheel, the other dialing a number he knew by heart before a text came through.

Sender has shared their location.

Devil pulled open the map, found Ellie's icon, and immediately slammed his foot on the gas. A growl barreled up through his chest before he yelled in the empty cabin of his truck.

"What the hell are you doing *there*?"

CHAPTER THIRTEEN

Ellie shivered and opened her eyes to darkness. Confusion and panic jolted her awake, and she clawed at the edges of the precariously nailed wooden slats to stop herself from tumbling to her doom. It took her a moment to remember she was in the treehouse, and even longer to register she couldn't hear kids playing anymore. Ellie frowned before looking at her phone. Ten fifteen p.m.

"Dang, Sash, I freakin' fell asleep." Her whisper puffed into the winter air as she inwardly berated herself much worse than her admission to a ghost. Night had settled into the air and the cold stillness gripped her, squeezing her heart with fear. She'd never been in the park so late and for good reason. She had to get the heck outta there, and fast.

Before stepping down the platforms, she held her breath to listen for anyone around her. The thrumming of her rapid heartbeat was so strong, she clutched her chest to cover the sound, praying it wasn't as loud outside of her body.

Her guard was always up whenever she was in public, but the addition of nearly pitch-black surroundings made her stomach churn with so much anxiety, the protein bar she'd scarfed down for lunch threatened to hurl itself back up. Thank God the tree kept its needles year-round or the platforms would be visible even in the dark.

Bolstering her courage, Ellie dried her sweaty hands on her leggings and tried to recall the path of rungs she'd need to find without her vision. She'd been up and down hundreds of times, but the overgrown tree had swallowed up the streetlight, and she'd never climbed down in the dark.

Ellie laid as flat as she could on the platform and felt for the edge, shining her phone light down to find it only illuminated one more rung. Each platform was two to three feet below the one above it, and none of them resembled actual stairs. She'd have to blindly feel her way with her feet all the way down to make sure she was landing on the platform.

Blowing out a breath, she spoke low to her friend, "This might've been a bad idea."

"What're you lookin' to score?"

Panic shocked down Ellie's spine and she gripped her hands around the edge of the platform. At the gruff question from the man she now realized was directly below her, barely visible through the branches but outlined by the moon, she turned off the flashlight on her phone, thankful she'd placed it light down onto the wooden slats.

"Anyone follow you here?" a smoker's voice asked. There was something familiar about the voice and Ellie narrowed her eyes as she tried to hear better. Maybe it was the hesitation and quick speech, but she couldn't match the voice with any of the faces scrolling like her contacts screen through her mind.

"Whatchu mean? You oughta be the one able to tell me if I'm bein' watched. Now what do you want, man? I ain't got all night." The first voice replied and Ellie peered over the edge of the wooden tree stand, still lying flat on her stomach, and strained her eyes to see two males directly below. One might've been wearing a hoodie and the other seemed shorter, wider, and from the sheen on his head, definitely balding.

"You'll stay as long as I want, you fucker," an older smoker's voice responded. "You know the drill. You supply, we leave you alone. I need more bars."

"Narcs been sniffin' 'round me anyway. I dunno, man."

"I'll steer them in a different direction, now do you have any, or not?"

There was rustling below while Ellie froze, hoping neither of them could hear her on the verge of hyperventilation.

"Nah. I brought glass. You got money?"

"No, that won't cut it. I need Zannies. I've had to resort to other shit already but I can't keep that up."

"Too bad, ol' man. You want it or not?"

The smoker growled. "Fine. How much do you have?"

"Well, how much do you got?"

There was a rustle below her and it sounded like one of the men grunted an assent.

"Half now? Half later?" the smoker asked.

"Shii-et, man. You know I don't play that way. All now or nothin'."

Another grumble. "Fine. Here." The smoker pulled out what Ellie assumed was cash and the other man examined it before giving up a bag himself. Curious, Ellie slid forward to look down. The inches her head extended past the plank made her dizzy and she hooked her feet on the other side of the platform to keep the falling sensation at bay.

Her foot tapped something and the subsequent cracking branches and twigs made Ellie wince as whatever she'd kicked plummeted to the ground. She coiled up on the platform, trying her best to hide.

"What the fuck was that?" The smoker's rough voice demanded an answer, but he sure as heck wasn't getting one from her. Ellie swallowed back her need for oxygen and covered her mouth from making any noise. The only thing she could hear was one of the men's labored breathing quickening before the crunch of dry grass. "What was... is that a damn donut? Where the hell did it come from?"

Ellie hoped he wouldn't connect a flying donut with someone stuck in the tree, but her luck had been craptastic so far, she didn't want to take any chances. She turned down the brightness on her phone and covered up the screen with her jacket so she could risk calling Dev. He picked it up mid-ring while yelling, but she didn't have time to listen.

"Dev?" Her whisper was hardly even loud enough for her to hear, but it worked.

"Angel?" When his nickname for her—the one that already made her heart skip a beat—came out in a bellow into her ear, her heart almost stopped completely, this time in fear as she paused for a second to make sure the men below hadn't heard.

"It was probably there from earlier in the day." The dealer's response made her think she was in the clear, so she rushed out her plea for help before hanging up.

She prayed the wooden slats and branches underneath her hid any light from her phone she wasn't able to smother and quickly sent her location, hoping that was all he needed.

"Nah, this is the only thing that looks like it coulda made those sounds. Did you hear it? It sounded like it came off the fuckin' tree."

The dealer barked out a laugh. "Man, you must be out your gott-damn mind if you think a donut came outta the sky. You sure you need this shit? You're already higher than I ever been."

"Shut the fuck up."

"Whatever, I'm out. I hate bein' in this park at night. It's straight-up haunted, man."

"And I'm the high one." The other man huffed out a laugh. "Get goin'. I'll be gone in a second."

The sound of grass crunching grew more distant and Ellie blew out the air threatening to burst from her chest. With a soft cry of relief, she rolled to her back to release all the tension in her arms and shoulders. She considered leaving, but there was no telling who else was hanging out in the park. If Devil had replied back, it was best to wait for him—

"I see you, girlie."

CHAPTER FOURTEEN

Icy fear stabbed Ellie's heart and she stared up in horror at the shining light on the pine needles around her. Her breath panted out in clouds and she covered her mouth with her hand to keep from screaming.

"Come on down, now. I don't bite."

Ellie refused to move. If he wanted her, he'd have to come get her. If he thought she'd go down willingly, he had another thing coming—

A click echoed through the tree and what it implied reverberated in Ellie's mind. Nausea roiled up her throat and she swallowed back her fear. Thanks to Devil, Ellie had heard that click hundreds of times before. At the shooting range.

"You know, the thing about parks at night... No one's surprised when bad shit happens. You'd think a place parents send their children would be safe at any time. But it's not, is it? Terrible things happen all the time in the dark, and people just... expect it. Wouldn't you agree?"

Ellie checked her text messages, but Dev hadn't responded yet.

"Not gonna talk, huh? Maybe you don't believe me. Well, let's say, for example, if some young woman, which I'm guessin' that's what you are from the pink on your tennis shoes. They're slightly bigger than a child's. Although, of course we ain't talkin' 'bout you. Just some poor unlucky lady. But if this young woman were to... I don't know, fall out of a tree in the middle of the night? Or hell, even if shots are fired, and a woman winds up dead... It'd be a travesty, certainly. But, a surprise? Nah. She shouldn't have been in the park all alone at night. She was careless. Naïve. Stupid. The media wouldn't go so far as to say she *deserved* it. But they might speculate what even the best of women woulda been doin' out that late. They'd probably resort to assumin' some sexual encounter, and you know how that always goes for women.

"But I'm gettin' ahead of myself. Bottom line, no one wants to think it could happen to them. Rationalizin' why it happened to you... I mean *her*... that's the game we all play, isn't it?"

Still lying on her back, cold sweat slithered down Ellie's forehead, making her shiver as it carved its way to the back of her neck. She checked her phone again, but there was no sign of rescue.

"Why don't you just show yourself? Then I won't have to accidentally shoot somethin' vital. Wouldn't it be easier to talk?"

Was this really happening? Could this guy really be threatening her right now? Threatening to *kill* her? In a public park? Ellie wiped her face and clutched her stomach as it twisted in fear.

Not knowing what else to do, she prayed. To God. To Sasha. Literally anyone who would listen.

"Suit yourself."

A sharp crack of air resounded and Ellie screamed as something *thunked* into the tree, only a few feet away from her head.

"I didn't see anything!" she yelled, enunciating the last word as tears streamed down her face. This lunatic was freaking *shooting* at her. "Please stop! I don't even know who you are! Please just leave me alone."

Tsking from below rattled her bones.

"That doesn't do me much good though, does it? See, I don't know you. Maybe you're a liar. You are a woman in the park in the middle of the night. Not too trustworthy, if you ask me. I'm gonna need me some insurance. That's all I do in my business. I learn things about people and decide what to do with them. Sometimes, I'll even help people out, if they help me. I think we can do that here. All I need from you is to see that pretty face of yours. And I'm sure it's pretty. I can tell."

Ellie grimaced as his words coated her and she desperately searched her brain for any way to escape.

"Just peek your head over that there floor you're sittin' on. I just need to see your face... for insurance. I need to know when I leave, you won't go to the police and tell them who you saw. If I know who you are, you'll know I can find you. And let's just say if you wind up knowin' who I am, well then you definitely know I can find you."

Ellie clenched her teeth to stop their chattering. His proposition made sense. Kinda. Right?

"How do I know you won't shoot my face if I show it?"

The smoker's responding chuckle devolved into a cough. She heard rattling like something against plastic and couldn't imagine what it was. She was racking her brain of what new weapon he was going to use when the man sighed.

"Let me explain how stupid that fear is. I could just send up a couple of shots into that flimsy wood right now and I'm sure I'd hit somethin' vital. It might be days before someone even finds you. Even if I don't hit you, you might fall out the tree. *Boom!*"

Ellie squeaked at his sharp yell but he continued to talk.

"All gone. No more whoever you are. Or I can wait for you to come down. Decide what to do then. You can't stay up there forever, girlie. And *brrr* do you feel that chill? It's supposed to get in the 'teens tonight. Wouldn't wanna get hypothermia.

"Or you could just show your face and I get my answers. I keep an eye on you, make sure you don't know who I am and that you don't squeal. Bottom line, I don't need to see your face to end you. The fact I haven't done it already proves what a nice guy I am."

Ellie continued to shake her head in indecision. He was right. The nine-square-foot platform she was clinging to like a life preserver was the same size as the targets she'd been taught to shoot on. Even if he was an amateur, twenty feet to aim would be a piece of cake.

The man sighed again. "Fine, have it your way. But for the record, I didn't want to do this." At the cock of the gun again, Ellie squealed and rushed to sit up, nearly falling off the platform and using nothing but bark and sap to keep stable.

"Okay, okay! I-I'll show you. But you h-have to throw the gun somewhere."

There was a breath of a pause before the man asked, "Throw my gun?"

"Um, yeah. I don't know. T-toss it over there, so I know you won't shoot me."

The man grumbled underneath her before she heard a click. "There, safety's on. I ain't throwin' my goddamn gun."

Ellie's stomach leadened. It really didn't matter if his safety was on, or if the gun was on the ground, or anything. Nothing mattered. He could still wait her out and shoot her. Or she could call 911, but then he'd definitely shoot her. Or maybe he'd run away if he heard sirens...

She mentally kicked herself. *Why the heck didn't I call 911 instead of Dev?*

Useless thoughts were coming a mile a minute until a thump farther away made her pause.

"I threw it. Happy? Now show yourself or I get it again and we do this dance all over. Don't even think of calling the police. You won't want to do that. Trust me."

Can he freakin' read minds? "W-why not?" It was probably a stupid question, but she'd do anything to stall.

"Let's just say, I've got an in there. They won't come if I tell them not to."

Ellie groaned and bit her hand to keep from screaming in frustration.

"Okay, okay. You threw the gun?"

She was met with a pause that was one of the least reassuring moments in her entire life, but no crunch of grass, no cocking of the gun.

"Alright... I'm doing it." Ellie's hands shook as she hooked them on the edge of the platform again. She leaned over, far enough to feel like she was going to fall from the vertigo. She winced at the bright light shining in her eyes, before prying them open to see who was down there. The flashlight blinded her instead and she brought her hand up to shield her eyes.

The smoker gasped. "*You.*"

Before she could question his response. Ellie jumped at the deafening sound of an engine barreling into the parking lot and again when a door slammed. The subsequent shout, though, soothed her.

The shine disappeared from her eyes, a balm on her nerves even though she'd been left blind with the afterburn in her retinas. Hasty crunches of grass faded away from the tree. Whoever was in the park must've scared the smoker.

A freezing cold gust rustled her hair in her ponytail. She shivered from the chill but was overcome by an overwhelming sense of relief when her name blew in on the wind in a demon's roar.

Devil found her.

CHAPTER FIFTEEN

Devil's truck skidded to a stop and he stormed out, slamming the door and yelling in frustration as he made his way inside the park. He never entered situations half-cocked, but lowlifes and dealers frequented Hatcher Gardens Park. He was alone so intimidation was more important than stealth. Announcing his presence as loudly as he could would hopefully scare them away, leaving Ellie safe.

Tucking low, Devil held his firearm at a ready stance. Whatever Ellie had gotten into, he sure as fuck wasn't about to be caught without a weapon. He scanned the park, checked his phone for Ellie's location, and cursed before stuffing it back into his pocket.

He was in the right place, but the app wasn't precise enough to get a good hit on her location. He blew out a breath, attempting to calm down before scanning the park. A gust of wind pushed at his back and the sound of footsteps several yards northwest brought his attention in that direction.

"Ellie!" he shouted her name so harshly it grated against his throat. Devil could see a faint light bobbing up and down away from him. If whoever was over there was anywhere near Ellie, he hoped his angry bellow scared the shit out of them. He sped his steps, forgoing caution in favor of catching the faint glow.

With about ten meters between them, the flashlight clicked off entirely, and it took a second for his eyes to adjust. When they did, he saw a short, wide silhouette run off into the thicket and Devil broke into a sprint after it. Whoever it was, sure as hell wasn't Ellie, but it was the only lead he had.

The figure stupidly tried to bulldoze through the brambles, probably attempting to hide, so Devil slowed to a stop outside the bushes. He tapped the trigger on his Glock as he assessed which way the person—a man, if the grunting and cursing was any indication—would escape.

The branches stilled and Devil held his breath as he tried to access all of his senses. When he heard a whimper, he tilted his head to listen. It'd sounded like it came from the large tree behind him.

Devil gritted his teeth and considered waiting out the man, but his ears were tuned into the soft cries coming from... *above?*

Was it Ellie? Was she hurt?

He waited another beat for the man to come out, before cursing under his breath at another sniffle. Backing away from his prey, he prowled backward to the tree.

Immediately, there was movement and rustling in front of him, and Devil bit back a groan, knowing the shady shit was clambering out of his hiding spot. He considered following the unknown target, but the medic in him was being pulled to check on the person crying behind—

"Dev?" The tentative whisper above him made the hair on the back of his neck stick up and settled his decision for him.

He kept his eyes forward to make sure the runner was fleeing in the opposite direction before he answered. "El? That you?"

"Yeah, it's me. I-I want to get down but I c-can't see."

"Down?" His gaze shot up and he retrieved his phone from his pocket to shine the flashlight up the tree. Blonde tendrils hung like tinsel from a crude makeshift platform in the tree. A head peeked over the edge and relief coursed through him when Ellie peeked over and shielded her eyes from the light. "Fuck, Ellie. What the hell are you doing up there?"

She disappeared from view, and after some rustling, yellow and pink tennis shoes slid into view, reaching down for the platform underneath it.

"Careful, angel." She was already halfway down and Devil still held his phone up to shine a path for her while scanning the park for threats again. He hadn't cleared the area and despite the fact he'd been below a teammate fast roping out of a chopper hundreds of times, covering for Ellie as she descended the tree made him edgy.

"Psh. I did this a million times growing up. Now that I've got light I'm good to g—" Ellie yelped as her foot slipped on a branch.

Devil cursed and positioned himself under where he thought she'd fall. Ellie yelped and groaned as she hit two branches. He shifted his weight to his back foot and bent his knees slightly, holding out his arms in preparation for her plummet.

His angel landed in his arms with an *oof* and Devil had to take a steadying step backward to keep from falling. When she was secure, he cradled her to his chest, bending his head low to smell her fresh spring scent in her hair until his rapid pulse slowed its painful beat. He brushed his lips over her forehead so lightly she probably didn't feel it. Too bad for her. His hold couldn't be that gentle.

"Ow, Dev, that's a little tight."

Devil loosened his grip, only easing up enough to make sure he wasn't contributing or exacerbating any injury she'd sustained. "You hurt?"

Ellie groaned. "Kinda." Her head lolled to rest against Devil's chest. He closed his eyes briefly in reverent thanks before making the trek to his truck.

"You can put me down now, ya know."

Devil grunted in response. "What're you doing in the park alone? At night? Are you fucking insane?"

Golden orbs shone silver in the moonlight before she averted her eyes. "I-I... I don't know, can't you put me down?"

"So you can do something stupid again? Not a chance in hell, angel."

"Excuse you. What right do you have to call me stupid?"

Devil shook his head. They'd finally reached his truck and he balanced Ellie against his chest to open the passenger door with the hand under her legs.

"Dev, this isn't necessary. I'm sore but I can—"

Devil raised her up into the truck and plopped her into the seat, making her grunt again.

"Really, Dev? You're being—"

Devil slammed the door on whatever she was going to say. On some deep level, he knew there had to be a logical explanation as to why he'd had to save her from the park in the middle of the night. But in that moment, when sweat was still fresh on his skin from the fear and anxiety threatening to boil past his defenses, he couldn't help but wonder how she could've been so careless.

When he slid into his truck and pulled out of the parking lot, he sure as fuck didn't expect the attitude radiating from her side of the cab.

"Mean."

He whipped his head in her direction. "*What?*"

"That's what I said. You're being mean."

Devil tightened his grip on the steering wheel and ground his teeth, trying to keep his cool. "Mean, huh? Well, I think you're being a bratty idiot. What the fuck were you thinking, Ellie?"

Ellie gasped and crossed her arms. "I know I said you could curse in front of me, but you can't curse at me, Dev. There's a difference. Try again without being a jerk."

He tried to focus on the road, and not on her tantrum. They were both reeling with adrenaline and he still didn't know what had happened. Ellie kept her face turned toward her window and absentmindedly picked bristles from her clothes with her still crossed arms.

"And I can smell your truck, by the way, even though I'm covered in pine needles. It smells like a sweaty homeless man chewing Big Red." She turned to face him, and her nose scrunched in his peripheral vision. "And wearing bad perfume." Before he could stop her, she leaned in to sniff him and wiped at his sleeve until he swatted her hand away.

"What're you doing?"

"Is that glitter?" She peered closer. "Oh, God, what happened to your lip? It's swollen!"

Devil growled. Hell—*the fuck*—no, they weren't talking about where he'd just left. "Stop trying to change the subject."

Ellie eyed him, and he could practically see her gears turning. He sat stock-still until she stared back out the front windshield. She huffed out a breath. "Right. Let's go back to you apologizing for calling me a 'bratty idiot'."

"I'll apologize as soon as you explain to me how you're not *being* a bratty idiot. What the hell are you doing in a park in the middle of the night? This park, no less. It's dangerous, Ellie."

The cab fell into a pressurized silence, as if they were both about to blow up, but neither of them wanted to cause damage. They fidgeted against the stillness until Devil couldn't take her quiet insubordination anymore. "Answer the question, Ellie."

"I had a reason, okay? But then I fell asleep—" Devil scoffed. "—on *accident*, and when I woke up there was some type of drug deal going on or something."

Devil's hands started to sweat on the steering wheel. "Was that who had the flashlight when I got there? Were you able to see them? Did they have any identifiable characteristics?"

Ellie nodded and looked out the window. "Yeah, that guy was the one buying I think. I wasn't able to see them or anything. I don't know much about those things but like I said, it seemed like a deal or something. The other guy—the dealer, I think—took off before you got there, but my donut fell—"

"Your donut?"

Ellie held up her hand. "I'll explain, I promise. My donut fell and I guess he noticed it. He stayed there and he, um... he threatened me."

Devil paused mid-scrub of his chin unable to keep from interrupting again in a low voice. "He fucking threatened you?" He tried to remain still and calm by channeling his breaths to keep from exploding. But her words were detonating in his mind and they made him physically itch to shield her from danger. "What'd he say?"

Ellie squirmed in her seat. "He... he made me... made me show my face, or else he'd shoot me."

The truck halted as Devil reflexively tapped the brake, almost as if his entire body was trying to keep the conversation from heading where he was afraid it would go.

"Did you do it? Did you see his face?"

Ellie nodded in the moonlight. "Yeah, I showed him. I didn't think I had any other choice. I didn't see his face though... the flashlight made it too bright. I thought about trying to ignore him, but then he shot the tree and—"

"He fucking *shot* at you? That's it. You're coming back to BlackStone, your brother's gonna want to hear about this. And you're never going back to that damn park again, you hear me? Especially not at night."

Ellie crossed her arms. "I'll call Jason tomorrow, but I want to sleep in my own bed tonight. You can't tell me what to do, Devil."

Devil. Not Dev. She'd only added two letters, but they were a one-two punch into his stomach. That, plus her insistence on staying at the dorm, was making him nauseous.

"I'll sure as hell tell you what to do if you can't take care of yourself! First you went to that stupid party and got taken, and now you were nearly shot to death—"

"Hold up." Devil stopped immediately at the command in her voice. "Are you seriously blaming any of this on me?" Ellie's voice raised steadily. "When I was kidnapped? Really? And just now? All I did was fall asleep. I went there when it was daytime and perfectly safe. It was an accident."

The pain in his stomach flipped in a dizzying sensation. He'd fucked up, but it was too late now. "Ellie, I..." He glanced over at her to see her eyes glistening back at him, wide with horror after his accusation. "Of course I don't think any of this is your fault. I just wonder sometimes if you paid more attention you'd realize when you're in danger, maybe you could prevent—"

Ellie's hand shot up. "Don't."

He shook his head and blew out a breath through his nose. "Ellie, I—"

"No. Don't, Devil. I already think it. I can't hear it from you, too. I just... I can't. Not from you. And not today."

Silence weighed heavy in the air, crushing the stone heart in his chest. He wracked his brain to connect the words left unsaid.

"Why were you there, Ellie?"

She narrowed her eyes at him. "I'll tell you if you swear to take me back to my dorm."

"Ellie," he growled.

"That's the deal. Besides, the guy just saw my face, it's not like he knows where I live or anything. It was probably just some junkie." Something about her voice made him wonder if she believed it herself, but she was so earnest, it was hard not to see how much she needed what she was asking for. "I want to sleep in my own bed, not the BlackStone guest room."

"I thought you didn't like your dorm," he hedged, genuinely curious by the change.

She sighed. "I didn't. I don't really. It's so... small. But I'm trying to do things that scare me." He could tell she'd turned to face him, but Devil kept his eyes on the road, trying not to read too much into her words. "Please, Dev. This is important to me. I finally got Jason to leave me alone. He convinced the university to let BlackStone install top-of-the-line security, which, if I'm right, BlackStone has access to the camera feeds. Yes, tonight scared the crap out of me, but I need to try to feel normal as best as I can."

Her wavering voice shook his resolve and he scrubbed his beard as he considered a compromise.

"I'll take you back to your dorm. But I'm texting your brother and telling him something at least. And I'm gonna sit outside and make sure no creepy asshole goes in."

Ellie scoffed. "Right, like some guy parked outside the dorm isn't creepy."

"Fair enough. You live in one of those fancy suites, right?" At her nod, he continued. "I'll sleep on your living room couch, then. Deal?" She opened her mouth to argue but he interrupted her with a *tsk*. "BlackStone or your couch, baby. Gotta pick one."

"Fine," she huffed. "You can stay on our couch. But I can't be held accountable for your psych bill if Virginia drives you crazy."

He barked out a laugh. "I think I can handle it for one night."

"'Mkay...'" Her exaggerated shrug didn't make her seem convinced, but Devil wasn't going to let her sidestep the conversation.

"That's the deal. Now talk."

Ellie's shoulders sagged back against the leather seat. For the longest time, he wondered if he was going to have to prompt her again, but then she finally spoke, and the raw, broken part of him he'd hidden since he was seventeen, almost wished she hadn't.

"It's Sasha's birthday." The crack in her voice stabbed his heart. "We went to our tree all the time growing up. It got less in high school, but we made sure to go at least every birthday." She pulled her ponytail to the front and picked out pine needles. "Ugh, my fingers are sticky from all the sap." She flicked the thin green sticks from her hands and chuckled as she brushed the two together to get the remnants off. "Back then, Sash and I didn't care too much about getting dirty from climbing. It didn't matter that the tree bark stuck to us like glue. We'd been thrilled when Jason secretly made a 'treehouse' for us—"

"Jaybird called that a treehouse? In a public park? How'd he get away with that?" Devil interrupted. "It was nothing but some two by fours slapped together." He shook his head at Jason thinking that shitty hack job was safe enough for his sister.

Ellie's laughter came out like a whisper. "It was enough for us. We practically lived in it. She lived in the Hatcher Gardens Neighborhood before it got to be the bad part of town." She sighed. "I wanted to be as close to her as possible today. I got us our birthday donuts—it was tradition—and I celebrated with her up there, the only way I could." Her voice trailed off softly and she leaned her head against the window.

Devil's stomach twisted at Ellie hurting. He could take pain, thrived off of it. But the emotional turmoil radiating off her and into the cabin of his truck was going to be the death of him.

Ellie turned her head. "Earlier... were you really mad at me?"

He glanced at her, longer than driving should've allowed, but there was no one on the road. "No, angel. I wasn't really mad at you. I was..."

"Annoyed?"

"Scared."

Her breath hitched. "But you're usually so... I guess I've never seen you lose your cool before. Jason says you don't feel anything." The last part was a tentative question more than a statement, but the indictment against his characteristic lack of reaction cut him as sure as the slice of a knife, but he didn't know why.

His lips tightened before he answered as honestly as he could muster considering the topic. "Not when it comes to you, angel."

She nodded, as if she could possibly know the hold she had over him. She laid her golden hair back against the bench seat and squared her vision on Devil.

"I won't go at night anymore. The daylight got away from me

today. But you can't expect me not to ever go there again. I was close to her for the first time since... a long time."

He shook his head, she had no idea how alike they were.

"Listen," he began, determined to get his point out before the memories threatening to tear down his peace of mind broke free. "I get what you're going through more than most. I had a friend, growing up. Troy. He was going through it at home. He started getting moody and turned into this angry kid. I didn't understand why at the time, just thought he was being an asshole. Come to find out, his parents were abusing him." The quiet hiss of breath beside him made him want to get the words out as quickly as possible. He'd kept the guilt in too long. Maybe getting some of that poison out of him would help.

"Their abuse drove him to abuse drugs. I lost my friend right before my eyes. I let him go, too. I thought he was the one who was fucked up, that he was a failure. Not that everything around him, including me, had failed *him*.

"We got into a stupid fight, I can't even remember what it was about anymore except that it was the last one. I let my emotions get the best of me. I lost control and let being angry and prideful distract me from seeing every sign right there in front of me."

Devil choked and cleared his throat, blinking his eyes several times to see the dark road better. Ellie patted his thigh, close to his knee, but he faced the street for the next sentence. He didn't want to get sidetracked. It was easy when he'd never wanted to be on the path in the first place.

"His emotions got the best of him, too. I lost him and... I found him." A creaking fractured his memory as the nightmare he'd lived at seventeen swayed on its rope in his teary vision, like a morbid transparent backdrop on the windshield. He clenched his hands around the steering wheel hard, until all he could focus on was the pain in his fingertips. Not the agony of seeing his best friend hanging from the ceiling.

"He took a bunch of whatever medication his parents forced

him on and when that didn't work, he took matters into his own hands. I never got to say sorry. I never tried to help him. Maybe I could've but—"

"You had no idea that was going to happen. You were just a —" Ellie paused and looked at him when he leveled his gaze on hers. "Just a kid."

"Yeah, baby." Devil nodded. "We were just kids."

The way she got to the point he wanted her to understand, it sounded so simple. Even if he didn't believe it himself, he hoped she did. She didn't deserve the same guilt he'd suffered.

It was Ellie's turn to sigh and she faced the road as he did. "Last week after I freaked out... is that why you did too?"

He jerked his head 'yes' even though he wasn't sure she saw. "You make me lose control, angel."

"And you think that made you miss the signs of my panic attack."

"I *know* it did."

"You didn't. But I'm sure." She sighed. "Losing control... I think that's why I got scared, too. I like things... regimented now. It helps me not have to think. Being in control now, I guess, makes me feel less guilty about giving in to feeling helpless then. I felt like I lost control of my body again in that moment and I think that's why I had my panic attack."

She felt like she didn't have control? So much of what she'd said fired off synapses and made connections in his brain. But the last was what sparked an idea in Devil's mind, one that wasn't fully formed but he wondered...

"She was cremated, you know." The sentence snapped him back to the conversation at hand. "There's nothing at her grave. Not even ashes. If I'm gonna be able to feel Sasha when I need to, I have to be where I remember us the most, where I remember her the best.

"The park... the tree. That was ours. Our safe haven. It saved us from all the stupid boys on the playground. We won every dang manhunt and hide-and-seek game." Ellie's voice became watery. "We became best friends in that treehouse."

Silence blanketed the cab of the truck, and Devil waited for her to finish. His body ached and he realized he'd been rigidly sitting on the edge of his seat cushion since they got in the truck. He settled back against the seat and glanced at Ellie, her eyes drifting closed as the lights of campus shone in the darkness. From the stressors she'd experienced, her adrenaline must've been through the roof. She'd been working herself to the bone lately. He was surprised she had any energy left at all.

She inhaled deeply before continuing softly. "It's something that helps me remember the good, even when everything else totally sucks. Don't you have anything like that?"

Her words drifted and he wondered if she was falling asleep. He grasped her small hand resting on the seat between them. His thumb traced her knuckles and he reveled in the softness of her skin. She scooted to his side, morphing to him in a sleepy daze, all the while still in his grip. The comfort in the simple touch soothed him.

"Yeah, angel. I've got something like that."

CHAPTER SIXTEEN

Deafening booms jolted Ellie awake, shooting her straight up into a sitting position and clutching her chest. Flailing around for purchase, her eyes widened to try to see as she was sucked down into the pitch-black room. She slapped her hands up and down her chest and legs, afraid of what she'd find.

I am wearing clothes.

I am in soft sheets... not on hard tile.

The last vestiges of hazy panic faded from her sight and she realized light filtered through yellow gauze curtains. Her breath whooshed out in relief.

I am safe. I am in control. I am in my dorm. I am in my bed.

The heavy banging that had jarred Ellie awake hammered at her bedroom door until she realized they were only normal knocks, not earth-shaking explosions.

"Ellie? It's Virginia." *Knock-knock-knock.* "Are you up?"

"Virginia, what the heck?" Ellie called out loud enough to drown her stuttering heartbeat.

"Oh good, you're up!" The knob on her door rattled. "Why's your door locked?" A dramatic gasp sounded through the thin doors. "Does your boyfriend seriously think you need to lock your door against me? How fuckin' rude!"

Ellie rolled her eyes but finally remembered how she'd gotten back to her dorm. She vaguely recalled Dev using her key to the back entrance of her dorm and he must've laid her in the bed.

"Ellie?"

"God, what, Virginia? It's..." Ellie looked at her watch to find it was already eleven a.m. She shook her head and hopped out of the bed to pull her door open during the middle of one of Virginia's knocks. Ellie ducked, but not before she swatted Virginia's fist hard enough for it to crash against the doorframe.

"Jesus!" Virginia yelped in pain. "What the hell did you do that for?" Virginia shook her hand and inspected her knuckles before turning back to Ellie with her eyes wide, asking for an explanation. "What, are you some kinda ninja, now?"

A blush heated Ellie's face, but instead of being ashamed, she stood up straighter. Virginia's fist had nearly used her own forehead as a door knocker. Dev would've been embarrassed if she hadn't blocked it.

"What do you want Virginia?" Ellie struggled to keep her sigh of annoyance in check. She didn't have time for her roommate's nosiness.

Ellie's phone vibrated on the desk behind her and she turned to check it.

17 missed calls. 10 voicemails. 28 text messages.

Ellie groaned and thumbed through a couple of the messages.

Jason: Ellie wtf happened?

Jason: Call me. Devil said he had to come get you?

Jason: Ellie call me, I MEAN IT.

Jules: Your brother's about to lose his shit, please call him when you can.

Jason: If you don't call me in five minutes, I swear to God I'm coming to your dorm.

Dev: Don't worry about your brother. I'll take care of him. Get some sleep, angel.

Dev: Leaving for BlackStone now. Call if you need to. PS your couch sucks ass.

Ellie snorted at the last one before tossing her phone to the bed. The final text was from the morning and Jason had stopped texting around three a.m., so she could only assume Dev had sufficiently calmed Jason down. It would have to do for now. She was tired as heck, and arguing with her brother might've literally been the last thing on earth she wanted to do. She turned back around to see Virginia was still standing in the doorway.

Nope. Scratch that. Second to last thing on earth.

"What, Virginia? I kind of have a busy day." It was only sort of a lie. Ellie didn't have anything on her agenda, but it wasn't like she didn't have anything to do. She had a crap ton of studying and she needed to check in at Sasha Saves.

Hurt flitted across Virginia's furrowed features. "Your boyfriend dropped you off late last night. I wanted to check on you. Make sure you're okay."

"I don't have a boyfriend." Ellie turned to grab her books from her bag. There was a test the following week she hadn't studied for yet. With her back turned to Virginia, Ellie safely rolled her eyes. She'd probably have to go to the library for some peace and quiet.

"Well, the hot redhead guy who looks at you like he'd burn the world down if anyone ever hurt you. You know the one?" Ellie turned to see Virginia's eyebrow perked up as she smirked.

"His name's Dev... or Devil, depending on who's asking."

"Yum-*my*. Sounds like I wasn't too off then. How fittin'."

A laugh burst from Ellie's chest and Virginia's smile widened before she spoke. "I think this is the first time I've ever gotten you to laugh."

Ellie's smile faltered as she climbed up to surround herself with books and sit on her bed.

"Oh, no you don't." Virginia entered the room and hopped into Ellie's desk chair. "You were happy for a second and I made you that way. Let's go back to that. It was nice."

"What was? Me laughing at you?"

"Laughing *with* me." Virginia scowled. "But I can see the

moment's gone. I'm glad you're okay or whatever." Virginia got up from the chair to leave the room and Ellie immediately felt like a jerk. Virginia only ever tried to connect with her and Ellie spurned her away every chance she got.

"Virginia, wait."

Virginia paused in the doorframe and huffed as she turned slowly, her arms crossed. Ellie wrapped a tendril from her ponytail around her finger and began to twirl. "Something crazy happened last night. Do you, um... do you wanna hear?"

Virginia's eyes widened and she nodded slowly before taking slow steps closer and putting her hand on the back of Ellie's seldomly used desk chair.

"Wait, can we, um... can we go to the living room?" Ellie asked.

Virginia narrowed her eyes before nodding. "Sure thing."

Virginia led the way and as soon as Ellie exited her bedroom, her chest expanded in the open space, breathing in and exhaling the air that was always trapped inside her lungs when she was in her tiny room. Ellie collapsed opposite of Virginia on the couch, still exhausted from the ordeal. When they were settled, Virginia turned off the TV from the news channel she'd been watching. The girl was obsessed with current events.

"Okay, girl, I'm all ears." Virginia curled up onto their couch, propping her elbow on a cushion and her chin up on her palm.

"Do you remember how I said my friend Sasha and I—" She cleared her throat. "Had a treehouse growing up?"

Ellie recounted being trapped and having to be rescued by Dev, all while Virginia sat in an eerie, raptured silence. By the end of the story, Ellie couldn't wait for her roommate to talk again.

"Holy shit." Virginia had moved during the story until her arms were hugging her knees. "That's insane... so... but like... you're okay, right? It was terrifyin' and totally shit-your-pants crazy-dangerous, but... you're okay?"

Ellie groaned before nodding, slightly embarrassed she'd needed to be rescued *again*. "Yep. I'm okay. No thanks to me, that's for sure. I don't know why the heck I keep getting myself into these crappy situations."

Virginia tilted her head. "No thanks to you? What the hell does that mean? If it weren't for you, you'd probably be dead meat being picked apart by a buzzard or somethin' right now."

"Um, did you not hear my story? I freakin' fell asleep in a park and got caught up in a drug deal! I could've died if it weren't for Dev!"

Virginia shook her head and waved her hand at Ellie like her point was total nonsense. "Nah, girl. That ain't how I see it, anyway."

Ellie huffed, a little annoyed she was having to convince this bimbo she'd been an idiot the night before.

"Fine, Virginia. How do you see it then."

Virginia's face scrunched up like she was trying to figure Ellie out. "You run yourself ragged, you know that? I hardly ever see you 'round here. It's like you don't like being in your own room."

Ellie felt heat rush to her cheeks at Virginia's accuracy. That was *exactly* what it was. Jason had done his darndest to get her into the biggest dorm. He'd convinced the university to make an exception and let Ellie and her BlackStone vetted freshman roommate stay in upperclassman suite-style dorms.

She only ever stayed in her room after waiting until the very last moment to go to sleep, and even then she needed constant background music or trashy TV to drown out her negative thoughts. But despite having more square footage, soft Target bedding, and cute aesthetic—thanks to pre-move-in shopping with Virginia—late at night, none of that mattered. Small was small, dark was dark, and cold was cold. Eventually she'd be reminded of the hotel bathroom she'd been locked inside for days. Her nightmares bled over into the physical realm, and she imagined the only warmth she felt was from the twisted up unconscious bodies around her. The night before was the first night she could remember sleeping soundly without music.

"I don't really. It feels... small. I don't... um... I don't like small spaces... a-anymore."

Virginia's face softened with sympathy. "Well, the point of my observation is you're tired, babe. You're everywhere for everyone else, and you won't even let yourself rest where you're supposed to be safest. Yesterday, you fell asleep after kickin' ninja ass, bein' a college student, and savin' the world with whatever that job is you go to all the time. You messed up. Big fuckin' deal. Tons of people mess up all the time and nothin' bad happens to them. Shoot, I should probably be dead ten times over for the stupid decisions I've been makin' at house parties since I got here."

Ellie chuckled but couldn't stop her confused frown. "What's your point?"

Virginia sighed and rolled her eyes. "The point is, you're a freakin' freshman in college. If you can't fuck up now, when the hell can you?" She reached over the couch and patted Ellie's sock-covered foot. "You're doin' good, babe. Real good. You fell asleep in a place you've always felt safe. Most people would've just been chilly. Unfortunately, your unlucky ass gets to have all the drama. You still handled it way better than I would've. Hell, you know what I would've done if I'd been up there?"

"What?"

"I'da've peed my pants, probably fallen to my death, forgotten I even had my phone... I don't know. Somethin' hella stupid, that's for sure. But nope. Your head was on straight and you kept it together to call for help." Virginia shook her head. "I know I wouldn't've done that. I'da've screamed bloody murder and that guy would've shot my ass before I got around to using logic."

Ellie rubbed her hand against her forehead and chuckled. "Okay, but that doesn't absolve me of being stupid."

Virginia lifted a shoulder and continued on. "Eh, maybe not. But don't be too hard on yourself. You're allowed to make mistakes and you did a hell of a job savin' yourself in my opinion."

"Virginia." She was now certain the blonde hadn't been listening. "*Dev* saved me."

Virginia shook her head. "He couldn't've done it without you, though. Besides, sometimes savin' yourself is all about findin' the right person to do the rescuin'."

Relaxing against the couch pillows, Ellie pursed her lips. "Huh... I guess that's one way to look at it."

Virginia shrugged as if she hadn't completely changed Ellie's perspective with one flippant explanation. "All I'm sayin' is give yourself grace, girl. You ain't perfect and it's no fun tryna be, ya know?"

A small smile stretched her lips. "This is nice, you know. Just... I don't know. Being normal? Talking with my roommate."

Virginia snorted. "Bless your heart, girl. It's darlin' you think bein' nearly shot to death in a tree thanks to a traitorous nasty-ass sour cream donut is dadgum normal."

Ellie barked out a laugh at Virginia's phrasing of Ellie's traumatic night.

"Traitorous donut? Sour cream is the best damn flavor and no one can convince me otherwise."

Well, Sasha, she does have a point. It didn't need to leap to my death.

Remembering she had a real-life, in-person friend in front of her, Ellie stopped talking to Sasha and rolled her eyes at Virginia. "You get what I mean."

Round cheeks framing a grin beamed back at her. "Yeah, I do. It's nice havin' my roomie."

"I like her, you know. This is good for you, girl."

Ellie sniffed at the thought and played with a frayed thread in her sock. "My best friend... Sasha. From before..."

"She's the one..." Virginia's soft eyes were understanding

when Ellie dipped her chin in confirmation. "If you ever wanna talk about her, Ellie, I'm here. I talk a shit ton, but I'll totally listen."

Ellie continued her nod and wiped away at the mist threatening her eyes before letting out a chuckle. "You're just like her, you know? Kind. Driven. You love people. Sasha was like that. She always said yes to everything. I was the scaredy-cat all the time. I never would've done anything if it weren't for her."

Warm manicured fingers wrapped around hers over her foot and squeezed. "Well," Virginia cleared her throat. "I think that's one hell of a compliment."

Ellie smiled wider and swallowed back her fear, deciding to finally be honest with her. "That's why it's been hard for me. To be friends with you. You remind me so much of her. It—" She blew a heavy breath out, imagining all her reservations flowing out with it. "It... h-hurts."

The hand covering hers squeezed again and Ellie finally looked up to see Virginia's eyes welling up with tears and sympathy.

Not pity. There's a difference.

Pity is lonely. People use it as a shield to reassure themselves the problems in someone else's life would never happen to them. The sufferer must've done something to deserve the karmic retribution they received and the pitying person inherently thinks of themselves as better than the pitiful one.

But when someone has sympathy, they're sharing in the pain, taking any of the burden they can, realizing it could've happened to anyone, and believing it definitely shouldn't have happened to the person suffering.

Pity wounds the ego, but sympathy heals the soul.

Virginia freed a watery sigh and Ellie felt her pain mirrored back to her.

"I'm sorry for everything you went through. I... I wish I knew what to say. But you are loved, you know. Sasha's gone. But people who love and adore you are still here. I'd love to be friends with you, whenever you're able. No pressure."

The last words were rushed out but Ellie hadn't needed them. She gave Virginia a small smile in return.

"I'm getting there, V. I'm getting there."

CHAPTER SEVENTEEN

Devil tucked his phone back into his pocket, thankful he'd seen the text in time to get back to BlackStone. He hopped the steps two at a time to the top floor and shouldered open the door to their war room.

Hands grabbed him by his coat lapels and slammed him up against the wall beside the entrance. He grabbed above his attacker's elbow with one hand and pushed the man's wrist upward.

"*Mother-!*"

A harsh slap landed on Devil's shoulder and he instantly released the pressure, realizing with his opponent's tap out he had his teammate in his grasp. He glanced past his attacker and saw Hawk, Snake, and Phoenix looking on, their expressions various shades of surprise and shit-eating laughter. That left—

"Fuck, man. I wasn't expecting that." Jaybird rubbed his wrist and shook it out.

"You should've." Devil shrugged, the attack and defense had been so quick he hadn't even had time for his adrenaline to spike. "You came at me, fucker. What the hell else did you expect me to do? At least grab my collar, instead. I know Draco taught you better." He and the rest of his teammates had been fighting each other for years and they'd all been taught their best moves by their teammate, Draco. "Rookie move."

Jaybird shook his head before wiping his face with both hands. "You're right. I'm just pissed."

Devil raised his eyebrows, expecting more.

Jaybird threw up his other hand. "About Ellie, goddamnit! She was in trouble last night and she fucking called you, of all people! Why the fuck would she call *your* coldhearted ass, for Christ's sake?"

The 'coldhearted' attack stung for some reason, but Devil would never reveal that wound. To be honest, he'd been surprised by that revelation as well, but he hadn't wanted to dwell on why Ellie would reach out to him above anyone else. Best not to dream when reality could slam you into a wall.

"She called you!" Their war room was virtually nothing but concrete and electronics, so Jaybird's yell reverberated around the room just as it did in Devil's chest. "And she didn't call me." Jaybird tugged his hair, making it wild. "I thought I'd been a good brother lately. I don't know, I guess I've been preoccupied with Jules. I never want Ellie to feel like I won't be there for her, again. To count on me being unaccountable. Like last time." Jaybird shook his head while mumbling the last, and Devil realized the problem.

When Ellie was kidnapped at the party she went to nearly a year ago, she'd used Jaybird as a ruse so no one would know she'd gotten a secret invite. She'd called her brother, banking on him to cancel a dinner they planned, and sure enough he did. Leaving Ellie free and clear to attend a party she had no business going to.

"It's not like that, man. I've been her trainer for weeks now. It was late, and I'm sure she didn't want to bother you with Jules. You've got a whole other family to think about. Ellie needs to grow up at some point and relying on someone outside her family would be good for her, you know?"

Jaybird nodded slowly, like Devil had said something wise

instead of pulling it out of his ass. "Yeah, yeah. I guess you're right. It's probably because you're my friend, too. Sorry, man. I should've known it was something like that when she resorted to calling you. I guess I let myself get carried away."

The hidden barb in Jaybird's words was unexpected and the pain was sharp in his chest. He clenched his fists until his blunt fingernails stabbed into the palms of his hands and he lost feeling in the tips of his fingers.

"Letting your emotions get in the way will get you killed." Devil nodded to Jaybird's hand for emphasis before pulling a chair for him to sit. "Or at least a broken wrist."

Jaybird shook his head before huffing out a breath. "You'll understand when you have someone you care about."

"What's that supposed to mean?" Devil's voice grated up his chest and into his throat.

"He already has someone he cares about, dontcha beautiful? Lil' golden angel, right?" Phoenix looked up from his texting and smirked before sliding his phone back into his pocket.

"What's *that* supposed to mean?" Jaybird demanded, his glare oscillating between Devil and the smart-ass with the backward ball cap and shit-eating grin.

Phoenix barked out a laugh. "If you don't know by now, dude, you're in for one hell of a surprise."

Jaybird's brow furrowed as he stepped toward Phoenix, but Hawk pushed himself between them and indicated a chair at the round table.

"Enough." Hawk's deep voice echoed in the concrete-walled room. "Ellie's safe now, right?"

Devil nodded. "Yeah she's safe. Once I found her, everything was fine."

"That's another thing..." Jaybird began before turning to their communications sergeant by his wall of screens. "Snake, you can hack into phones and do that thing where you follow people's location, right?"

Snake gave a slow nod. "Yeah... whatcha getting at?"

"I want every one of us to have her location. That way if she calls any of us we can find her. Or her roommate... they're friends, right? Do her too."

"Dude, that's a serious invasion of privacy." Snake argued.

"I don't give a flying fuck. We'll only use it when we need to. Can you do it or not?"

Snake shook his head with a frown. "I'm not doing it. Come back to me when you get her permission—or if there's an emergency."

Steam was practically coming out of Jaybird's ears. Devil didn't mind the plan but he understood where Snake was coming from. Granted, Devil didn't give a shit if the rest of the room had Ellie's location. He'd made sure to keep following it after Ellie sent it to him the night before. There was no way he was telling her brother, though. Devil had it for an emergency and that was enough for him.

"Moving on." Hawk sat in his usual place at whatever the hell the head of a round table could be called and crossed his arms. "I called a meeting for a reason and it sure as fuck wasn't to stalk a coed. Sit your asses down."

Jaybird grumbled to his seat between Phoenix and Devil at the table. Everyone faced Snake as he swirled around in his rolling chair, his back to the computer screens lining in stacks above his desk.

"We've got a lead on the Ashland elite scholarship party."

Devil's back straightened. If they were finally making plans to find the bastards who stole Ellie, maybe he could put his obsession with her aside. Everything surrounding her felt like unfinished business, so putting her to bed would be a relief.

He sucked in a breath and ground his teeth to the point of pain.

Not the relief I should be thinking about.

"We always thought the assholes would be stupid enough to

try the same stunt again, but we haven't had much to go off of," Hawk explained. "Which means they probably have help from people above our pay grade—"

"Or we're losin' our touch," Phoenix piped in with a shrug as he leaned his chair back on two legs.

Hawk narrowed his eyes at Phoenix, but their cocky teammate seemed unfazed by Hawk's death glare. Their team lead huffed out a breath before continuing. "In any case... I got to thinking after our last meeting with Burgess... he really put emphasis on the party. We've always suspected he was a player on the other side, but with that comment, it made me wonder if he's too dumb to realize he's tipped his hand."

Jaybird scoffed. "Abso-fucking-lutely he's that dumb. The guy tried to pin my own sister's kidnapping and her best friend's murder on me." His finger jabbed into his chest and Devil winced at the power behind it.

"Well, now we have proof he's onto something, at least." Snake cut in. He swiveled his chair around and after a few swipes of the keyboard, what looked like a professional database took over the nine screens in front of him. "This is the room check-in log at the McIntosh Hotel." He cleared his throat and swallowed. "The one where..."

Snake faced Devil and completed his sentence as Devil trailed off. "Yes, that's the one. Where the party was held just shy of a year ago. Where the girls were taken. Where we raided without any luck. All in the same, my friend." He turned back to the screen. "I'd hacked into the system last year, and I've been keeping track of the hotel database and this new entry caught my attention and, specifically, when it is booked."

Despite the large collection of screens, Devil still had to squint at the tiny writing. Give him a target through a scope eleven hundred meters away, and he'd hit it every time. But tiny words ten feet away he'd miss every other letter. Finally he got the right amount of squint to eye-opening ratio, but Phoenix ended up narrating it for him anyway.

"Vaz-yay Pup-kin? Room 307," Phoenix sounded out.

"No, it's pronounced like voz—as in the fancy way to say vase —yah, poop-kin," Snake clarified.

"Poor guy." Phoenix snorted back. "Sure it's not my way? Your way sounds—"

"Moving on." Hawk's dark eyes may not faze Phoenix, but they shut Snake's mouth mid-retort. "Snake says they're using another dummy name."

"Like Ivan Ivanovich last year?" Devil asked, recalling how, before they realized the name was a fake, Devil had wanted to beat the fuck out of the guy last year in retaliation for finding an empty hotel room when they were supposed to be saving Ellie.

Snake nodded. "Yes, exactly." He pulled up the floor plan of the hotel. "According to the booking itinerary, this Mr. Pupkin is booking room 307 for only two nights around the same time the fundraiser was held last year."

Jaybird shook his head. "It's fucking incredible these bigwigs are able to keep parties like this secret. In the past, we knew the players ASAP and picked these assholes off easier than finding... uh... that guy." He snapped his fingers. "The one with the red and white hat?"

Everyone cocked their head at Jaybird.

"You mean... Where's Waldo?" Snake sounded out slowly.

Jaybird threw his hands up. "Obviously! Who the fuck else would I be talking about?"

"I'm not really sure *why* you're talking about him." Snake pushed up his glasses. "Usually Phoenix says the stupid shit."

"Hey!" There was a thump as two of Phoenix's chair legs returned to the ground. He opened his mouth but Hawk cut in before Phoenix could retaliate.

"That was MF7. We were backed by the United States and the subjects we were dealing with were third-world ops entering or exiting our country, with the occasional US-international trafficking ring. This is our home. We have to play by different rules now. Unfortunately, since the government seems to be

MIA on this, that means figuring out who is involved all by ourselves. "

"I get it, but it fucking sucks ass," Jaybird grumbled and Devil grunted in agreement as he shook his head slightly.

"We have to make do with what we've got. Speaking of which..." Hawk leaned back in his chair and scrubbed his hand against his fade before nodding at Snake to continue.

"From the hotel log, we know when, or at least we can infer, the organization behind the kidnappings will be at the McIntosh. Now we can plan accordingly to surveil and extract, if necessary."

"We can have an actual plan instead of like last time where we were fucked from the beginning. They've kept real damn quiet for nearly a year. I'm glad we're finally gonna go somewhere with it," Jason said.

Snake clicked on his keyboard and mouse and another screen pulled up. "There's something else we didn't have last year. Now we have the list."

"The list?" Phoenix asked.

Snake nodded. "Yep. We have the list of donors, invited guests, eligible 'scholarship recipients.'" He used finger quotes because young women, like Ellie, who'd just turned eighteen at the time, were fooled into thinking they were planning their future while the assholes in charge of the party were planning on stealing and doing God knows what with them.

Devil popped a piece of Big Red into his mouth, attempting to keep his mouth busy and avoid being a smart-ass. But he couldn't help himself. "Does anyone even actually get scholarships from this shitshow or are the elite Ashland assholes fucking *everyone* over."

"Surprisingly enough, there is some legitimacy to the scholarships. They've raised and donated over a million dollars to local Ashland high schoolers." Snake pushed his glasses up on his nose and shrugged.

"For real?" Jaybird asked, his eyebrows up to his hairline. "How are they keeping this all under wraps?"

"Big money in high places?" Snake answered. "It's how these things get by cops and the general public. They probably use the scholarships as a guise for when people find out about the party, and they don't spread the word about their charitable donations to make sure no one looks into it too hard. Choose the right people to be involved and boom, you've got yourself a covert operation to do whatever the fuck you want."

Hawk exhaled a deep breath before shaking his head. "Anyone can be bought."

"Exactly. But we have last year's list and this year's." Snake continued. "Now I need to cross reference them and figure out who our players are. Jaybird, maybe Ellie can help—"

"No." The anger Devil had felt rumbling the entire conversation finally escaped in a growl and he felt the heat of everyone's stare as all eyes drew to him.

Jaybird's brow raised. "No?"

Devil crossed his arms and stopped chewing his gum to stare right back. "I said 'no.' Ellie's not getting anywhere near any of this ever again. I won't allow it."

"*You* won't allow it?" Jaybird scoffed. "Who the fuck are you to say anything about her? What, you teach her some self-defense and all of a sudden you call the shots when it comes to her?"

"Guys." Snake raised his voice, as if he was trying to drown out the anger flooding the room. "I hate to break it to ya, but Ellie's an adult. Don't you think she should be the one calling the shots? She at least deserves to be informed and have the choice of whether or not she wants to be involved."

"She's too fragile. She can't handle being brought into something like this. She was fucking gunned down in a tree just last night—"

"Fuck, Devil, don't put it that way, goddamn." Jaybird's groan ended as a harsh rebuke.

"—Involving her is out of the question."

"Effing men. Ellie wants to be involved, you idiots."

Devil stiffened at the new voice, but his alert posture relaxed when he recognized the newest arrivals. Snake, however, was funny as fuck as his pale face reddened all the way up to his blue-black hair.

"How the fuck did *you* get in?"

CHAPTER EIGHTEEN

Devil glanced up at the newest arrivals in the room. How Nora had snuck herself, Assistant District Attorney Marco Aguilar, and Officer Henry Brown into their fucking war room was beyond him. The quirky woman was a magician with technology so he'd learned not to question it. He wouldn't understand the explanation anyway.

That didn't stop Snake though. "I told you to text me so I could get you a temp code."

"Who the fuck is with Jules, Nora?" Jaybird demanded.

"What the hell are you doin' here, Henry?" Phoenix sputtered out. "What are any of you doin' here?"

"I invited them," Hawk explained. "Nora, Marco, Henry, why don't you have a seat." He gestured to the table.

"And Jason." Nora pointed her finger at Jaybird as she walked to her seat. "Why don't you do your woman—and me—a favor and leave her the eff alone, you godsdamned stalker. She's at home and just fine."

Jaybird snapped his eyes to Hawk. "We need to get this meeting over quick. I can't be having Jules alone. She's pregnant for Christ's sake."

Nora rolled her eyes. "Pregnant, not an invalid, ya crazypants.

You need to chill out." She pulled a chair from the table and plopped into it. "And sorry we're late, Cap'n. I had to bypass your security."

"Bypass secur—" Snake swiveled in his chair and typed away at the keyboard before huffing out a surprised laugh. "I don't even have you on any of our cameras. Damn, how did you do that?"

Nora shrugged. "I have my ways." Her smile was wide like a cat that got the cream. "I'll show off after the meeting, babe. Can't be having just anybody off the street come bee-boppin' up in here, can we boys?"

"Nora..." Hawk lowered his eyes at her. "Stop antagonizing Snake."

Her mouth opened but she must've seen Snake's scowl because it quickly shut again. Instead, she sobered, as if realizing she was toeing the line marking Snake's bad side.

"Sorry, Snake. When I actually pull one over on ya, it feels good to rub it in. You know this game we play is like one of the highlights of my week."

Snake's foul expression immediately relaxed as he snorted and shook his head. "Mine too, if you weren't so damn good at it. Don't say you won this round yet, though. If I fix the breach before you tell me how you did it, then the score stays zero-zero."

Devil never understood where the Nora and Snake dynamic came from, but they fought like siblings. It was a constant back and forth, but they always eventually hugged it out.

"Fair enough, Superman." Nora pointed a finger gun at him.

"Back to the list..." Hawk began. "Marco, Henry, and Nora, as you've probably gathered, I've invited you here today to help us make plans for the scholarship benefit. We have a hunch the same bastards as last time will make the mistake of trying again."

"Bold move," Marco replied, his lips pursed as he nodded.

"Yup." Snake's expression mirrored the ADA's. "But this time we have the guest list and we can vet people. We'll have a plan instead of going in blind like last time."

"How'd you get a guest list?" Henry asked.

Snake's pale skin turned a new shade of beet red as he straightened his collar. "Um, my, uh friend works for a company that helps throw it every year."

Devil felt his brow raise slightly, but he quickly schooled his face. He'd never seen Snake bashful before. *Interesting.*

"Is this *friend* the one who recently started volunteering for Sasha Saves and is gorgeous and funny as Hades with a daughter that's just as fiery?" Nora waggled her eyebrows before giving Snake a pronounced wink.

"That's awfully specific," Marco laughed.

"Yes." Snake cleared his throat. "It may or may not be the woman you're speaking about, but she's taken. And honestly, 'friend' might be generous." He grimaced before mumbling. "I think she might hate me."

Nora waved her hand at the air as she blew a raspberry. "That woman does not hate you. She's a little sassy, but who here among us boss ass bitches isn't sassy every now and then, amiright? Give her time and keep fixing Sasha Saves's oh-so-spotty security, lately." She gave Snake a knowing grin. "Seriously, Superman. What is *up* with our wiring lately?"

"That's been you?" Snake snapped his fingers and pointed at her before a bark of laughter escaped him. "Ha, I knew it!"

Nora beamed and gave a small curtsey. "What can I say? Somebody's gotta play cupid 'round here."

Snake's smile lit up his face before he took off his glasses and massaged his closed eyes with a chuckle. "God, Nora, you're like the kid sister I never wanted."

"In any case." Hawk emphasized the words, cutting off the faux family banter. "Snake's going to go through the guest list and vet all the attendees. No one will go in or out of that hotel without our knowing about it. Nora." He paused and turned to her before speaking. "We might need you in the field."

Nora's smile vanished, but she nodded as she brushed her newly dyed black hair behind her ear.

"Nora, really?" Jaybird looked to Hawk while he pointed to the woman whose face had turned a sickly pale. "What if anyone recognizes her?"

"I doubt they would." Snake pushed his glasses up on his nose. "Last time she had a very distinctive shade of purple hair. This time it's a faded black, the most common hair color all over the world."

Hawk's brow furrowed and he lowered his voice as he directed his attention to Nora, as if Snake and Jaybird hadn't spoken. "It's okay, Nora. We'll all be there in some capacity. Nothing will happen to you."

"That's what you said last time." Her whisper was barely audible. "And now you have one fewer agent to make the same promise."

The room quieted at her point and Devil felt the weight of Draco's absence heavy on his chest. She was right. The Crew had promised her the same thing last year, but Draco was shot and Nora was kidnapped and almost lost for good, along with Ellie and the rest of the trafficking victims.

Devil and the rest of the men shifted and fidgeted in the silence before Hawk finally spoke up on a deep sigh. "I'm sorry Nora. If we can get around it, we will. But for now, we might need you in there, at least with an earpiece. Having a woman in the mix will put less suspicion on the agents in the field. Do you think you can do it?" Nora pinched her eyes closed before nodding again once. "Thank you." He turned to the other men. "Marco, Henry. You're going to be there, right?"

"Yeah, they're actually using security this year, so I'll be there," Henry offered.

Marco nodded as he explained, "Apparently I count as the 'elite' this year. I received a verbal invitation yesterday from *the* Mitchell Strickland, himself, if you can believe it." Everyone groaned at the mention of the biggest jackass in Ashland County

—one who had been acting like a fucking choir boy since they were given a clue about him the year before—and Devil couldn't help but join in. Marco shifted his head in the direction of the computer screens. "All your intel is right from what I know, which, admittedly, isn't much."

Hawk tapped his lips as he thought. "Excellent. For now, Snake and Nora, you get together and go through this list. Run a background check on everyone. Dig deep. Remember what that Ascot kid said last year. He said Strickland has a brother, but maybe he got the name wrong. Dying men aren't infallible. Still, go through extended families, friends, jobs from high school, shirt size. Anything you can get, we need to know about it."

Snake winced. "That'll take a while, Hawk."

"We've got a month to plan in advance this time. Like you said, things have been quiet in Ashland lately." Hawk turned to Marco and Henry. "You guys haven't heard anything right? I know Burgess was a dead end again last time we met with him. But when he mentioned looking into the party more we got serious about—" Henry shifted in his chair. "What? What is it? You both looked at each other." Hawk crossed his arms and adopted his deep commander voice.

Henry exchanged glances with Marco, apparently for a second time since Devil hadn't seen them do it the first time. "It's just..." Henry began and rubbed the back of his head. "Burgess has been actin' real weird lately. I'm not sure he's as reliable as y'all think. Maybe even unreliable. This party might be just 'nother red herring like he's been givin' y'all the entire time."

Hawk's sharp eye stabbed into Marco. "Is this true?"

Marco's lips tightened and he rubbed his goatee. "Last time I saw him, he was jumpy, seemed cagey—"

"—pale, sweaty." Henry grimaced.

Marco continued on. "He was in the evidence room for a case that's not even on the trial docket, even though he said it was. I don't know, man. Brown's right, Burgess was acting pretty strange."

Devil recalled their last meeting and cleared his throat to speak. "I've always thought he was a little off. Last time we met with him he was relatively calm, which I actually noticed only because he's usually fidgety."

Elbow propped up on his crossed arm, Hawk tapped his lips. "He might be questionable but he's our only lead in the sheriff's office who has any real power" —he winced— "no offense, Henry."

A look Devil couldn't decipher passed over Henry's face before it went blank and he shrugged. "I'm still technically a rookie, so you're right. I've been keepin' an eye on him though. I'll let y'all know if he starts actin' even weirder."

Hawk nodded. "Thanks. Hopefully we won't need that intel. I'm not sure what's going to go down in that hotel during the party, but I know for sure we're going to use the swiftest, safest, and most effective measures to extract any and all victims. It might not be what you want to be a part of in your positions in the government." He sighed and leveled his gaze. "I'm going to be real with you. We need you and Marco to sort of turn the other way, if you feel me."

Marco's lips tightened again and he nodded once. "I'm not comfortable with that, but I also know when you guys had a hard time depending on the Ashland cops last time, women were abducted and murdered. I'm doing my job for justice, not to ensure the law is followed if *you* feel me."

"We're not going to go out of our way to break the law, but we're sure as hell going to get in the way of someone who does. By whatever means necessary."

Devil nodded his agreement along with his teammates.

"Now, going back to Ellie…" Hawk turned to Jaybird and Devil bristled at the thought of what either of them would say next. "Snake and Nora are going to go through the guest list to cross reference everyone who was there last time, but we really need Ellie to help us. If she remembers anything, *anything*, about who attended that party, her going through the lists of faces would be invaluable. We need whatever her memory will give us."

Devil opened his mouth to say no but Jaybird glared at Devil before cutting him off. "I think I know what Devil's gonna say, and I'm actually with him on this one. I don't want her anywhere near this. She was re-traumatized less than twenty-four hours ago, and I don't want her to go through her nightmares again. I don't know if you guys remember Ellie after the kidnapping—"

"I fucking remember." The words slipped out before Devil could catch them, but they were the truth. For over six months after Ellie had been rescued, she'd suffered night terrors and panic attacks. She wouldn't sleep away from BlackStone or her brother's apartment and Devil had talked her through more than one.

He cringed inwardly as he recalled the attack *he'd* caused the week before when he'd come onto her, making her feel helpless. It'd been forever since he'd seen her that broken, and he'd be damned if he allowed her to break again on his watch.

The idea he'd been cooking up ever since he talked to her last night percolated again. It never dawned on him she might've felt out of control in that moment, but if he made sure she knew who was really in charge, maybe they could work. He wouldn't spring it on her yet though. He'd bide his time and wait until it seemed like she was ready again. Hopefully his solution worked.

"Keep Ellie out of it, for as long as we can." Jaybird's tone was on the verge of begging but Devil wasn't very far behind him.

Phoenix whistled. "Dayum... what're y'all fools gonna do when your girl starts datin' some dude? You won't be able to call all the shots then, ya know."

"The fuck?" Devil barked out. Ellie dating? No one was good enough for her. They wouldn't begin to know how to appreciate what they had with Ellie in their arms. No one else knew the extent of what she'd been through, how to get her through the pain when the past was too much, or how hard she'd worked to get in a better place. How hard she *still* worked.

But I do...

The words were a gentle nudge in his mind, but they crashed into every one of his last hard-fought convictions to stay away from Ellie.

Snake lifted his glasses and wiped at the bridge of his nose. "I guess... I guess I could ask Naomi. She had the list—"

"Naomi? Who's Naomi?" Henry butted in.

Snake paused as he returned his glasses to his nose. "The woman who gave us the list. Anyway, she was there last year, too, so I'll ask her to sit with me—I mean us. Hopefully, she won't bite my fucking head off again."

"I still think you Neanderthals are making a colossal mistake not allowing Ellie to make this decision." Nora tapped her long nails on the table and raised a black brow in Devil and Jaybird's direction.

Devil clenched his fist as he spoke. "Naomi will have to do until you absolutely need Ellie." Jaybird nodded his assent.

Hawk steepled his fingers in front of his chin and tapped his lips with the side of both pointer fingers before shaking his head. "It is what it is. But if shit hits the fan and something she knows could've prevented it, whatever happens is on you two." He narrowed his eyes at Devil and Jaybird, emphasizing his point before continuing. "In the meantime, when you two bastards want to let a grown ass woman make her own goddamn decisions, let us all know so we can help save those who aren't as lucky as she was to have a team of ex-soldiers dedicated to looking for her."

Devil's lips tightened and he could tell Jaybird was equally offended at the truth of their situation. But it didn't change anything. It might be the wrong choice, but if he could protect his angel in any fucking way, he damn well would. If that meant making sure she never had to see the face of one of her perpetrator's ever again, even if it helped someone else, that was a decision Devil was willing to go down for. He would carry that burden to make sure she never had to carry one ever again.

Phoenix's words had clicked something in his mind and he realized what he had to do. There was no just getting Ellie "out of his system". If nothing else had taught him that, his limp dick at a strip club sure as hell made him learn that lesson. He'd been afraid of damning his angel, but maybe giving in to temptation was what they both needed after all.

Jaybird looked at the table before speaking in a low voice. "It's nonnegotiable at this point."

"So be it," Snake replied. "But for the record, you're making a mistake."

Resolve settled over Devil's soul, finally at peace with the choices he was making regarding Ellie. He narrowed his eyes at Snake, challenging him—hell, the whole goddamn world—to fight his determination to keep her safe.

"So fucking be it."

CHAPTER NINETEEN

The euphoria jolted through Neal's body like a wave of cool salt-water over paper cuts. He was still getting used to the new stuff. The first time he'd used, he'd bled like a gunshot wound. Since then, he'd perfected his methods. It was a different, shorter high than he was used to, but at least it kept him functional between hits. He liked the peace and quiet, too.

Going to the park two days ago had been a bad call he'd regretted every hour since. He'd never wanted to take his addiction this far, but fuck did the ice flowing in his bloodstream make the guilt burn a little less.

He pulled out his cigarette lighter and alternated between flicking it and twirling it in his fingers as he sifted through the files in front of him on his kitchen table.

What he had could damn the entire city. So many people would be ruined with the black-and-white words in front of him and he felt the weight of his responsibilities even with the drugs coursing through his veins.

That brat blonde in the tree was another worry. The look on her face of pure confusion and fear had convinced him she didn't know who he was, but the uncertainty of having another person out there who knew his business ate at him like the ulcer in his stomach.

"Dammit, Cici. What am I supposed to do with all this."

"Do the best you can, baby. I believe in you."

The words sounded odd in his head. He hadn't heard them in so long they'd become a foreign language.

"I'm tryin' Cees. I'm tryin'."

He rubbed his chest, trying to make the pain go away. It wouldn't. He knew that. The doctors could say it was his bad diet, vices, and poor health. But he knew the score. His heart was ripped in two when Cici left him. Despite his best efforts, misery tore at the peace he'd tried to sew into himself. The needle on his side table wasn't doing the job anymore.

Time passed, but he wasn't sure how much. He only knew that it did from the shifting shadows on the green carpet. He'd forgotten to close the blinds all the way again. That shit was gonna get him in trouble with a nosy neighbor someday. Not that anyone in the old neighborhood bothered him. He was given an extra stipend to help control crime and everyone knew he was a cop so they left him alone.

A harsh shrill of a phone grated against his nerves. He dug into his holster, only to realize his cell was already in his hand. He lifted it up to his ear with disjointed movements, as if someone else was controlling his arm.

"Burgess."

"Do not 'Burgess' me. You fucking called me, *durak*. What is wrong with you?"

Neal bristled at the accusation and sat up in his threadbare chair. He'd had it since the day he and Cici had moved into the house. "I'm fine. I don't know what the fuck you're talkin' about but get to the point."

"Calm down, Neal. You need him. Make sure he feels like he needs you too."

Neal inhaled Cici's words deeply only to exhale on a cough.

After his fit, he realized the phone was nearly silent on the other line.

"Hello?" he asked, half expecting to have to call back.

"Speak to me like that again Burgess, and you are fucking done. Do you hear me?"

Neal shivered at the panic shooting down his spine and he gulped on impulse. "Y-yes, sir." The manufactured respect soaking his words made him want to vomit. But Cici was right. Neal had to make sure the boss felt like he needed him.

A frustrated sigh pushed through the earpiece. "Do you have anything new?"

"No." Neal fumbled with his excuse. He had no recollection of calling the boss, but it must've been for some reason. "I-I was checkin' in. Seein' if there's anything y'all need from me for the, uh, the party." Neal twisted the empty medicine bottle that still stayed with him. There hadn't been Zannies inside in a couple of weeks. Now it was where he hid whatever his dealer could offer. For once, Neal was thankful meth was so pervasive in the rural south.

"We have a good lineup of product to choose from—" Neal winced. "Have you gone through the list of applicants? Their backgrounds? We need that information. Another disaster like last year and all of us are through. You need to make sure these ones will not be missed. Obviously the contact we had last time was unreliable so we are depending on you."

Neal flicked the lighter and watched the flame. Who was the contact last year? He put that on his mental list of things to look into. It was getting rather long, but hopefully he had time.

"I asked you a fucking question. When I ask a question, I expect a fucking answer you fucking idiot."

"I-I haven't finished it yet. But I'll get to it, I swear."

The man on the other end sounded like he was cursing in his language. "Burgess, if you fuck this up, it will be your ass up for the next auction. If you think what these buyers do to women is bad, you do not want to know what they will do with a useless, fat, old junkie. These men have fucking islands. I would hate to imagine what they do with all the product they collect. I am sure they get creative, though."

Neal gulped, nearly choking on fear. "I understand."

"Good. And by the time of the party, I would bet money the BlackStone group figures something out. But have someone to help make sure we can get past them this time. I am getting pressure from the boss to change the location, drop, and time, but I think we have planned better this year and there is more involved here than the Ashland County operation."

Sweat pricked his brow as the information burned his conscience. Helping a human trafficking operation went against everything he ever stood for, but he was in too deep. And he needed them. At least he was shoring up ammo to fire back if he ever needed to. Police raids had taught him it was always good to have a backup plan.

"So what am I supposed to do?"

"Keep using your excellent investigative skills." The man on the other side laughed harshly and Neal's face scrunched up in confusion.

Why is he laughing?

"I-I can do that. But is there not anything else you want me to do? I mean, for the scholarship party?"

"Get us that fucking information like I asked you weeks ago, you idiot. Why have you not—" The man sighed and groaned. There was an awful long pause before the Russian spoke again in an almost cordial tone. "You know what? I have an idea. Follow through on getting us that information and I'll have Vlad ready an exchange for you. How about that? I understand you have changed your drug of choice? We can get that for you. High grade too. Better than what our own dealers have."

Neal's fingers twitched on his lighter as he glanced around for the spoon and dwindling baggy he'd just used. He hated giving up the background information of potential victims, but maybe nothing bad would even happen. Maybe if they got the information, they'd see the women weren't good fits for the operation. Maybe he could even alter the information to make that happen.

He searched the side table next to him. The bag had somehow gotten lost in the tissues and newspapers he'd strewn about. Lately every time he got home he laid whatever he was carrying on a random side table or on the ground, needing to get to his chair as soon as possible to light up and get his fix.

The place was a mess. Even worse than usual. Cici would have a fit. He fingered the small, almost empty plastic next to him. He had no choice. The evidence room was out of the question. For some reason they'd made policy harder recently to get inside without a reason, a monitoring officer, or an evidence deposit.

The man on the other end went silent and Neal once again grew scared he'd accidentally hung up.

"I have to get off the phone, I cannot sit here on the other side while you jerk off doing what the hell you do in your own time. I need an answer, Burgess. If I cannot depend on you, then—"

"Alright... I'll get the information. Backgrounds, next of kin, and homelife, right?"

"Yes, those things and anything else you might find of importance. I cannot stress to you enough how crucial this is. We need to get this to the buyers as soon as possible for their perusal." Sweat ran down Neal's face and he wiped it off with the back of his hand before drying it on the upholstery. "If you fuck this up, you know what you will be to me? A loose end. Do you know what happens to loose ends in my world, Burgess?"

"U-um... no, sir?" *And I don't want to know.*

"They get cut."

CHAPTER TWENTY

"Look alive, Ellie."

Ellie blocked the blow at the last second but Dev still clipped her in the ear with the mitt, making it sting. They'd been training for a month and he still got the drop on her ninety-nine point nine percent of the time.

"Ugh." She backed away and rubbed at her ear, but Dev closed the gap, coming at her with the pads again. "Dev, stop, I need a break."

"No breaks, El. We don't have much time left in this session. Try to finish strong. If you're up against somebody, they won't stop and wait for you to lick your wounds before they stab you again."

"Blech." Ellie grimaced and stuck her tongue out in disgust. "God, how morbid."

"You're stalling." He slapped the pads together and turned them to her again. "Now get back in here."

"Come on, Dev, I didn't sleep well. A survivor came into Sasha Saves last night right before the store and clinic closed. She agreed to do a rape kit at the hospital so I stayed with her half the night."

Because Ellie hadn't slept, she'd had to rush out of the dorm when Dev picked her up. And because she had to rush, she hadn't had a chance to eat anything but one of Virginia's weight loss energy bars. Even her skin felt tired.

Dev tilted his head. "I thought you weren't on call last night."

Ellie blushed, knowing she was about to get caught. "That's beside the point."

"No, no, no." Dev turned the mitt in a way that let him swipe his hand down his face, pausing to massage his eyes before pointing at Ellie. "We all created schedules to make sure this type of thing didn't happen because you were spreading yourself too thin. You're not on call when you have early mornings. That's the deal. How did you even get to the hospital? Your bike got stolen at the park."

"Ugh, don't remind me." Ellie groaned for what felt like the umpteenth time that training session. She hadn't even thought about her bike after all the chaos of that night. By the time she remembered and Virginia drove her by to look for it, the bike was gone.

Dev gave her a pointed look, obviously still waiting on her answer. She refrained from groaning one more time and looked away, drinking some water before mumbling, "Don't get mad at her, but Naomi picked me up."

"Naomi? If she was available, why didn't she take care of the call?"

Ellie shook her head as she answered. "Not yet. Naomi's doing a really great job, but she's still a brand-new volunteer. I couldn't leave her there by herself. Besides, she doesn't work the late shifts and had to leave to pick Thea up. It was just me the rest of the time until the survivor was ready to leave and Nora came to drive me back to my dorm."

"Well..." His shoulders rose and fell on a deep sigh. "Since you're not listening to anyone else telling you to slow down, I guess I'll be the asshole and tell you that you brought this exhaustion" — he scanned her body with the mitt— "on yourself. You guys could've called Nora from the start, and you know that. You need to think about what's best for *you* sometimes, at least for the fact that an attacker won't care if you're tired. He'll use it against you."

Ellie grumbled. "This morning I would've chosen an attacker over you picking me up and making me work out. This is dang torture."

When she saw Dev's smirk grow on his face, she realized it was no use. She'd tried every complaint and excuse in her arsenal over the past month and he never gave her an ounce of leeway. It would've been a nice change of pace from how everyone else treated her if she wasn't so exhausted.

She huffed before finally putting her hands up in a blocking stance. "Fine, let's do this, then."

When she pulled her whole focus back on Dev, she bounced lightly on her toes to get her mind back in the zone. Sure, she was struggling from lack of food and sleep. Unfortunately, there was also the added complication that Dev was shirtless. With his abs and pecs staring right back at her, Ellie had almost no chance of paying attention.

God he's so hot.

"Hell yeah he is."

Sasha's voice purred in her mind and she giggled until she noticed Dev narrowing his eyes at her. When he smirked, she bit back an embarrassed groan, knowing what was about to come next.

"Whatcha thinking, there, angel?"

Ellie felt her blush flood her all the way down to her toes. "Leave me alone, Dev." She'd gotten better at keeping her emotions in check, but with how tired she was, and how Dev already seemed to always know what she was thinking, Ellie wasn't surprised every lust-filled thought was written all over her face.

A low rumble from Dev erupted into a roar of laughter, making Ellie chuckle too. It'd been a long time since she'd seen him laugh like that. If ever, now that she thought about it. His deep bellow echoed across the gym and Ellie's grew, too.

Until she realized she had an opening.

She dove in with a left hook, skimming the top of Dev's mitt as he reflexively brought it up to his head.

"Shit!"

"Look alive, Dev." Ellie did a little shimmy and started to back away as Dev's eyes darkened. A mischievous smile widened across his face and sent shocks of anticipation right to her clit.

"Oh, so it's like that, huh?" He tore off his pads and stepped toward her, an odd determination in his eyes. "Okay, we can play that way."

"Wh-what're you doing?" Ellie's voice wavered, unable to hide the thrill of excitement shooting in every nerve.

"We've only practiced with protective gear up until now. Let's graduate you to some actual hand-to-hand combat. Don't worry, I'll go easy at first." Dev's slow, lazy steps made her stomach flip and she matched him step for step in the opposite direction.

"Combat? Like actual fighting? So, um, I'm not watching myself in the mirror this time?"

"We'll be doing more than that, baby." Dev's low voice made her core throb. But his slow pursuit hadn't stopped, and instinct told her she didn't have time to squeeze her thighs together to ease the ache.

"As much as I get off watching you learn the way your body moves," his eyes drifted down her body before he licked his lips, like he'd just drank in every drop of the arousal pooling in her panties. "I want to see what your body does when I'm against it."

"For the love of GAWD, and all that is motherfuckin' holy, if you don't fuck him, I will."

Ellie's back hit something solid as Sasha yelled at her, and she realized she'd bumped into the mirror. She was trapped. Her pulse beat all the way down to her core while her confused mind played catch-up.

Half of her wanted to run out of BlackStone and never come

back, afraid of what Dev would do to her. The other half couldn't wait to find out.

He was feet away from her, but she couldn't take her eyes off the forest green orbs mesmerizing her in their hold.

"You remember, angel? Fighting is the last resort. What's before that?"

"H-hide." She darted her glance around the room, automatically trying to find safety.

"That's right. But you have to be smarter than your attacker." He tapped his head as he closed the space between them. "And if I were your attacker, you'd do well to remember that I would turn over every—" His fingers grazed down her throat, but she couldn't stop watching his eyes. "—inch... of this facility looking for you." Dev trailed his fingers back up her neck and his thumb pulled her lip from between her teeth as he leaned in. "So, Ellie... if you can't hide. And you can't possibly beat me in a fight..." His breathy chuckle puffed against her hair and his lips lingered over her ear. His words rang in her mind like a challenge, so she closed her eyes to try to block out the heat consuming her from his touch. "What... should... you... do?"

There was no way out and as much as she wanted to be beneath him, something inside her desperately wanted to escape. So she did what she had to do. She thrust her knee up into Dev's crotch and ran like hell.

Dev growled out a yelp and reached for her, but she was able to scoot around him thanks to his agility training and new injury. She didn't know where she was going and she didn't fully understand why she was running, but every instinct told her she needed to make him chase her. That she *wanted* him to chase her.

The gym wasn't that big and the door was only a few strides away. She turned around to see if Dev was following and—huge mistake. The six-foot-four monster of a man was recovering way too quickly and already almost right behind her. And she'd just given him the advantage.

Ellie faced the door again and dug her feet into the ground to pick up speed. She rounded a power squat machine and lifted her legs to hop a bench... only to be captured mid-flight.

Muscular arms wrapped around her in a bear hug and turned her around. A strong hand circled her throat. She began to hyperventilate and her stomach flipped, whether from the adrenaline or the desire pooling in her core, she wasn't sure. He turned them around and there in the mirror she was captivated by seeing Dev holding her against his hard body.

Watching the Dev and Ellie in front of her was surreal. The man's hungry gaze down on the woman made Ellie squeeze her legs to ease the ache throbbing between. He looked at her with a mixture of awe and desire, like he'd been starving his entire life, and he'd finally found the sustenance he craved right there in his arms. Like he *needed* her.

His lips hovered over the shell of her ear. "Come on, angel. Push past the fear. Breathe for me."

Had she quit breathing? The edges of the world were turning black and panic shocked down her spine. She hadn't noticed before, but the gentle command accompanied by the soft stroke down the column of her throat reminded her to suck in a breath. The air invaded her lungs, too much at once.

"Ellie, come on. You've worked so fucking hard at the physical fighting, you've got this." Her breathing came in fast gulps but the world came back into focus. "The rest is all in your head, baby. You have to remain calm, logical, and be the proactive person in this situation. Whatever your next step is, you have control. You hear me? *You* are in control."

You are in control.

Ellie hesitated, unable to quit staring at the image of them together. His grip adjusted and his whole hand encompassed her throat, still tender against the skin.

"Come on, Ellie. What would you do? Fight the fear."

I have control.

A tinge of defeat tainted Dev's words. "We have to work on

this, baby. I'll work on it with you, but in the real world... fuck, I've been holding you for half a minute. A lot can happen in half a minute."

"I-I'd..." Ellie inhaled a calming breath against Dev's forearm, but only got cinnamon. She leaned on his chest and squeezed the corded muscle with her hands.

"Ellie?" The surprise in his tone made it obvious he didn't know what she was doing. When he released his grip on her throat, she embedded her nails into his arm.

"No," her whisper carried a command, and feeling Dev follow it by tensing his fingertips against her made her heartbeat thrum with power. "Stay..." Ellie watched the Dev in the mirror lift his gaze to meet hers. "Please..." she begged.

They shared several breaths in tandem before she felt him swallow against the crown of her head. "Okay, then, baby... I-it's just us. Just you and me. You still have the control here, angel. If you trust me then whatever we do, whatever *I* do, know you have the power to stop me."

Dev tightened his biceps and forearms around her chest encasing her in a feeling of comfort and safety she wasn't sure she'd ever had. His grip was firm against her throat... But *she* had control in this situation. If she said no—not that she wanted to —or even if she didn't say yes, he would respect her. She could give in to this man, trust him completely, and know she was in good hands.

Ellie felt his length hardening behind her. The empowering beat in her chest pulsed in her clit as she pressed her butt farther into him. Dev closed his eyes on a stuttering exhale, giving Ellie the satisfaction of knowing she had an effect on him.

"Ellie... I can't play games with you..." Dev's voice was impossibly lower and made her core ache.

"Who's playing a game?" Ellie whispered. "I want this."

Dev shook his head, but didn't let go. His hips pushed into her until they were in an unfamiliar dance that felt as natural as breathing.

"I... can't." Dev's forehead leaned against the back of her head, making it impossible to see what he was truly thinking. "You make me lose control. Last time... I didn't even see the signs you were about to have a panic attack. Then I lost my shit knowing I did that to you—"

Ellie tried to turn around, but he kept his hold. "Dev, none of that is your fault. I feel safer with you than anyone."

"What if I break you, angel?"

His last words whispered over her, like that was the last thing he wanted. But Ellie blushed in the mirror at the thought of what being broken by Dev would mean. It should've scared her. But it didn't. She attempted to turn to talk to him face to face, but Dev tightened around her neck until it was harder to breathe. She swallowed against his hand and couldn't help the moan that escaped her as desire throbbed at the emptiness inside her.

Dev tilted his head and she could almost see the spark of— was it excitement or satisfaction? She couldn't tell, but she got the overwhelming sense she'd passed some sort of test. "You like that, Ellie?"

Instead of nodding, Ellie pushed his forearms with her hands, still bound by his biceps. She was on the verge of being in pain, but God, it felt good. His fingers dug into the sides of her throat until her chest was heaving and the world felt fuzzy again. But *she* was pushing him further. She could stop it at any time.

"You like when I do that? You like knowing that even when I'm in charge, you're in control?" His teeth nipped her ear. "That I'm *begging* you to be at my mercy?"

She nodded before moaning again at the thickness grinding between her butt cheeks.

"Say it, baby."

"Say what?" She closed her eyes at his slow thrusts against her, but his fingers moved up to her jaw and he tapped her lower cheek until she opened them again to face the mirror.

"Tell me what you want. I'm warning you, after that, you're

mine. But I need to hear it from you first, angel. Now..." Hungry eyes caught hers in the reflection, keeping her captive just as much as his embrace. "What... do *you*... want?"

Ellie licked her lips and as this focused man's control slipped to follow the pink muscle, pride rippled through her. He shook his head imperceptibly and brought his attention back to her and growled.

"What do you want, angel?"

She bit her wet lip and took the plunge.

"You."

CHAPTER TWENTY-ONE

Dev's gaze darkened right before he spun her around. He brought her chin up with his forefinger and captured her lips with his, setting her on fire when his tongue met hers. Melting in his hands, she moaned and buried her short nails into his pecs. He broke the kiss to scoop her up with his forearm under her butt and walked them to the other side of the gym.

Without putting her down, he locked the door and turned back around. She was about to ask him where they were going when a low rumble vibrated her breasts and his hand tugged her hair free from her ponytail.

"You know what I've fantasized about since the first day I trained you?" His intensity bored into her, sending shivers traveling underneath her already sensitive skin. She shook her head as much as the grip on the back of her nape would allow before kissing her way around his jaw and neck so he could still see.

"You... in the corner of this gym."

Ellie turned her head to see where he was taking her. The mirrors on the wall met at the edge of the room, and in them, she saw Dev carrying her from two different directions. "Why here?"

"Because angel, with mirrors on each side, you'll have no

choice but to watch yourself come the first time I taste your sweet pussy."

His words went straight to her clit and she dove in to kiss him again until the sudden sting of the cold mirror hit the bare skin of her back. Her feet touched the ground again, but her mind was floating away from reality. She braced herself for an onslaught of flashbacks until Dev bent down until the only thing in her vision were the hard lines of his determined face.

"Look at me, angel. It's you and me. I see you going off in that space in your head to protect yourself. But you are safe *here*. In BlackStone, the safest place on earth. *You* are in control. Say it."

The words mumbled from her lips but Dev pinned her chin between his forefinger and thumb and forced her to focus back on him.

"Say it, *you* are in control."

His head nodded up and down, and hers joined in as she swallowed and repeated after him.

"Again. *You* are in control." The words penetrated through the fog and she blinked back into her body, where arousal was consuming her from the inside out.

"*I* am in control."

"Good girl." Dev's thumb stroked her chin as he searched her eyes. Her empty core clenched desperately, as if those two words alone could fill her up. "Now kiss me, angel."

Ellie licked her lips and tugged his face to hers, threading her fingers through his short hair. Their mouths met like two lovers in a dance, and she opened her lips when he tongued the seam. Heat rolled through her and her sex ached with need.

Dev's hands feathered down past her sports bra and along her naked torso, making goose bumps bloom in their wake. Gratitude flickered through her mind that he was leaving her breasts protected by the thin fabric. She didn't understand the feeling, and when Dev skimmed his finger inside the seam of her shorts, she didn't care to analyze it. She didn't care about anything except for his rough fingertips against the sensitive skin on her hip bones.

"Trust me, Ellie. Relax your back against the mirror, okay?" Ellie's already swollen lips brushed against his as she nodded and did as she was told, secretly hoping for another 'good girl.' His eyes and smile turned cocky, as if he knew she already craved the words.

"Do you like it when I tell you what to do?" She grinned back at him, and he chuckled. "I'm sorry to say that I'm not gonna be able to give you much more instruction."

She couldn't help her frown or the breathiness in her voice. "Why's that?"

That wicked grin again. "Because, baby, I don't like to talk with my mouth full."

Lowering to his knees, his hands skipped past her shorts and scooped her legs up onto his biceps. Ellie squealed with laughter as she tried to keep her balance against the mirror and her thighs on his shoulders. Her hands delved into his hair and held on like reins.

"Shh, shh, angel, we don't want to call the calvary in here."

Ellie snapped her mouth shut. Getting hot and heavy in a semi-public area was one thing. Making sure everyone left in the building knew about it was another.

Dev laid open-mouthed kisses up the inside of her thigh, taking turns on each one and sucking as he went. Even with her newfound resolution to be quiet, Dev's name stuttered out of her in ecstasy. How had she never known the skin of her inner thigh was so sensitive?

"God, I love my name in your mouth." He nipped at her thigh. "I can feel your goose bumps form when my lips leave your skin. Like every inch of your body can't wait to touch me."

Ellie's mumbled assent ended on a higher pitch as he bit and sucked underneath the loose hem of her shorts, hard enough she knew it would bruise. While she was recovering, he hooked his finger into her loose shorts and panties and pulled both to the side, exposing her sex to him. She unintentionally tried to push him away, but the sting of his slap on her butt made her stop.

"Don't get between a man and his meal, Ellie. I've been starving for your pussy."

She opened her mouth to object when Dev opened his. His soft tongue lathed up her core and Ellie tugged on his hair, gritting her teeth to keep from crying out.

"Goddamn, you're so wet, I could drink you all day." His tongue played along her seam, dipping and teasing, making her thrust into his mouth, searching for something to fill her. His free hand dug into her thigh, no doubt leaving fingerprints.

"Baby, hold your panties to the side for me so I can use my fingers, too."

"Yes, sir." The growl against her slit pushed her close to the edge, but she did as she was told. When she heard a whispered, *Good girl*, her sex tightened in response.

Dev swirled his now free finger in her arousal before teasing the tip of his finger in her opening. She watched in anticipation, unable to look away, as his forefinger entered her. Her core fluttered around the welcome invasion, and her hips began to move on their own, thrusting into his finger. His tongue returned to her sex, but this time, it concentrated on the bundle of nerves he'd been teasing around.

His finger feathered inside her for a second longer before he pulled it out, leaving an ache stronger than before.

"Dev!" His name began in a groan but ended in a sigh, as Dev flitted his tongue against her clit, and massaged her entrance with his fingers again. She tried to swivel her hips but Dev circled his arm around her thigh to still her. He thrust one finger inside her channel, but his thumb continued its pursuit down to the spot where absolutely no one had been. She tensed up at the realization but Dev slapped her butt again, making her yelp.

He left her clit and squeezed her thigh, turning her focus back to him. "Trust me, angel. I won't do more than you want, I promise."

Ellie nodded quickly and tried to relax. He watched her as he continued to work her with his fingers. They were soaked from her arousal and his thumb massaged the untouched rosette and... *God*, it felt *amazing*.

He must have understood her reaction because the cocky man had a smirk of male satisfaction on his face. But good god, she didn't care about that when he dove in with his tongue and continued his dual massage.

His tongue homed in on her clit and Ellie squirmed under the attention. Her body was on fire, everywhere he touched, her skin was hypersensitive and she felt herself climbing higher to a peak she'd only ever been by herself.

"Dev... I-I—"

"I know, angel, I'll get you there. Just open your eyes." She did as she was told and opened them to see herself in the mirror beside her. Her eyes were like molten caramel from her heated desire and she was instantly captivated by watching the Ellie in the mirror's reactions.

Dev's tongue pointed and vibrated on her clit and her reflection went rigid as she reached for the summit. But when Dev sucked on her clit and his thumb pressed on the sensitive pucker, she exploded. She watched her mouth stretch in a silent scream. It was easy to see the euphoria wash over her body as her reflection trembled from her orgasm. Her fingers of her free hand dug into his hair for dear life and she crashed down, her body jolting from the tremors of pleasure.

Ellie was at Dev's mercy until the tension in her muscles finally eased. She let go of her panties, letting them fall back over her sex as she collapsed against the wall. Her thighs were still so close she felt Dev's cheeks widen in a smile before he pulled her panties to the side again and swiped his tongue up her seam.

"Dev! No, i-it's too much. I can't." His chuckle puffed warm air against her wet core and she squirmed, afraid he was going to try to tease her again. She heaved a sigh of relief when he let go of the fabric, but her adrenaline spiked again when he began to freaking *stand up* from his kneeling position despite the fact Ellie's legs were still wrapped around his head.

She squealed but Dev gripped her waist and pulled her high and off of him as he stood up the rest of the way, before depositing her safely to the ground. As soon as her feet hit, her knees buckled, and Dev hooked an arm around her waist to pull her close.

He kissed her, hard against her lips, and she tasted herself as his tongue slid over hers once before pulling away.

"Careful, there, angel." Dev's soft smile glistened with her arousal and sent her core fluttering, the empty feeling not so profound now that her inner muscles were spent. The man hardly ever gifted anyone with a smile, so when he did, Ellie felt a sense of pride. But good *Lord*, the one he had on now made her feel deliciously sinful.

Dev settled her to the ground but didn't let go until she stood on her own. Once steady, she lifted her head to thank him but paused mid-word as she watched him use his thumb to swipe the moisture left on his lips before licking it off his fingers.

"Most satisfying meal I've ever had." Ellie's jaw dropped and his smile grew wider. "I love that you blush even after I've just had my head between your thighs."

She groaned and rolled her eyes. "Keep talking to me like that and I'll make you go back for seconds."

His forest green eyes darkened. "Don't tempt me, baby." He moved to grip her waist again but she backed up and held him off at arm's length.

"No, stop." His hands leaped off of her like she was on fire, but she shook her head to relieve his concerned frown. "No, you're fine, it's just... what about..." She trailed off, not entirely sure how to ask him.

"'What about' what?"

She inhaled and decided to go for it. "What about you? Don't you, um, get a turn?"

Heat flashed across his eyes and he bent to give her a scorching kiss that left her breathless. He pulled away and twirled a strand of her loose blonde hair.

"As much as I want you to put that ponytail back up so you can suck my cock, I'm gonna have to take a rain check since you kneed me in the fucking balls less than..." He checked his watch. "...Twenty minutes ago."

Oops. Forgot about that.

Wait.

"Twenty minutes?" Her pitch went up and she grabbed his wrist to check the time for herself. "Oh, crap. I've got class in like fifteen minutes! I can't believe I forgot!"

"Don't worry, El." He chuckled and waved her off. "I'll drive you. Get your things and we'll go."

Ellie nodded and met him at the door. As he unlocked it, her hand acted on its own volition and drifted to his, holding it before she registered what she was doing. As if it was the most natural thing in the world. It even felt like it was until she noticed Dev looking down at their connection like he'd grown another appendage.

"Oh, um... sorry." She loosened her grip and tried to pull away, but Dev's hand tightened around hers.

"No, don't." His whisper was soft. Vulnerable? She couldn't quite place it, but it made her heart ache. "It's nice." He pursed his lips and studied her with a serious look for long enough she began to fidget under the attention. "I want to take you out on a date."

Ellie perked up. "For real? Like a *date* date? Like a real dinner and a movie kinda thing?"

Dev laughed and opened the door. "If that's what you want, then sure. I just want to spend time with you."

"What? Does all this time beating each other up not count all of a sudden?" Her smile was so wide she was sure she looked like a loon, but heck, she was so excited she didn't care.

"Ha ha." He rolled his eyes. "Joke all you want, but I'm taking you out. Friday work?"

Ellie's smile became brittle at the edges. She tried to keep her lips firmly curved up and forced her lingering happiness to bleed over the wounds that were still too fresh. "That's my birthday, actually. I-I was planning on staying in—"

"Excellent. It's settled. I'll take you on a date for your birthday. We have to celebrate another year. Not everyone gets those, you know."

Unspoken grief settled over his words like a shroud, and she wondered if he was remembering his friend like she was remembering Sasha. They'd both lost so much already in their lives and she knew he was right. She should try her best to celebrate life when she could. But it was going to be tough celebrating on the anniversary of the day Sasha was... But she didn't expect him to remember. She wished she didn't have to.

He squeezed her hand again and she returned it automatically, trying to live in the moment and get out of her head as he led them down the hallway to the garage. They were at Dev's truck before she knew it and he opened the door for her, pausing to brush his lips over her forehead before helping her up inside. He closed the door and Ellie's fingertips ghosted over the spot he'd left, sparking a hazy memory of the first time he ever kissed her. She brought her hand to her heart, trying to calm it to keep from shouting what she felt for the whole world to hear.

What if he didn't feel the same? Sometimes his cold exterior was so invulnerable even Ellie forgot the warmth he hid inside. She didn't believe for a second he was incapable of love... But what if he'd convinced himself she wasn't worth the risk?

"There's only one way to find out."

Ellie nodded at her friend's advice. She'd tell Dev how she felt someday, but not yet. Then she'd find out if putting her heart into this giant's hands would set her soaring or crush her spirit. She wasn't sure she was ready for the answer.

CHAPTER TWENTY-TWO

"Ellie, come *on*. Pink or blush?"

Ellie opened her eyes to see Virginia holding up two semi-formal dresses that looked suspiciously like the same color.

"Honest to God, Virginia, I can't tell the difference. You'd look great in both."

"Jesus, girl, were you sleepin' standin' up?"

"Maybe." Ellie groaned and pretended to snore against the wall. It wasn't actually that uncomfortable.

Virginia tsked and tossed both dresses back over the changing room stall. "You need to sleep, girlfriend. You can't be out all hours of the night." She went into the changing room and poked her head out. "At least not for work. You should do somethin' fun." She popped her head back in.

"I'm here, aren't I?" She didn't want to be anywhere near the mall, but she needed an outfit for her date with Dev. What she actually wanted to do was curl up in bed and forget about the fact that for the first time she could remember, she wasn't celebrating her birthday with her best friend.

"Oh my God, do you think this is fun? 'Cause I think it's fun!" Virginia called from behind the door. "Be still my beatin' heart. I'm officially havin' fun with my roommate." Ellie snorted and rubbed her aching eyes.

"But seriously, I'm worried about ya, girl. You've been burnin' the candle at both ends. Eventually, you're gonna run outta wick."

Ellie huffed in annoyance before replying in as dry a voice as she could muster to hopefully steer the conversation away. "I know what I'm doing."

"Okay, but like, what if you fall out and I'm the only one around? I'm not like you. I don't have a sexy giant teachin' me how to lift buses and shit. I can't carry you!" A sharp gasp behind the door made Ellie jump and dart her glance around. "Oh my God, I bet you could totally carry me! We should try it on the way to the food court."

Ellie placed a hand over her rushing heart and tried to relax again by forcing herself to concentrate on laughing at Virginia's joke. "He uses tires to train me, not the whole bus. And no thanks, I'll pass on dragging your butt around the mall."

"Such a party pooper. But on the real... isn't there someone else who could do your job? I don't know what all your sister-in-law's got you doin' at her law firm, but doesn't she see you're workin' yourself to death?"

Ellie frowned for a moment until she remembered the job at Jules's firm was the lie she'd told her roommate to help explain why she was gone all hours of the night and couldn't go to any parties.

The secrecy behind Sasha Saves was perfect for survivors, but the result was Ellie having to lie to everyone around her. Yet another strain on her psyche.

"There's no one else to do the job." There, she didn't have to lie. It was partially true, at least. The whole truth was Ellie didn't *want* anyone else to do her job because no one could be as good at helping survivors than a survivor herself. No trauma was the same, but at the core of it, survivors spoke the same language. No one else at the clinic was as fluent as her.

Well, except for maybe Nora... and Naomi... She shook the reasoning away.

"But, El—"

"Leave it, V. 'Kay?"

Virginia sighed in defeat. "Fine. But will you at least try on that gorgeous dress? That green will bring out your eyes. And with those kick ass gold heels from the store next door? Your man's jaw is gonna duh-rop."

Ellie glanced down at the wrap dress. It was nicer than any she'd ever worn, and it looked like something that might even be comfortable to move around in, but it was no Sasha original. The last time she'd needed a fancy outfit, she was going to that stupid party where her whole life changed.

She'd wondered over the past year if she and Sasha were the first to be stolen at a party like that in Ashland County. It was a yearly party, so to think it was a pattern sickened her. The thought had crossed her mind to try to go again this year. She'd even hinted and outright asked Dev if the Crew was going to do anything about the scholarship party, but he always went tight-lipped. At the time, she didn't push for more answers because she hadn't had anything to offer to help stop it from happening again.

But now I do...

She'd been practicing self-defense and all manner of survival tactics for the better part of half a year. Maybe she should approach Dev about doing a little recon to help figure out who was behind it all. Familiar faces at the party might even help jog her blotchy memory. She shivered at the thought. She'd purposely avoided digging too deep into her memories out of fear of the panic attacks they caused. But now that she was stronger, she'd go through it a thousand times to prevent someone else from suffering like Sasha had.

"El!" The creak of Virginia's dressing room door cracking open brought Ellie back to the moment. "Girl, are you fallin' asleep with your eyes open now? Jesus, I'll get you home so you can nap before your date. Let me finish tryin' mine on while you try on yours and we'll go, 'kay?"

Ellie glanced around the changing area at all the tiny stalls and slowly shook her head.

"Nah, I think this one will fit. I'll just take it home."

Virginia groaned and closed the dressing room door again before tossing a dress over the top. "God, to have your body. I've never been happy with anything I haven't tried on. Must be nice to have the body of a mannequin."

"Please, I'm not the size of a—" Ellie looked down at her baggy sweatshirt and glanced to the side at one of the aforementioned mannequins. She pulled the bottom of her sweatshirt tight and her jaw dropped as she realized her sweatshirt wasn't just baggy, it swallowed her whole. Even though she'd grabbed the size she'd worn forever, the dress in her arms might not even fit her.

She'd always been slim, but never skinny. Granted, it'd been hard to find the time to eat lately because she was always on the go. But, heck, now that she thought of it, she couldn't even remember the last time she had something more than a protein bar.

Ellie dropped the hem of her sweatshirt and sighed. The weight of the breath leaving her body made her dizzy enough to feel like she was about to tip over. The lounge chair in the corner of the changing area was practically calling her name, so she opted to take a seat while Virginia tried on her eleven hundredth outfit.

"Gah, I love shoppin'. Thanks for comin' out with me today, by the way. I really needed a dress for formal and the ones I brought from home wouldn't do. Plus, we got to hang out *and* you got a new dress, too."

"I don't even need this dress," Ellie mumbled. It had to be too fancy for whatever date Dev had in mind. There was no way he'd opt for a candlelit dinner.

"Girl, no one ever *needs* a dress this pricey, but it can't hurt to

have one just in case so you don't have to come back out here."
Ellie heard the door open but didn't feel the energy to look.
"Hey, what do ya think?"

Ellie peeked an eye open at Virginia's newest dress. The long,
pink, one-shoulder chiffon and lace dress had an asymmetrical
hem which was "in" right now, or so she'd been told when
Virginia picked it out. It fit Virginia like a glove. Sasha definitely
would've approved. The thought made her smile and didn't hurt
nearly as bad as she expected it to.

"It looks gorgeous on you, V. I like that one."

Virginia squealed. "Yeah, I agree. I love this one!"

"Awesome." Ellie shifted to stand up. "You ready to go?"

Virginia's mouth fell open. "Go? But I've only decided on one
dress."

Ellie stared at her and waved her hand to indicate Virginia's
whole body. "But you found the dress you love..."

Virginia busted out laughing. "That doesn't mean I'm done.
I've got like ten other dresses in here. I'll try these on real quick
and we'll go. Promise."

Ellie groaned and Virginia laughed as she shut the door. After
a moment Ellie began to rest her eyes again until Virginia
spoke up.

"So... how 'bout that redhead, bus-flippin', giant trainer of
yours? Y'all goin' steady, yet? What the heck does that even
mean, anyway?" She giggled and Ellie couldn't help but smile
along with her.

"No. But things have, uh... sorta heated up." The memory of
Ellie watching herself come with Dev's mouth on her flashed
across her mind.

Now, these are flashbacks I don't mind having.

Virginia squealed and Ellie heard her muffled clapping.
Maybe a dress was in her hands? "Oh my *gawd*. That's excitin'.
Have y'all gone on a date yet or will tonight be y'all's first one?
Where will it be? I need all the details."

"First one and I'm not sure."

"Ugh, okay, fine, Miss Silent Violet. Keep your secrets. I see that *I'll* need to be doin' all the talkin' in this friendship." She opened the door and did a twirl in a flowy—but still pink—dress. "How's this one? Cute, right?"

"Very cute. Just as cute as the last one."

Virginia gasped and her face crumpled. "El! Don't say that!" She stomped her foot. "Now it's gonna be hard to choose. Ugh." Virginia slammed the dressing room door after her and Ellie giggled at the theatrics.

The changing room grew silent, with only the susurrus of fabric in the background. Ellie searched for something to say to keep from being a "Silent Violet", but her brain wasn't functioning properly.

She had two tests coming up, one in Russian and one in psych that she needed to study for. But she hadn't had the energy after running, training, class, therapy, and work to go to the library. And studying at her dorm was impossible. She couldn't stand being awake and staring at those walls. She only felt comfortable enough to sleep once she was dead tired. Which coincidentally she was at that moment. Virginia's suggestion of a nap sounded perfect actually.

"All done."

"All done?" Ellie asked and glanced at her phone to see what time it was.

Dev: Hey angel, what're you up to?

Ellie felt her smile grow as she typed back.

Dress shopping

Dev: Nice. What's the occasion? Birthday date with me? ;)

Ellie felt her lips widen on impulse but stopped as soon as Virginia crooned, "OoOo" in several different notes. "Is that the boy?"

"Maybe." She did a little dance with her shoulders as she

stood up, only for the world to fade in and out at the edges. She took a few steadying breaths and her vision cleared again.

"Hey girl, could you help me carry some of these? I think I bit off more than I could chew."

"Uh, yeah, sure." Ellie walked the few feet to Virginia's open dressing room before shaking her head to clear the fuzz. Big mistake.

Her body felt lighter than the gravity pushing it down, and as she leaned against the open door, a hand grabbed on to her arm.

"Good, God, El, are you alright?"

Ellie nodded but quickly regretted that decision. "Yes... yes, I'm fine. Just stood up too fast, is all."

Virginia's brow furrowed in concern like she didn't believe her. "You know what? Let's get somethin' to eat on the way home. You're scarin' me."

Ellie's stomach twisted with guilt at the worry etched on her friend's face. "It's alright, V. I promise. I got up too fast."

Virginia shook her head and led Ellie by the arm away from her dressing room.

"No ma'am, it's your birthday and you've got the rest of the day off. I'm forcin' some Chick-fil-A down your throat and then tuckin' you in for a nap before your hot—"

The world was going by quicker than her eyes could adjust. "V, can you slow down?" she mumbled but wasn't sure if the words came out right. The twist in her belly roiled up her throat, making her feel like she was going to get sick. Ellie covered her mouth with one hand and tugged the other away from Virginia's grip.

"Please, V. Stop."

"What? We're not movin'—Oh my God, Ellie!" Virginia dropped the dresses and grabbed Ellie by both arms, but it was too late. Ellie fell backward, hitting something on her way down. Three white walls stretched over her, caving her in.

"Someone call 911!" Her friend bent over her. Ellie was on the floor, but she wasn't certain how she got there. Before she knew it, hands passed over her and Virginia was being peppered with questions too fast for Ellie to register.

"I'm okay…" The words mumbled past her lips as she tried to sit up. She was grabbed from all sides and she tried to shake them off and push the panic away. The world came back into blurry focus only to have a stranger in her face shouting something at her and one yelling behind her. There were people everywhere, crowding her. She tried to see past them but the only things in her vision were walls and people grabbing, pulling, holding her down, closing her in. Trapping her.

"Ma'am. Ma'am, we think you passed out. We're gonna check your— ma'am? Oh shit, she's hyperventilating."

"What the fuck is going on?"

"Dev?" His name came out of her mouth all fuzzy. He was yelling but he still sounded too far away.

"Sir, we're gonna check her out. We think it might be exhaustion but she's hyperventilating so it might be—"

"She's fucking claustrophobic and you assholes have her in a goddamn dressing room. Get the fuck out! I've got this."

"Sir, she fell here. We shouldn't move her until we've—sir, wait—"

"I found you, angel. You're safe." The deep voice coated her like a salve before strong arms cradled her. She nestled into the cinnamon scent, relaxing to the gentle, warm vibration against her ear. She reached her hand out and only felt air. She was free.

Her vision came back into focus, and the rumbling grew louder until she could tell what it was.

"You are safe. You are in control. You are safe. You are in control. You are safe. You are in control."

She mumbled the words back and the soothing effect on her nerves was instant. They repeated the mantra until cool air blew on her cheeks.

"I'm safe. I'm in control. I'm with Dev."

"That's right, baby. You're safe with me. Just breathe. We're outside and you're safe. Breathe deep for me."

Her eyes had been open but on the first big inhale of cold air it was like a shock to her system and she could see for the first time. It snapped her back to the moment and she concentrated on breathing at the same speed as the man holding her.

"You are safe. You are—"

"I'm okay, Dev. I'm okay." She wrapped her arms around his neck and pulled herself up farther in his arms.

"Thank God." Dev moved his hand to cradle the back of her head. His lips whispered over her forehead and she closed her eyes at the overwhelming sense of peace and security cleansing her body of tension.

"Ma'am? Who is this? Do you know this man?"

"I'm her boyfriend and a naval medic. Get the stretcher out and you can check her vitals before we go." Whoever he was talking to, must've sensed the authority behind his command because soon enough she sat on an upright stretcher outside of an ambulance.

Multiple EMTs took her vitals, fed her a fake sugary, chocolate substance, some beef jerky, and a Gatorade while asking her questions—most of which Dev answered for her—but it was nothing like the crowded feeling she'd felt right after passing out.

It could've been because she was finally feeding her body, but it also could've been because she was safe. Dev's hand never stopped touching her. He moved to accommodate the EMTs but they stayed connected and he remained in her vision at all times.

After a while, a portly medic approached her with a clipboard. "Ma'am, we think you suffered from exhaustion and then a panic attack. We don't think you need to go to the hospital, but we can take you if you want."

Dev's hand squeezed hers and it was the only answer she needed.

"No. I'm safe with Dev."

The stranger nodded but Ellie checked out of the conversation, trusting Dev to take care of the rest.

Eventually, despite the fact she'd been given the all-clear to go, Dev insisted on carrying her off to his truck. The gentle sway of his footsteps lulled her eyes closed. She was functionally okay, but she was still exhausted from... *everything*. He set her in her seat and clicked the seat belt in, kissing her forehead before he left.

"Rest, angel. I'm taking you home."

CHAPTER TWENTY-THREE

"I can't believe you fuckin' punched him, dude. That was aggressive as hell. He's one of your best friends and you're usually all I-am-robot." The last few words spoken in Phoenix's crappy robotic impersonation woke Ellie fully from her nap. There was a low rumbling growl in response and Ellie lifted a bleary eyelid.

"I'll do it to you too, if you don't fucking leave. I wanted her change of clothes from her roommate and you gave them to me. That's all I need right now."

"Sheesh, alright. But you know Jaybird's gonna have your ass for keepin' her from him. That and I'm sure as hell he knows you're in love with her by now."

Love.

The word lit a small flame of hope in Ellie's soul and cleared the sleepy fog in her mind.

"Leave. Now." The rumbled command came before the slam of the door and a deep exhale.

Ellie opened her eyes completely to find Dev's back up against the door. She felt around and fingered the soft comforter she was burrowed in and soaked in the cinnamon smell from her pillow. Slowly she remembered she was laying in Dev's bed in his studio apartment at the BlackStone Securities facility.

She glanced back at the man who'd saved her once again and met his deep forest green eyes.

"Some birthday, huh?" The brows and muscles around Dev's eyes were weary and tense as he spoke, and Ellie's stomach twisted with guilt.

Was that because of her? Stupid question. Of course she was the cause. She had a million questions, so instead of filtering them, she blurted the first ones that came to mind.

"How did you know I'm claustrophobic? Or where I was?"

He shoved his hands in his pockets and chuckled. "Your roommate texted me from your phone. And as for the claustrophobia... I had a hunch it was one of your triggers after your panic attack at the shooting range. Then I started paying more attention and noticed you spend as little time as possible in that tiny dorm room of yours. You also gravitate toward people you trust when the room is too crowded. My theory was confirmed when I realized you don't like your movements restricted—"

"Unless you let me feel like I am in control."

"No, you *are* in control. Even if you don't have control over the physical situation, control over your mental state is the most important. You could train to fight back an entire army but if you don't focus and think logically then one guy will beat you every time."

"Ugh, but I got beat by a freakin' *closet* today."

Dev huffed another laugh and paced toward her until he sat on the bed, one knee up and one leg off the side. His weight made the mattress dip and her body fell closer into the lowered space until it met Dev's thigh. He laid a hand on her shin and gave a gentle squeeze. "Fair, but only after you deprived your body of the proper ammo. You're taking shit care of your physical self. You finally lost the battle and everything shut down on you."

The denial she'd been asserting for a year wanted to push back but his words held on and she bit her lip from fighting the truth.

"Oh and heads-up... your brother's a little mad about my decision to monitor you. We came to... terms. I told him you would see him after you've rested. I know his hovering stresses you out sometimes."

Ellie tilted her head and gave him a smile. "You're right. It does. A lot of the time, actually." She scanned her surroundings and waved her hand. "I like your place."

He smiled and gestured to the room. "I'd give you the grand tour." He emphasized the words like there was more to it than the all-in-one room. "But this is it and you need your rest. I was hoping to have you here under much better circumstances." His wink made the sudden butterflies in her lower belly go wild. "But here we are."

"I'm sorry," she whispered before sitting up against the wooden headboard.

"Why are you apologizing?"

"I don't know. I freakin' passed out. I feel like I worried everyone—"

Dev patted her shin. "Stop. Alright? We're giving you time to rest. No need to apologize to anyone but yourself."

It was Ellie's turn to raise a brow. "Myself?"

He jutted his chin to the open space beside her against the headboard. "Mind if I sit?"

"Oh, of course not. It's your bed." She tried to laugh but she was still exhausted by everything she'd been through and it took too much effort.

Dev scooted beside her and crossed his arms. His fingers tapped against the curve of his large biceps and Ellie had to snap herself out of staring when he spoke again.

"I'm sorry."

Ellie felt her face contort to show the confusion she felt. "*You're* sorry? You got me out of there today."

He sighed and scrubbed his face. "I've let my emotions get in the way of your health and—"

Ellie's hands shot up. "Hold up, hold up, hold up. You think what happened today was *your* fault?"

His brow furrowed as he nodded. "If I'd been paying better attention—"

"No, ugh. Your emotions aren't the problem here. *Mine* are. Or at least, me trying not to have them is the problem." Ellie groaned. "I need to fess up. If today didn't wake me up, nothing will."

Dev sat beside her silently as she gathered her thoughts.

"You noticed. You think you let your feelings get in the way of seeing the signs of my future breakdown, but you didn't. You've confronted me about it and I swept it under the rug." Ellie blew out a heavy breath, hoping it would center her. She was even tired of the question but after the day she'd had, she wasn't confident in her answer anymore.

"I'm just... exhausted, I guess. That's not your fault, it's mine. I've closed myself off. Pushed everything away. I thought, if I worked hard enough, fixed everything—every*one*—around me, I wouldn't have to think about it anymore. I wouldn't have to feel so guilty... But it's not working."

His face remained unnervingly impassive but she knew he was waiting for her to get everything off her chest. She bit her lip before resting her head against the headboard and closing her eyes. Even then she had the overwhelming urge to change the subject, to keep putting off having to deal with the turmoil inside, but the weighted silence made her feel like she couldn't breathe until she released the burdens suffocating her.

"You know... I didn't really want to go on a date with you tonight." Dev frowned but Ellie waved his concern away and continued talking. "I'm supposed to be honoring tradition in a childhood treehouse with my best friend right now. Eating a donut and planning our lives out. Promising each other we'll grow up to be mean ol' biddies together and swear we'll still climb up that treehouse to celebrate our birthdays."

Dev's brow relaxed in understanding and she was glad he didn't say anything because the next part was going to be the hardest.

"A year ago... today... Sasha was m-murdered." Ellie fought to say the word as quickly as she could, but it still stabbed her in the chest on its way out. "For the rest of my life... today will always be my birthday and it'll *always* be the anniversary of my best friend's death." She wiped at her suddenly stinging eyes. "And I can't stop thinking... what if I'd done more to stop it. What if I hadn't been so scared. Would she still be alive?"

Her voice warbled with emotion and she wasn't sure if she could say any more. Wasn't even sure what else she could say. Several minutes passed while she tried to analyze her feelings and fight the pressure to blurt anything else out. But she didn't have to worry because, like always, Dev filled the empty space.

"Damn, we're more alike than I thought." He closed his eyes and rubbed them with his thumb and finger as he mumbled to himself. "Fuck, it *doesn't* work, does it? I thought shutting down worked. But it doesn't if it looks like this."

Confused, Ellie stayed silent as Dev's exhale deflated his body until he seemed to be as exhausted as she was.

"Before our last mission, my teammates were my brothers."

Ellie's heart skipped a beat but she didn't say anything, afraid it'd break the rare moment when Dev opened up to her. She knew her brother was haunted by their last mission but he refused to talk about it. The prospect of getting to hear more about what made Dev tick and the details about why Jason was so distant when he came back made her anxious.

"When Troy committed suicide, I closed myself off. I'd missed all the signs warning me he was in trouble. That guilt screwed me up and it took a long ass time to let people close again.

"And I did eventually. With my team. We lived, we died, we killed... for the team. Everything revolved around my brothers and our purpose.

"But on that last mission, somehow the bastard knew we were coming..." He sighed and shook his head. "We were there to help save victims—"

"Women like me and Sasha."

He grunted his assent, and his hand found her blanketed thigh. "But nothing went as planned. Jaybird, Hawk, and Eagle—"

"Eagle?"

He nodded. "He was our team lead, then, not Hawk. Phoenix piloted our chopper, Snake was back on base with the commo—um, sorry, the comms system. He was our eyes from a drone above and talked to us through our headsets. And I remained by the Bird for medical support with Draco as QRF—the quick reaction force if shit hit the fan... Which it did.

"Something went wrong with the commo... Snake was having a hard time getting through to Hawk, Eagle, and your brother. There was static and it cut out completely for me and Draco. I didn't know anything was wrong until everything blew up."

Even knowing Dev, her brother, and the rest of the Black-Stone Crew got out, Ellie still felt a frisson of fear. But while her heart was racing, Dev recounted his story in a low monotone, as if he was reading a medical report aloud.

"The target had set his own home as a bomb. Civilians we hadn't known would be in there were trapped when the explosion went off—"

"Oh, God. Were they okay?"

Dev's lips tightened and Ellie shut her mouth. She knew better than to interject during a traumatic story and she could handle his. She'd listened to traumatic stories day in and day out, but it was something different altogether to know the survivor personally.

"Seeing that bomb go off with three of my best friends inside scared the shit out of me. It was only a moment of being frozen in fear for them, but it was long enough to miss what happened next.

"Hawk, Jaybird, and Eagle made it out, but as soon as they did, we caught fire from who we thought were friendlies... people Jaybird and Draco had trained to take care of themselves against the men terrorizing their village.

"Your brother and Hawk made it to the Bird. Eagle was behind them and caught a bullet to the thigh. The wound wasn't life-threatening, except for the fact it slowed him down during a firefight. Hawk went back to help him. I couldn't move. I *should've* moved. It was literally my *job* to react quickly and act as backup, and prevent what happened. But I fucked up because I couldn't shut off the emotions that paralyzed me.

"They were almost at the Bird when they were attacked. I'd even seen the local coming, but I still couldn't fucking move. He pointed his AK right at them, but Eagle pushed Hawk down. He took the bullets straight to the chest."

Ellie covered her mouth to keep from interrupting with a gasp.

"If I'd gone to help sooner or picked off the guy before he took the shot... it was seeing Eagle fall that snapped me back into the moment. I guess my medic training finally overrode my fear.

"I hopped out and we pulled him into the Bird. Phoenix flew us away while Jaybird and Hawk fired back down below. I did the best I could. I've seen horrible things. Fucked-up things people do to each other and I'm their goddamn cleanup crew. Or the grim reaper. It never sits right with me when I lose someone. But, Eagle?" He shook his head and his lips flattened into a thin line. "I did the best I could and failed. After that, I shut down again."

Ellie grabbed his hand from her thigh and squeezed. "But, why?"

"I kept thinking, if I'd been paying attention, if I'd kept my teammates at arm's length and hadn't been distracted and frozen with fear that they'd been injured, maybe I would've realized that the friendlies around us were about to turn. Maybe Eagle would still be alive.

"I couldn't make mistakes. Let emotional attachments get in the way. If I do, people get hurt. It's why I freaked the fuck out and ran away when I let my need for you blind me from the signs that you were about to have a panic attack—"

"Dev, that wasn't—"

"Not caring enough made me ignore signs with Troy. Caring too much had me blind to see the danger that killed Eagle until it was too late. Turning everything off and operating on facts and logic, that's how I could stop the death around me."

"Dev, stop. None of that is your fault." Ellie sat up from sitting beside Dev to turn and face him head-on. "Obviously I've got my own issues, but you've taught me how to fight back, in every way. You've given me control back that I thought I'd lost. Caring about your teammates didn't kill Eagle. You were *ambushed*. There's no way you could've known that was gonna happen. And you did care about Troy, but there's no way to know when someone's desperate enough to take their life."

His fingers stretched to lace farther into hers until every inch of their palms were touching. "I'm telling you this because... I think you're like me, a little, at least. I haven't really analyzed what I was doing until I realized I understood your coping mechanisms perfectly. You're doing everything you can not to think about your loss and even more to try to cure the guilt from it. But refusing to face it is killing you, baby. And you definitely don't deserve that guilt."

"But with Sasha..." she whispered and shook her head. "No. Our situations are nothing alike. You did everything you could to help Eagle, but you had enemies bent on killing y'all. I didn't do anything to stop her from getting... I didn't stop it. I just lay there."

"How are they not the exact same situation?" He reached up with his free hand and brushed her cheek. "Listen to me, El, you were barely eighteen, drugged, and untrained. It's okay to not know what to do in that situation. All we can ever do is our best and it's okay if the best you can do is self-preservation. Sometimes the opportunity to save ourselves is all we get."

The air caught in her throat and Ellie found it hard to breathe, but in a much different way than a panic attack. It was almost like she was tasting the air for the first time and it was cleansing, even as it burned. Tears stung her eyes as she pulled away from his hands.

"But how? How do you live with that? Knowing people are gone and you didn't stop it? I don't want to feel it anymore and I've tried turning it off but i-it's not working."

She couldn't help the hitch in her voice at the end but she blinked back the moisture in her eyes to meet Dev's. His eyebrows raised, as if he was thinking about her questions, then furrowed as he shook his head.

"You're right. Turning it off doesn't work. I think seeing you in so much pain is what's making me realize it, but you're right. I've tried turning it off for years. I thought if I held everything at a distance, I wouldn't ever miss clues like that again. I wouldn't let my emotions get in the way of seeing what was important, and honestly, it protected me too. If I shut down, it wouldn't hurt as much when the people around me died."

"And that's worked for you?"

Dev continued to face forward and nodded imperceptibly. "Yes... I'd say it's worked to a certain extent. But only because I didn't let myself feel anything at all. I wouldn't want this for you.... This *emptiness*. Darkness." He finally met her gaze. "I don't think I want it for myself anymore, either. Not when I've felt what it's like to care about someone who's full of light."

Ellie's heart stuttered but she was only ready for one epiphany for the night. "So... what do we do?"

Dev swiped each tear from her cheek with his thumbs. "I'm figuring it out too, by watching you and realizing what I want for you. I guess, what I want for you is... to fill the emptiness with everything we feel. Hurt. Grieve. Let it all in. And then when that's done..." His hands caressed the back of her head and he pulled her close to kiss her forehead before tucking her in to his side. "When that's done... I guess, we live. That's all we can do, right? We live for those who left life too soon. And we live because we owe it to ourselves to try."

Ellie wrapped her arm around his waist and let the tears flow freely as she nodded her agreement.

"I-I miss her, Dev. I miss her so much." She stared at the cream-colored wall as she cried until there was too much moisture to see anything but the blank space. "Sh-she's gone and every day a new memory happens, something I wanna tell her about and I can't. Not really. I tell the sky. I pretend she talks back. But it's not enough. She's gone and I don't just miss her," Dev rubbed her back and with the encouragement, she continued, voicing words she'd always been too ashamed to say out loud. "I'm *missing* her. She was the part of me that made everything colorful and now the world is... dim. Like everything bright was burned up with her and now I'm dark inside."

In one swift motion, Dev pulled her up from under the comforter and Ellie found herself sidesaddle on his lap. His hands held her face close to his, fierce and commanding, forcing her to keep her focus on him.

"Don't think that, Ellie. You've gotta fight against that." His fingers stroked her cheek, soothing the pain inside her. "You are the strongest woman I know, and one day this fight won't seem so hard. One day you'll be able to breathe easy again. But, promise me, angel, promise me you'll fight that darkness."

She bit her lip and closed her eyes before nodding, but Dev took her chin in his thumb and forefinger.

"Say it. I have to hear you say it."

Ellie's chest pounded with emotion, and her exhausted body ached. From the conversation, from rehashing the past, from *life*. But she opened her eyes and swallowed. "I-I'll fight it."

Dev searched her face as if he was trying to find the truth there. Whatever he saw, he accepted, and dipped his chin. He wrapped his hand around her nape and kissed her, melding his body to hers until he broke away. His eyes burned with intensity as they met hers as what he said next seared her soul.

"You might think you're the darkness, Ellie, but to everyone else, you're the goddamn sun."

CHAPTER TWENTY-FOUR

Neal stabbed his hands through his thinning hair and screamed at the top of his lungs. It'd been too long since he last shot up and this time the wait would kill him. Ever since that little blonde bitch saw him weeks ago, he'd been extra careful about going to dealers. Unfortunately, the ones he trusted most worked for the Russian. They'd all been instructed to cut him off. Thankfully he'd kept a stash, but rationing it out was a goddamn bitch.

"It's fine, Cici. I'm fine. We're fine. Look." He stumbled through the room to the piles of files he had surrounding his chair. "I've got all this dirt on everyone. I'll make them give me the meds. They can't do anything to me after I show them all this."

He twirled around in the middle of his living room, uncaring about the piles of paper he tripped on, or the used paper towels and various bits of trash that had accumulated around him. He laughed loudly and slapped his hand against a large file he'd packed in his briefcase from the precinct. No one there was trustworthy, so while he ultimately kept all the files hidden away in various parts of his office, he had to work them up at home with his corkboard. The only truly safe place was his house.

There were eyes everywhere else and no one fucked with him in the neighborhood. They were all too afraid of the cop.

It didn't used to be like that. When he and Cici first bought the house, police officers were revered across town. Now he was lucky to get a smile, let alone a first responder discount.

"But this... this will change everything, Cici. I just need to get better. Just one more dose and I'll get well. This will do it." He waved the file at the woman in the mirror above the couch before turning and muttering so she couldn't hear. "All this'll damn me one way or the other."

"Don't say that, Neal."

"Why not?" Neal whipped around to yell at her, pointing his drink in her direction, but she was gone. He staggered back, pivoting with each step, trying to find the embodiment of the voice that was becoming more and more real to him every day. She was nowhere to be found so he leaned against his side table and tipped the glass back and patted the last remnants of the 'shine down his mouth. He swiped the back of his hand against his mouth and yelled at nothing. "Why the fuck can't I say things like that, Cici? *You* sure fuckin' did!" He threw the empty mason jar against the wall, shattering it into thousands of little pieces before he mumbled. "You said 'em 'n left."

He walked into the kitchen to get another jar to take the edge off. The first one had only dimmed the edges of his memories. He needed full obliteration.

Before the Russians cut him off, he hadn't had a proper drink in years. But the time between hits made it hard to think of anything besides getting his next doses and getting well. He'd decided to trade one demon for the other. A sip of his cousin's moonshine here and there did the trick. They'd been Christmas gifts for decades, and Neal never had the balls to tell him he'd quit.

"Good thing I never threw this shit out." He pulled more moonshine from the pantry and unscrewed the wide mouth aluminum top for a large swig. It burned, but he'd gulp down the delicious heat as long as it promised oblivion.

Neal slammed the mason jar on the kitchen counter a little harder than he meant to. He picked up the glass and examined the bottom, making sure he hadn't cracked it. Wouldn't do to waste a good batch of hooch.

Seeing no cracks, he shrugged before taking the few strides to the entryway between the living room and the kitchen. From where he stood, the profile map on his corkboard stared back at him from the living room, mocking him with all the answers he couldn't share. Not yet.

As he was about to cross the threshold into the living room, a shadow passed on the mirror above the couch. A sharp chill rattled through him and he shivered.

"What was that? W-was that you, Cici?"

For the first time in months, only silence answered back. Neal whispered a silent prayer of thanks that he always carried his holster with him now that people were following him. He gripped the butt of his gun and swiveled his head to scan the perimeter, making sure he was flush against the kitchen wall beforehand so any intruder who came in wouldn't catch him from behind. A drumbeat echoed in his mind until he realized it was his labored pulse, filling his body with its own adrenaline high.

Leaning against the doorjamb between the living room and kitchen, Neal's eyes flicked around to try to find the shadow he'd seen.

"Cici?" he whispered, even as he knew it was pointless. She only came to him on her terms. Neal couldn't blame her though. He was a sorry SOB now, but he'd never been good enough for her to begin with. Hell, Cici had suffered the pain of her body constantly fighting against her, and she'd still stayed a saint. If the tables were turned, Neal would've gone batshit.

He shook his head. He was being stupid. Whatever he'd seen was a figment of his imagination. Cici wouldn't play tricks on him. He just needed his medicine. Everything was better when he had medication running through his veins.

He brought the glass up to his lips, only to find his hand empty. He whipped around to the kitchen where the 'shine still sat on the counter.

He stared at his empty hand and the counter before doing another double take. "How the fuck did you get there?" he mumbled. He shoved his hand in his pocket and retrieved the lighter that calmed him with its consistent flicker. Every time he ignited it, it followed through. There were few things in life that reliable.

He trudged to the kitchen and got the jar, shoving it up to his lips and clipping his teeth on the mouth of the glass. It was heavier than he'd remembered but it didn't matter. He walked back to the living room, kicking at the wads of trash that had collected.

"Need to clean up," he mumbled as he rubbed his aching head. "Cici will have my hide when she gets home."

He swigged the moonshine and swished it around his mouth. The more it burned, the less he noticed. Neal gazed over his hard work over the last year. The red strings illustrated a map to nowhere if you didn't know your destination. But he knew exactly where each red vein led, and he was *this close* to figuring out who was at the heart of it all. Once he did, he'd decide who to take the information to. One thing was for sure, he wouldn't be caught with his pants down again. Hell, if he got well in the meantime, it'd be a no-brainer where to send the files to.

"We can only hope, ain't that right, Cees? Just dial it back, one step at a time. We'll do it *together*." Neal mocked the last slurred word as he spat it from his mouth. She definitely wasn't going to like that. The last time they'd gotten into it, she'd said it was her or the alcohol. He'd taken a swig just to spite her. He thought he'd won when she didn't say a word back.

Maybe if he'd looked closer, he would've seen her quit in that moment. Maybe if he'd listened, he would've realized the silence afterward wasn't the same thing as peace.

"You know... I imagine it sometimes. When we fought last. If I hadn't been such an ass. If I'd been lookin' right at ya instead of thinkin' about my next sip. If I'd had——" He waved his hand up to the board in front of him. "If I'd had little red lines to show me what road you went down after that fight... maybe I could've stopped myself. Maybe I could've stopped you."

"We can't change the past."

"I know..." Neal sighed and lay back in the chair, crossing his legs at the ankles and once again following the red trails with his eyes. The lifeblood of Ashland County was implicated before him. He flicked the lighter in his hand and leaned back, holding it straight out in front of him. He was far enough away that the flame encompassed the entirety of the board. He couldn't see the fucked-up history of his town. The town he'd sworn to love and protect. The town he'd failed.

"It's like you, Cici." The monotone of his voice sounded odd and tinny in his ears. Like a man he no longer recognized was speaking through him.

The heat of the flame burned at the pad of his thumb, but he didn't care. The burn peeled away at the layer of shame he'd carried with him for eight years.

If he'd listened to Cici. If he'd listened to anyone. Stopped drinking when she'd asked. Paid attention when she'd begged him to notice her. Not have been so damned selfish. Maybe things wouldn't be so fucked up. Cici might be alive. That girl from last year... the dozens of women he'd lost under his watch...

"You didn't know."

"Exactly." Without the hit to take away his thoughts they ran rampant in his mind, running at a pace he couldn't keep up with but the ideas were all the same.

Failure.

Failure.

Failure.

They died.

Because of me.

Finally the heat grew to be too much and he dropped the lighter. It fell inert on his lap and he swiped it away to make sure it didn't burn through his trousers.

Another small burn mark formed on aged green carpet. He imagined it spreading up to the edges of the board, across his shoes, up his legs, deep in his gut, all the way to ravage the empty hole where his heart was supposed to be. He'd been so empty, so cold, for so long. It was nice to feel something again. Even if it was all in his imagination.

CHAPTER TWENTY-FIVE

"You're not effin' banned from Sasha Saves, ya drama queen. You just can't bebop up in here at all hours of the night anymore, 'kay?" On the last word, Nora sounded like she blew a piece of bubble gum just to pop it for emphasis.

Ellie massaged her brow as she sat on a stool at her temporary apartment at BlackStone. There was a strange mixture of understanding and frustration swirling inside her. She'd been relegated to being a part-time, first-shift employee at Sasha Saves and it drove her bananas. Naomi now had her work cell phone and—somehow—Nora had found all the numbers from survivors in Ellie's personal phone and redirected them to the work phone.

"But it's been a whole month since I passed out. I'm feeling great." Ellie wasn't even lying this time and was better rested than she'd ever been. She'd even gained back the weight she'd lost.

"Hmm... been going to therapy?"

Hope sparked in Ellie's chest. "Yep, twice that first week and once a week since."

"Mhm, mhm... sleeping?"

"Yep."

"Eating?"

"Yep, yep, yep, and going to class, and training, and studying. All the good things."

"That's great, girl! I'm proud of you."

Ellie shimmied her shoulders with excitement before bringing her phone back to her ear. "So I can come back full time?"

"Hmm... what? Oh, no way."

"Ugh, come on, Nora. I need to get back in there."

The pixie on the other line chuckled. "The fact you think I have any say over this is effin' hilarious. Your brother and Devil are calling the shots. Apparently, I'm the damn messenger."

Ellie groaned again, louder to match Nora's growing laughter. "Okay, fine. But who went last night? I checked the email this morning before class and there was a confirmation from the SANE nurse at the ER that a kit was sent off to the Ashland County Sheriff's Office lab?"

A sigh resonated on the other end, and when Nora spoke again, she'd sobered for the topic. "Yeah... Naomi actually went to the hospital and spoke with the sexual assault nurse and helped explain the rape kit and process to the survivor. She's got a, um, history with the woman, so she took the reins. She's been pretty godsdamned invaluable here."

Ellie sighed. She was glad Naomi was having a bigger role in the clinic, especially considering how her relationship with Sasha Saves started on such a tumultuous note. But Ellie still couldn't help feeling like she was doing the survivors a disservice by not being there for them when they needed her.

"I feel... I don't know. I feel useless when I can't be there."

Nora *tsked* on the other end. "Ya gotta let it go, babe. I get it. Trust me. I don't get exactly what you're going through, but I'm pretty sure I get the gist. Every moment I'm not doing something for the clinic or sitting at the hospital beside the comatose man who saved my life? I'm fighting with the part of me that screams I'm being lazy or I'm failing them. Those are my own issues, but for you? Taking care of you, going to school... Hades, girl just being a frickin' college kid... That's your job right now, 'kay?"

"I know, I just—"

"*Bup-bup-bup*. Brace yourself for some harsh words comin' at ya, sister. I'm sure Little Miss Barbie and that redheaded devil of yours don't want to be picking up pretty little Ellie pieces from the floor anymore, capeesh? Does that help put it in perspective? When you weren't taking care of yourself and only worrying about others, you made it so others had to worry about *you*."

Ellie paused, her mouth open. She hated to admit it, but it made sense. Nora was always down for the tough talks and sometimes when they burrowed under Ellie's skin, Ellie dug her heels in right back to withstand the truths. But this one...

"I-I never thought of it that way..."

"I know. We love ya, girl. It's time for you to join the party."

Ellie nodded as if Nora could see her on the other line.

"Listen." Nora coughed on the other end and whispered into the receiver. "I gotta go. I'm about to have lunch with Matt."

"Matt? Draco's nurse from the hospital?"

"Yup." The word came out slow and popped at the end.

"Bowchica—"

"Abso-effin'-lutely not, little girl. He's just a friend."

Ellie snorted. Nora commenting on anyone's size was hilarious considering she wasn't much bigger than Tinker Bell.

"Well lunch sounds... nice? It's always good to have friends, I guess," Ellie offered, only to have Nora grunt on the other end.

Ellie looked at the watch she'd been patiently attending to the past hour and a half and hopped off the stool. She'd be fifteen minutes early, but since Dev had BlackStone business to take care of before her classes, she'd had to wait all day to find out whatever "special training" he'd planned that night.

The last 'special' training they'd had a month and a half ago, he'd given her the best orgasm of her life while he held her up on his shoulders. It was too bad she'd kneed him in the balls so hard she couldn't reciprocate, but since then, she couldn't get the thought of returning the favor out of her head.

"Yeah, yeah, friends are great. Gotta go, babe." Nora already sounded distracted.

"I gotta go, too," Ellie replied as she left her apartment and took ten strides to the studio next door.

"Peace out, Girl Scout."

The call ended and Ellie shoved her phone into the side pocket of her leggings as she delivered two hard knocks on Dev's steel door. On the third, she nearly slammed her fist into Dev's chin in the newly open doorway, but she retracted her hand with an agility she hadn't dreamed of before her training sessions.

His brows raised as if he was impressed before he glanced at his watch. "Getting better every day, El. You're early *and* you stopped yourself from clobbering me. You might save a life with those reflexes." Dev winked at her as he stepped aside for her to enter past him.

"Goddamn." He sounded like he was choking and she turned around to see him staring at her butt. "Ellie, those leggings are..."

Ellie laughed and twirled like she was wearing a dress. "Thanks, they have pockets. And I'm not *that* early." She blushed at being caught, but didn't disagree with the reflexes compliment.

She'd become strong over the past couple of months, and the last month she'd strengthened herself mentally and emotionally, too. After finally truly embracing her therapy sessions, and after her therapist insisted they meet in person again, Ellie could admit she felt the difference inside and out.

"Well, whatever they have, they're, um... working. Anyway, you're early enough that I haven't gotten the supplies out, yet. I was finishing cleaning my gun." He pointed to his dining table where his gun was laid out in pieces on a towel. "Have a seat and I'll be ready in a minute."

Ellie nodded and walked by him until she felt the hair on the back of her neck prickle.

"And see—" Dev's sudden closeness right behind her made every nerve tingle. "I can come behind you like this and you don't even jump anymore."

Ellie exhaled a breath and whipped around to see his small smile, the one that sent flutters low in her belly. Trying to play off the fact he'd set her off guard, she feinted a punch at his arm and giggled when he jumped back, rubbing his arm, pretending like she'd hit him.

"Yes, perfect. Instead of getting overwhelmed, now you can punch their lights out. Progress."

Ellie snorted. "Some would argue whether that should be considered 'progress'."

Dev waved away her point. "Nah, they'd just be mad you got the drop on them." He went to rummage through the closet in the corner of the room while Ellie sank into one of his dining chairs and pulled her phone out of her leggings to lay it on the table. His voice was slightly muffled as he called out from inside the walk-in. "Still liking the apartment?"

Ellie nodded. Nora was partly right that other people were calling the shots, but Ellie had agreed to every suggestion on how to get healthier, and made some of her own. Dev and Jason were just better at keeping her accountable.

Part of their agreement was staying at BlackStone. Her dorm was doing her more harm than good, and Jason was convinced she needed constant monitoring. His original plan was for her to stay with him and Jules, which Ellie said a gentle but firm 'heck no, thanks anyway'. Staying with her overbearing brother would've made her crazy on its own, but being there while he obsessed over his pregnant fiancée? That would've been a complete disaster for her mental health.

The compromise had been to shack up temporarily in the studio apartment that would've been Jason's if he'd signed onto BlackStone when the security firm began. It was downright spacious compared to her dorm room.

The only person she'd been afraid of disappointing was

Virginia, but her roommate had assured her she didn't even notice Ellie was gone. Which surprisingly hurt for Ellie to hear until Virginia explained it was only because Ellie had never been there in the first place. In fact, they were talking more than ever thanks to a constant stream of texts and FaceTimes back and forth. Virginia was thrilled.

"What about your neighbor? He still driving you crazy?" Dev peeked his head out and smirked while Ellie rolled her eyes.

Having Dev as her neighbor was... interesting. It was nice to know she was safe, but it also meant he was just a wall away. Still, their schedule hadn't changed much. She either saw him at Sasha Saves or when they trained three times a week. The only difference was every time they did see each other, Dev had been distant, treating her with nothing but respect and professionalism.

Obviously, she freaking hated it.

Some days she was sure her eyeballs were going to dry out from staring at the wall between them while trying to imagine what he was doing on the other side, and what she wished he was doing with her. Now that she had a full belly and a month's worth of good nights' sleep in her system, every time they trained, she couldn't keep the idea of a heavy horizontal workout out of her dirty mind.

"I don't know, I hardly ever see him. Seems like he's gone all the time." She cupped her chin and leaned on her propped elbow while trying to listen for any hint at what their lesson would be.

"Aw, you noticed? That makes me feel all warm and fuzzy inside." His quiet chuckle at her expense got on her nerves and she narrowed her eyes at his closet door until he finally emerged. "Believe it or not, I have other responsibilities here *besides* training you."

"I get that but, um..." Talking about Dev's hot and cold routine was the last thing she wanted to do, but he seemed more receptive than he had been in over a month, so she ventured in. "We had some" —she cleared her throat— "*very* hands-on training a while ago. And since then, you've been very... hands-*off*."

Dev stepped outside the closet and leaned his shoulder against the side of the open door and tossed something in one hand to the other. "Sorry, El. I've wanted to give you space, is all. I don't want to interfere with your health and I figured..." He shrugged a shoulder. "I figured when you were ready you would come to me."

Ellie gulped and nodded but couldn't draw her stare away from the items in his hand. He walked to the dining table with his brow furrowed before depositing them onto the surface. Her mind raced with possibilities of using either the rope, the tape, or the handcuffs in front of him to bind her in the next 'exercise.' Her core pulsed with need and she crossed her legs to keep from dampening her panties.

"Right... makes sense..." She cleared her throat. "So um, not judging or anything, but why the heck do you keep shady, serial killer crap in your closet?"

"Oh, you know. In case I'm in the mood for a little something... hands-*on*." Dev's voice was pitched low, and Ellie finally looked up to see his eyes burning with intensity, and the heat there sent a warm blush creeping up her chest and into her cheeks.

Ellie's eyes darted to the bed, where she could easily imagine herself tied while Dev tasted her arousal again. She'd been craving him since he'd made her watch herself come. "L-like what... exactly?"

A wicked smile inched across his face. "Unfortunately, the things I have in mind today are not nearly as fun as what's going on in your head. Although, I'd be really fucking interested to see where that imagination is taking you right now."

Disappointment twisted up in the lust consuming her body, but when Dev snapped the rope like a folded belt, the clapping sound made her thighs quake from how hard she was squeezing them together.

Ellie closed her eyes and took a breath to center herself. If he was going to keep teasing her, she wasn't going to take the bait anymore. Two could play at that game.

She opened her eyes and adopted a smirk before crossing her arms. "Whatever, get on with the lesson then, *sir*."

A rumbling formed in Dev's chest and fire lit the forest green in his eyes. Why she'd chosen to poke the demon, she had no idea.

"You know exactly why, girl. And I fuckin' approve."

Sasha whistled inside her mind, and Ellie braced herself for the wave of misery that accompanied their inner conversations. Ellie had started hearing less from her friend in the past couple of months and Sasha had been radio silent since the store incident. The only thing Ellie could do in the moment was hope all the self-help had prepared her for the worst.

But when her pulse remained calm and her heart didn't try to tear itself out of her chest to get away from the pain, she let the tension in her muscles relax. Dev was looking at her with a tilted head, but said nothing as she smoothed down her loose midriff hoodie for something to do with her hands. Inside, she didn't know how to feel about... *not* feeling guilty.

Deep down, she knew it was healthy for her to move on, and fewer talks with a ghost was a good step in the process. Even with all the talks with her therapist, cognitive-behavioral exercises, and meditations, on some level, Ellie had still expected to regret the moments she didn't think about her friend. To feel remorse over being the one left behind, and having the audacity to forget her for a second. But all she felt was gratitude. For who Sasha was, the friendship they had, and the person she'd help Ellie become.

Ellie closed her eyes and spoke to her friend, at peace with the fact their conversations were getting few and far between.

Thanks, Sash.

She looked up to find Dev watching her with soft, knowing eyes. "That's... nice."

"What?"

"That." He stretched across the small table and brushed her bottom lip with his finger. "This smile. It's nice to see. I've been seeing it around more lately and it's a relief." He stroked her cheek, sending shivers down her spine, and dropped his hand before turning back to the props. "Today, we're going to work through escape techniques." He picked the handcuffs up and twirled a cuff around with his index finger. "Pick your binding, angel. First one's your choice."

Ellie gulped and looked at the item until her eyes stung. What a freaking choice indeed.

"What's it gonna be, baby?"

"Uh..." She sifted through all the scenarios in her mind, spending a little extra time on the ones involving handcuffs. And while each fantasy made her clit throb with anticipation, her anxiety and adrenaline got the best of her and she blurted out the worst possibility. "That one. The duct tape."

CHAPTER TWENTY-SIX

Devil's smile lessened and he tried not to read too much into the look of panic that crossed over her face. He grabbed the tape and tossed it in his hand, attempting nonchalance and trying his best not to look disappointed. If she wasn't ready, she wasn't ready, and he sure as hell wasn't going to pressure her. How fucked up would that be?

"Alright, let's do this. We're going to simulate a kidnapping situation."

Ellie pursed her lips and shook her head. "But I wasn't tied up when I was kidnapped. Just high."

What she said didn't surprise him, but how she said it was a kick in the gut. He'd figured they didn't tie her up. Most trafficking situations don't require ropes and duct tape. Drugged, pliable victims were easier to move in plain sight.

No, it was her casual delivery, like they weren't talking about the most traumatic event in her life, that made him want to burn the McIntosh Hotel down to hunt and kill the assholes who'd done this to her.

Good thing he wouldn't have to wait long. Tomorrow was the big day. If everything went smoothly, they'd save victims *and* rid the world of a few more demons.

His fingers itched at the prospect but he had to tone down his anticipation. Ellie couldn't know about the plan, not yet anyway, so he cleared his throat and moved on.

"I know, baby. But not every situation is the same. Go ahead and lay down."

Ellie hesitated and looked around. "O-on the floor? Or..." She pointed and did a one-eighty until her finger indicated the bed.

Devil hid a smile. Fuck, he couldn't wait to try *anything* with her on the bed, let alone bondage. "The floor will do... for now." He watched her carefully and his cock twitched at the crestfallen look on her face. Did she want him as badly as he wanted her?

It'd been thirty-one days since he'd tasted her and twenty-eight days of pure torture keeping his hands off her since she fainted. For twenty-eight *fucking* days he'd backed off, letting her focus on herself so he wouldn't interfere in her recovery.

And fuck, she seemed fully recovered now. Her skin had its healthy golden glow back, and the sunken bags under her eyes were gone. She seemed happier, too. No, she *was* happier, he could tell. Earlier, when he'd said it was nice to see her smile, he hadn't been blowing smoke up her ass.

Her ass.

Visions of when he'd massaged the untouched rosette in the gym thirty-one days ago flitted across his mind and shot straight down to his cock.

Fuck, she looks good.

Ellie gained weight over the past month and she'd filled out here and there. Devil thought she was gorgeous as sin before, but goddamn, he couldn't get the thought out of his mind of tugging those leggings over those plump cheeks and getting between. He'd be in heaven.

A moan so faint he thought he'd imagined it made him realize the look he was giving her wasn't too far off from what he was thinking. She sat on the floor, biting her lip, and from the molten caramel in her eyes, he knew the flush of her skin was from need.

Unfortunately, they'd both have to wait. This lesson was important. He'd waited long enough to show her escape techniques, afraid teaching her too early would set off her claustrophobia. Now that she was healthier, it was time to show her the ropes, so to speak. Or at least how to get out of them.

Her breaths were coming in pants and Devil decided to at least give her a taste of her own medicine with her cheeky 'sir' comment earlier. He'd tried to hide how that word was his kryptonite, but apparently she'd been studying him as much as he'd been studying her.

"Don't worry, baby, when I take you, you'll be more than willing. I won't need to tie you up to get you into my bed, but I'll keep you that way so we can have some fun before I make you come."

He enjoyed the thick gulp that traveled down the column of her neck and his fingers twitched at the thought of pinning her to the bed by her throat, making her swallow around his hand. Or his cock. The thought made him thicken and he adjusted his sweatpants so they didn't get off track... yet.

Ellie nodded slowly, as if she didn't know how to respond to his threat, and patted her hands on the ground. "'Kay, now what?"

"This." He bent down and began to wrap the tape around her ankles over her tight leggings. "What's the first rule of kidnapping?"

"Um... don't get kidnapped?"

He snorted as he rounded the tape over her lower calves and did the same to her wrists. "Touché. Well, the second rule of kidnapping is: never go to a second location." He tapped her shins and stood up.

"Never go to a second location. Got it." Ellie looked down and raised her arms and legs like a floppy mermaid learning to swim. "Is this why I was supposed to wear long sleeves and leggings."

"Yes. Alright, your task is to get free in three minutes. What-ever you do, don't quit. This will also be a good exercise for adrenaline, and thinking calmly on how to use available resources." He raised his watch.

"What? Three minutes? How?" Her scrunched-up face was adorable, but if he kept looking at her like that he wasn't going to be able to let her finish the exercise.

"And..."

"Wait! Hold on—"

"Go!"

Ellie huffed but attempted to get up. She had a time of it, rocking on her ass and pulling at the tape around her legs with the tips of her unbound fingers.

"Two minutes left."

Ellie groaned and collapsed onto the ground with a dramatic flair, irritating the fuck out of him.

What the fuck? She's giving up already?

"Dev, this is impossible. You tied me up to make sure I couldn't get out of it." She waved her arms. "How am I—"

"Come on, Ellie." Devil couldn't help his growl. He was riding the line of encouragement and hard-ass and if she didn't kick *her* ass into gear, he was going to have to go full hard-ass. "Don't quit. Try to be resourceful. You've got one minute now."

She grunted before shoving her fists into her mouth and trying to tear her hands loose. As she did, she kept trying to talk through gritted teeth.

"You were... freakin'... Navy... if you... wanted it on... How could I—*oof...* take this off?"

The way she attempted to rip the industrial-strength tape with her canine teeth would've been painful to watch, if Devil wasn't already grinding his into dust.

"Fifteen seconds." Anger built inside him as she started to whine in frustration.

"Ugh, Dev!"

Ignoring her tantrum, he kept counting. "Ten seconds—"

"Stop, it's impossible!" She swiveled and got on all fours as he counted down. He thought that was at least better than being flat on her ass, until she collapsed back on her calves and threw her hands in the air.

Un-fucking-believable.

"Five... four... three—"

"You win, dangit!"

"Two—"

"I quit, okay! Just tell me how to do it, already."

"One." Devil shook his head slowly, his jaw tight with the disappointment tensing every muscle. "What the hell was that, Ellie?"

When Ellie rolled her eyes and lifted her arms in question, Devil wanted to tangle her pretty golden hair in his fist and force her to see how serious he was. "What do you want from me? I did my best."

"Your *best?*" Devil scoffed and propped his hands on his hips. "You quit a minute in!"

Ellie huffed and brushed away a phantom loose hair, a habit Devil noticed when she started pinning her hair back.

"Why would I try hard if you're gonna tell me how to do it when the time's up? So... you know, go ahead and tell me how so I can do it during the real thing."

"*The real thing?*" Devil slammed his hand on the concrete counter, making her jump. "Goddamnit, Ellie, do you think all of this is a joke?"

Ellie straightened up and her eyes widened before she furrowed her brow and frowned. "No, of course not."

"Then what the fuck was that?"

"I told you! Why do I need to bust my tail if you're gonna tell me how I should've done it all along?"

Devil grunted and scrubbed his beard so roughly his skin hurt. "Fuck, Ellie. *Fight.* Have these past two months been completely pointless?"

"No!" It was only when Ellie yelled back at him that he realized how loud he'd gotten. "I've busted my butt for these training sessions and this *always* happens. You have me do something. I do it the dumb way, and then..." She pointed in one direction with her duct tape hands, before pointing in the other as she spoke. It seemed like she was trying to bring levity into the argument, but Devil wanted to turn her over his knee. "You swoop in and save me and teach me the right way. I just wanted to skip to that part."

Devil shook his head with his eyes to the ground. "You didn't want the right way. You wanted the *easy* way." He emptied a harsh breath from his lungs. "That's not what you should've been learning at all."

"No, I was saying I've learned a lot and—"

"Then save yourself, Ellie! Fucking *fight*. Don't give up when it gets hard and expect someone else to come 'swoop in and save you.'" He said the last with finger quotes and he knew he'd hit the mark when her face turned a pretty shade of crimson.

"I didn't mean it like that—"

"You know what? I think you did. I watched you give up a minute in. In a real situation, you might not even get that long. Every second counts. Three minutes was generous and you didn't even try for half that."

"I didn't know that was part of the test," Ellie objected while she hit her thighs with her duct-taped hands.

"It doesn't matter. You've heard the saying, 'practice like you're playing the game,' right?" At the downward jerk of her head, he mimicked the motion. "Well, the stuff I've been teaching you? What you've been training for? Isn't a game. It can be real life or death situations and goddamnit, what if something happens to you and you're not prepared because I went easy on you? And you just... give up? What if someone else's life is on the line? If this had been the real thing, you would've squandered the last few seconds you had to get yourself free. In these situations, you have to always be thinking. Always be on. You can't expect someone to come save you every time. It only takes once for that not to pan out and you're running out of lives, baby."

Ellie closed her eyes and rolled her shoulders back before opening them again. "Fine. I'll do it again."

Devil's eyebrows ticked up but he nodded at the resolve she carried. "I'll tell you how to get out of it, but you have to do it full force. Not the *easy* way. And once you're free, act out how you would escape from this room. Go through all the motions."

Ellie lowered her chin once in a nod and Devil sat down beside her to show her the steps.

"Stand up this time. You were on a good path getting on all fours, but keep going." He moved his body to do the same. "When you're up here, cross your feet the best you can. Even when you're duct-taped you should be able to do that within the tape. Once you've done that... fall straight down—" He dropped into a cross-legged sitting pose. "Like this."

"Crisscross applesauce?" The words were ridiculous and Devil couldn't keep from snorting even though Ellie's face was serious.

"I don't know what the fuck that is, but if it looks like this, then sure."

Ellie did a thumbs up with her hand and blew out a breath. "Okay... okay. I can do that. What about my arms?" She held up her taped arms.

"Those..." He leaned forward to grab her by the forearms. "You do like this—" He kept hold and shoved her hands into her stomach, stopping before he slammed her wrists into her belly. "... as hard as you can. Don't break speed and make sure your elbows are out. That's how you make sure you're getting the right angle to tear the tape."

Ellie's gaze was unfocused, like she was envisioning it in her mind. "Got it." Her shoulders raised and fell with her exhale of determination.

"Alright, try it again."

At Ellie's nod, Devil stood and backed away to give her room to sit her ass back on the floor. He held his watch up to monitor the time. "Three minutes. And... go."

This time, it seemed Ellie didn't focus on the tape as much as on her exit strategy. Single-minded conviction to fight through the moment creased her forehead as she maneuvered to get on all fours and struggled to stand up. Devil glanced at his watch.

"Two minutes, thirty seconds."

Instead of whining or signaling her frustration, she stuck her tongue out slightly between her lips in concentration. Her perseverance was hot as fuck and Devil's mouth watered as he watched her pink tongue gloss over her bottom lip. When her teeth dug into the plump flesh, he desperately wanted to tug it free.

Fuck, I'm being an asshole. I literally just yelled at her for not having her head in the game. Focus.

He folded his arms and leaned against the wall, creating some distance to keep from pouncing on her.

Ellie moved her feet around like Devil had taught her and all of a sudden she fell to the ground in "crisscross applesauce," whatever the fuck that was. The tape made a satisfying rip as it split down the middle.

Ellie squealed and looked up at Devil from the ground. "I did it!"

Her enthusiasm was contagious and Devil barely kept his composure. He dipped his chin in a gesture of approval but that was it. He couldn't distract her or slow her down. But all he wanted to do was lift her up from the ground and show her how sexy it was to see her overcome adversity. Instead, he did the responsible thing and glanced at his watch.

"Two minutes, Ellie. The bad guy's in the next room taking a piss. Gotta hurry."

"Ew." Ellie grimaced and he rolled his eyes.

"Come on, what're you gonna do? Stay in the moment. He's coming back any second." He glanced at his watch. "One hundred and five... to be exact."

"You got this," she whispered to herself and Devil tilted his head to analyze her. He'd noticed her do it before, talk to herself almost as if she was expecting someone to talk back, but fuck, whatever she needed to do to beat any assholes trying to steal her away again, he was all for it.

She stood back up on her unbound feet and pointed her elbows out to the side.

"One shot, El, it might be all you got," he encouraged her in a low voice. "The tape could roll up and make it harder to tear. Give it everything, baby."

Ellie watched her hands and nodded, breathing out.

"Forty-five seconds left."

Ellie suddenly slammed her wrists so hard against her stomach, Devil involuntarily reached out for her with concern, but she only gave a soft grunt. The tape ripped on the first try and Devil whooped. He leaped toward her to celebrate her escape, but Ellie whipped around and his open arms missed her. Before he could follow the direction she fled, he heard the rack slide on his Glock.

Ellie held the gun with precision and, but for her hand gripping the handle far from the trigger, she had perfect form as she raised the pistol at him. With a fucking smirk on her face.

Devil slowly lifted his hands out to the side, playing along. He'd been cleaning the gun before she arrived, so he knew it was empty. He also knew she'd racked the slide to double-check before she pointed it at him. When his gaze met those pleased, delicious caramel eyes, a smile of pride formed on his face, despite the fact he was essentially caught with his pants down.

It was interesting because, when he fucked, Devil thrived off control. Truth be told, Devil thrived off of control at all times, but seeing this woman play with the illusion of their power dynamic? Fuck, his cock was threatening to stand at full attention.

"What're you gonna do now, Ellie? You've got the bad guy in

your sights." He licked his lips, letting his thoughts linger in his gaze as he ate her up in his mind. "What would you do next?"

Ellie kept the gun steady and breathed deeply through her nose, blinking slowly before glancing around the room. "I would... I would've already checked all available exits. If there were other people with him, I'd have tried to keep tabs on them. But he's by himself, so... I would—"

"Act it out, Ellie. Follow through with it." Devil spoke low and she nodded before gulping. His hand twitched to feel the motion under his palm as it traveled down the column of her neck.

Without skipping a beat, Ellie kept the gun pointed at him and sidestepped one foot next to the other slowly, her back facing the wall as she traveled to the door. She curved her trajectory, keeping well within the safe zone as she passed him. Her breaths were calm, slow, like they'd practiced during her training. His chest filled with so much fucking pride, he nearly broke the moment again.

Finally, Ellie reached the door and tapped the knob. She paused before lowering the gun. Her lips curved up as she whispered, "I did it?"

Devil felt his cheeks widen in a smile of his own. "Yeah, baby, you did it. You fucking did it. You'd be free right now as long as—"

"—I ran like hell."

Devil burst out laughing. "Exactly, as long as you ran like hell."

Gun in hand, Ellie fist-pumped the air and waved them around. "YES! Heck yes! I did it! I did it! I really did it!"

Devil lowered his arms from their position of faux surrender, knowing this moment was bigger than just getting out of the tape. She laid the gun down on the counter and as she made her way toward him, he could see her courage and confidence building right before his eyes. He had no doubt she would bring that same energy in a crisis.

"You did angel, you—*oof*."

Ellie ran at him and leaped into his arms, encircling her long legs around his waist. Her lips crashed onto his and her taste was the cool water he'd been thirsting for during their thirty-one-day drought.

CHAPTER TWENTY-SEVEN

He'd been caught off guard by her throwing herself into his embrace, but goddamn if that girl wasn't made for him to hold. His arms wrapping around her body felt as natural as breathing.

Devil returned her kiss, teasing his tongue against hers until she pulled away from him. He tugged her back by her nape, but when he was met with some resistance, he immediately let go.

"Can we—um, can we do another one... before?" She looked down and he realized his hard cock was insistent against her clothed pussy. If they'd been naked, he could've sunk into her with one stroke.

Shit. I was wrong. She doesn't want it. I need to stop. She doesn't want this—

"No, don't look at me like that. I want... I want to try... another one, is all."

Relief she still wanted him coursed through his body. Devil grunted his agreement and eased her off of him, enjoying her shiver as her pussy grazed over his cock on the way down.

He cleared his throat and readjusted his sweatpants, securing his tip behind the drawstring. Still noticeable as fuck, but at least not obscene anymore. Even though he wanted to lick every inch of her body until she was wet enough for him to slide into her, if she wanted to learn more about how to save herself, he sure as fuck wasn't going to hinder that. He'd never forgive himself if he missed the opportunity to teach her something that would've saved her life.

The thought jolted him back to their purpose. "Alright, let's do it. What'd you have in mind?"

"Um... how about the h-handcuffs?" A strange look passed over her face. Her smile was innocent, but her eyes were wicked, confusing the hell out of him as he tried to silently figure out if she had a hidden agenda.

"Okay..." He went to the table and grabbed the cuffs, going straight into instructor mode. Anything to get his mind off of burying his cock inside Ellie's soaked pussy.

Fuck.

"So what you do with these... I'll go ahead and tell you because it's hard to figure this one out. Let me have your bobby pin." She tugged the pin from her ponytail and gave it to him. "So what you do..." He straightened the pin and held one of the closed titanium cuff loops, pointing to the shim and mechanism. "There're teeth that make the handcuff tighter, see? You wedge whatever straight, thin metal you have between these two to split the arm and the ratchets. One click is all you need. Any more and you could jam the pin inside, making it tighter, and much harder to escape. I'll teach you how to work around that problem one day but practicing would require you not to give a shit about pain and I don't what to put you through that."

He gave her the pin and locked the handcuffs around her wrists. "Here, you try now. I won't time you this first time. The duct tape was about speed. You wouldn't be able to do that in front of a kidnapper. But if your captor has you in cuffs, you could be working on it without them knowing."

Ellie hesitated with her head bent low and the silver rings around her wrists. Her breaths came at a quicker pace. "Um... what if... what if you had me in cuffs?"

A bolt of desire heated through his body, but he didn't want to assume what she was getting at again. "Uh... you're already in them—"

"No, I mean. What would *we* do... if *you* had me in cuffs?"

She raised her head and when he saw her molten caramel eyes hot with desire and that plump bottom lip being held hostage by her teeth, his breath hitched. All the blood in his head went straight to his cock and he grew light-headed with anticipation.

As soon as the feeling passed, he stroked down her cheek and spoke in a low voice. "I would have you at my mercy..." His thumb and forefinger caught her chin. He lifted it and bent to force her to look in his eyes. "But *you* would still be in control." Her breathing grew ragged as he continued. "I would spread those pretty thighs and bury my tongue in your sweet cunt to taste what I've been missing for thirty-one goddamn days. You're heaven in my mouth baby, and I would take you there with me in every stroke... Would that be something you would want?" At Ellie's nod, he growled and gripped her chin tighter. "You have to say it, angel."

Her warm, breathy sigh sent shivers across his skin. "Take me, Dev."

Devil scooped her up, with one arm propping her ass. He ducked his head between her cuffed arms as Ellie left small, wet kisses along his jaw. Her ponytail had loosened from the exercise and Devil wound his free hand up her spine to sink into her scalp until those long locks were freed. He pulled her away by the base of her neck, tangling the strands until they got caught between his fingers, like rays of sun peeking around shadows. With her neck in his grip, he bent her head to take her lips between his.

When her tongue devoured his, he growled into her mouth and turned, walking her to his bed a few steps away. With one arm tucking her lithe body against him, he crawled across the mattress and stroked his hand up against her skin in a fluid motion to lay her ass down first, followed by her back, and ending cradling her head to the pillow.

Devil started to back away, but she fucking bit his lip. He groaned as his cock surged, painful in its already fully-alert state. He tore his lip free and kissed her before grabbing her thighs with both hands to grind his length against the warmth between her legs. She broke away on a moan and he took the breath to duck out from underneath her handcuffed grasp.

"I need to feel you come, baby. Just remember, you're in control, okay?"

She whispered it back and at her dazed nod, he immediately tucked his fingers in the elastic of her leggings and slid them down over her lean hips and thighs, letting his fingertips drag against her soft skin and reveling in the goose bumps he left in his wake. As he rolled the fabric down, she lifted her waist and her round ass popped free from its confines. His cock surged against his sweatpants and he nearly came right then and there.

He took a steadying breath before continuing to unclothe her and dragged open-mouthed kisses down her bare skin until he tugged her legs free.

Devil kneeled between her legs and trailed his tongue as he traveled up. His hands glided behind the touch of his lips and every time Ellie made any sound of pleasure, he squeezed—hard —making her gasp.

She reached down with her handcuffed hands and tugged at his hair, pulling it by its roots. He had no idea how the fuck she knew exactly what he wanted—the act, the pressure—but god-fucking-damnit did he love when she added a little pain in her touch. Most of the time, if a woman touched him, he'd push her away like she was on fire. But Ellie? He wanted her touch to sear into his skin, branding him as hers and hers alone.

When he got to her mound, he nipped through her cotton panties to where he knew her pretty bud was hidden. Her cry electrified his skin down to his tip and he thrust against his comforter to alleviate the pressure.

"Dev—"

"Fuck, I love that you call me that." His fingers curled around the waistband of her panties, grazing the golden curls underneath, until she stopped him.

"No, wait—"

His hands nearly leaped from her body.

"No, I actually... I want you to... teach me something else." Her shy smile made his cock weep with precum, but his brain couldn't catch up.

"Teach you? *Now?*" He sat up on his knees to question her further, but she pulled his shirt so he had to catch himself with his hands on either side of her shoulders. Her bound hands tucked under his shirt and scratched down his abs, making him groan. Blunt nails ended on the waistline of his sweatpants and his cock jumped as she scratched the sensitive skin outlining his Adonis belt.

Now that he had an idea of what she had in mind, his voice was like sandpaper as he worked past the need to moisten his tongue with her arousal. "What is it you want to learn, angel?"

Ellie pulled at the string tying his sweatpants and cool air kissed his tip. A shudder rolled down his spine and he closed his eyes to soak in the sensation. The cold metal of the cuffs shocked his skin as her index finger swirled around the head of his aching cock.

"I want to take you in my mouth."

He'd expected her words to come out as a tentative whisper, but the conviction there opened his eyes to see a woman more confident than she'd been the entire time he'd known her.

"With the cuffs on? You sure?" *Please for the love of God, say yes.*

She nodded and bit her lip, pulling the string loose on his pants until the air told him she could fully see his length peek over the top of the gray fabric. "I want to... I want you to teach me what you like, Dev."

A groaned curse rolled out of his mouth in several syllables before he dove in to let his tongue dance against hers.

He snuck his arm behind her back and the other wrapped around her ass, pulling her up into his kiss until he flipped their positions. She landed straddled on him, but kept the kiss going without missing a beat. Her nails stabbed into his scalp and he loved that every time she bit his lip, she left a salving lick. Eventually she sat up and scratched her fingernails underneath his shirt, watching his reaction the entire time.

"You can do more than that on me, baby. I'm a fighter, I like a little pain with my pleasure." He winked and Ellie's eyes widened with... intrigue?

"I-I think I do, too."

Devil's breath caught in his chest. He held her hips down on his half-naked cock and bucked up into her heat, making sure to use a little force behind the thrust. She moaned even though he had to have bruised her inner thighs.

Fuck, if she likes pain... he couldn't think about it. One day he'd flirt with the line to see what she liked. But no fucking way was he going full tilt on her before she was ready.

Ellie bit her lip and maneuvered off his cock to kneel between his legs. Her fingers returned to his waistband and when she tugged him free, her sharp inhale was nothing short of satisfying. His thick length bobbed against his stomach and Ellie sat mesmerized.

Devil chuckled at her expression. "Get beside me." He tugged his pants off the rest of the way before grabbing the back of his shirt and pulling it off. "I want to make you moan around my cock while I fuck your mouth." Ellie's eyes widened but she did as she was told. "Good girl."

She bit her lip and Devil smiled with satisfaction. He'd noticed what those words did to her and fuck if he didn't love the accompanying blush dusting her skin every time he said them.

He tugged her lip from her teeth with his thumb. "Can't be doing that, baby." He smirked. "You'll bite your pretty lip off before I can feel it around my cock."

Ellie pinkened even more, but she kept him from chuckling when she stroked her fingers up his thighs, leaving the metal chain of the handcuffs trailing behind her. The titanium rolled over his cock, making him jump and hiss from the cold.

She encircled his length with both cuffed slender hands, leaving the tip bare. Her grip was soft, tentative, like she was awaiting instruction. He was about to tell her what he liked, but her nails bit into the skin just beneath his head. His hands desperately gripped the comforter with the urge to hold on to ride out the delicious pain, but his girl didn't let up. She stroked him slowly, going back and forth between a strong grip and a slight pinch from her nails, seemingly taking cues from the faces he couldn't help making.

Her hands left his shaft to help prop herself on the bed and she bent over his cock to lave the top. Devil fought against closing his eyes to feel it more intensely. He had other plans.

"Yes, keep doing that." He leaned up and she tried to sit up with him, but Devil smacked her ass and she yelped. "Nope, I said keep doing what you were doing." He didn't stop to take in her expression and instead reached his fingers to unzip her midriff hoodie while she slid her tongue around the head of his cock.

Thank fuck she's wearing her front zip bra.

"Don't stop, Ellie," he ordered her as he tugged the second zipper down. Her breasts fell out and he twisted a nipple until she moaned, vibrating around his cock.

"Goddamn, that feels good." With his hand around the breast closest to him, he kneaded the soft mound and circled its dusty rose tip into a peak. "I wish I had this in my mouth." He pinched her slightly and her eyes relaxed closed.

Her tight mouth slid down until his cock nudged the back of her throat. She was at a disadvantage needing to use both cuffed hands to hold herself up, so when Ellie tried to push past the resistance, Devil threaded his hands in her hair to pull her up. He was too long for her to deep throat, at least for the first time.

"It's okay, baby. The tip is fine."

He let go of her hair, but kept his hand on the back of her head. She returned to his cock and fucking *watched* him with her molten caramel eyes as she slid her lips down his length. Her tongue stroked the bottom of the head, sliding the sensitive skin there up with the suction and Devil groaned—loud. He felt the slight difference as she fought back a smile.

"Fuck, yes. That's it."

He closed his eyes and bucked slightly in and out of her mouth as she kept pace. There was a small *click* and suddenly, the grip changed when one of her hands joined her mouth.

Devil looked down in surprise to see her hand sliding up and down his cock underneath her mouth. "You got loose from the cuffs." He growled his approval as she tightened her lips around him and showed off the pin she'd kept somewhere the whole time. "That calls for a reward."

One brow raised but he didn't give her enough time to ask any questions as he sat up and palmed each hip. He picked her up and whipped her around so her panty-covered mound was positioned over his waiting mouth.

Air caressed his cock and he heard her yelp. "What the—"

Devil slapped her ass. "Keep going and you'll get your prize." He couldn't see her face, but she sucked him deep into her mouth again and he groaned into her panties.

With his index finger, he slid them to the side, revealing her pretty pink cunt. With one swipe of his tongue, he tasted her sweetness and moaned along with her in pleasure.

"Angel, you're like goddamn candy." Devil gripped a cheek with one hand and cut right to the chase, spreading her legs apart to swirl his tongue around her clit. He was seconds away from finishing and he needed to get her up to the same speed.

She grazed him lightly with her teeth and he bucked into her mouth. It wasn't enough to choke her, but when his tip went past the tight muscles in her throat and she didn't gag, he tried again, thrusting farther in. He cursed at the tightness strangling his tip, and he drove his tongue into her core, lapping at the arousal filling his mouth and striving to get her to come before he did.

She whined and matched his intensity, swallowing his head down as she took him. The vibration in her throat threatened ecstasy before he could get her hers.

"Ellie, I'm gonna come. You should get—baby... I—" He tried to get her attention so he didn't come before she was ready, but she kept bobbing up and down on his cock.

Deciding the best course of action was to get her distracted with an orgasm herself, Devil continued to hold her panties while he thrust a finger into her core. He feathered her G-spot while his tongue tapped her clit so fast it had to feel like he was pulsing against her. Ellie undulated over him, grinding her cunt into his face and goddamn was it sexy. She was already so fucking ready, Devil could feel small contractions as she tightened on his finger. He joined another finger with the first and increased his speed.

Ellie slipped and her lips met the base of his cock. Her legs trembled around his head and her pussy clamped down as she rode his fingers.

Ellie choking and swallowing him whole was too fucking much and Devil lost it. He closed his eyes and roared her name as pleasure cascaded out of him and into her wet mouth. She drank up his cum as he pistoned into her until he was spent.

He dropped his hips back to the bed and he lazily trailed his finger down her cunt as he caught his breath.

The wet heat left his cock. "Please, I can't. Oh God, Dev." She leaned away from him and he grabbed her thighs, pulling her back until he could suck her clit between his teeth one last time. His name erupted from her in a long moan and her thighs trembled as he drew out the last remnants of her orgasm. After, she collapsed onto his chest and he lifted her from her straddling position.

"Come here, angel."

Devil used his abs to sit straight and pull her sated body up by her upper arms to straddle him again, this time with her soaked panties against his semihard length. A sleepy grin took over her face.

"I love that smile." Despite his words, he kissed it away, forcing her mouth open with his tongue, not caring that he tasted himself. Fuck, it was hot knowing she took him in her mouth. He gripped the front of her neck and lifted her up to look into her eyes. "I want to give you that 'just fucked' look every day for as long as you'll let me."

Forever.

The thought flitted through his mind, but he quickly pushed it away.

"If it's like that every time, I wouldn't mind that at all." Her smile widened and he released her with a peck on her lips. She sighed before laying her cheek and half-naked body on his bare chest.

He was gone for her and he knew it. But she was only a freshman in college for fuck's sake. Cornering her into a serious relationship, assuming she'd even want one at nineteen, would make him one selfish son of a bitch.

As if she read his mind, she spoke softly against his chest. "You know... when we, um... when we have sex... ugh, sorry. I'm awkward." She slapped her hand over her eyes. He chuckled and peeled her fingers away from her face before she exhaled and continued. "It'll be my first time and, um... I'm on birth control. I don't want anything between us... if that's okay. I don't know what you wanna do with that information. Just thought I'd tell you."

Devil tamped down the sudden urge to roar and beat his chest like some testosterone-driven gorilla. It wasn't necessarily that he would be her first that made him apeshit, but the hope that he could have the privilege of being her *only.*

"I'm clean. I'd never risk anything with you, but if you're sure... it's your call." He cleared his throat. "We do this at your pace, El. You're in charge." Devil stroked her spine with both hands as she nodded. He felt her cheek lengthen as she yawned and he tugged her closer against him, enveloping her in his hold.

He wouldn't tell her, not yet anyway. But she was full of firsts for him, too. The first hand he could remember holding, the first time he'd given the reins over to a lover. His first relationship—if what they were doing was even a fucking relationship. A wave of shame passed through him as he realized they never did go on that date.

He was about to try to plan another one with her, but her breath was already slow and steady, a rhythm he could listen to for the rest of his life if she let him. He rubbed her back softly, more for himself than for her. He didn't want to wake her, but having her in his arms eased an ache in his soul he'd developed the first moment he saw her.

"So glad I found you, angel," he whispered against her golden hair.

"I love you, Dev." Her voice was so faint, he thought he'd imagined it, especially when the lazy cadence of her breaths never changed.

He wanted to say them back. The words itched to get out from the back of his throat. But that one last step to opening himself up after closing himself off for so long was a leap into a fucking canyon. After ten years, thinking emotional attachments were distractions was deeply ingrained in him. When he'd told Ellie after she'd passed out that he didn't want to be that way anymore, he'd meant it. But old habits die hard and he'd been convinced for too long that caring too much made him make mistakes that wound up hurting people.

Can't risk it until after tomorrow. I'll tell her after.

BlackStone had a big day the next day. He hoped to God Ellie was kept busy enough by classes the next day to not worry about what the Crew was up to. He needed her as far away from him as possible. Hopefully nothing bad would happen, but with a mission, you could never be too sure. And he needed as few distractions as possible.

Ellie was strong, but Devil sure as fuck wasn't strong enough to keep his head on straight if she was somehow involved. And if she knew they were crashing the scholarship party, there was no way she'd be willing to stay out of the thick of it. He understood though.

When you have skin in the game, it's hard not to want your pound of flesh.

CHAPTER TWENTY-EIGHT

Ellie extracted her Russian book from her backpack and tossed the bag on her apartment floor.

Professor Novikov had been in rare form that day, full of energy and refusing to speak at any normal pace in Russian. It was a miracle she'd passed last semester with her absences, and Ellie was embarrassed at how lost she'd already gotten in her schoolwork within the first two months of school. While she got healthier over the past month and a half, Ellie had thought she'd done a fair job catching up. But then Professor Novikov went on a million-word per minute Russian tangent. She'd been ashamed again until she realized Virginia's eyes had glazed over and she'd given up taking any notes—along with the rest of the class.

With a sigh, Ellie opened the book to teach herself what Professor Novikov had been too quick to explain but her mind kept going back to the night before, like it had all day.

Ellie had woken to cool cinnamon scented sheets. She'd basked in the comfort and feeling of security until she'd reached to the side, only to feel an even colder empty space.

She'd slept safe in Dev's arms last night after he'd brought her to yet another 'best orgasm of her life.' A cheeky grin widened Ellie's face and a sense of feminine pride warmed her all over as she thought about how she'd finally been able to return the favor. She bit her bottom lip and propped her chin with her elbow as she tried to focus on the Cyrillic alphabet allegedly written in sentences.

But it was no use. She'd been preoccupied all day, and knowing Dev might be in the room next to her was driving her crazy. Tilting her head toward his wall, she listened to see if she could hear him, but it was silent. The type of silence you only get when you're completely alone.

It'd been like that all day. Normally, Ellie and Dev texted back and forth throughout the day, but he'd been radio silent. That, and the fact he'd left her in his bed alone—hurt more than she wanted to admit.

Of course, it happened all the time. Sasha and Virginia both talked about it, not to mention survivors at Sasha Saves, and pretty much every TV show targeted to her demographic. For the first time she realized she was one of those girls that was surprised she might be getting ghosted.

Is that what he's doing? No... Dev wouldn't do that... right?

But was that how *all* women felt the morning after a hookup? She'd always watched or listened with an air of disdain. Judging the women for not expecting to be left. As if it was their fault the man they'd chosen was the type to leave before they woke up.

She shook her head. *So he didn't wake up with me. Big deal. I can't be sad about that. We haven't even talked about being together or had sex yet. Get a grip.*

Ellie groaned and collapsed her face into her hands.

Oh god. What if I am too innocent for him?

He'd said it plenty of times. Maybe it was her dang fault for not listening when what the man told her was obviously the truth. Who could blame her when the guy looked like that, though?

Ellie rolled her shoulders back and hopped off the stool, deciding in the moment she needed to go for a run. She already had the mysteries of body language and a man's silence filling her brain, retaining any other foreign languages was going to be impossible until she worked out the stress.

Clad in her normal athleisure wear, Ellie left her apartment, opting to get a snack from the residence floor kitchen before she went to the first floor and worked out on one of the treadmills in the gym.

On her walk to the communal kitchen, the halls were eerily quiet. Even though the residence floor of BlackStone was homey in a masculine, industrial way, the concrete and steel design made the silence so profound, it felt like she was the only one in the building. It even had a weight to it, like a hot lazy wind before a storm in the summertime.

When she reached the kitchen, Ellie grabbed two bacon and cheese egg bites from the fridge and popped them into the microwave. When the bites were warm enough, Ellie hopped on the same black concrete counter that was in every apartment kitchenette and scarfed the protein down.

When she was finished, she grabbed a banana and tucked it into the pocket on the side of her leggings. Pockets and leggings were truly gifts from God, and whoever combined them deserved their spot in Heaven. She didn't know who that genius was, but in the meantime, she'd thank Kate Hudson for the pair she was wearing.

While Ellie made her way down the halls to the center stairs, she felt the ridiculous urge to tiptoe. Giving in, she took the stairs slowly until she reached the first floor. She carefully pushed the door open and looked around. There were finally voices to the left of her as she emerged from the stairwell, and she helped the door close behind her without a sound. Tiptoeing around had been a weird impulse at first, but now that she knew she wasn't the only person left on the planet, she wanted to see if she could sneak up on some of the stealthiest men alive.

Ellie followed the voices to one of the rooms she'd never

visited. She and Dev had passed it a thousand times, but she hadn't thought to ask what it was.

A metal door, stronger looking than every other bulletproof one in the place, was cracked open and Ellie crept closer and pinned herself against the wall so she could surprise whoever was in the room. Getting the drop on any of the BlackStone Crew would be hilarious, so long as Hawk wasn't in there. If he was, she'd pass. The guy was too serious to function.

"—head into the hotel tonight for the scholarship party—"

All thoughts of playing a prank left her mind completely and she listened in on what Hawk was saying.

"—we'll be able to intercept the room before they can leave with the girls. From what we can tell, that big bastard from last year came in with a few full canvas bags early this morning."

"I've been in and out of there all day ever since we saw them arrive," Snake spoke up. "Under the guise of security and making sure we have every possible eye and ear we can in there. No one's been in or out of that room except the big guy and another one who looks like a minion. I'll be here but online with you guys tonight. Marco, you'll be there as an expected guest—"

"Yep. Like I said, I've made it to the Ashland elite apparently." Ellie vaguely recognized the prosecutor's voice, but identified with his sarcasm. "I'm sure it's a keep your enemies close situation and I sure as fuck plan on doing the same. I've got my contacts on speed dial when y'all are ready."

"Yeah, about those contacts..." Phoenix's drawl had a hint of annoyance. "Why are they sittin' this one out?"

There was a sigh before Marco spoke. "I'm frustrated too, but the feds can't send people in on a hunch. They're on call if you find concrete evidence of criminal activity."

"So basically we're gettin' stuck doin' all the dirty work?" Phoenix scoffed. "Typical."

"If we want this done right, we'll have to do it ourselves. What about you, Henry? You'll be there?" Hawk's question came out sounding more like a command.

"I'll be there too. Burgess has me scheduled for security, so I'll be hit or miss with helping y'all since I'll be where they post me."

"What's he been saying about all this?" Hawk asked.

"Um... well, we told y'all he's been kinda off lately..."

"It seems like it's getting worse." The prosecutor finished.

"Worse how?" Dev asked. His voice sounded harsh to her, maybe even angry.

"I don't know, man. He seems like. I don't know. Tweaky?"

"Like he's on drugs?" Dev's question was more of a statement, like he was expecting the answer.

"Yeah. I never noticed him doin' any or anything but he sure as hell is actin' like a crazy addict."

"The sheriff's been eyeing him, too," Marco offered.

"No shit, for real?" Henry's voice perked up. Ellie tilted her head at the door, surprised the officer knew less than the ADA.

"He told me yesterday he's thinking of pushing Burgess into early retirement. The investigator's been fucking up royally lately and is now missing whole damn shifts. From what the sheriff was saying, if it wasn't for government red tape, he'd have been fired a while ago."

"At least we weren't depending on him," Hawk's deep voice murmured.

There was a pause before Snake cleared his throat. "Right then. Hawk, you, Phoenix, and Devil will be at the hotel—"

"I still say I need to be there." Ellie's brother's growl interrupted, but sounded off for some reason. Still, a shock of apprehension over getting caught jolted her skin like static.

"We've been over this, Jaybird." The amount of power behind Hawk's cool reply was enough to make Ellie's knees weaken. "Jules was just put on bed rest. You didn't even want to leave her long enough to come to BlackStone for this meeting. You'll be distracted and you're needed if your fiancée goes into labor. Besides, you're recognizable. These bastards probably have their own personal version of 'Wanted' posters and the man they failed to frame has got to be number one."

Jason sighed. "Fine. Can you program the headset I've got at home so I can listen in?"

"That'll be easy," Snake confirmed.

"As long as you fuckin' charge them this time..." Phoenix's statement was uncharacteristically abrasive. "Can't have another Yemen."

"You know I fucking charged them then and I fucking charged them now. How many times do I have to tell you that? I think the question is, are you going to fucking wear yours this time, ass—"

"Enough." Hawk's reprimand quieted the room. "The party starts at seventeen hundred hours. We need to be ready to go well before then."

"Can, uh, can I get a headset? That might help me with y'all." Henry's tentative question was met with Snake's curse.

"Oh, fuck. Sorry, man. I don't have one for non-agents."

"Nora's gettin' one, right?" Henry reasoned.

Nora? Nora's in on this?

Ellie tried not to feel hurt the BlackStone Crew was depending on Nora and not her. Did they really think so little of Ellie that they couldn't trust her?

"She's a practicing agent today," Hawk replied. "Nora?"

"Hm?" Nora's voice was quiet, subdued.

"You'll be Phoenix's date, arriving with him twenty minutes into the party via taxi. Devil and I will arrive separately, park the van in the parking lot... here." A tapping sound punctuated Hawk's instruction.

"We'll be ready to go at fifteen hundred so we can gear up and take turns scoping out the hotel one final time before we attend the party," Hawk said.

"Ellie will be at BlackStone... she doesn't know anything, right?" her brother's low voice asked. "We need to make sure it stays that way."

Ellie's breath caught and she tiptoed closer to the cracked door. Whatever she wasn't supposed to know, she sure as heck was going to find out everything.

"I don't think she has a clue," Dev responded. "She hasn't talked about the party since I shut her down our first training session."

"Nora, you haven't talked to her about it?" Jason asked.

"No." Nora cleared her throat and spoke louder. "We talked yesterday, but we've been ships in the night at Sasha Saves. I haven't told her, but I think you should."

"I agree," Snake chimed in. "If she just went as recon, like a fake date or something, maybe someone or something there would jog her memory."

"That would be the worst thing for her," Jason argued. "We can figure shit out ourselves. You've already been through the entire damn list. If we don't know who's there by now, she definitely won't."

Snake sighed at Jason's response. "That's the invite list, though. And Naomi, Nora, and I have been over it, but we all know hit men and henchmen aren't 'cordially invited' to this shit. You know she'll hurt you left her out. At least let her know so she can be at Sasha Saves when we take the women there afterward. Don't you think she has a right to know?"

"She's too fragile still. She just fainted from overworking as a coping mechanism from all this shit." Jason's point made Ellie seethe. What the heck did he know? Ellie had been training daily, eating better, and going to classes and therapy. Heck, she'd even made a friend. He'd been holed up with Jules.

"That was over a month ago," Snake reasoned. "It seems like she's doing much better—"

"Exactly," Dev responded, and Ellie beamed. Finally, he was sticking up for her. She could maybe go as his date and point out if she saw anything or anyone familiar. She'd stay near the exits in case she needed to hightail it outta there for some reason. Or heck, she could even ride with the women to Sasha Saves and be someone they could trust.

The other women Ellie had been kidnapped with had been overwhelmed when they were rescued. Ellie had had the benefit of being able to trust the Crew right off the bat. The other women had a hard time, but maybe Ellie could help these survivors.

"She's been working hard and doing much better," Dev continued, and anticipation tingled in Ellie's fingers. "But I still don't want her anywhere near this shit. She couldn't handle knowing about this..."

Ellie clutched her chest as her heartbeat thrummed in her ears, muffling the rest of the conversation, which was just as well because she didn't want to hear anything else Dev had to say.

Did he really think she was still so incapable of defending herself? Still so weak she couldn't even handle knowing about the dumb party, let alone help do something about it? They didn't even think she was useful enough for recon, for crying out loud. What if she could recognize someone that they didn't? And Snake was right, she could at least be at Sasha Saves when they needed her.

Ellie's eyes pricked with tears and she shut them tight.

They didn't know the trauma these survivors had gone through. Ellie did. When she'd been saved by her brother's Crew, she was lucky enough to know immediately she was in good hands. But even after their rescue, when the drugs wore off, the other survivors wore looks of pure terror on their faces. They hadn't been able to trust that they were in safe hands, despite all the reassurances from their new saviors.

No, she didn't want that for these women. They needed her. She wanted to make sure they had an empathetic female face telling them they were finally free and safe whenever they were rescued.

Ellie turned, refusing to listen to anything else. Resolve filled her as she tiptoed up the stairwell and took her phone out of her pocket to text.

Hey, can you bring my dress to BlackStone HQ tonight? The one you went back and got me from the dress shop?

Virginia: Uh, sure. I have class rn. After? When do you need it?

Ellie looked at the clock on her phone. It was already fifteen 'til three. The party started at five and the BlackStone Crew was leaving the facility at any moment. She'd have to navigate around the BlackStone Crew when she got there, so right on time would be better. At this point they could be leaving any second to go scope out the hotel according to Hawk's instructions.

ASAP after your class, pls. Oh and do you mind giving me a ride?

Since Snake would still be at BlackStone when the Crew left, she'd have Virginia come by and change in the car. She didn't want to risk being seen in her dress on her way out so she'd have to make do in the car.

Virginia: What's the occasion?

Ellie cringed. Virginia was gonna flip, but there was no way around it. The girl would find out after she dropped her off at the McIntosh in her fancy cocktail dress. A vague answer was the best choice.

Going to a party.

Virginia: YAASSS QUEEN. Fking finally!!!!!

CHAPTER TWENTY-NINE

"It's like we mapped out." Hawk's voice came in tinny over Devil's headset as the BlackStone leader confirmed their recon. "Four exits, two leading outside, two to the hallway, and one door to a room I've seen multiple older men and a suspicious number of young women go into." Devil took a sip of the glass of whiskey he'd gotten for a prop.

"Saw that too," Phoenix answered. "So far Nora and I've only heard borin' ass bullshit about life goals with zero chance of pannin' out." Phoenix's uncharacteristic growl was low in their headset. "Oh, I gotta target by the south door. At least I think he's a target. Shit, for this party to be so hidden, they sure don't give two fucks about disguisin' their men."

"Their MO's all about hiding the party until the actual event. Then everything is in plain sight, I suspect to hide the real reason behind it," Snake murmured.

Devil glanced at the target closest to him. A big fucking son of a bitch in all black. "He's right though. They definitely stand out."

"You said there was a room people were going into?" Jaybird asked over the set.

"Yeah. My count is six men, each with a woman who looks about half his age on his arm," Hawk replied.

"Ellie said something about how she and Sasha were brought into what they called an interview room... maybe that's it?" Jaybird responded.

"Fuck, do you think one of us can get in there?" Devil asked.

"Interview room? Lemme see what Nora and I can do," Phoenix answered over the set. "I can act like a sleezy ol' bastard if I need to."

"That's an act?" Nora's quick quip made Devil smile behind his glass as he watched the couple head to the door in question where a balding linebacker type dressed in all black guarded the door.

"What're you doing Phoenix?" Hawk hissed. "We don't know what's going on in there."

"Gettin' us in, now shut up."

Devil had to hand it to the man, Phoenix was charming as fuck and Nora was a natural, smiling in a demure black cocktail dress and laughing at the jokes coming over the headset. Devil casually strode closer until he could hear them in person in case there was any trouble.

The bald guy's mouth was razor thin and his eyes bore into Phoenix completely unamused. Devil patted his chest for his gun holster, appearing to be searching for a handkerchief, but ready to have Phoenix's back.

But as if on cue, the guy tipped his head back to laugh and stepped aside. Phoenix and Nora sailed into the room, no sweat.

Snake laughed over the set. "Well, fuck. That was easy."

"Yeah... very easy..." Hawk's voice was a low rumble and Devil had to agree with the skepticism laced in it.

"There aren't too many people in here," Phoenix said casually over their headset. "It looks like there's some seatin' to our left, but I'm not feelin' too chatty right now, are you, dear? Let's head over near the outside exit about ten meters straight from the door—"

"Why are you narrating everything to me, Phoenix—"

"It's not for you, Nora, it's for *anyone* who might be interested."

"Oh, right. Sorry," Nora apologized before Devil heard the smallest whisper. "I'm nervous."

"It's alright," Phoenix answered back. "I think we can talk better here, just get close like you like me." There was a laugh before Phoenix spoke low. "Looks like some pretty big names in here. The ARShole firm showed up."

"Makes sense. We figured the Ascot, Rusnak, and Strickland law firm partners would be there. Marco said Strickland invited him," Snake offered. "Andrew Ascot's been laying low since his son was murdered last year by those 'drug dealers.'" Devil could hear the sarcasm in Snake's voice. To keep the human trafficking investigation under wraps, the media had been told Andy Ascot was killed in a drug deal gone wrong. Terrible cover for a man who'd saved Jaybird's life. "It's been impossible to catch them with their pants down."

"Fuck, man. Phrasing." Jaybird growled.

"You're right. Sorry. Poor word choice. But Phoenix, can you hear what they're saying?" Snake continued. "Who they're talking to? Who are they with? Do they have women with—"

"You're doing it again," Hawk quietly pointed out Snake's tendency to talk nonstop when he was nervous or excited. It was often helpful to hear a genius's stream of consciousness, but on missions, it was annoying as fuck.

"Shit. Sorry," Snake apologized but kept speaking at a quick pace. "But isn't it weird? You'd think after his son was fucking murdered last year after this party he'd keep a low profile."

"Sloppy is what it is," Devil responded and turned to mill around the ballroom.

"One of the big ass dudes in black just talked to Rusnak, but it looks like the big guy's been dismissed. Oh, wait, shit. Fuck. We got movement," Phoenix said over the com. "Strickland's leavin'. Looks like he's goin' out the service exit."

"Follow him, Phoenix," Hawk ordered.

"On it—Oh, wait, shit, what about Nora?"

"Naomi is on her way to come pick Nora up to head to Sasha Saves. We only needed her as a decoy," Snake answered.

"But what do I do until then while Phoenix goes to follow him? I don't want to be left alone, not here."

"It feels like something's about to go down." Hawk was thinking so loudly, Devil could almost hear him tapping his lips. "Phoenix? Escort Nora to the front exit so she can leave with Naomi. Devil, see if you can find Strickland. You're closest. That hallway should be connected to the one lining the entire ballroom. Follow him, but don't blow your cover. Snake, you got him on cameras?"

"I-I don't yet. But I'm sure I will, just... hold... on... and... there you are, motherfucker. Yeah, he's entered the main hallway. Looks like he's heading to the elevator. Devil, when you exit the service hallway, you cross the main hall and the stairs are directly in front of you. Hey, do you guys think that's how they take the women from the party to the room? From the service hallway straight up the stairs?"

Devil didn't respond but kept his focus down the small corridor with its plain white tiling and bright lights. It didn't make sense they'd use such a well-lit hallway, until Devil realized he didn't pass a single soul on his way out. If the service hallways weren't monitored, it'd be a piece of cake taking the women up the stairs.

"Where are you, Devil, I don't see you on any of my cameras."

"Still taking that service hallway."

"Copy," Snake answered. "Should lead you right to the exit on the south hall. From there you'll go up the two flights of stairs to room 307."

"Got it," Devil answered, but before he turned, he noticed a slender woman with golden hair enter from the exit.

"Ellie?" The angel turned his way and her normally tan skin paled to a sickly white.

"What the fuck, Ellie's there?" Jaybird growled from the other end.

"Oh, um. Hi, Dev." She brought her hand up at an awkward level and gave a small wave.

Devil blinked back at her to confirm she was really standing in front of him. His jaw ticked with anger and every muscle in his body tensed.

"Ellie, what the—" Devil approached her only to hear footsteps on the carpeted main hallway. He grabbed her by her upper arm and snuck her back into the service hallway, suspecting it was Strickland.

"What the fuck's Ellie doing there, Devil? I thought we agreed she'd stay out of this." Jaybird demanded.

"Believe me, I did, too." He brought his finger up to the small button on his clear earpiece and spoke before he pressed it. "Going offline, guys. Call me if you need me ASAP."

"Devil, don't you dare turn your headset off," Jaybird yelled.

"You getting emotional is exactly why I'm turning this thing off. I'll handle it."

"I'm still heading up there, with or without you, Devil," Hawk said. "Deal with Ellie and make it fast."

"I think we have some time. Looks like Strickland's making friends in the hallway before he goes up there. Besides, it might be good to catch him with his pants down."

"*Dude...*" Jaybird groaned.

"Sorry." Snake's voice came out apologetic.

Devil pressed the button on his earpiece, silencing Jaybird's voice before an employee approached them in the hallway.

"Um, excuse me, sir. Y'all can't be down here. No guests allowed."

Devil grunted, not wanting to give any energy to the waiter. Checking that the coast was clear, Devil tugged Ellie by the arm to the nearest alcove and tucked them in.

Ellie tried to pull her arm from his grasp, but he held it tight, afraid she'd get away.

"Dev, what're you doing? Let me go."

"Ellie, what the fuck are you doing here?" Devil hissed and peered out of the alcove before speaking to her in a hushed—but firm—tone. "You could ruin this whole mission."

"Dev, I need to be here." Determination set in the scrunched and crinkled lines in Ellie's forehead and frown. "You might not think I can handle it, but I deserve to help and I know how to defend myself."

Devil's heart raced painfully at the thought of her being involved in any of this shit and his chest rumbled with his frustrated groan. "This is exactly why I didn't want you to know about this party, Ellie. Goddamnit." He lifted his hands and scrubbed his beard and face. "You have to leave, now."

"No, if there are survivors here, they need me. I can help!"

"The fuck you can, Ellie. *I* can't have you here. You have to go."

"No!" The little minx punctuated her yell with one gold heel slamming into the carpet.

"Did you literally stomp your foot? God, Ellie, come on—"

Someone passed by the alcove and Devil turned with his arm up the wall, cornering Ellie in the alcove, and pushing her close up so they looked like lovers in a tryst rather than a spat.

Unbidden, the realization her breasts were flush up against his chest came through his mind. When Ellie shivered against him, he noticed his thumb was drawing circles on the bare skin of her shoulder. Her trembling against him reminded him of a very different tremor he'd felt less than twenty-four hours ago. Her legs wrapped around his face. Her sweet taste on his tongue.

He closed his eyes to gather focus.

When he opened them again to reprimand Ellie, heat was in hers. She was obviously feeling what he was and it had to stop immediately, but goddamn did she feel good against his body. Unable to control himself, he brought his head down low, brushing his lips against hers and moved his hand to stroke the bare skin of her collarbone. She looked fucking amazing in her green form-fitting dress.

"Fuck, Ellie, if we were anywhere else, I'd—"

"What? What would you do?"

Helpless to the adrenaline coursing through him and the sudden spike of fear for Ellie's safety, Devil couldn't resist sucking her lip between his, reveling in her body melting against him. Her legs had gone lax, and it seemed that but for his grip on her lower neck, she'd be a puddle at his feet. He ground his cock into the V between her legs and tightened his grip against the sides of her neck, completely at his mercy and trusting him.

An elevator dinged and Devil cocked his head to listen to two men in the main hallway.

"Going upstairs already, Mitchell?"

Devil bristled at the laughter that followed as he realized one of the men was his target.

"Yes! I've gotten word—excuse you, sir! Hey! Stop! I'll be contacting your boss! Good Lord, Andrew, the manners on people. Anyway, I'll be back down to the soiree shortly. I've been told we have some *fruit* waiting upstairs and I'd like to get that first little taste."

The other man barked a laugh before replying, "Don't have too much fun without me!"

Devil could hear the elevator doors close but not before his target's snickering made the hair on the back of his neck stand on end.

He returned his attention to Ellie only to find her golden skin now a sickly pale as she pointed behind him.

"What is it? Angel, what's wrong?"

"Th-that's him, Dev."

At the terror in her voice, Devil spun around, using his body to shield Ellie behind him, but there was no one there. He positioned himself to see Ellie out of his periphery. "Who? I don't see anyone."

Ellie's fingernails dug into Devil's forearm. "No, I recognized his voice... the one going up the elevator. Th-that was the man who... who—" She swallowed. "Sasha—" She choked out the name and understanding washed over him in an icy wave as he turned and tugged her in a tight embrace.

"Fuck, I'm gonna fucking kill him."

"No, Dev, you can't." She pushed away. "It's bigger than him. He knows who's behind all this. He has to. Just figure out a way to turn him in. It's the only way to stop everything. Promise me, Dev. I can't have another death on my conscience, not even his." He paused, still unconvinced until her caramel eyes pled with him. "Sasha didn't get any justice, but she believed in fate. Don't take this into your own hands. Let justice and fate decide what happens to him."

Fuck, she was *begging* him. He nodded once, still holding at bay the fury in his chest. It wasn't like him to get emotionally involved, but where Ellie was concerned, he was a live wire.

"I'll do my best not to kill him, that's all I can promise you—"

"But Dev—"

"Angel, do you trust me?"

Ellie nodded her confidence without hesitation. Devil tried not to let the gesture go to his head, but there was no hope for his heart. He'd been drowning in the silence of detachment for so long, her faith burned in his chest, making him feel like he'd just taken his first deep breath.

"Good." He coughed to clear his throat of emotion, but his voice still hitched when he spoke. "You have to leave. I can't be thinking about you when I'm trying to focus on the mission."

His phone buzzed and he cursed before releasing her and getting his phone.

Snake: We hear fucked-up noises from 307. Get up there NOW.

Devil shoved his phone into his pocket and grabbed his gun. "Leave, Ellie. You have to get out of here right now."

"No, I can help! I already did!"

Anger pierced through reason like a hot poker, and words he didn't believe forced their way out of his chest. "Christ, Ellie, leave! I can't have you fucking up and getting yourself kidnapped again on my conscience."

Ellie recoiled like he'd struck her. "God, Devil, that's awful." Her face crumpled, but he couldn't stay there. On one level, he knew he'd fucked up everything, but his logical side told him it was too late and he had to fucking go.

He shook his head, hating himself, but hoping she'd listen. "There are victims to rescue, Ellie. I can't worry about saving your hurt feelings, too."

With that, he turned out the hallway and ducked into the adjacent stairwell across from the alcove. He hopped the steps two at a time on silent feet until he reached the top. He opened the door slowly and quietly, only to be greeted by the barrel of a gun.

CHAPTER THIRTY

Neal paced to calm his nerves instead of leaning against the wall. He'd already attempted that once, but his blood was crawling underneath his skin and adding even the slightest bit of pressure almost made him lose his shit.

Music from the ballroom blasted in his ears even from his position farther down the hall, but he tried to focus past his headache. It was imperative he keep his cool for as long as he could while he monitored the lobby entrance to the McIntosh Ambrosia Room.

He was looking for a Russian, but he had to pretend like he was running security. He was supposed to be off duty, but no civilian would question him while he was in his uniform, right? He was an officer of the law, they'd expect him to be part of the security to protect the people inside the hotel.

"They don't know you can't protect anyone."

The biting judgment in Cici's voice tasted like acid in his mouth. She knew he'd come to the conclusion that if the Russians didn't pull through this time, he'd have to resort to helping them again before striking back. He needed to get them more women... just once, so they'd have to thank him somehow.

"It's not like that Cici. Just this one last job and they'll give me more medicine. You know I can't go without my medicine."

It'd become nearly impossible to go a single moment without craving the newest poison he'd resorted to feeding into his skin.

"You've always been weak. It was alcohol then. Drugs now. Your vices are gonna kill you."

"No... no. It'll help. Just one more hit and I'll get well. I-I'll go to rehab this time. I swear."

You didn't get help then. What makes you think you will now? If you hadn't been so selfish, I would still be alive.

"It's different this time, Cees. It's different."

"Your fucked-up decisions are going to get someone killed again."

The words were in Cici's voice, but they sounded wrong and loud in his head, halting his racing thoughts. Neal stopped to look around to see if anyone else had heard her. There were men and a few women in dressy clothes milling in front of the ballroom entrance. Drinking. Laughing.

Were they laughing at him? No. But the couple heading straight toward him were looking at him. No, *staring*. They wouldn't take their eyes off of him. They must've heard Cici.

Could they tell how much he'd fucked everything up? Anyone who heard the hate in her voice had to know he'd ignored her. Fought against her love for him until it was broken and twisted into brambles that scratched at his heart every time he breathed.

If he'd fought *for* her, instead of against, they could've fought her sickness. Together. But she gave in.

No. She ran away.

The afterlife had seemed like a better alternative than fighting the cancer killing her slowly. The depression had set in long before the cancer, but the pills she took—all at once—those were quick. Using his favorite poison to wash them down her throat was poetic justice as she swallowed the pills that drug her to her grave.

Neal hadn't even known she still had a prescription for

Xanax, or that she'd stockpiled it over the years as a nurse. Her general practitioner hadn't either, considering how many pills had kept Neal afloat before he resorted to drug busts and Russians.

He thought she'd gotten over the anxiety she'd developed a few years into their marriage, but he hadn't paid enough attention. Cici might've wanted help with her mental health in the beginning, but in the end, she'd refused to acknowledge her depression until its hooks were embedded in her, dragging her down deep until she drowned.

"You still don't get it... I was tryin' to get away from you."

She spat out her words.

"Shh, be quiet Cees. They'll hear you."

He ducked into an alcove in the hall, behind a tree, willing his body to stay still as he closed his eyes and collected his breath, hoping no one heard her.

"Burgess, what the fuck are you doin' here?"

Neal snapped his head up and attempted to calm the instant rage that sliced through him when he saw his boss.

"Sheriff, what're you doin' here?"

"I asked *you*. I'm the one here monitorin' security for the Ashland elite scholarship party."

"I-I'm here for that, too." As soon as he said it, he cringed, knowing what was coming.

"I told you to take time off, Burgess. You're obviously" — Sheriff Motts waved his hand out at Neal— "unwell. Besides, after you fucked up so royally last year? These people would never vote me back in office if I had you run security on this event."

"Sir, I—"

"No, you need to leave. Now. Consider this an *order* for you to take some paid leave for the foreseeable future."

Neal's face flushed with embarrassment.

"He can tell you're sick. He can tell you need your medication. Just leave. Or wait in your car until the Russians need you."

Neal nodded at Cici's whispered suggestion. "I'll do that."

"Good. Take that time off seriously, Neal. I'm worried about you."

Sheriff slapped his hand on Neal's shoulder, stabbing little needles into his skin. But he at least had the wherewithal to know he couldn't sucker punch his boss, so he shoved his hands in his pockets and grunted instead.

"Yes, sir." Head bowed, Neal marched past the sheriff down the end of the hall, bumping into yet another pompous prick on his way to the hotel exit. Ignoring the reprimands, whispers, and chatter droning on around him, Neal continued toward the exit to the alleyway where he'd parked his vehicle.

When he was finally outside and in front of his patrol car, he pulled his phone from his pocket. Now out of earshot, he pressed the button on his chest and called the Russian as he paced in front of his vehicle.

"What do you want?" The low gruff voice on the other end irritated Neal's eardrums, and he tried not to focus on the delayed echo of the small orchestra in the ballroom.

"I've been waitin' for one of your men, to get the stuff for the information I gave you, but there's been a problem—" He didn't want to tell the Russian why he was leaving. That'd be humiliating, and there was no way he'd get his medicine if the Russian thought he was a liability like the sheriff did. "I have to step out for a little while—"

"For the last time, I do not give a fuck what you do. I have to go—"

"But the-the bag... one of your goons is supposed to get me a bag. I did everything you asked. You got your women in the room—"

"Neal, shut the fuck up—"

"—is it because I didn't get you more? I-I can get you more." He cringed at the thought but it had to be done. "You have this p-party tonight. But I can get you more women, Mr. Rusnak—"

"Do not ever use my name." The rushed whisper hissed

through the phone and Neal bit his cheek so hard at his slipup, he tasted metal. "Neal, if you do not shut the fuck up I will come find you and personally rip your tongue out of your head." Neal swallowed at the gory vision in his head.

But he could get on their good side again, if he got them more women. That'd be good. They'd probably supply him for life. Like they'd promised once before. He wouldn't even need rehab then.

There was a sigh on the other end before the Russian continued. "If you go home like a good little soldier... I will have Vlad drop something off for you."

Neal nodded at a speed that felt like his head was going to bobble off. "Yes, sir. I'll go right home." The Russian hung up and Neal pressed the button on his chest again before pocketing his phone.

Easy enough. He just had to go home.

But was that really all they wanted him to do? Was this actually a test? If he followed their orders blindly, would they come through? Last year when they'd framed Jason Stone, Neal had been kept out of the loop and only on a need-to-know basis. Neal had trusted them without question as they'd fed him lies about Stone being the perp he'd wanted. Turns out, Neal and Stone had both been easy scapegoats to ensure the Russian could get off scot-free.

Sheriff was right about last year. When Neal realized he'd been taken for a fool, and that his other employers had been funneling women in and out of his county right under his nose, he spiraled. Taken more pills than he ever had before.

The operation he'd signed on for was never supposed to go that route. Just drugs. Last year he'd realized it didn't stop there. Now he was too wrapped up in it all to stop anything. Somewhere deep in his mind, he knew selling his soul for his next hit was gonna kill him one way or another. But if he was going to go up in flames, he was going to take every goddamn one of those demons down with him.

Until then, he would do whatever he had to do to stay alive. And goddamnit, he needed his medicine. He was losing himself every second he suffered without it.

"You lost yourself a long, long time ago, Neal."

"Shut up, Cici." He growled. He had to think of something to get the Russians back on his side. First, he needed to go home so Vlad would drop off what he needed.

He kicked the tire of his patrol vehicle. A glimpse of gold shined in his periphery, stopping him in his tracks. It took him a second to register who the young woman was, staring at her phone, until the glow of her cell phone lit her face in the waning evening light.

It was the same woman who could single-handedly take him down. The one the Russians might still be interested in. His ticket to getting back in their good graces. He realized what he had to do and rested his hand on the butt of his gun.

"Hello, Miss Stone."

CHAPTER THIRTY-ONE

"Fuck man, I almost offed you." Hawk lowered the gun but quickly shifted back to join Phoenix in front of room 307. Not having time to worry he'd almost had a GSW to the head, Devil pulled his gun from its shoulder holster and followed Hawk's lead, getting on the other side of the door across from him. They usually cleared rooms with a four-man team, but three would have to do.

He tuned into the yelling on the other side. The sound of flesh meeting flesh was followed by a muffled scream.

"Gotta go, Snake," Hawk whispered and Dev turned his earpiece on again to hear the reply.

"I can't override the system again, someone's locked the door back—"

Devil stepped out from his post beside the door and kicked left of the doorknob. He ducked low for balance and below normal aiming height. The door swung open and hit the opposing wall.

"One, hallway!" Devil shouted and Hawk pivoted around the door into the room and ran at the man Devil had indicated. Screams filled Devil's eardrums. Hawk pushed the tall man in black against the wall and shouted as Phoenix followed suit as their number two.

"One, left corner!"

Hawk's yell was Phoenix's command. Phoenix followed the directive and held his gun steady at the only other man in Devil's vision. The bathroom door was ajar, revealing another unclear sector Devil needed to check before he continued to clear the remainder of the corner-fed room.

Phoenix went to corner target two while Devil pushed open the bathroom door. The door hit something on the other side and Devil peered in to find women piled on the floor, discarded like rags.

Turning off his medic side, he detected no immediate threat and backed away before taking measured steps to the remaining uncleared sector. Pushing past Hawk and pinning his foot for a low, wide, balanced pivot to face the threat. Devil turned the corner and raised his gun at a familiar shirtless man. The man raised his arms in surrender. A woman on the bed scrambled to the headboard while holding her face on the bed.

"On your knees! On your knees!" Devil yelled and the man backed into the nightstand before collapsing to his knees. "Hands up! Hands where I can see them, asshole!"

The nearly naked woman's eyes had the glazed look of someone high on drugs. Her body struggled to follow Devil's orders while strangled screams and weak cries escaped her.

Devil scanned the rest of the corner-fed room and found no other threats. He kept his Glock on the man and took in the lack of movement at his back, indicating Hawk and Phoenix had their targets secured.

"Thank God you're here." Devil pivoted to the blubbering man kneeling on the floor. "I-I've been kidnapped! I-I'm Mitchell—"

"Shut the fuck up, Strickland. I know who you are. Stay on your knees, hands behind your head."

Strickland began to make moves as if he was going to stand. "B-but I told you, I've been kidnapped—"

Devil kicked him in the chest so his ass landed harshly back onto his calves. Outrage was written all over his face.

"What the—"

"I said, 'hands behind your head.' You don't wanna test me. Only the idea of you rotting in a jail cell forever is keeping me from shooting you in the head right now."

Mitchell narrowed his eyes and watched Devil before lifting his hands behind his head, seeming to take in the reality of his situation in the same moment. His face twisted in resignation as he slumped against the nightstand.

So weak. He hadn't even fought back. "What a little bitch," Devil muttered.

Devil heard movement behind him. He maintained the wall at his back and the rest of him was poised for an attack, while aiming at Strickland's head.

Phoenix dragged his unconscious target by the scruff of his neck to the opposite side of the bed. Devil had missed when Phoenix knocked his man out, but it made sense to secure the safety of the room. Hawk emerged from the room's short hallway, leading his target at gunpoint to the diagonal corner of the room before commanding him to get in the same position as Strickland.

"Snake, targets have been subdued," Hawk informed the rest of the team. "We're gonna need to make that call."

"Copy." After another moment, Snake spoke again. "Got 'em en route."

"Good," Devil responded. If the feds were on their way, they only had a few minutes more of complete control of this situation.

He glanced at the dark-haired woman on the bed, trying to sit up. Her movements were slow and erratic as she tried to stretch the T-shirt over her bare legs. Her left cheekbone was busted and spilling a steady stream of blood.

"Who gave you that?" Devil asked and watched as the girl's eyes flitted around the room, probably unsure of who the bad guy was in the situation.

Hawk's voice was low and menacing as he spoke to his target. "Who touched her?"

Devil's eyes cut to Strickland's look of panic on his face.

"I did not." The heavy Russian accent came from Hawk's corner.

"Can't ask my guy." Phoenix shrugged, indicating his still passed out conquest with the muzzle of his gun.

"Guess that leaves you." Devil donned his mask of detachment and addressed Strickland. "Show me your hand."

"I-I am, they're behind my head—"

"Right hand. Palm down, then back to your head."

Strickland glanced at the man on the other end of Hawk's gun.

Phoenix scoffed. "He ain't gonna save ya, coward. Do as the man said."

Strickland slowly followed Devil's command, showing the corresponding split knuckle Devil had expected on Strickland's doughy middle finger.

Devil glanced again at Phoenix and Hawk, both of whom had their guns and eyes half on their targets and half on him. He bent down to Strickland's eye level and pointed at him with the muzzle of his Glock. "You know, I heard something about you."

Strickland gulped, his terrified eyes staring between Devil and the weapon.

"This isn't the first time you've done this." Devil tilted his head at the bed before caressing Strickland's cheek with the muzzle of his gun. "Is it?"

Hawk and Phoenix cursed. Sweat puckered from Strickland's blanched forehead.

"Thought so. See, I wanna kill you. I do. It would be a motherfucking pleasure to wipe your pathetic ass off the face of this planet. But there's a woman I love who's a fucking *angel*. And she asked me to spare your life."

Strickland relaxed a fraction, maddening Devil even further. How dare this murderer get a breath of peace when he strangled it from innocents?

Devil stood and aimed for the dead center of Strickland's chest. Just below his evil heart.

"Too bad for you, I'm the devil."

Boom.

CHAPTER THIRTY-TWO

"There are victims to rescue, Ellie. I can't worry about saving your hurt feelings too."

Dev's words shuddered through her but she couldn't shake them. He was right and she freaking knew it. She could help and she already had. But believing she was the only one who could help was ridiculous when trained professionals were involved. She was trained but no professional. She'd never thought about being a liability to the team.

The memory of the panicked faces of her fellow survivors had been the driving force behind her stupid decision to go to the party. She'd been consumed by her need to help these new survivors as soon as they needed her. Pulling Dev's focus away from saving them was the exact opposite of what she'd wanted. But she'd done exactly that.

Ellie breathed in an even rhythm to manage the adrenaline and guilt burning through her veins. She'd had a myriad of emotions in the five minutes she and Dev spoke. Lust, fear, anxiety, terror... mostly the last three, but the lust on top of it was very confusing and none of it was helpful.

The whole thing was a bust. She'd already gotten caught and

she'd only been at the party for a few minutes. And, to top it all off, she'd made her friend mad.

When Virginia showed up with Ellie's dress, Virginia had been in one, too. While Ellie changed en route, she'd argued with Virginia about crashing the party. The poor girl had believed Ellie's text was an invitation. When she'd dropped Ellie off, Virginia had huffed and puffed reasons as to why she should go with Ellie, until Ellie slammed the door shut. Her stomach had twisted with guilt as she watched Virginia peel through the back parking lot.

She'll get over it... hopefully.

Ellie didn't want Virginia anywhere near the party Ellie had been kidnapped from. If being mean to Virginia saved a life but lost a friendship, that was a sacrifice Ellie was willing to make. She wouldn't go through losing someone again.

She'd meant what she'd said about Strickland. Ellie couldn't have someone else's death on her conscience. Not even the man who murdered her best friend. It was better to have kick ass lawyers like Jules keep him in jail forever instead.

Ellie smoothed her hair back out of habit, only to remember it was pinned up. Still, the gesture was soothing in its ritual. After finding her bearings, Ellie stepped from the alcove and rolled her shoulders back. It was time she faced facts. She'd thought she could help, but if she were honest with herself, she was more a liability than a lifeline.

Ellie sighed and turned to the exit, only to bump into someone coming out of what looked like a storage room.

"Oh, I'm so sorry, I—Henry?"

Officer Henry Brown gave a forced laugh and nodded to someone behind her as he balanced her.

"Whoa, hey Ellie. I'm, uh, workin' security for the function."

"Oh." Ellie scrunched her eyes, trying to hide the fact she already knew. "Where's your uniform?" It was odd to see him dressed in a black suit. She'd only ever seen him in his uniform.

"Ya like?" He smoothed down his tie before looking back at

her and smiling, winking his dimple at her. "They didn't want us wearin' our dress blues. Probably to avoid making the guests nervous."

"Oh, right." Ellie nodded. "Makes sense, I guess."

"What're you doin' here? I thought your brother didn't want you to come."

Ellie felt her cheeks redden. It'd been embarrassing that her brother still treated her like a child, but it was mortifying that now she'd earned it with her poor decision to crash the party.

"I, uh. I forgot," she explained lamely. "I was just leavin'." She pointed to the glass door behind Henry and shuffled around him.

He moved and laughed, letting her pass by. "I won't tell Jason I saw you if you won't." He put his finger up to his lips and smiled.

Ellie cocked her head to the side and forced a laugh, not really sure what he meant, but deciding to play along. "It's too late for me, I think. I saw Dev, so I'm sure Jason already knows."

"Ah, well too bad. Sucks you might get in trouble. See ya, Ellie." He waved to her and turned down a small, brightly lit hallway.

Ellie waved back and leaned against the silver bar on the door to go outside. She pulled her phone out of Virginia's borrowed clutch to call her to come take Ellie back to Black-Stone. V was going to flip. Ellie would make it up to her, though. Probably by agreeing to go shopping on demand at Virginia's every whim, but Ellie had earned the punishment.

Can you come pick me up? Same alley you dropped me off in? I'm ready to go.

Va: WTF? Really? I was just starting to have fun :(

'Just starting to have fun'? What the heck does that—

"Hello, Miss Stone."

A memory of that smoker's voice clawed against Ellie's brain, and she dropped her phone to the ground in shock.

She bent down to pick the phone up before realizing she should've left it, but on her rise up, she met the man's eye.

It was him. The man from the park. The investigator on Sasha's case. Even though she'd thought the man's voice at the park seemed familiar, she hadn't seen the investigator in a year and had never put the two together. He'd lost weight over the year, and his cheeks were sunken in while his sweaty skin was a sickly shade of yellow. The two sides of Investigator Burgess collided in her mind, confusing her to the point of indecision.

The investigator *tsked*, snapping her out of her assessment, and shook his head. "Oh, so you do remember me? Not good, I'm afraid. Not good at all."

The threat in his voice was clear and fear skyrocketed Ellie's pulse, making her dizzy enough that the world faded at the edges.

Run. Hide. Fight. First priority is escape.

Dev's mantra settled her and she glanced around after taking a breath, her thoughts racing over possible exits. It was an alley behind the hotel leading to nothing but open space and parking lots on either side of the building. The only thing big enough to hide behind was the dumpster directly to her right. Her only option was the exit behind her.

"Whatcha doin' there, girlie? You ain't got nowhere to go. We're gonna figure this out, right here, right now."

"O-okay, I'm here. Wh-whatcha wanna talk about?" Ellie slowly backpedaled to the hotel door. If she was around people, he couldn't do anything to her. It was a short-term plan, but it was the best she had in the seconds she'd been brainstorming.

Ellie tried to blindly swipe numbers over her phone to unlock it and call Dev. But the screen was cracked and a tiny glass shard pricked her finger. Would telling the phone to call Dev work? It was worth a shot.

She watched the investigator as she thought, but his eyes had glazed over.

Is he paying attention anymore? Maybe I should run for it...

He was muttering under his breath faster than she could attempt to read his lips. Actually, now that she thought about it, his mouth had been moving constantly since she'd seen him. Ellie was watching so intently, trying to figure the investigator out, that she didn't realize his hand was on the butt of his gun until it was too late.

It only takes a second for a pro to take his gun out of his holster.

She risked turning her head to see how far away she was from the door. Just enough.

Ellie turned and ran on her toes, praying her pretty gold heels wouldn't literally get her killed. Her dress tightened around her knees but she used quick steps to get to the door. She was about to open it when gunshots reverberated in the alley. One sounded off in the distance, but the other was close. She would've wondered if he intentionally tried to miss her, if the wall beside the door didn't also have a new bullet hole in it.

"Try'na leave? Nope. Can't let you do that. And there's five more where that came from."

Five? Revolvers have six. Who else is shooting?

The door in front of her opened wide and Ellie tensed to run through it, but a beautiful blonde in pink chiffon crashed into her. Ellie steadied her roommate by the shoulders so neither of them would fall.

"Virginia! What are you doin' here? We have to—"

"Holy shit, what was that?" Virginia interrupted her and did a three-sixty. Ellie watched with a shock of panic as the door shut behind her friend. "The ballroom was crazy loud, but I could've sworn I heard a gun—um, what the hell is goin' on?" Virginia lowered her voice to a whisper. "Why is a cop pointin' a gun at us, Ellie?"

Ellie cupped Virginia's face with her hands and forced her to look at Ellie and not the investigator. "Listen to me, V. Turn around and go inside. I'll be right behind you."

The investigator *tsked* behind her again. "Sorry, can't do that either."

Ellie turned around to face the investigator. *"Please,* she doesn't know anything. Just let her go." Virginia's fingernails dug into Ellie's shoulders as she spoke and Ellie used the pinch of pain to ground her.

"Nah, see, she definitely just saw somethin'. People inside might not've heard the gunshot 'cuz of all that damn music, but she'll go on in there and tattle." He made a show of waving his gun around. "And as for you, I told ya if ya recognized me, we was gonna have a problem. Welp. Seems like we have a problem."

"There's no problem." Ellie shook her head as she tried to wrack her brain for an escape route. Virginia's presence folded a wrinkle in the clear-cut map Dev had drawn for her on how to defend herself. "Just let us go. I promise I won't say anything about the park."

"That's the guy who shot at you in the park?" Virginia hissed in Ellie's ear and Ellie watched as the investigator shook his head and shrugged, like he had no other choice but to do what he had to do.

"Seems you told someone, huh? Can't have loose ends, Miss Stone." With the gun pointing at them, the investigator pulled his handcuffs from his tactical belt. "So why don't you come on over here and we'll go down to the... uh, station and figure all this out."

Never go to another location.

The investigator was too far away for her to disarm him.

But, if he comes closer...

It was risky, but Dev had taught her how to steal an attacker's gun as a last resort. Running and hiding were out. Fighting was the only option.

"We're not comin' to you. Y-you have to come to us."

"What're you doin', El? We need to get outta here."

It was another tactic. If she stalled enough, maybe someone else would come and interrupt. She was biding time she wasn't sure they had, but she sure as heck was going to try every weapon Dev had stocked in her arsenal.

The investigator huffed, but took the bait, slowly pacing

toward her with the gun poised to fire, as if he was afraid she had some trick up her sleeve. Hopefully, she did.

"*Ellie*, what's the plan. He's gettin' close."

"Shh. Trust me." Ellie concentrated on the trembling hand aiming the gun and mentally played through the motions she'd need to use to disarm him.

"Ellie..."

He was about to be within her reach when he lunged for her. She moved the way Dev taught her to divert any shot he could take, but Virginia screamed and tugged Ellie to the door, making Ellie crash to the ground.

A loud crack above her head deafened her senses. Virginia fell to the ground beside her and the crimson stain forming on her pretty pink dress made the edges of Ellie's vision fade away.

Ellie's arms were wrenched behind her back as hundreds of pounds kneed her in her spine. The investigator crushed her under his weight, but when Ellie saw Virginia laying on the ground, her friend's blue eyes wide as she held her hand against her upper chest, holding back thin rivulets of blood seeping slowly through her soft hands, Ellie felt like she was going to break in half.

"No!" Ellie moved, kicked, and screamed, did everything she could but the knee in her back made her hips grate into the asphalt. Her hands were locked into handcuffs and the world began to cave in around the edges.

No. No. NO. Not now.

"Keep screamin' and I'll put another one in her."

Ellie went silent and breathed sharp quick breaths through her nose to keep from passing out. The tinny smell of asphalt smelled awful, but she focused on the scent filling her lungs. She couldn't have a panic attack. Not then. Where was everyone? Why was no one coming to help?

"Now, play nice and come with me—" The investigator heaved her up. Ellie began to kick him with her heels and writhe, until he continued. "—and I'll even call 911 for your friend.

Wouldn't that be nice? Damn chivalrous, if ya ask me. 'Specially for what I could probably get for her. I'm sure my visitor will be fine with gettin' you though."

The investigator grunted as he dragged her to the back of his police vehicle. The rough cement bit into her skin, but Ellie gritted her teeth and kept her body limp. She'd stopped fighting, but that didn't mean she was helping the man dig her grave.

Virginia's bright blue eyes squinched in pain, and the hand that wasn't holding on to her chest reached for Ellie.

"Come on, you don't want to be actual dead weight, do you? You're lucky they still want ya. I wouldn't even bother with ya if I didn't think they'd pay me back."

The investigator pulled her up by her handcuffed arms, pulling them out of socket and Ellie yelped.

"Help.... Someone.... Help." Virginia's sobs tore at Ellie's heart. When the investigator attempted to shove her in the back seat of his patrol vehicle, Ellie finally kicked and screamed against him, knowing if the investigator was dealing with her, he couldn't bother with Virginia.

All we need is time. Just a few more minutes until someone comes to get us.

Ellie fell on the ground and it took her a second to stop screaming and realize why the investigator had dropped her. He cleared his throat and aimed his gun at Virginia. Ellie stilled, every muscle in her body so tense she felt like she'd snap at any moment.

"Get in the fuckin' car. Now. I ain't playin' no more games. If you don't get in there right now, I'm gonna actually finish her off."

Ellie shut her mouth and backed awkwardly into the car, desperate to keep that barrel off Virginia.

Sirens blared in the distance and relief flitted across Ellie's chest. Even if it was too late for her, hopefully it wouldn't be too late for Virginia.

The investigator paled even more. His face poured sweat despite the chill in the air. "Looks like we'll have company soon."

"Please, somebody... *help*."

Virginia's weak cries were strong enough to give Ellie hope until the investigator's face hardened.

"Can't have that either."

"C-can't have what?" Ellie asked, not sure she wanted the answer.

"Guess she's gonna have to come with."

"What? No! You said you'd leave her!"

"Welp. I lied. Can't have loose ends. She seems like she might make it." He kept the gun pointed on Virginia and seemed to be thinking as he talked to himself out loud.

"They want women, Cici. One more and we'll be set..."

"Who are you talking to?" Ellie asked before she could stop herself.

Instead of answering her, he nodded to himself and slammed the door on Ellie. He turned and picked Virginia up, grabbing underneath her arms and dragging her limp, eerily silent body to the front of his police car.

"What are you doing? Stop! Just leave her!" Ellie kicked at the cage separating her from the front of the car as the investigator shoved her friend in and slammed the passenger door.

He slid into the driver's side and Ellie shifted to kick behind his head.

"You can do that all ya damn well please. Won't do ya no good."

The car jolted forward and Ellie screeched as she fell to the floor. The sirens became deafening and Ellie screamed as loud as she could to be heard over them. With every turn and brake, Ellie moved until she finally sat upright and realized the cop was using his own lights and sirens as he sped through Ashland to God knew where.

Ellie dedicated every part of her to driving the investigator crazy. But as he ignored her and kept up a steady stream of chatter with someone who wasn't there, she wondered if he already was.

"We're here," the investigator finally screamed over her.

The old brick sign for Hatcher Gardens Neighborhood with its missing white letters passed by and Ellie stopped screaming. The investigator had turned off the sirens and lights too, and the eerie silence inside the car made Ellie's heartbeat thunderous in her ears.

Panic and confusion crept over her bones like a freezing mist. They definitely weren't going to a police station—not that she'd actually thought they would.

Where are we going?

For the first time that day, her best friend responded in her mind.

"Looks like we're about to find out."

CHAPTER THIRTY-THREE

The three BlackStone men hung back as federal agents took over the scene outside room 307. Phoenix texted in the corner of the hallway, waiting for their next move. Hawk spoke with the agents, and Devil had done what he could for the women until paramedics arrived to take them to the hospital. ADA Aguilar was fielding press reports to spin the event how the government wanted.

The cat was out of the bag, so to speak. Last time, when the Crew had rescued Ellie and the others, BlackStone went through the entire operation under the radar. They'd only involved the local government after Marco convinced the sheriff to ensure them clemency and support.

"I hate we had to get the feds involved this time. I wanted to take care of things myself."

At Devil's complaint, Hawk gave him the side-eye. "You nearly did."

"Hey, they said Strickland will live, didn't they?"

Hawk scoffed. "No thanks to you."

"No. Ellie told me not to kill him. She said all this is bigger than Strickland and he could lead us to others."

"Smart." Hawk nodded.

"I promised her I would try not to kill him and agreed to let fate decide."

Hawk snorted and shook his head. "Good thing fate knows where all the vital organs are." The corner of his lips perked up at Devil and Devil allowed a sliver of a smile in return before Hawk continued. "I agree with Ellie. This is bigger than Strickland. Finding out everything he knows is key. Besides, at least now if fate decides it's his time, at least Strickland's death won't be on our hands."

"What do you mean, 'our'? He would've been my kill."

Hawk turned and clapped him on the shoulder. "We're a team, man. We live. We die. We kill. For the team."

When Hawk crossed his arms again, Devil cleared his throat. "I-uh, I think I want more than that."

"What do you mean?" Hawk's eyes barely flickered to Devil, but his body stayed facing forward.

"I think... I think I want more than..." Devil waved his hand toward room 307's door. "This. The job. The training. The missions... and honestly the team." He closed his eyes and soft, golden hair filled his vision. "There's someone I care about more now. More than all of it."

Hawk chuckled beside him. "And to think you told Strickland before you even told Ellie."

Devil whipped his head to see a big grin on his leader's face. "How... how did you know?"

Hawk barked a laugh before federal agents gave him a look that could kill. He sobered, likely remembering where they were. The hours after a successful mission were the strangest feeling. Adrenaline slowed down to a halt, but the mind was still keyed up from everything going right. It reminded him of floating in crystal clear, warm water.

"Let me tell you, brother, there are cameras everywhere in BlackStone. What'd you think, you were being sneaky? Don't worry, Snake scrubbed the feeds and started turning off the cams where you were training." Hawk's chest rumbled with laughter and Devil felt his face redden. No use denying it now, not that he wanted to anymore.

"Does Jaybird know?"

Hawk shook his head. "If his confusion over you talking to Ellie is any indicator, then no. And that's one conversation I don't mind missing."

"Tell me about it," Devil muttered as ADA Aguilar walked up to them with a smirk on his face.

"Just so y'all know, it might be harder to swing a 'defense of others' argument if you keep attempting to murder people. You might've used your last get-out-of-jail-free card." Aguilar's words were serious, but his eyes looked like he'd be laughing if they were in better company. "In any case, Strickland's in a hospital bed with warrants for the rape and murder of Sasha Timmons. We'll need Ellie to testify..." Aguilar looked at Devil with a weighted question.

"Fuck, does everyone know?"

Hawk chuckled. "Seems like you, Jaybird, and your poor angel were the only clueless ones."

Devil shook his head and met Aguilar's silent question. "She'll be fine. I know she'll want to help any way she can—" He held up his hand and pulled out his phone. "Speaking of which, I'm gonna try to call her and get her to meet the women at the hospital."

Aguilar nodded and Devil walked off to the other end of the hall and called, only to hear a dial tone and Ellie's number recited back to him.

What the fuck? Why wouldn't she be answering her phone in a time like this?

Unease prickled up the back of Devil's neck and he opened up Ellie's location from her contact profile. Her blue circle hovered over the hotel.

"Hawk, something's wrong." Devil pressed the button near his ear until he remembered their headsets had gone offline when the feds arrived. "We need to call Snake."

Devil turned to elaborate, but Hawk already had the phone up to his ear. His dark brows raised in question and Devil answered, waving his screen with Ellie's location. "It's Ellie. GPS is saying she's here, but she should've left by now. I need Snake to do whatever magic he can and try to find her. Whether by her phone or the hotel cameras."

Hawk relayed the message verbatim. Sweat made Devil's palms sweaty and he dried his hands on his dress pants. He was trying to listen to what Hawk was saying on the phone, but Devil's pulse raced inside his chest, like it was trying its best to flee and run after hers.

After a minute, Devil waved his phone at Hawk and pointed down. "I'm gonna keep calling her and try to trace my steps. It's still ringing so I'm going to see if I can find it."

When Devil got downstairs, there was no one to be found. Before the feds had cleared the hotel, every single party attendee and hotel guest had been required to stay and be accounted for before they could leave. They'd gotten quite a few Russian body-guards and were still detaining some of the high-powered officials. Whether as suspects or witnesses, Devil didn't know. And at that moment he didn't care.

"Pick up, goddamnit, pick up," he whispered into the phone, making sure he wasn't louder than any ring or vibration.

"Any luck?" Hawk and Phoenix emerged from the stairwell. "Snake said she's gotta be at the hotel. She's not at BlackStone and Naomi and Nora said she's not at Sasha Saves. This hotel is as close as he can ping her. He's sifting through video now."

"Is this where you last saw her?" Phoenix asked after a moment of Devil walking in circles.

"Yeah... I was coming through the service hallway." He pointed to the entryway and acted out the encounter before indicating the exit door. "She'd come from that door, I think, and was trying to crash the party." He walked back to the alcove, searching for her phone and not hearing any sounds. "We hid in this alcove and that's when she heard Strickland

and ID'd him as Sasha's murderer. I told her she had to leave..."

"So she'd have gone out the door she came in right? If she listened to you, at least," Phoenix offered.

She had to have listened to him, right? He'd said hurtful things, but surely she understood the gravity of the situation and how important it was for her to help in the ways she truly could. He wished he'd explained it better, but the pressure to stop Strickland and the men upstairs was too great and he'd snapped.

He nodded to Hawk's suggestion and pushed the door open. It was the same back alley they'd used last year when they'd tried to save Ellie the first time. He glanced around the spartan area, searching until he noticed something shiny on the ground.

"Is that—"

Devil ran the few steps to what had caught his eye. He bent to retrieve the phone lying on the ground, its screen shattered. There was a stain in the cracked glass, and he could barely make out his name as the caller. He brought the phone closer and shined his phone on it to see what was covering her phone and swallowed bile when he recognized the substance.

Blood.

He turned to face his teammates' grim faces before he spoke aloud his worst nightmare come to life.

"She's gone."

CHAPTER THIRTY-FOUR

"This is wrong, Cici. It's too much. The Russian ain't even here. What if Rusnak was lyin'."

The rip of tape around Ellie's bare legs punctuated each sentence the investigator was rambling. He'd apparently given up mumbling and muttering to whatever apparition was following him around and had gone into full conversation with... Cici?

"Can't really judge him, can ya, girl?"

Guess I can't, can I?

As soon as they entered Sasha's old neighborhood, Ellie's best friend was back to her talkative self. It honestly couldn't have come at a better time. Sasha's voice was like a calming, meditative breath, keeping Ellie's mind on track and out of the worst possible scenarios threatening to drive her to helplessness.

"This house looks just like mine did, doesn't it? Same layout and everything."

Ellie huffed a laugh and the investigator paused to look at her and give her a bug-eyed glare before going back to wrapping the tape.

He'd parked behind some old house that reminded Ellie of the one she'd practically lived in growing up, except the inside was a time capsule from decades ago. There was shag carpet, wood-paneled walls, brown, green, and yellow hues.

Looks exactly like yours. Except for how outdated it is.

"*True. The kitchen seems smaller. Probably 'cuz of that pantry over there.*"

At Sasha's words, Ellie looked to the small double doors, but cringed when she saw Virginia breathing heavy as she leaned against the wood. "*And at least mine wasn't fuckin' gross. What is that smell? Can't be bleach...*"

Sasha was right. It was why Ellie thought they were in the investigator's house. It reeked of the same tobacco and alcohol scent seeping from the sweat dripping down his forehead. The underlying cleaning odor was hard to believe since the place was a total pigsty.

Newspaper and trash were everywhere, like whatever he hadn't wanted to hold anymore, he'd just dropped straight to the ground. The two biggest concentrations of debris were around a corkboard she couldn't see the front of, and his chair centered in the living room. It was disgusting. At one point she could've sworn she'd seen something move out the corner of her eye.

Ellie sighed before yet another wrap of duct tape stuck to her skin. She glanced at Virginia. The investigator had carried her in first and dumped her in the corner of the small kitchen, much like he dumped everything else in his house. She was sickly pale and sweating and her labored breathing hurt just to hear. Ellie couldn't imagine how it felt. She looked so broken the investigator hadn't even bothered to bind her.

His mistake.

If Ellie was going to get them out of there, the less she had barring their escape the better.

She glanced around the house for the umpteenth time for exits, hiding spots, and potential weapons. There were drawers in the kitchen she could grab a knife from. A half-full jar of moonshine.

"*Your kick ass heels, obvi.*"

Ellie tucked her chin to hide her smile. Sasha had always had the knack of making even the worst moments seem manageable. Looking back, its absence was probably why Ellie was paralyzed with fear in the hotel when they were kidnapped.

"It was also a real fucked situation and you were drugged. Don't beat yourself up, babe."

Ellie nodded to herself. Y*ou're right. I've been working on that… I just think the situation is starting to get to me—*

"Don't let it. Focus. Breathe. You've learned a lot of shit from that man of yours. Don't let it go to waste."

"There, that should do it. That'll keep her still until we figure out what to do with her." The investigator's knees creaked as he stood up. He tossed the duct tape on the counter in front of him and took a heavy swig from the mason jar of moonshine before taking out a medicine bottle from one of his uniform pockets. His thumb stroked the paper on the outside and he opened it, only to close it again.

"Where are they, Cici? I don't want all this shit to be for fuckin' nothin'. What do I do with them if the Russians don't show?" He pulled out his phone and started typing on it. "I don't know if I can do this. Can I leave them somewhere? What do I do?"

The line of questioning was like a lifeline, and Ellie grabbed on and held tight. Dev's words from her countless hours of training filtered through her mind and came out in Sasha's voice.

"Remember: negotiate. Humanize. Make the captor feel bad for takin' you."

"Who's Cici?"

The investigator stopped typing and laid his phone on the counter to turn to her. "None of your fuckin' business, girlie." He tilted his head to the side, like he was craning to hear something. "I don't care if it wasn't fuckin' nice."

Ellie looked around to the dusty pictures hanging on the wall. There were a few where she could barely make out the pretty woman in the frame with the investigator's arm wrapped around her.

"Is Cici your wife?"

The investigator grunted and swiped down his face, smearing the sweat accumulating there. He pulled out a lighter and started to flick it, on and off, on and off. A habit. He seemed to get lost in the flame.

Doesn't that hurt his thumb?

She needed to get his attention. If she got through to him, maybe she could negotiate their way out. "Is that her? The happy woman in that picture?"

He grunted again and looked up at the picture Ellie had nodded to since her hands were still handcuffed behind her back. A problem she'd been trying to work out a solution for since he'd slapped them on. Dev had only taught her the one front hand-cuff and then she'd gotten him a little... sidetracked.

The investigator walked up to the picture and used his fingers to clear the grime from her face. "Cicilia."

"Um... sorry? I didn't hear—"

"Cicilia. She's my wife." The investigator staggered back and took another swig from the moonshine. He'd already depleted over half the thirty-two-ounce jar in their short time together.

"Cicilia is your wife?"

"Was. Gone now." He pulled his phone from his pocket.

"Don't let him make that call, girl. Whoever he kidnapped you for could be waiting on the other line."

"H-how long were you married?"

He huffed and lingered his gaze over the picture again. "Thirty years." He took another sip and sucked in a breath through his teeth before exhaling.

Despite everything, Ellie's heart ached for him. "H-how long has she been gone?"

His wistful stare grew watery. "Eight."

"I'm sorry." She couldn't imagine losing the man she loved

after so much time. Or ever. The thought of Dev going into that hotel room flashed into her mind.

Was he safe? She hadn't even thought of the danger he constantly put himself in. She'd just trusted he'd make it through. But God, what if he didn't?

He has to be okay.

Ellie bowed her head and breathed in deeply to envision him safe and healthy, but the stench of ammonia choked her instead.

"We were happy, ya know."

Ellie stilled and watched the investigator as he washed his depression in moonshine and leaned against the counter for support. The lighter was quiet in his hand.

"I'm sure you were," Ellie offered.

"We got married at eighteen. Too damn young, but happy. I went into the police force. She became a nurse. It was perfect."

"That sounds nice. Did, um... did y'all have any kids?"

The silence went on so long Ellie found herself searching for something else to say until he filled the empty space with three simple words.

"We'd wanted them."

Ellie's lungs twisted, both out of sympathy and fear she'd asked the wrong question, but the investigator continued.

"I got promoted to investigator. We were happy about that for a while. But the job... it ain't easy. 'Shine's doin' the trick right now." He lifted up the jar. "Back then, Jack and Jim were my closest friends. That's when everything got fucked up."

He buried his face into the hand holding the lighter and whispered. "I'm sorry, Cici. So sorry. It's all my fault. If I'd been there... I know. But if I'd been there more... come home earlier. Been home. You woulda stayed..."

The pain laced in each word ripped at Ellie's heart and she looked away. She could never hold back tears when she saw a man cry, but it was more than that. Even with all her work at Sasha Saves, she'd never seen someone more broken.

A crash of glass against the wall made her yelp, but the sound was drowned out when the investigator screamed at the thin air.

"You left me! And now look at what I've become. Without you, I am *nothing*. Why did you have to go? Now I'm neck-deep in somethin' I can't swim out of." He slid down to the floor. "You always had the answers, Cees. Always. If you were here, you'd know what to do..." Tears streamed down his face, but he wasn't sobbing. It was almost as if he didn't even notice them anymore. "I know... I know. Rehab. You've been tellin' me for years." He sighed and leaned his head against the counter island. "You're right. You're always right. Fuck."

Everything was silent again, but Ellie didn't feel the need to fill the air with noise this time. It seemed like there was a full conversation going on in the investigator's head anyway and she was afraid to interrupt.

"Maybe that'll work. What does this life have to do for me anyway? I'll plead guilty. They'll send me to rehab..." He sighed. "I'm gonna die in there though, Cici." He paused. "But I guess I'm dead already."

Ellie wasn't sure what he was talking about but she let him go. She looked over to Virginia, whose eyes were back open. She gave a subtle thumbs up with her right hand before closing them again. She didn't look any better, but maybe she was better off than Ellie thought.

"You ready to go?"

Ellie whipped her head back to the investigator, who was now staring at her.

"Um... go?" *Uh... Sash? What'd I miss?*

He sighed and slapped the ground before grabbing the counter to help him stand back up. "To the station. Let's get this over with before I change my damn mind."

"Really? Uh, why?" Ellie winced. *Why did I ask that? How freakin' dumb—*

"'Cuz you got an angel up there, is why."

Ellie had no idea what that meant, but she didn't question it.

Hope and relief washed over her as the investigator pulled out what she guessed was the key to the handcuffs. She maneuvered her duct-taped feet to sit up on her knees.

"Thank you, oh my God. Thank you. I'll do whatever you want if you get my friend to the hospital."

He paused. "Shit, fuck. I forgot about her." He wiped his face. "We'll take her to the hospital first. Lights and sirens should get her there quicker than waitin' for EMS."

Ellie was dizzy with gratitude. "Thank you."

"Don't thank me, thank Cici—"

A loud pounding on the back door froze Ellie's blood.

"Who the fuck..." He moved to look out of the grungy curtains covering the small window next to the back door. A hushed curse escaped him before he turned to Ellie. Whatever he'd seen turned him whiter than a sheet. His lips were working before his words were audible.

"Hide."

CHAPTER THIRTY-FIVE

Ellie was surprised the small room wasn't making her hyperventilate. But maybe it was because she was holding her breath as she watched an even worse nightmare unfold. Through the crack between the pantry doors, Ellie watched as the investigator let a big, tall man in all black inside his home.

Who's that?

"No one good."

"I-I didn't think you were comin'. I left as soon as Rusnak told me to."

"I do not care." The heavy Russian accent tripped a circuit in Ellie's brain.

Is that the same—

"Yep. That's one of the guys who took us."

"Um... right. Well, I was actually leavin', so, um. You can too. I-I'll call Rusnak later."

She couldn't see the Russian's expression. The men had moved into the living room and all Ellie could see was half the investigator scratching his arm.

"You do not want this?"

There was a deafening silence in the room and Ellie imagined she could almost hear the investigator arguing with his wife in his mind.

"Is that—"

"Da. Boss said you want good stuff." Ellie heard a faint rustling. "You do not want this now?"

Ellie could hear the investigator whispering.

"Who is this you are talking to? Is there someone else here?"

"No! No, I um... I talk to myself sometimes."

The Russian grunted. "I tell boss you do not want good stuff."

Muffled footsteps grew louder as they moved from the carpet to the linoleum in the kitchen.

"Wait!"

The footsteps stopped.

"H-how good?" The investigator gulped so loudly it hurt Ellie's throat. "It looks smaller than normal."

"Pure. You do not need more now."

The investigator cursed. Ellie thought back to the park. Was this another drug deal? Her heart sank as the realization slowly dawned on her that her easy out was dwindling away. She had no idea what he was like when he was high. If he was hallucinating, shooting people, and acting irrationally while sober or coming down, she didn't want to wait to find out.

Trying to ease the pain from her awkward position, Ellie shrugged her shoulders. At least she'd become much more limber and flexible over the past couple of months. Still, having her arms wrenched back for what felt like hours was getting hard to endure.

She was exhausted, physically and mentally. She closed her eyes but refused to sit. She didn't want to be caught in a worse physical position by sitting down with her hands tied behind her back.

She looked at Virginia. The poor girl was still breathing just as heavily, and her eyes were still closed. While the investigator had helped Ellie hop to the pantry, he'd had to drag Virginia. All she'd let out was a weak moan. As bad as it sounded, the low wail was still music to Ellie's ears. Being in pain meant she was still alive.

Ellie caught movement in the sliver of light she had and she watched as the investigator sat down with his hand outstretched. The Russian placed a small bag into his hand and the investigator clutched it to his heart.

"I-is this gonna be all of it? Or can I have my supply back." The investigator's smoker voice came out warbly and hopeful.

"Boss is pleased with you. You work hard for—" Ellie frowned, trying to understand the word but caught back up when she realized it couldn't have been English. "—They thank you with product you want from now on."

The investigator paused from rustling around his side table from his chair and gaped. "Forever?"

"*Da.*"

The investigator huffed and gave a little laugh. "Ha, no shit. Hear that, Cici? We're gonna be fine. We're gonna get well and everything will be okay."

"Who is this person you speak to? It is only me, *durak.*"

"S-sorry. Nobody."

After a pause, Ellie's pulse spiked with the fear she'd been found out. She took measure of her breaths to make sure the Russian couldn't hear her.

"What is all this?"

"All what?" the investigator asked, sounding like something was in his mouth.

"This."

"Oh, uh, my board?"

"*Da.* You have pictures and string on this... *board.*" There was a *tsking* noise. "Boss would be interested in this information, I think."

"No... No, no, no. Uh, you won't tell him, right? It's just somethin' I've come up with... Ya know, so Rusnak can have all the dirt on everyone he's workin' with?"

"You have many people on this board. Does boss know this thing?"

"No, oh, God no. Just me. I'm keepin' tabs on people for Rusnak, like I said. I'll be gettin' him this info as soon as I'm done. No one needs to know yet. It can be just me and you. You won't tell him, right?"

The Russian grunted. "I will leave you now."

"Vlad! Vlad, you won't tell him, right? P-please uh, I'll get rid of it all, I swear. If he doesn't want me lookin' into things I'll get rid of it."

"Do not worry, *durak*. I will not tell boss about this thing."

The investigator let out an audible sigh. "Th-thanks. Thank you, buddy. I owe ya one."

"I will leave now. You are... busy. I will go leave by myself."

"Oh, yeah, sure. Um... tell Rusnak I said thanks... please?" the investigator said it with a question in his voice.

The Russian grunted again and heavy footsteps came nearer to the pantry. Ellie backed away from the crack. She heard the rustling of plastic quickly followed by the flick of a lighter. Ellie heard what she assumed was the back door creaking open before she moved back to her position at the light.

The investigator had his sleeve rolled up and a rubber tie wrapped around his bicep. He was pulling the end with his teeth and held a shiny needle in his free hand.

Ellie backed away from the pantry doors. She wanted to get out of her hiding place, but not only did she need to make sure the Russian left, she also didn't want to see the investigator inject poison into his skin.

Memories of needles pricking into her skin pushed to the front of her mind, but she fought back the panic usually accompanying those thoughts. Part of her wished she could stop him, encourage him to go to rehab like the ghost in his mind tried to do. But the part focused on survival and saving Virginia, knew the moments after he injected would be the easiest window of opportunity to escape.

As Ellie brainstormed, a long, loud, satisfied groan rattled through the house before it abruptly stopped. Ellie peeked between the doors to see the investigator with his head lolled to the side, mouth open, and the needle still in his arm.

"Holy crap," Ellie whispered.

Is he dead?

"I don't know. But there's nothing you can do for him in here."

Ellie turned to Virginia, the crack shining enough light in the small room for her to see her friend's pale face and closed eyes.

"V, we gotta get outta here. Come on," Ellie whispered, hoping she would wake up. A thought crossed her mind and she didn't know why she didn't think of it before. Not that she'd had a whole lot of opportunity to think rationally. "Wait, do you have your phone?" Ellie didn't know anyone's numbers by heart but maybe they could call 911?

Virginia swallowed and she responded with a hoarse whisper. "Yeah, it's..." Virginia's fluttering eyes flashed wide. "El, I-I can't move my left arm..."

Ellie glanced to see Virginia struggling, trying to roll over to seemingly free her right arm, but her left arm was flopping uselessly. Blood trailed down it and Ellie realized the problem.

"The gunshot... Virginia, I think the bullet did something to your arm."

Tears streamed down Virginia's paling face. "I'm tired, Ellie."

Ellie squeezed her eyes shut as she thought. She was hand-cuffed and couldn't get Virginia's phone, wherever it was, nor could she retrieve her bobby pin from her hair. Could Ellie leave Virginia to run to find help? If that was the best option then she'd do it, but it seemed risky. But maybe a neighbor next door would be home and Ellie could ask them to call 911—

A loud squeaking stopped Ellie's train of thought dead in its tracks. The back door closed softly, and the owner of heavy foot-steps darkened the pantry before passing by. Ellie tiptoed to the sliver of light and saw the same monster of a man looming over the frighteningly still investigator.

"He's back."

Unease slithered down Ellie's spine.

Why?

Sasha was silent as Ellie watched the Russian circle the recliner. He studied the room, a look of disgust staining the hard angles of his face before settling his stare on something out of Ellie's vision.

He faced the board he'd spoken with the investigator about and fished his phone from his pocket before holding it up for a few minutes.

Is he taking pictures?

He shoved his phone away and rounded the chair to enter the kitchen again, out of Ellie's sight. Something scraped over the counter and Ellie strained her eyes despite the man not even being in her field of vision, until the Russian got back in her eyesight. She watched, horrified and helpless, as the Russian unscrewed the mason jar lid he carried, sniffed it, and poured it over the investigator's still body.

Once the jar was empty, he tossed it behind him, causing a *thunk* where the glass must have fallen to the carpet. The Russian passed by the door again, making Ellie even more on edge. He went back to the living room, with a large mason jar in each hand. He emptied one in the direction of the board before shaking it all over the living room. There was another *thunk* followed by more splashing. The man had developed a rhythm, but the beat stopped just before Ellie saw him take the investigator's lighter. She bit her lip from screaming out, as her tired mind finally connected what was happening.

With the lighter in his hand, the Russian continued his deadly cadence, leaving a trail of liquor in and around the kitchen and punctuating the end of each jar by shattering the glass onto the linoleum. His shadow darkened the pantry, and Ellie slowly moved out of eyesight to lean against the wall.

With each crash, slow tears leaked down Ellie's face, no doubt from the alcohol vapors and the helplessness of her situation. Finally, the morbid song stopped. She closed her eyes, saying one final prayer that she was wrong.

The Russian's deep voice interrupted Ellie's thoughts and she had to strain to understand the foreign language.

"Tell the Pakhan he knew too much, but it is done."

The back door squeaked open and Ellie continued her fervent whisper, hoping saying it out loud would encourage the universe to tell him to leave.

But then there was a *flick*. The world erupted and Ellie's hell came to life.

CHAPTER THIRTY-SIX

The sweet euphoria that always flowed in his veins after he shot up, halted at once, freezing his blood in place. Neal opened his eyes to his empty living room.

Well, it wasn't really his living room. It couldn't have been. But it reminded him of his living room from the past. Back when Cici was still alive.

Brighter. Cleaner.

Neal sat up abruptly in his chair and searched the side table. No bent spoon. No baggie. No trash on the floor. His eyes scanned the rest of the room and found no cork board covered in his obsessive search for freedom. He glanced into the kitchen and blinked rapidly.

"C-Cici? Is that you?"

The love of his life stood behind the kitchen counter as if she'd never left. She lifted her serene smile but continued to knead the bread in front of her. "Well, of course it is, silly."

Cici turned to an awfully familiar teenaged girl in the corner of the kitchen. "Hurry, dear. It's not their time. She needs your help."

The girl's dark curls bounced as she nodded her head and gave a wistful smile, mischievous and sad at the same time. "One last time," she whispered before breathing deeply. After a quick exhale, she opened the door to the pantry and closed it behind her.

"W-who was that?"

"Oh, don't worry about it, dear. We have to be quick, too, I'm afraid."

The Cici of more than a decade ago stopped kneading the dough to tuck a short curl behind her ear. She looked happy, young, healthy. The sight brought tears to his eyes.

"But y-you're..."

"I know, sweetie." The faint wrinkles around her eyes crinkled in worry. "I know."

"You know? You know you're... gone?"

Cici gave a faint smile and brushed her hands against her apron, leaving flour just like old times. Whenever she'd baked, he'd always teased her because while the welcoming scent of bread filled the air, clouds of flour covered everything else.

She took a step toward him, but he staggered back when she all of a sudden appeared in front of him with her hand stretched out.

"It's time to go, Neal. We can go together now. I've been waitin' for you."

Neal blinked at her hand in confusion.

"I'm sorry, dear. But we have to go. It's now or never."

"You're... gone. I saw you..."

He blinked and he was in his bathroom, watching the past unfold like a movie. One that had been a constant rerun in his mind for eight years.

He pushed his fingers down her throat and shoved her head into the toilet before she threw up on him. The hacking and choking hurt his heart, but losing her would kill his soul.

"Leave me alone, Neal! Just let me go! I don't want any of it anymore!"

"No, stop." Cici's command killed the vision and walked behind him in the now empty bathroom. "Don't think about that. Not now. It's all over. Just come with me and you'll never worry again."

She stretched out her hand and he stared until another vision took over and he found himself in their bedroom.

He stretched his open palm, waiting for Cici to give him the orange bottle. She'd been hiding the pills under the mattress again. As a nurse, it was easy for her to get them and he didn't want to rat on her and get her fired. Besides, sometimes her job was the only thing that got her out of the house. She'd sworn she'd stopped and he'd checked around the house, but the pills kept turning up, like weeds choking the life out of his beautiful garden.

"All you have to do is clean yourself up, Cici. You can do it. Just dial it back, one step at a time. We'll do it together." His hand twitched as he tried to be firm, but not so insistent she shut down, or snapped and refused to listen.

"The physical pain was less." The memory evaporated and a healthy Cici stood in front of him. "But the emotional..." She clutched her heart, leaving powdery flour on her chest.

"You got dependent on the pills. And the depression got worse," he muttered.

She gave a small smile. "Not a great combination, huh?"

"God, you were so sick for so long..."

He was an apparition in the bathroom again, watching the scene they'd gone through in real life more times than he could stomach.

He pulled her head from the toilet after she'd finished coughing and wiped her lips with a cool cloth.

"Say it with me, baby. I can get better. We'll do it together."

"No, Neal, I can't. It's too much. It's all too much. You don't understand. Please, just let me go."

"No, Cici, you can beat this. Let's do it together."

She whipped her head up at him with a hateful glare. "Don't you get it? I'm tryin' to die to get away from you! Just let me go!"

"I tried to hurt you that day." Cici sighed and shook her head. "I said the worst thing I could think of."

"It worked," Neal mumbled and swiped a hand down his face. "But you were right. I didn't realize what pain you were talkin' about... until I felt it myself." He sighed and they were back in the living room, with him sitting in his chair and her holding out her hand. He looked up in her adoring eyes and felt peace... and regret.

"I'm sorry, Cees. So sorry I pushed you to that. If I'd been sober sooner. If I'd been there for you, seen the signs."

"Shh, shh. No, Neal. It wasn't your fault. I was sick."

"The cancer... I know. That's what snapped me out of it—"

"No, Neal. Before that." She tapped her head. "My mind was sick. My heart..." She brought her hand down to her heart and covered it as she shook her head.

"Because of me, right?" His heart ached for her answer. "I was distant. A drunk. I pushed you away."

"No, honey. You can't blame yourself for the things in my mind that made life unbearable. The cancer was just the tipping point. I couldn't hold on anymore. But stop blaming yourself. You've been living off of my worst moments for too long. It's time to give that guilt up. I'm at peace now."

"You are?"

She nodded with a gentle smile and held her hand out again. "Come walk with me, Neal."

He looked up from her hand and they were in the field where they'd married, behind the church they'd faithfully gone to. He looked at her face and she was skipping backward through the wheatgrass. It was the Cici from their wedding day. Young and vibrant. Full of life.

"Come Neal. It's so peaceful." She giggled and twirled in her simple ivory gown.

He choked on emotion. It was such a relief to see her smiling again. He took a step forward to follow her, but a hard tug at his back kept him from moving. "It's been so hard without you Cees."

She stopped running and the older Cici was in front of him

again in a blink, still just as beautiful.

"I know. And I know why."

"You do?"

She nodded. "I was never mad at you before I was sick. You were sick then, too, with your own demons to fight." She sighed. "You've been living with my last words playing like a record. But there were so many good ones before that. We both could've done that more I think. Focused on the good. It might've helped." She held out her hand again. "But none of that matters here, Neal. It's wonderful. Peaceful. I want this for you."

Neal looked at her hand and stepped forward, fighting against the pull at his back but it was too strong. "I can't go with you Cees."

"Why not? Just take my hand." She looked behind her and faced him again. "Please Neal, we don't have much time and we can't stay here."

"I-I'm scared."

She smiled. "Come on, honey, we'll do it together." She took small steps backward, her hand stretched to him. "Walk with me in peace."

His feet were glued to the ground and no matter how hard he tried, he couldn't pull them from the dirt.

Her sigh reached him and blew against his skin. "I love you, Neal." The light behind her shined so all he could see was her dark outline. He covered his eyes to keep from being blinded. When he lowered his hand, Cici's shadow was nearly gone, faint against the bright background.

What was he doing? His wife was in front of him. Why wasn't he going after her? He could be with her again. Cici didn't blame him, like he'd thought. She'd forgiven him before he even realized. What was stopping him from doing the same? From forgiving himself?

Neal tried to step forward, out of the mud. He looked down to try to free his foot, expecting a dirty, watery current holding him back. But there was nothing but tall grass.

He huffed his frustration and lifted each foot with all his might until each step was easier than the last. Neal laughed, triumphant he could race after her, but when he looked up even Cici's shadow was gone. He turned around, unable to remember which direction she'd left.

"I'm comin' Cees! Wait for me!" Neal yelled as loud as he could, coughing past the hot wind forcing its way down his throat. He hoped Cici would call back for him, but there was nothing but the whooshing of the wind.

Choosing the direction he thought she'd gone, Neal ran as hard and fast as he could until he couldn't feel the grass against his feet anymore. The hard dirt underneath him vanished and he felt nothing but warm air underneath his legs.

The sky stretched forever, above and below him. There was nothing but white light everywhere he could see, so bright it almost burned and he had to blink moisture back into his dry eyes.

"Cici?" Neal called out but choked on an acrid burning sensation in his lungs. He opened his eyes, widening them past the smoke to see an inferno raging around him. He tried to get up, but his pleather chair glued him to his seat. The crackle of fire around him pulled him under and heat washed over him like scorching water, consuming every pore.

He was encompassed in pain, so intense he couldn't even scream, and for moments that seemed like lifetimes it was all he knew.

Until it stopped.

Neal opened his eyes. The silence rang in his ears and the darkness blinded him, swallowing him whole. But at least the pain was gone. The euphoria he'd become addicted to was back.

Cici was right. It was peaceful.

It was terrifying.

He screamed.

And then there was nothing.

CHAPTER THIRTY-SEVEN

"Come on, Snake, do you have the location or not?"

"Been working on it since you asked me to hack into Virginia's phone and pinpoint it two minutes ago, Devil. You know this shit takes longer in real life than in the movies."

"He's got it, man. We'll find her," Hawk murmured to Devil as they and Phoenix ran to the parking lot where Hawk had parked the BlackStone SUV. Snake was on Hawk's speakerphone while Devil checked his own phone every fifteen seconds to see if Ellie had called him from a different number.

When the car was in view, he raced ahead to the driver's side. He wrenched the door open only to have Phoenix slam it closed.

"Fuck no, dude. You're in this too deep. I'm drivin'."

Devil growled and opened his mouth to object.

"Get in the passenger seat, Devil. Phoenix drives," Hawk's command came out as he hopped in the back, and Devil followed out of habit before he knew what he was doing.

He rounded the SUV and hopped in just in time for Phoenix to peel out of the parking lot.

"Why the fuck didn't I ever ask for Virginia's number?" He shook his head and punched the glove compartment box.

"If you make the airbags go off and slow us down, Jaybird's gonna kill you," Hawk warned.

"Does he know?" Phoenix asked, looking up at the rearview mirror.

"I texted him. Told him to go to BlackStone ASAP and we'd meet him there until we figured it all out," Hawk answered.

"He just walked in. Devil, how sure are you she's with Virginia?" Snake asked over the speaker.

"Zero percent sure. It's just a hunch because Virginia's been driving her everywhere since her bike got stolen."

"Copy," Snake responded. "Let's see... huh... looks like she's near that park again."

"What the fuck?" Jaybird's voice was loud and clear. Like he'd grabbed the phone from Snake. "Why the hell is she there at night again?"

"I don't know," Devil growled, wondering the same thing. "She wouldn't go there at night. Not again."

"How do you know? If she was that careless the first time, why not this time, too?" Jaybird asked, obviously fuming.

Devil bristled at the accusation. He would've thought the same thing at one point, but it wasn't a fair assumption anymore. "That was weeks ago. She wouldn't do that again. Besides, last time was an honest mistake." Ellie had worked hard and Devil felt the need to defend her. She'd earned the benefit of the doubt in his eyes. "She's smart. Whatever happened, it was either out of her control or she fought like hell."

Jaybird grumbled on the other end, obviously unconvinced. But he didn't know Ellie like Devil did.

"Directions to the park, somebody?" Phoenix prompted. "I haven't been on a swing in fifteen years."

"Already sent the location to the SUV GPS system," Snake replied.

"Turn right in... two miles," a robotic female voice commanded over the speaker. "With traffic, you will reach your destination in... twenty minutes."

"Twenty minutes? Goddamnit." Devil scrubbed his beard. A lot could happen in twenty minutes. "Snake, do we know if she's at the park exactly or are you still pinpointing her location?"

"It keeps narrowing down to that location... oh, wait. I read it wrong—"

"What the *f*—"

Snake cut Jaybird off. "You're going to the Hatcher Gardens Neighborhood, approximately one klick from the park."

Devil grimaced at the update. "Why the hell would she be there?"

"Remember, this is only Virginia's location," Snake answered. "They might not be together."

"They're together," Devil said before muttering to himself. "They have to be."

"We'll find her." Hawk's declaration was said with such conviction it felt like a command to the universe. Devil didn't usually believe in that shit, but if it would listen to anyone, it would be Hawk.

Hawk leaned forward between Phoenix and Devil in the front. "Who lives in the neighborhood. Do we know anybody there?"

Everyone answered Hawk's question in the negative before Snake spoke. "Well, we know they were likely at that party. Naomi and I looked up every single person on the guest list. I'll cross reference the locations we have for them."

"Good idea," Hawk said. "Is there any other way we can figure out ASAP who lives there?"

"Not quickly enough," Snake groaned. "Fuck, from my files no one who was invited to the party lives in Hatcher Gardens Neighborhood."

"Makes sense," Phoenix grumbled. "That neighborhood's like a shit place now, right? The party only had rich jackasses and high school girls there."

"Can you drive any faster?" Devil's temper was electric on his skin and he tried to calm it down before he lashed out. "This town is an inch wide on a map, it shouldn't take us this fucking long to get across it."

"Dude, chill. You heard the lady, it's Friday night traffic. What do you want from me? We're already farther than the bitch said we'd be."

Devil huffed and leaned back in the seat, studying his phone like it had all the answers.

If Ellie wasn't with Virginia, if this was a wild-goose chase, he didn't have any other ideas. What if he couldn't find her this time?

No. I can't lose her.

Devil closed his eyes and tried to think of anything useful, but all he saw was her smile. How she lit up every room like the goddamn sun.

He'd shut everything out years ago. His world had been dark for too long, but Ellie made him realize how much better life could be if he let the light in.

"If I lose her..." he whispered.

"I know, man. I know." Hawk clapped him on the shoulder.

"So... it's like that, huh?" Jaybird growled over the speaker and Devil shook his head.

Fuck, guess everyone knows now.

"Dude, so not the time." Phoenix groaned.

"No, I want to know. It's my sister and I need to know why Devil's getting to call the shots." There was silence before Jaybird sighed on the line. "Are you in love with her?"

Devil swallowed. "Yeah, man. I love her."

Jaybird sighed again. "Devil, she just turned fucking nineteen. What the hell, man?"

"Weren't you like a billion years older than Jules when y'all met? Wasn't she nineteen?" Phoenix reasoned, and Devil raised a brow. He hadn't thought of that.

"Exactly, and I fucked up big time with Jules. I'm lucky as hell she forgave me after the shit I put her through."

Phoenix tilted his head in a nod. "And now you're happy as a blue jay... havin' a baby with her. A whole goddamn life right?"

Devil wasn't sure why Phoenix was coming to his defense, but his own emotions were all over the place, so he didn't mind the reprieve. He hadn't let himself feel so much in a decade. It was fucking overwhelming.

"Yeah, and you have no idea how lucky I am with *that* in particular," Jaybird mumbled and Devil wasn't sure if they were supposed to hear, or what he'd meant, but Phoenix kept talking.

"Don't you want that for your boy? Your sister's an adult and Devil's a few years younger than us, bro. He may look like a thirty-five-year-old and act like he's a thousand, but he's still only twenty-seven. Half-plus-seven rule, my dude."

"That's not a real rule, Phoenix," Jaybird grumbled.

"Plus, math, idiot. He'd have to be twenty-four for that to work with a nineteen-year-old," Snake reasoned and Devil snorted.

Phoenix shrugged. "Meh, same difference. Trauma ages you. With what we've all been through, *including* your sister, we've got much more important shit to worry about than numbers."

Devil sighed and closed his eyes. "I love her, I'd live for her. Die for her. And I would've killed for her today if she hadn't saved Strickland's life. What more could you want from someone who loves your sister. Isn't that enough?"

There was silence on the other line and Devil waited. Normally he wouldn't give two shits about what any of his friends thought, but Ellie adored her brother, and if Jaybird didn't approve, Devil wasn't sure she'd give him a chance.

Fuck, Devil didn't even know if she was *going* to give him a chance after the way he'd talked to her at the party. He'd gone about everything all wrong. Hadn't even officially taken her on a date. And to top it all off, now that he'd told Jaybird, Ellie was truly the last person to know how Devil felt about her. He shook his head. He'd fix it all as soon as they found her.

I'll find you, angel.

He sent it out as a prayer and hoped Ellie could somehow know. Meanwhile, he'd wait to see if her brother would doom them before they started.

"You're emotionless, though. I'm not sure I want that for her."

Phoenix and Hawk both barked out laughs, making Devil jump in his skin.

"What's so funny?" Jaybird demanded.

"Man, the boy is *gone* for his girl," Hawk managed to explain through his chuckle. "He doesn't have emotions at work, but goddamn the man is a fucking sap for Ellie."

"Really? I haven't seen it..."

"'Cause you've got pregnancy brain, my dude," Phoenix joked.

"That's only for the woman, asshole."

"Sure it is." Phoenix laughed and Hawk joined in again.

A resigned sigh came through the speaker. "Fine. You can date her. But I swear to God, if you hurt her I will hunt you down. Friend or not."

Devil shook his head but smiled as he spoke. "Man, I wasn't asking for your permission, but glad to have your blessing. It'll make it easier to convince Ellie to go on our first date."

"You haven't even been on a fucking date with her yet?"

"Shut up, Jaybird," Snake interrupted. "I've got something."

"What is it?" Devil sat up farther in his seat, clenching his fists to the point of pain.

"I've pinpointed the house down to a cluster of addresses from Virginia's location. Do you want the good news or the bad news?"

"Cut the shit, Snake, just tell us," Devil growled.

"I think you're right and Ellie's with Virginia. But you're not gonna like who else they're with."

"Okay..." Devil waited for the shoe to drop.

"Investigator Burgess's house is dead center of the cluster."

"What the fuck? That shitty house on the screen is his?" Jaybird yelled on the other side.

"We don't know yet, but we always thought he was a shady fuck," Hawk answered. "Whatever's going on can't be good."

Devil closed his eyes in agreement, trying to push every worst-case scenario out of his mind.

"Send us the exact address, Snake. I'm about to turn into the neighborhood."

"Already did."

The SUV told them where to go and they weaved around the neighborhood until they pulled up to a small dilapidated house. It didn't look as bad as the ones around it, at least Burgess's house had all its windows and the door was still on its hinges. There was also a light on whereas the other ones were pitch black.

"Looks like Burgess is the only one home... in the whole fuckin' neighborhood." Phoenix joked and Devil would've punched him to shut the hell up if he hadn't seen something that made his blood freeze.

Tendrils of smoke were escaping through the roof of the house, and there was an eerie glow behind the blinds. Devil worked against the icy paralysis and opened the door, nearly falling out before going into a sprint.

"Dude, what the—"

As Phoenix yelled for him, the windows on the house exploded. Devil fell back and covered his eyes from flying glass and blistering heat. When the cloud of fire dissipated, Devil lowered his arm to see the house in front of him engulfed in flames. Strong hands gripped both of his biceps and Devil kicked and tried to dig his heels in to keep from being pulled away.

"Stop, we'll get her, alright?" Hawk yelled over the crackling wood. Devil had forgotten how loud a fire can get. "Not like this. We weren't trained for this."

Neither was Ellie.

The thought sent icy shards of panic through his spine, and

he had to fight the paralysis and his teammates. "No! I have to get her! Let me go!"

Hawk and Phoenix held him at bay as his whole life evaporated into smoke. His breath came in spurts and the pain in his lungs had nothing to do with fire.

"I can't... I can't... just watch... her die." The words were ripped from his chest and he collapsed to his knees. The fire licked at the tops of the windows, lighting up the night.

"She'll... she'll... be alright." Phoenix struggled to comfort him, but Devil shrugged off his hand.

A cool wind drifted over his body, making Devil shiver. All the air around him that wasn't coming directly from the fire felt practically chilly.

"I have to go. Let me go."

"No." Hawk's voice brooked no argument, but Devil didn't give a fuck what his leader said. "We can't let you go in there. It's not safe and we can't go in to save you if you do something stupid."

Sirens reached out to them from the distance but Devil couldn't stop the urge to get up. To do *something*.

Another blast from the house brought on new heat and Phoenix and Hawk let go of him to shield their eyes, but Devil widened his. A hazy figure stood on the right side of the house, but the fire was too bright to see if it was Ellie.

"There she is!"

He leaped up and sprinted to the side of the house. Footsteps tried to match his speed, but he'd been running with Ellie in the morning. The girl could run like the wind, and he harnessed that energy to get to her.

More flames exploded around him, but he didn't care. Ellie had been *right there* at the side of the house. He'd seen her. Devil didn't know why she wasn't running to meet him, but he knew she was there.

When he got to the place he'd seen her, he backed up and did a three-sixty with his hands on his head. He scanned the length of the house and backyard. But there was nothing.

When Phoenix and Hawk caught up to him, they tried to pull him away, yelling at him about getting burned, but Devil shook them off. The cool breeze in the night added a thin layer of protection against the heat.

"Don't touch me again." His growl vibrated in his chest and for some reason, they listened and let him go.

The heat licked at his face and he kneeled down, following the cool air, hoping Ellie could feel it wherever she was.

His teammates yelled behind him, but he ignored them. The heat was a wall he had to fight against and he covered his eyes as he followed the inexplicably cool air leading him closer to the house.

I'll find you, angel.

He said it over and over again, hoping she somehow heard him.

Something inside the house thundered so loudly it cracked his eardrums. The walls collapsed inward as the roof crashed in. Devil flattened himself to the ground to avoid the burst of hellfire.

No one could survive those flames. The house fell in on itself and every hope Devil had collapsed with it.

That was it.

It was done.

She was gone.

He fell to his knees. What was he going to do without her? She'd become everything to him in such a short time. If his words hadn't been so mean. If he'd trained her differently. If he'd trusted her enough to tell her about the party. Would they be at BlackStone right now? In his apartment?

Fuck.

This one would break him. Every death he'd witnessed had taken a piece of his soul, but Ellie's death would kill him.

Devil roared and slammed his fists down on the ground. He

laid there, breathing in the dirt, not caring anymore that the world burned around him. What did that matter when everything he loved was already ash?

His chest pounded and his breaths came in spurts. It had to be his tie strangling him. Devil tore at the fabric until he was free, but it wasn't enough. He shredded his dress shirt, hoping the pain would stop once he was free. It didn't. He kept clawing at his chest until the thin fabric of his thin tank top ripped under his fingernails. But it was no use. Without Ellie, he knew the ache in his chest would never go away.

Something inside the house banged and rattled and he knew he needed to get up. The fire was consuming the house just feet in front of him, and he didn't know what direction the walls would fall when they finally did.

But his muscles wouldn't listen. The grass brushed his face. Tears stung his eyes just before they watered the ground. The chilly night breeze lifted his hair in a gust—

"In here! In here!"

Muffled shouts electrified his limp body. They were so faint, Devil wasn't sure if what he heard was real or the hope of a desperate man. He lifted his head and swiveled around but couldn't see where they came from.

Cool wind buffered him from the heat and cleared away smoke with the breeze. As he blinked back the sting from his eyes to see better, his gaze caught on something in front of him. He stared at the ground in confusion for a moment until it finally registered that he was witnessing a miracle.

CHAPTER THIRTY-EIGHT

Ellie didn't need to look out the pantry doors to know the world was on fire. Heat from the flames seeped through the crack and Ellie fell back against the wall. There was no way out. The alcohol vapors wafted between the doors and a golden glow lit the small closet.

The light rested on Virginia's deathly pale face. Her eyes were sunken in and her mouth was partly open. Blood outlined her shoulder as she laid down on the ground from the bullet wound still slowly seeping from her.

Tears streamed down Ellie's cheeks and she coughed back emotion and fumes until a wail emptied from her lungs. She slid down the wall and silent cries wracked her body before she landed hard on the floor.

She'd thought she was going to break in half when Virginia had been shot and the investigator's knee was on her spine back at the hotel. But as the air grew too hot to breathe, and the acrid smell of burning wood and linoleum filled her lungs, and her friend's eyes fluttered open for maybe one final time...

Ellie broke.

Her best friend's dark skin tone was nearly purple.

Her chocolate eyes glazed over. They closed.

Her body spasmed and went limp.

Ellie screamed silently against paralysis. There's nothing I can do to save her. There's nothing I can do to save her. There's nothing I can do...

No.

Fuck. That.

Ellie forced her eyes open against the flashback, against the burning air, and against her fear.

"I'm getting us outta here," Ellie told herself as much as she told her dying friend. Now to find an escape route.

Ellie lifted and looked outside, only to see a scene nothing short of hell. There was no way out of the pantry. She screeched and looked around but it was practically empty. Nothing but rice and cans from what she could see.

"Somebody help me!" she screamed at the top of her lungs, careful not to breathe in any more toxic air. She didn't know how far away the Russian was, or if he'd even left the premises. But if the Russian grew a conscience in the next five minutes and was the one to save her, then so be it. She'd cross that bridge later.

"Somebody, please! Help me! Help us!" In an anguished yell, Ellie reached out to her best friend. "Sasha, please help me. What do I do?"

Ellie held her breath to listen, but there was nothing but the billowing flame outside the thin doors.

"Sasha! Help me, please! I don't know what to do! Help me!" Crackling wood and plastic answered back. "Come on! *Now* you're silent? When I need you?" she screamed again and threw herself down on the ground.

"Ow! Son of a—" Something hard poked Ellie's butt and she leaned to the side but her body was in the way of the firelight. She leaned back to feel with her hands until her fingertips grazed over a metal loop.

"This house looks just like mine did, doesn't it? Same layout and everything..."

"Except for the kitchen..." She reached back to her childhood and recalled the root cellar she and Sasha used to be obsessed with when they played manhunt. No one ever found them there because the entrance was a small trapdoor hidden in the corner of the kitchen.

"Holy crap, Sasha, you did it. Oh my God, thank you, thank you, thank you."

Ellie wriggled to her knees and whispered, "I can do this," before crawling to Virginia.

"V, V. We gotta get outta here, and I have an idea. Please, can you help me? Does your right arm still work?"

The only sign of life Virginia gave was a nod downward. But awareness was all Ellie needed.

As gently as she could, Ellie pushed Virginia to her back. A low moan pierced Ellie's chest with guilt, but she couldn't stop to comfort her friend. Ellie bent her head low and into Virginia's limp—but working—hand.

"Grab my bobby pin, V! Hurry!" Ellie shoved her head where she knew her bobby pin was against Virginia's hand. Featherlight fingertips touched her hair and Ellie pushed her head farther into her friend's hand. "Come on, V, grab it with your fingers. That's all you gotta do and I've got the rest."

There was a small tug at her hair and Ellie pulled away slowly, hoping her friend could keep a hold of the metal pin. When Ellie sat up, the blood rushed out of her head and she felt faint from the angle. But there it was, the small shiny piece of metal that would get them out of there.

Ellie swiveled around on her duct-taped legs and stretched her arms back to the point of pain until she finally felt Virginia's hands. She found the bobby pin in her friend's grasp and yelped with excitement. Careful not to drop the pin, she unbent it and hooked it between the arm of the handcuffs and its metal teeth to separate the mechanism from the ratchet.

"Remember... just... one..." *click*.

There was blessed relief in her left wrist before pins and needles shot up her arms. But she was *free*. Ellie laughed into a groan as she stretched her arms in front of her. Her groan turned into a cough as the heat burned her lungs.

"Gotta keep goin'."

She helped herself up and stood tall, knowing this was about to hurt. The investigator had wrapped tons of tape on her bare legs. It would require all her strength and gravity to rip it.

"Okay, one. Two...." Ellie shook her hands and breathed, only to pull in more heat. "Three," she coughed and collapsed cross-legged onto the ground, landing hard on her butt. She looked down at her free legs and pumped her fist in the air. They were red and the skin was abraded but she couldn't feel it yet.

"Adrenaline. Gotta keep goin'."

Something crashed outside the pantry door and the heat felt close to blistering her skin. Virginia coughed.

"Gotta go, gotta go."

She got up and felt for the loop again she'd landed so hard on before. Her fingers searched and searched until finally, the cool metal was in her hands. She tugged, but it refused to lift.

"Oh, hell no." Ellie bent her knees and leaned forward so she could fall back and pull with her entire weight. "One. Two..." She heaved and stumbled backward. The door was still in her hand and off its hinges.

Ellie laughed again, and part of her wondered if she was getting hysterical, while the other part of her told her to shut up and keep going. She looked in the dark abyss below and couldn't see a dang thing.

"Oh!" She stood up and turned on the light she'd been afraid to turn on while the Russian was there. A wooden ladder showed their escape.

"Come on, V. We gotta go."

Her friend's eyes opened a fraction and she held her right hand open for Ellie. Ellie went into a squat and scooped her friend up by the armpits to drag her the few feet to the opening. It was only big enough for one of them at a time and she knew Virginia wouldn't be able to do it herself.

"V? I'm gonna do my best, but whatever strength you've got, I need you to use it now, okay?"

"'Kay," Virginia whispered.

Ellie got behind Virginia's back and started to drop her into the darkness, hoping it wasn't too far of a drop. Fire licked through the crack in the doors and her skin felt tight from the heat, but she focused on the cool sheen of sweat trying to protect her body.

Inch by inch, she dropped Virginia until Ellie was half in the hole herself. "Okay, I'm gonna drop you!" She let go and there wasn't a big thump, so Ellie counted that as a win.

A loud creaking moved the walls around her.

"Gotta go, gotta go," she repeated and swiveled her butt around to descend legs first.

The ladder whined from age and Ellie reached for the pantry wall to gain balance. The drywall burned her fingertips and Ellie yelped, pulling them back. Her momentum slid her down the ladder all the way, and she hung on with one hand until she was able to regain her footing, somehow not rolling her ankle on her heels. Ellie righted herself and followed the ladder down four more rungs before feeling the ground beneath her.

"Whew that was—"

A loud crash above her shook the world, and dust fell in a cloud from the ceiling. Ellie jumped over Virginia and protected her in case anything fell. She stayed huddled over her friend until the dust literally settled and the debris stopped collapsing around her.

Heat scratched at the thin fabric of the back of her dress and Ellie hissed at the sting. She felt the urge to turn around, but knew it would only slow her down. Still, in her mind's eye, she imagined fire falling down the ladder, chasing her. The floor was cement, so at least there wasn't anything for the fire to catch on and escalate.

Except for them. Ellie had to work fast to keep from becoming tinder.

"Keep movin'." Ellie pushed her hair back. She stood and breathed through her nose, trying hard to ignore the bitter burned plastic odor.

The only good thing about the fire being inches away from her was that it put everything else around her in stark relief and she found her escape. The cellar doors.

Ellie dodged a falling ember and pulled Virginia by her waist until they were both underneath the cellar door. She turned to the doors above her and pushed. Only to meet resistance.

"You gotta be kidding me."

The ceiling was low where the door was flat with the ground, so Ellie stooped to get into a modified squat lift. When she was in position, she used her feet to push with all her might against the ground with her back against the door.

Nothing.

She thought about screaming for help, but the fire behind and above her was so loud, she was sure if anyone was dumb enough to be in or around the house, they wouldn't be able to hear her.

Better to use all my energy where it counts.

Ellie pushed her back against the door again, groaning with the effort but showing nothing for it.

"One more Ellie, you got this. Just one more." She moved back to the best position and counted. "One... two..." On three, she pushed and screamed with the effort. The weight of the door disappeared, throwing half her body out of the cellar. But she was on the ground. Free.

Hands scooped under Ellie's armpits and she yelped. She fought and screamed against the arms until she realized they were broken wings wrapping her in an embrace. Soft lips crushed against her forehead.

"Dev?"

"Angel, oh thank God."

Dev's hold tightened and she swung her arms around his

neck. She looked up from his tattooed wings to see a figure in the smoke.

Ellie whispered against Dev's neck, not entirely sure who she was talking to. "You found me."

He squeezed tighter and threaded his hands in her hair. "I found you, angel. And goddamnit I'm never losing you again."

Cool air brushed against her face and lavender tickled her nose.

Ellie gulped and blinked back tears as she whispered again. "Thank you, Sash."

"What, baby?" Dev stood up from his kneeling position. "We gotta get you outta here."

Ellie watched as the figure melted away and two more appeared.

"Dude, let's go. I don't think this place is done blowin' up." Phoenix bent to pick her up but Dev snatched her away. That's when she remembered she wasn't the only one who needed saving.

"Virginia!" she yelled into a cough and pointed behind her. "Virginia's in there."

"Shit." Hawk took two strides and hopped into the cellar feet first. He came back within a second carefully holding Virginia against his chest.

"Come on. Let's get outta here." Phoenix jogged into the smoke, leading the way.

Ellie reached her legs to the ground, only to have them wrapped up by Dev's arm.

"If you think I'm letting you go after that you are out of your goddamn mind, angel."

Ellie only nodded and returned her arms around his neck, taking in the soothing cinnamon she'd come to crave the past year. Dev ran them up a hill and Ellie watched the house as it collapsed even farther in on itself. Sirens and fiery winds filled the night.

The dark shadow figure formed in the new billow of smoke beside the house and Ellie blinked back tears.

Love you, Sash.

"Love you, too, El."

A cool tear trailed down Ellie's cheek as she said goodbye for what she knew in her heart was the final time.

CHAPTER THIRTY-NINE

Devil paced as Dr. Layton pulled the stethoscope away from Ellie's chest and hung it around her own neck. "Except for your knuckles, Devil, there's hardly a scratch on either of you. From what y'all are telling me, it's miraculous you came away with only pink skin to show for it. I'd say you're completely fine, but doctors are at least supposed to say 'take it easy for a few days.' It's in our oath." She winked at Ellie and gave a warm, reassuring smile that eased the tension in Devil's body.

He'd known Ellie was okay. The paramedics even cleared her on scene, but Devil had wanted a second opinion and insisted they take her to the hospital. There was no way in hell he'd have let her leave there if she hadn't been given a clean bill of health.

Jaybird had been a wreck. He and a very pregnant Jules had sat with Devil late into the night while Ellie was overseen in the ER. As soon as the doctor was finished with her, Jaybird hovered, asking her a million questions and not letting her so much as fucking breathe. Devil had wanted to tell him to back the fuck off, but he understood Ellie's brother was just as worried as he had been.

When he noticed Ellie getting tired from having to convince

Jaybird she was fine, on top of the fact that she was already exhausted from fighting for her life, Devil had stepped in. She'd tried to say she was fine, that she didn't need the rest, but the fatigue in her posture said otherwise. He'd told Jaybird to leave, reassuring him that he could see her in the morning. Whether it was Devil's clenched fist, or the catch in his throat as he'd told Jaybird they needed time to decompress, for some reason, the man listened.

After Jaybird and Jules left, Devil had to practically pry Ellie from the hospital waiting room. She'd been waiting there with Virginia's parents, but they'd insisted Ellie go home and rest, reassuring her they'd call when Virginia woke up from her successful surgery.

When he and Ellie were finally on their way back to Black-Stone, Ellie coughed and Devil had flipped his shit, terrified he, the doctor, and the paramedics had all missed something. He'd called the doctor the BlackStone Crew had on retainer for serious injuries, or for when Devil was compromised. At the time, Devil was worried both might be true.

"Thanks doc." Devil shook her hand before walking her out. When they got to the door, he turned to watch Ellie drink a sip of water before triple-checking with Dr. Layton. "You sure she'll be fine?"

Dr. Layton smiled and followed his gaze over his shoulder. "It's nice to see you care. Your bedside manner is usually so... detached."

Devil's lips tightened as he silently swore to change that about himself. It wasn't fair to him or even everyone else that he held them at arm's length. After Draco, the closest man he had in the Crew to call a best friend was Jaybird. And even Jaybird had been the last to know about his feelings for Ellie.

Well, next to last.

He glanced back again before turning to Dr. Layton.

"She's different, huh?" The knowing smile got on his nerves but he grunted his assent. Dr. Layton chuckled. "I'll leave y'all be, then. Remember..." She lowered her voice. "Nothing *too* strenuous."

Devil groaned. "Goodbye, doc." Dr. Layton laughed on her way out and Devil closed the door behind her. He leaned against it before scrubbing his short beard with both hands. Finally, he looked up and narrowed his eyes at Ellie.

She sat on Devil's bed, freshly showered and wearing his T-shirt and boxers. He hadn't been able to be in his apartment while she'd washed up. His emotions were too raw and he knew if he was alone with Ellie, he'd smother her before the doctor even had a chance to listen to her lungs. After he'd laid Ellie on his bed and given her clothes to wear—despite the fact she had her own just next door—Devil had run to the gym and beaten a punching bag with his bare fists while he waited for Dr. Layton.

But now they were alone and Devil had some things he needed to get off his chest.

"Don't you ever do that to me again, Ellie. That's almost three times now I've been afraid for your life."

Ellie averted her eyes and played with a loose thread on his comforter. "I know, Dev. I'm sorry. I should've stayed home—"

He was in front of her and lifting her chin in two strides. "No, you don't know the terror I went through when I realized you were gone. The panic that almost gave me a heart attack when we realized you were at Burgess's. The way my heart *ripped open* when the fucking roof collapsed in on that house. You don't know—"

"I know..." Ellie's caramel eyes widened with tears and her lip trembled as she tried to look away. "I'm sorry. I get it—"

"No, you don't get it." Devil tightened his fingers on her chin to keep her from looking anywhere but at the sincerity on his face. "You couldn't because... I haven't told you yet."

She tilted her head in question. "Haven't told me what?" She bit her trembling bottom lip and his desperate need for her shot straight to his cock.

Using his thumb, he tugged her lip from between her teeth

and bent to meet her gaze. With one hand on either side of her hip, he caged her in before brushing his lips against hers and pulling back to look in her eyes.

"That I felt all those things because I was so scared of losing someone else I care for. Someone I love." He cupped her jaw with one hand. "Especially before I even got the chance to tell her."

Ellie's breath hitched and he took the opportunity to dive in, to drink her in like the water his body was so parched for ever since that damn fire. Adrenaline still raced through him, mixing in with the relief she was safe and *alive*.

He threaded his fingers into her hair, loving that it was already down so he could twist the tendrils in his grasp. His other hand lifted her ass and she encircled his waist with her legs. Just like everything else about them, their bodies were already so in tune with each other that she seemed to know what he wanted before he had to ask.

With her in his arms, Devil climbed one knee after the other and laid her out on his bed, gently so she wouldn't be jostled.

He bent to her ear and bit the lobe before growling, "I need to be inside you, Ellie. I need to feel how fucking alive you are."

"God, yes, Dev. Please, I want you."

Without wasting another second, he stripped her down completely, tossing the clothes to the side before doing the same with his tank top.

When she lay back against his pillow, he kneeled between her inviting legs. Ellie gulped and he grazed the column of her neck with his fingertips as she swallowed. She reached for him and he intercepted her hand with his before continuing his trail with the other to trace the valley between her breasts. They were already a warm, rosy pink from the fire and desire for him.

"Need to feel your skin against mine." He blanketed her body with his and whispered over her lips before sucking on the plump bottom one that always drove him crazy. Dancing his tongue against hers, he swallowed her gasp as he teased her nipples into peaks with his fingers.

Leaving one last deep kiss with her lips, Devil dipped down to capture one of her pretty rosebuds in his mouth and his hands curved underneath her soft mounds.

"These..." He sucked a peak into his mouth and swirled around the bud with his tongue. When he'd earned a breathy moan, Devil flicked his tongue over the bud the same way he had her clit, and loved the way she whispered his name as he let the soft mound escape his lips. "These are the perfect size for my hands. When I see you, my fingers ache to tease them into hard diamonds." He blew at the wet peak, playing out the fantasy he described and rolled the other between his fingers.

Pushing her breasts together until they almost touched, Devil left small nips around each bud, trading back and forth. When he released them, he continued open-mouthed kisses along the outline of her breasts. His fingers pinched her buds and she hissed his name in pleasure underneath him.

She squirmed and dug her fingers into his shoulders before wrapping her legs around him. From his position, her wet heat against his abs promised warmth as she began to undulate under him, no doubt searching for him to fill her.

Ellie trembled and moaned his name into a whine. Knowing she was ready for more, Devil gave her a final wet kiss on each nipple before spanning his hands across her torso and sucking a wet path down her body. When he got to the golden curls between her legs, he dove his nose in and breathed his own shower gel mixed with her natural essence. "I've been dying to taste you again."

He dove his arms under her legs and positioned her over his shoulders before spreading her center with his fingers. "Your pretty clit's glistening for me, baby." Using his tongue to trace her slit, he chuckled against her as she writhed and moaned under his attention. When she almost wriggled out of his grasp, he tapped her clit with his fingers and she yelped with surprise.

"Stop moving, angel." As if his words controlled her movements, she went limp in his hands and he smiled when her fingers held on to the bedspread for dear life. "Good girl," he whispered and smiled against her pussy as her breaths came in pants.

"Remember, our rooms are soundproof. I want to hear you scream my name." Devil shifted his elbows on the bed, propped her ass in his palms, and used his hands like a table for his feast. He massaged her entrance with his tongue before he pulled her hips closer to his face so he could pierce his tongue deep inside her.

Ellie called out his name and tugged at his hair in a painful grip making Devil close his eyes as his cock wept from the tip. He swiped his tongue up her center, drinking in her sweetness before laying her back down, taking a finger and pushing it into her tight channel.

"Fuck, baby. I want the first time you come tonight to be on my cock, but I want you to be ready for me more." He caressed the inside of her pussy. "Although... you're soaked for me, aren't you?"

"Yes, Dev, please... I want you inside me. I'm ready." Her breathy moan went to his cock as she lifted her head to watch him and bit her lip.

He grinned, but shook his head. "Not yet. But you will be."

She *was* ready, but he wanted her to be so blissed out when he entered her for the very first time that she only felt pleasure. With that goal in mind, Devil stroked her clit with his tongue at a new speed until her body started to tremble.

She clamped her legs around his head and he slapped her ass to get her to relax, loving the yelp she gave him. He curled his fingertip up to focus where she was most sensitive, ready to hear her scream so he could finally push inside her. Grinding his slacks against the bed, he almost groaned out in frustration at the lack of relief. Nothing else would do at this point except for her tight grip. But he had to wait.

When Devil added a second finger, she squeezed hard on his hair. Little pinpricks of pain from her blunt nails digging into his scalp made him harder. A long moan escaped her and he sucked her clit between his lips before vibrating his tongue against the tight little nub.

"Dev!" At the scream of his name, she trembled around him and he let her ride his face until she collapsed back against the bed. When she finished, her gorgeous face was flush from her orgasm, but her hungry eyes said she was ready for more.

"Dev please. I need you inside me."

"Believe me, I need that more than you right now." He stepped off the bed to pull off his slacks and boxers. When he was naked, her eyes went wide and he palmed his cock. "Baby, you mentioned before... I'm clean, but I've got condoms—"

She shook her head. "No. I want to feel *you*. I trust you."

Devil gave a swift nod. Of course, he would've done whatever she wanted, but fuck was he glad she wanted to go skin to skin with him. He rubbed his shaft roughly up and down, spreading the moisture from the tip to help him slide inside her. Not that he needed it. She was already dripping for him.

"Before we do this, I need to tell you..." He climbed over her and settled between her legs. Lining his cock up with her pussy, he dipped shallow strokes at her entrance to soak his shaft in her arousal. He pushed back her hair to watch her face as he tested how deep he could go before he met resistance, making sure he didn't thrust until she was ready. "I'm so fucking proud of you. You fought tonight. I'm not ready to hear the whole story yet. But I know you fought for your life and goddamn am I grateful."

He smiled, hoping he was showing her what he felt for her before he said it. "I heard you yesterday before you fell asleep." Her eyes widened with surprise and her cheeks tinged pink. "I heard you and I should have told you then, too, but you were braver than me." He brushed his lips over hers before whispering in her ear. "I love you, angel."

At the same time as his confession, he gripped her hip with

his free hand and on the last shallow dip of his cock inside her, he pushed into her tight wet heat. She drew in a sharp breath and he grabbed her lip with his, sucking it in as he stayed still inside her. Her channel squeezed around him like a vise, prompting him to moan against her lips. He'd never been bare with anyone before and fuck, did it feel like heaven inside his angel.

"Tell me when I can move, baby." His breaths came out in shudders as his entire body fought not to come on the one thrust.

She settled her hands on his shoulders and wrapped her legs around his back before taking what seemed like a fortifying breath of her own.

"I-I'm ready."

Devil dragged his cock out of her tight sheath before easing back inside her, already holding on to his release by a thread. Ellie moaned his name low and he couldn't stand it anymore. "Fuck, Ellie, I'm trying to be gentle, but I almost lost you tonight." He kissed up her neck and whispered into her ear. "I need to feel you come alive on my cock."

His name moaned on a breath was his only response and he began to move inside her at a harsh cadence. Despite his warning, he gauged her reaction to make sure she wasn't in pain. Each plush muscle squeezed his cock like a fist as he plunged inside her. Still, she hung on to him, her eyes closed in rapture as she whispered *yes* under her breath. Her fingers dug into his back as her legs clamped against his ass, helping him keep a swift pace.

His woman was a fucking natural at knowing exactly what he needed. She moved against him, her lithe body meeting his, stroke for stroke. Pleasure rippled down his spine with every thrust, threatening to make him spill inside her too soon, but from her quickening pants he could tell she was seconds away.

Letting go of her hand, but keeping his speed, Devil cupped her jaw before tracing her neck. "One day I'm going to choke you while I come inside you. Would you like that, angel? Being completely at my mercy while I fuck you?"

Ellie's breath hitched as she nodded before giving him a delicious moan, "Yes, sir..."

"*Fuck*, baby. That fucking word." Holding her collarbone, Devil left his thumb in the vulnerable little valley between her neck and her chest and used the angle to his advantage. He pulled back, and pushed into her tight sheath at a punishing speed, working to get that spot deep inside her.

"God, oh, God."

"Not, God, my angel." He thrust in and ground against her clit. "I'm your fucking Devil."

"Dev!"

"Good girl." His words came out in a harsh breath as her body vibrated against him, choking his cock inside her tightening channel. "That's it, baby, come all over my cock. Let me feel how alive you are."

Her body danced against his as she gave in to her release. The bottom of his spine tingled until he lost all the control he possessed. His speed grew slow and inconsistent until he grabbed her ass and tugged her body flush to his, leaving no space between them. Light flashed in his eyes and he was blinded by the pleasure.

"Fuck, angel," he growled as he came, still dragging his cock in and out as her pussy milked the last drops of his cum. When he was spent, he collapsed over her, barely catching himself before he fell.

He stayed inside her and flipped them over to lay her on top of his chest. As he brushed his lips over her hair, he lifted her head up by her nape so he could kiss her sweet mouth again.

"I don't think I'll get over seeing it, you know."

Ellie peered down at him between the lashes of hooded caramel eyes. "See what?"

He stroked his thumb down her cheek and took a mental

picture of the soft, sated smile on her face. The one he was quickly becoming addicted to seeing.

"Heaven, angel. I see Heaven with you."

CHAPTER FORTY

Soothing warm cinnamon filled Ellie's nostrils. Her eyes fluttered up and she breathed in the scent as she slowly came to realize she was lying on Dev's bare chest. Strong arms wrapped around her tighter in confirmation.

"How're you feeling?" His chest rumbled under her cheek as he spoke. He began to rub slow circles on her back, making the T-shirt he'd given her to wear roll up under his hand.

"Fine, actually." Ellie lifted her head from his chest and pulled at the T-shirt fabric. "This yours?" She smiled at her joke, knowing good and well it was, but she wasn't prepared for Dev's eyes to wrinkle with worry.

"Yeah, do you not remember?"

Guilt pricked her heart and Ellie tried to laugh it off, but the huffs turned into a cough. "Of course, I remember everything. I was teasing you, silly."

And she did remember everything. Even the parts she wished she could forget.

"I wish we'd stayed and waited for Virginia to wake up." She'd been rushed into surgery for her bullet wound and loss of blood. Ellie would've stayed there all night if Virginia's parents hadn't told her to go home and rest.

Dev slipped his hand up her shirt and continued the circles on her bare back. "The doctors said she needed sleep. Besides, her parents were there."

"You're right." She sighed. "They needed their privacy."

Dev nodded and continued his smooth circles, making Ellie shiver.

"You cold?" He sat up against the headboard and tugged her close before pulling the covers up to her neck.

"Around you?" She giggled. "Never." His skin scorched hers every time they touched, burning underneath her skin in ways a fire never could.

"Just making sure. You've been through a lot. It'd be okay, you know, if you wanted to talk about your feelings or anything."

His stilted—but sincere—offer to talk made her grin, until she remembered their fight at the hotel. She felt a frown form on her face as her muscles tensed. Rolling her shoulders back, she tried not to show how much her thoughts were affecting her, but as always, Dev saw right through her.

"Come on... what's on your mind, angel?"

Ellie raised her head from his chest again and sat up. Dev's arm fell loosely at her hip. "I was in a fire last night."

"Yes you were." He sighed, his eyes were downcast and full of... what, guilt? Worry?

"And I got myself outta there..."

"Yeah... what're you getting at?" His head tilted as it laid against the headboard.

"I can take care of myself, ya know."

Dev cocked his head and huffed out a laugh. "I know that."

"You taught me how to, and I used everything you taught me to get outta there all on my own. And with Virginia. I saved us both. And..." She braced herself with a deep inhale and slow exhale. "I saved myself yesterday, and you didn't even think I could handle even knowing about the party yesterday."

Dev's brow furrowed and he sat up until his back was flat against the headboard. "Angel, what're you talking about?"

"I know you told everyone to be quiet about the party so I wouldn't find out. Did you really think I couldn't handle even knowing about it?"

He shook his head slowly, as if he was trying to catch up with her logic. "No..."

"I've been working hard on myself. In training. In therapy. You have to believe in me sometimes!" Ellie raised her voice, trying desperately not to sound too emotional and sticking with logic. The best way to get through to Dev.

"You're right... and I do."

"And—wait... you do?"

Dev laughed and shrugged while he shook his head. "Yeah of course I do. Why do you think I don't?"

"I-I thought you told the Crew I wouldn't be able to handle knowing about the party... isn't that why you didn't tell me about yesterday?"

Dev frowned again. "You keep saying that... I don't know where the hell you got that idea, baby. But what it sounds like to me, is you didn't hear the whole conversation *and* you were somewhere you weren't supposed to be..." He raised his eyebrow in accusation and Ellie felt her cheeks redden.

"That's beside the point."

He nodded. "Fair. But, if you'd listened to the whole conversation, you would've heard me say I thought if we told you anything, you wouldn't be able to handle knowing without insisting on coming to the women's rescue at the hotel. Which is *exactly* where I didn't want you to be."

"Why not, Dev? I could've been there for the survivors to help them know they were finally safe and you've taught me how to fight."

Again, Dev adopted a look of confusion before agreeing with her. "Of course you do."

Ellie stopped again. "Okay... then what's the problem? Why didn't you want me to come help? I'm more than capable of holding my own."

"Aside from the fact that defending others is an entirely different animal than defending yourself and that you're well-trained by a professional, but not a well-trained professional, and that you have emotional ties to this situation, *and* that I was going to call you immediately after we saved those women to let you know that we needed you at Sasha Saves... I can't lose you, Ellie." He shook his head. "It wasn't that *you're* not capable. But I knew *I* wouldn't be able to stand it if something happened to you. That kind of fear has no place in a mission."

"Oh." She didn't know what else to say. Last night when he'd spoken to her soul and told her how he felt, she'd half convinced herself that was his adrenaline talking, or an amazing dream after a really god-awful nightmare. "I-I'm sorry. I never even thought of it that way."

Dev stroked her cheek with his fingertips. "I meant what I said last night, baby. If things went south on a mission I was on, one where I'd felt like I was in charge of your safety? Shit, Ellie, if I lost you, that'd fucking end me. I love you, Ellie."

Ellie's heart literally skipped and she squeezed his hand. "I love you, too, Dev." Dev gave her one of his small smiles and leaned in for a kiss and swept his tongue against hers. He wrapped his hand around the back of her thigh, pulling her to straddle him. Her sensitive skin tingled in anticipation, needing a repeat of last night. He threaded his fingers through her hair and pulled her in just as his bedside table vibrated.

"Shit... That'll be the meeting."

"Meeting?"

"Yeah." He leaned over and grabbed his phone and typed in his password. "Yep. Meeting in the war room."

"Oh." Ellie tried not to show how disappointed she was that he was leaving already. "Will I see you after?"

He whipped his head up from the phone. "What, you're not coming? Do you have class or something?" He looked at his watch. "Wait, no it's Saturday."

Ellie laughed and shrugged. "What am I supposed to do? Go with you to an official BlackStone meeting?"

He raised an eyebrow as he nodded, like she was supposed to know the answer already. "Yeah, baby. Don't act like you haven't listened in on one before." At his wink and teasing smirk, she rolled her eyes. She could already tell he was never gonna let her eavesdropping stunt go. "It's our after-action report. You were part of the action."

His words meant literally nothing to her. "Uh... you're looking at me like I'm supposed to know what that is."

He huffed and started talking as he climbed out of the bed, butt naked—*how had it not registered that he was naked this whole time?* —before pulling on gray sweatpants. She could see the outline of his cock as he turned around and Ellie felt her cheeks redden.

"...make sense? Baby, you listening?" He laughed. "Like the sweatpants?"

She looked up and knew her cheeks were officially red when she saw the smirk on his face. "I-I'm sorry, what were you saying?"

Dev's eyes narrowed as she bit her lip and she couldn't help but notice the length in his pants began to tent.

He adjusted himself. "Fuck, yeah maybe sweatpants aren't a good idea."

"Um, disagree. Sweatpants are *always* a good idea."

He laughed at her assessment and she joined in until both of them ended with short coughs. "Unfortunately, we'll probably be able to behave if we keep hacking up lungs." Dev reasoned with a grimace. "What I was saying is, an after-action report is a meeting where everyone on the team recaps the mission, or the action, so to speak."

Ellie tilted her head and frowned. "But I wasn't on the mission."

"Might as well have been," he joked. "Go, get changed. I'm sure they'll want to hear how everything went down. Once you start telling your story I won't have to worry about my sweatpants."

"Why's that?" Ellie asked as she got up, smoothing Dev's T-shirt down over her bare butt.

He pulled a Henley over his head and scoffed. "I imagine hearing how you were abducted, *again*, will make me want to go on a killing spree. My name might be Devil, but I don't get off murdering people. I'm fucked in the head, but not that fucked." He opened the door and peered his head outside. "Go get changed. I'll wait for you to go to the meeting, but be quick. Hawk's a stickler for punctuality."

"Is the coast clear?" Ellie asked.

Dev barked a laugh. "Yeah, but apparently we haven't been as sneaky as we thought. Everyone knows about us. But as much as I'd love to see you only in my clothes, I think that'd be pushing it with your brother."

Ellie's jaw dropped and she felt her skin flame. "Jason knows?"

Dev nodded. "Yup. Even gave his blessing."

She rolled her eyes. "Not that we needed it." Her brother's take on protectiveness was so outdated.

His small smile made her belly flip. "That's exactly what I said. It's better this way though."

Unable to argue with his logic, Ellie stood on her tiptoes and gave him a quick kiss and a smile before she went to her apartment next door. She changed into her staple black leggings, with a normal long-sleeved T-shirt covering her butt. She put on socks with skid pads and opened the door to see Dev leaning against the wall, already chewing gum.

"Ready?"

"Yep, let's do this."

They made it to the "War Room," as Dev called it, with a minute to spare.

"Glad you could join us," Jason muttered and her cheeks heated as she realized everyone was already there.

Like, *everyone*. The rest of the Crew, including her brother, Jules, Nora, ADA Aguilar, Officer Brown, and heck, even Naomi was there. It was a tight squeeze with all the people, but Dev led her in and pulled out a chair beside Jason for her before standing behind it.

"You two beautiful gems live in this complex and you were still the last ones here... how is that exactly?" Nora smiled and Ellie couldn't hide her grin, ready to turn Nora's teasing right back at her.

"I don't know, Nora. How was your lunch date with Matt?" Nora scowled as Ellie giggled. It was going to be so fun teasing Nora about her new boy *friend*.

"Let's get started men... I mean... everyone." Hawk cleared his throat. "I'll start with the mission..."

He recounted the events at the party, much of which Ellie had heard in the war room the day before. According to Hawk, they'd saved eight women, caught two Russians red-handed, and Mitchell Strickland. The new information lifted a weight from her shoulders she hadn't realized she'd been carrying all that time.

"Mitchell Strickland must be the man from last year," Ellie offered.

Hawk nodded. "Devil told us."

"That's why he's in the hospital right now." Phoenix laughed and nodded toward Dev as he leaned back on two chair legs. "Good ol' angel of death."

"What?" Ellie whipped her head at Dev who at least had the decency to look contrite.

"I may or may not have let fate decide what would happen to Strickland."

"What's that mean?" Ellie asked, annoyed Dev was choosing then of all times to be cryptic.

"It means he knew exactly where to put a bullet to keep him alive and also make him wish he was dead," Phoenix answered and Ellie narrowed her eyes at his attempt at dark humor.

"You shot him?" She turned her glare on Dev. "But you promised you wouldn't shoot him."

"I said I'd do my best not to *kill* him." Ellie shook her head at his reasoning, but Dev just shrugged and smirked at her. "What do you want from me? I did my best, El."

A laugh huffed from her at her words from their training session two days ago getting thrown back at her. She was tempted to make a sassy retort but ADA Aguilar spoke up.

"He's in the hospital for at least the next few weeks, but he'll live," ADA Aguilar offered. "He'll be using a colostomy bag in prison, but he'll live."

"Well, at least we'll see justice for Sasha," Ellie said.

"And justice for the other survivors." Nora's voice lowered and she looked at Ellie with soft eyes and a small smile. "Like you, babe. You deserve that, too."

Ellie felt her eyes prick. It'd been a year. A whole year and nothing had been done at all. She knew BlackStone had been working on finding the true culprits of the trafficking, understood that a bigger picture was at stake, that justice takes time, but the silence had been deafening. She was glad they were finally on track.

"The other two were also served warrants and are currently in jail without bail. I'll be doing my damnedest to make sure that's the case for all these *cabrónes*." ADA Aguilar's voice hardened at the end.

"Ellie, what we want to know is how you got mixed up with Burgess." Hawk propped his elbow on his crossed arm and tapped his lip

"Yeah, what the actual fuck happened?" Jason looked as if he was going to ask more but Dev's chest rumbled.

"Show her some respect. Ellie didn't just save her own life, she also saved Virginia's. She deserves to be treated like a hero, not a child."

Ellie's heart fluttered that Dev came to her defense and she was sure the moisture stinging her eyes was going to escape at any moment. But she rolled her shoulders back and cleared her throat, intent on telling them the whole story. How the investigator, or Burgess as they called him, had kidnapped her by shooting and using Virginia as leverage. How he'd seemed sick and was talking to his dead wife.

"Sheriff Motts thinks Burgess had early onset dementia. He wasn't even supposed to be at the party yesterday, apparently," ADA Aguilar offered.

Ellie noticed Snake's brow raise, but she wasn't sure of the reason, only that she disagreed with the prosecutor. "I don't think it was dementia," Ellie explained. "Investigator Burgess was gonna let me and V go, but he got a visitor."

"A visitor? Who?" Hawk straightened and crossed both arms.

"A Russian guy named Vlad. H-He's the same one who kidnapped me. Probably you too, Nora."

Everyone looked to Nora and she paled before she swallowed and spoke in hushed tones. "Then he's the same one who shot Drake... Wh—What happened?"

"He gave Investigator Burgess drugs, I'm very sure they were drugs. I watched him shoot them up in his arm." Everyone in the room swore. "Then Vlad took pictures of Burgess's board he had in his living room and set everything on fire."

"What the fuck, that's messed up," Officer Brown said. "I-I thought he'd overdosed and accidentally set his house on fire with that damn lighter he's always flickin'."

"Was he alive?" Jules asked.

"He's not now," ADA Aguilar muttered and Ellie's heart cracked at the heavy blunt finality in the statement. Investigator Burgess was sick, not evil. Or at least she hoped.

She swallowed before speaking again. "I don't think he was alive when the fire happened. It seemed like whatever he shot himself up with either put him out, or was... bad. I'm pretty sure he was gone before the fire was started."

"How did you get out?" Jason asked in a quiet voice, as if he wasn't ready to hear what she had to say.

Ellie recounted how she got out of handcuffs, duct tape, and got Virginia out of the pantry and into the root cellar, and how Dev found her after she'd fought her way to the surface. When she finished, everyone in the room but Dev had varying expressions of shock. His hand rested on her shoulder and he drew small circles on the back of her neck with his thumb.

"Well, I'll be damned." Phoenix said. "Hawk, we got any openin's? Might could use a pretty face around here other than just mine and Devil's. Oh, and sweet baby Nora's, of course." He shot a teasing grin at Nora.

Jason smacked him in the chest and the jokester shot his arm out and grabbed the table to catch himself from falling from his two chair legs.

"Nope, no siree, absolutely not," Nora laughed and crossed her arms. "I've retired from the game, boys. You'll have to drag me back in, kickin' and screamin'."

"I am curious, Devil," Hawk began. "How did you know she was in there? I didn't even notice the root cellar door, but you were right there seconds before she escaped. It was flat to the ground and covered with dirt. Did you hear her?"

"Yeah, how did you know?" Ellie looked back at him to see confusion written on his face.

He scrubbed his beard and tilted his head at his teammates. "I heard you screaming, 'in here, in here.' I'm surprised you guys didn't hear her, she was loud as hell."

Hawk and Phoenix both shrugged but Ellie shivered and turned around to look up at Dev.

"You heard me screaming 'in here'?"

Dev nodded and laughed. "Yeah, it was hard to hear over the fire but when I saw the cellar door, I realized I wasn't just hearing what I wanted to hear. Then I saw you pushing your way through the doors to get out."

Ellie pursed her lips in thought and turned back around. She didn't recall screaming anything, except when she was exerting all her strength on pushing up the door. But maybe she wasn't remembering it right. It all seemed to be a blur.

"Can we circle back to something?" ADA Aguilar asked.

"Sure, take the floor," Hawk offered.

ADA Aguilar turned to Ellie. "You said he had a board in his living room?" Ellie nodded. "What was on it?"

Ellie wracked her brain to remember. "I didn't get to see it much. The Russian said their boss wouldn't like it... and he said a few things in Russian I think I remember, hold on." Ellie scrunched her eyes closed and tried to remember back to hearing Vlad talk on the phone. "He said something on the phone like... 'he knows too much' and 'it is done.' From where I was it sounded like he was talking about the investigator, and... maybe Vlad did something about that."

Her belly twisted up and she felt queasy, thinking the investigator might've been poisoned after all, but tried to remember the other thing she'd heard. "The investigator was obviously working with them though. The Russian guy said the boss was pleased with him for working so hard for... *someone.*" Ellie frowned, trying to understand the word but caught back up when she realized it couldn't have been English.

ADA Aguilar's brows raised. "For who?"

She shook her head hoping it would rattle the words free from her memory bank. "Vlad said Investigator Burgess had done good work for..." She searched her mind for the Russian word he'd said but she couldn't remember it more than sounding it out. "I wish I'd studied better, but it sounded like uhlayuh... yactuh... est, or something—"

"Alea iacta est?" Snake asked, animated as he turned in a circle to the computer, not even waiting for Ellie's agreement and nearly bumping Naomi beside him in the motion.

"Um, yeah. Sounds like it, I guess. Then Vlad looked at the board, I think. Investigator Burgess said he was 'keeping tabs on people for Rusnak' but then Vlad said the boss wouldn't like it.

Investigator Burgess begged him not to tell. Guess that doesn't really matter now."

"Sorry, Ellie, but did you say 'keeping tabs on people for Rusnak'?" ADA Aguilar asked, and Ellie nodded slowly.

"Excuse me." ADA Aguilar pulled his phone from his pocket as he walked out. "Agent Kuo, yes ma'am, it's Aguilar. I need your guys to search the station..."

The door closed behind him and the room was silent for a moment before Hawk spoke. "Well, if that's everything—"

"Hold on." Snake typed three keys hard and the screens all filled up with various articles. "*Alea iacta est*, it means something close to, 'The die has been cast.'"

He turned to them proudly, but the room was silent. "Well, it's a Latin phrase, originally from the Greek, attributed to Julius Caesar when he crossed the River Rubicon—"

"Ugh, no one cares, Snake. Get to the juicy meat." Phoenix pulled his ball cap around and used the bill to cover his face before acting like he was asleep. "What does it mean in connection with all this?"

Snake narrowed his eyes. "I don't know yet..."

"It's somethin' though, isn't it?" Naomi asked. She leaned closer to Snake but seemed careful not to touch him. "I mean, it's somethin' you can look into, right Wes?"

Ellie's brows raised.

'Wes?' Interesting.

"You're right," Hawk muttered before tapping his lips. "It's something to look into. We'll add it to the list. Is there anything else to cover?"

Everyone grumbled in the negative. "Alright. As you were men—I mean, ladies and uh, gentlemen."

"Smooth," Nora laughed before everyone stood up and milled around.

Jason came up to Ellie and pulled her into a hug. "You okay, El? Promise?"

Ellie smiled and let him hold her for as long as he needed.

He'd done good giving her space, even though Ellie knew it had to have been killing him inside. "I'm okay. Dev's been taking care of me." She gave Dev a sideways glance and grinned at his blush.

Jules bumped Ellie's shoulder and gave her a knowing smile. "He's been doin' that from the beginning, I think." She turned to Ellie's brother and rubbed her large pregnant belly before leaning against Jason. "Come on, Jay. Your daughter is kickin' your fiancée's bladder and if they both don't get a cheeseburger ASAP there *will* be hell to pay."

Jason laughed and gently wrapped his arm around Jules, as if he was afraid she might literally pop if he handled her too roughly.

"See ya, El. Devil, take care of her." Jason tilted his chin up at Dev before lifting an eyebrow at Ellie. "I don't want to have to hear about you getting kidnapped again." Jules gave Jason a playful slap and turned him to exit the room.

Dev glanced at Ellie and her skin tingled as his fingertips trailed down her arm and squeezed her hand before yelling at Jason's back. "I don't think we'll have to worry about that. Haven't you learned by now?" He grinned wider than Ellie had ever seen him as he looked back down to her. "She can take care of herself." He squeezed her hand and brushed his lips over her forehead. "Isn't that right, angel?"

Ellie smiled and squeezed back. "Yep. But it helps to have the devil on my side."

EPILOGUE

One week later

"El! Are you ready? Your boy's eatin' all our food in our kitchen! Hey, I was watchin' that!"

Virginia called to Ellie from their kitchen like she wasn't ten feet away in her adjacent dorm room.

"Hawk said there's about to be an update." Dev's low grumble made Ellie smile.

She'd moved back into her dorm after the fire. Figuring if she could get out of a burning closet with her hands tied behind her back, she could handle a ten by ten–foot room. Naomi and Thea had also needed the BlackStone apartment to stay at after—

Ellie shuddered. She couldn't think about that. Everyone was safe now and that's all that mattered.

Besides, on top of everything else, Ellie had wanted to move back because she'd missed Virginia and wanted to give the friend thing a good ol' college try, literally.

"Ugh, I can't stand to watch the news ever since I became a current event myself. Now give me back my remote or I'll—" It sounded like something was thrown and when Virginia grunted, Ellie cringed, hoping her friend hadn't hurt herself. But that was much more likely than her throwing something hard enough to injure Dev, especially in her state.

It'd been a week since the fire and Virginia was looking at being in a sling for at least five more. The doctors said the bullet was a through and through near her shoulder, and she was lucky to have any function at all in that arm. She'd need physical therapy for the next few months to get back to normal, but they'd warned that normal might not be realistic.

"Don't you know we're college kids?" Virginia huffed. "Why ya gotta eat us outta house and home ya lil' devil."

Ellie snorted at her friend's attempt at scolding and smoothed down her golden empire waist dress. She'd bought it with Virginia at a store Sasha used to be obsessed with.

"You woulda loved this one, Sash."

Ellie listened into the silence and felt a sad smile grow on her face. She hadn't heard Sasha's voice since the fire, but she was at peace with it. Something told her that night was the last time she'd hear from her. Her therapist reasoned Ellie had grown in her therapy to the point that she'd moved past depending on a mental discourse with a fictitious iteration of her best friend. She'd also explained that all the conversations she had with her best friend were Ellie's thoughts, but she'd used Sasha's voice as a coping mechanism.

Ellie knew all that was bull.

Without Sasha, Ellie and Virginia would be the ashes of burned toast about now. Ellie couldn't help but think how Dev claimed to have heard her yelling from the cellar. She'd turned her memories over in her mind thousands of times and she knew without a shadow of a doubt she hadn't yelled for him. Whether it was in his head or not, Ellie wasn't sure, but she chose to believe Sasha had helped save them. Ellie closed her eyes and thanked her friend again, but was at peace with the silence.

She opened her eyes and turned in the mirror on the back of her door and nodded once to herself. "Ready." Ellie walked out of her dorm room and into the kitchen suite. Dev was ridiculously good-looking in a navy button-down, tie, and slacks. He also looked just plain ridiculous sitting in their small dorm-issued chair at their small dorm-issued table.

"Girl, you look sexy as hell. And I would kill for those shoes."

Virginia whistled and adjusted her sling, grimacing when she apparently moved it wrong. Yeah, she'd definitely hurt herself. Ellie winced in return but Virginia snapped her fingers and pointed at her.

"Hey! Stop it right now, girl. At least we're alive."

At least we're alive.

Ellie swallowed and smiled before she turned on her gold heels. "Speaking of which, you *should* love these shoes. These were the ones I was wearing that night."

Call her sentimental but Ellie had taken those shoes to a cobbler the following Monday to have them fixed. They were a little darker gold than when she'd bought them, but again, she'd been able to save herself from a burning house with her hands tied behind her back in them, so heck no she wasn't going to just throw them away.

"Goddamn, angel." Dev leaned back in his chair and scrubbed his beard before seemingly snapping out of whatever he was thinking. "Um... these are for you. They, uh, made me think of you."

He shoved a bouquet of marigolds at her and Ellie hid her smile behind them as she smelled their sweet scent. It reminded her of her shampoo she loved so much. She lowered the flowers to thank him, but he was looking away and fiddling with his cream tie.

"Is the devil nervous?" Virginia teased and his face went three shades darker. "Haven't you ever been on a date before?" Virginia laughed until Dev's light skin was practically maroon with embarrassment. She gasped and covered her mouth while Ellie bit her tongue, not entirely sure how to save him. "What? No... you've actually never been on a date before? Holy shit."

"Har, let's all laugh at the twenty-seven-year-old date virgin."

He waved his hands and got up from the chair. "Let's go, angel. We've got dinner and a movie to catch—"

"—This just in, Andrew Wilton Ascot, the Third, is now the third Ashland County elite to be implicated in the Ashland County Human Trafficking ring."

"Hold up, turn that up," Ellie commanded Virginia but took the remote and did it herself, unable to stop staring at the TV.

Plastered on the left side of the screen was a picture of a man who looked exactly like an older version of the Andy Ascot she'd known, the one who'd helped save Ellie and had died for her brother. In the background, ADA Aguilar spoke with an officer while more officers and federal agents carried boxes out of the Ascot, Rusnak, and Strickland building.

"Mitchell Strickland was arrested the night this news team first reported the trafficking ring that has been insidiously invading the county. Ashland County residents would be surprised to know who's on the suspect list. Thanks to the hard work of police officers and district attorneys, they are drawing up arrest warrants for more of Ashland County's more influential residents as we speak. Ascot is the second member of the law firm that seems to be at the pinnacle of it all and officers are on their way to arrest him now.

"Federal agents are still looking for this man..." A picture of Dmitri Rusnak filled the screen. He looked incredibly familiar, but Ellie couldn't place his face.

"Authorities believe Dmitri Rusnak is one of the leaders in the trafficking ring, but this news team has to ask just how far up the ladder this ring goes. Are the authorities *part* of the problem —Oh—Assistant District Attorney Aguilar! Do you have a moment?"

The news anchorwoman ran up to ADA Aguilar as he finished shaking a crime scene investigator's hand. ADA Aguilar turned to the camera and pasted a winning smile on his face, but even Ellie could tell from the crinkles around his eyes he was stressed.

"Assistant District Attorney Aguilar, can you comment on the rumors that Ashland County Sheriff's Department's Investigator Burgess was in the thick of this trafficking ring?"

ADA Aguilar's wince was slight, probably not even noticeable unless you knew him. "From what we can tell, Investigator Burgess was heavily involved in the inner workings of the trafficking ring, but in what capacity we're not sure. We think Dmitri Rusnak might've been blackmailing Investigator Burgess. But it should be known that thanks to Investigator Burgess's meticulous notes, reports, and body camera footage of numerous phone calls with who we believe is Rusnak on the other line, we now have a clearer picture of who has been involved in this case."

"And that's a good thing I take it? Even though he was working for them... he was helping Ashland County?"

Aguilar shook his head. "Whether Investigator Burgess was keeping records to put these guys behind bars or whether he was trying to blackmail them back, we're not sure. But what I do know is, we have a lot more people we are looking into, and when we find Dmitri Rusnak, his case is gonna be a slam dunk. Thank you, that's all the time I have—"

"Wait! Sir, people are wondering how long this has been going on. Can you tell us if Investigator Burgess was part of the trafficking ring *last* year?"

ADA Aguilar sucked in a breath and shook his head again. "All I can say about it is, it looks like he only got in deep with the human trafficking side recently. It seems as though he was mostly involved in the drug trade that Rusnak also has his hands in. Maybe he was as surprised as the rest of us about the human trafficking and how entangled it is with the Ashland elite, but he was too wrapped up in it to get out. We're not sure at this time. Thank you, that'll be all today, Morgan. Thank you for your work at Channel Seven."

The anchorwoman's mouth fell open as ADA Aguilar walked away. "Oh, uh, th-thank you, sir." She turned a slightly flushed face toward the camera again. "Well, AC listeners, we'll be keeping you updated here on—"

Ellie turned off the TV before looking at Dev and Virginia's stunned faces. "Well, dang."

"Sounds like Burgess was a fucking double agent," Dev grumbled in disbelief.

"Something like that," Ellie said, her voice quiet, too stunned to know what to do with herself.

A large, strong hand grabbed both of hers before squeezing. "Still want to go, angel? I know bringing stuff up can be—"

"I'm fine, just give me a second first." Ellie curved her free hand over the one Dev was using to hold hers. She took a deep breath and mentally repeated the mantra she now used to center herself.

I am safe. I am in control. I am here, in this moment.

She opened her eyes and saw Dev's small smile.

And I'm happy.

MEANWHILE

He turned the flat screen TV off and slammed his fist down on his home desk, glad he'd decided to take a sick day. It surely would've left a dent at his work desk. He wiped his face with his hand before looking at the pathetic man he'd mistakenly depended on.

"You fucked up. *Again*, Dmitri. I told you we needed to be discreet this time. Fewer women, not the party. But you went and fucked it up with that stupid little group of yours insisting on fucking tradition."

"I'm sorry, sir."

Is he crying? Pathetic.

"The BlackStone group... have you given me the dossier on them?"

"Uh... yes sir. We worked on compiling it. They and a deceased teammate were part of a paramilitary team that operated under a clandestine branch of the military—"

"Yes, I fucking know about MF7. Do we know anything about them since they were kicked out of MF7?"

"Yes, sir. I'm sorry, sir. They've entered private security and since we uh, accidentally kidnapped one of the team's sister, they've had it out for us."

"You know..." He massaged his eyes, sore from having to look at the sniveling incompetence in front of him. "Just a thought, Dmitri. But, it would be in your best interest not to remind me of more of your fuck-ups when I'm already reaming your ass for this one."

"Yes, sir. I'm—"

He slammed his hands down again. "Are you a fucking broken record, Rusnak? I don't need sorrys. I need answers. I don't need mistakes. I need results. I have buyers wrapping a noose around my neck and sellers looking to bury us. We don't have the luxury we did years ago of eliminating competition. And product is harder and harder to come by these days even on the drug side since you've gone and shit all over that too. That fucking imbecile cop blew your whole fucking cover."

There was silence and he sighed. He turned to look at the man and saw he was white as a corpse.

Good.

"What would you have me do if you were in my position? Hm? You fucked up yet another auction. You revealed both of our operations in Ashland County, which was one of our most prolific counties thanks to your stupid little club. And now your cover has been blown." He templed his hands and leaned on his thumbs, before softening his voice and using the same soothing tone he did on his wife when she tried to leave him. "What should I do?"

"I'm sorry, sir. It won't happen again."

He nodded and laid his hands flat on the desk. "You're right, Dmitri. It won't." He nodded at the Russian behemoth who was somehow still hidden in the room. The man was the perfect employee.

Dmitri followed his gaze and turned to see his maker, the weasel turned back to him and got on his knees and fucking begged.

Disgusting.

"Please, sir. Please. It won't happen again. I swear! I-I can get new buyers and we'll get new product. Please sir, I beg you, I have a son—"

"And I have a brother. But you won't see me giving him any more chances either." The Russian held up his gun and Dmitri looked back and forth at the Russian and him before he screamed.

"Please, sir, *no*! I have a family!"

"What is it your people say? You've 'passed the point of no return?' I'm sorry, Dmitri, but my hands are tied."

He nodded and the gunshot deafened him as it went out. Small splatters of blood coated his desk and he took out a hand-kerchief to wipe his face of the failure on the floor.

"Thank you, Vlad." He stood up. "Please see that this gets cleaned up."

"*Da, ser.*"

"Oh, and Vlad? I think you know what to do with the rest. We can't have any loose ends."

The Russian holstered his gun under his coat. "*Da, ser.* No more problems."

∽

-THE END-

∽

Breaking Conviction Coming September 13, 2021

ALSO BY GREER RIVERS

Conviction Series

Escaping Conviction

Fighting Conviction

Breaking Conviction – September 13, 2021

Title TBA - Releasing Winter 2021

Ashland County Legal Short Stories

A Tempting Motion: An enemies-to-lovers, office romance

Thank you for reading!

Please consider leaving a review on Amazon, Goodreads, and Bookbub!
Even just one word can make all the difference.

BE A DEAR AND STALK ME HERE

Be a Boss Babe and join my Facebook group
Greer Rivers Babes
Sign up here to become an ARC reader
Subscribe to my newsletter
TikTok
Instagram
Amazon Author Page
Goodreads Author Page
Facebook Author Page
Bookbub
Website

ACKNOWLEDGMENTS

I'm a words of affirmation girl, so bear with me. I love to give shoutouts and I'm super blessed which means there's a TON of gratitude to go around but it's impossible to mention everyone without writing another 110k words. The tl;dr version of this is: if you know me, I'm more thankful for you than you could ever know.

First, and almost foremost (sorry, the hubs is always my #1), thank you READERS! The dream makers and Boss Ass Bitches. I know your time is precious, so to have you spend it on something I wrote is a true damn honor. If you are also a booktoker/bookstagrammer/faithful reviewer, holy crap, let me just tell you that you make an author's world go 'round.

Hanging out with y'all is why I do this and I love hearing from readers: good, bad, or ugly, although admittedly I'm always fingers-crossed for good. You rock my world with your encouragement and I'm truly so surprised every single time someone says something pretty about my words. I wouldn't be able to pursue this dream without y'all so thanks for making my dreams come true!

To Marisa at Cover Me Darling: Thank you so much for putting up with me! I was a stressed out wreck and you held my hand while making a cover that was better than I could dream of!

Many thanks to Elle McLove, my editor at My Brother's Editor, and Rosa Sharon, the Fairy Proof Mother: Y'all are the freaking best and I'm so thankful to keep working with MBE. Elle, I'm so sorry I tortured you this round, but I need you to still love me and make my shit pretty. Rosa, it makes my damn life when you say you like something! PS I also need to get your addresses so I can send y'all well-deserved tiaras!

To FC's alpha and beta readers:

Payson, Jessica B., Lee J, A.V., Salem, Ashleigh, Whitney, Kristen, Randi, Sierra, Jessica S., Carrie, Janet, and Melissa

This book would be an absolute disaster without y'all. Payson, your tough as nails alpha reading is literally making me a better writer, and no matter how many tears I cry, that one 'The part above this is GREAT!' comment made it all worth it. Thank you betas for telling me 'plush mounds' was an icky description (I agree, idk what I was thinking), reminding me about the bike, breaking it to me when something sucked, and reassuring me with pretty words of your own. I couldn't do this without y'all's compliment sandwiches and you were exactly what I needed to publish this book. I was terrified and your encouragement helped me keep going. More than that, I feel like I've made some great friends and that means everything.

To my TikTok author friends: Many of you have been encouraging as hell and also hilariously fun to get to know. Booktok is my people and I'm so glad I joined and met all you other thirsty bitches. This has been such an incredible journey and I am so very grateful to call y'all my friends! I can't wait for ORLANDO! It's gonna be the bomb.

To Lee J: You are the sun, my friend. Thank you so much for loving me even though I'm your Simon Cowell alpha. I'm so proud of you and so excited to continue our writing journeys side by side. Thank you for telling me my words are pretty and being gentle with me when I need it. This one was rough for me to write, but you kept me going and I freakin' love you for that and so much more.

To Kayleigh: Girl, I couldn't do this without you. Thank you for putting up with my *constant* bitching and stressing and meeting me on that level when I need it (#spiralsquad), but also picking me up when I need that, too. Our deadlines are crazy and I am PUMPED to accomplish all the goals we dream about at 1AM EST. You are seriously one of the best friends a girl could have and 1. I can't wait for the beach, and 2. I can't wait to keep being friends with you.

To my OG BABs/Dinner Divas: Katie, Sydni, and Liz: For some crazy reason, y'all accept me for my flaws and keep loving me through my crazy. Including you guys, I can count on one hand the people I feel confident in being totally myself with. I'm not crying right now, I swear...

Thank you, Katie, for being the type of bestie who lets me be unapologetically me. Idk how you always intuitively know what I need or how I'm going to react, but I'm so grateful for it. Thank you for always texting me ahead of time to let me know where to park and I'm so glad that Goose and Evie are the best of friends, aka not enemies.

Thank you, Sydni, for being the type of bestie who not only remembers I don't like olives, but makes a whole 'nother damn batch of pasta salad without them. It was fucking delicious. On the way home that day, I teared up because I was so over-whelmed at your thoughtfulness with *everything*. It's honestly healing to have an awesome friend like you and so encouraging to have you in my corner.

Thank you, Liz, for being the type of bestie who never gives up on getting me out of the house. There are literally days I can't remember when I've left it, but I try my best to always say yes to you. I never, ever expected to have a book release party but you selflessly planned and threw the best one I could ever ask for. Drunk chatting with you in the back seat while we waited for them to get pizza will forever be one of my favorite hazy memories.

I've never had a solid group of ride or dies until y'all, and now I'll never go without. I'm so thankful to have friends that come up with excuses like book release parties with tiny red paper shoes and dog birthday parties in order to drink the rest of a wine advent calendar. Next time we go to that Alice in Wonderland gin restaurant with food just as tiny, let's get a burger first, then dessert after.

To my wonderful family, my momma, sisters, BIL, and precious baby angel face niece: if y'all ever read this, I'm sorry I've been MIA writing 110k word book in a month. In my defense, y'all know good and well I'm a "dilly dally" and you're deoxyribonucleicly obligated to still love me. May you always and forever be my oblivious supporters. I love y'all with all my heart but I mean it with all sincerity when I say please, for God's sake, do not read my books. If you are in these acknowledgements because you have indeed read a book or two, well, sorry-not-sorry and hope you enjoyed it, at least, lol. Keep your judgments, but I'll take your prayers. Lord knows I need them.

To Maria: the fact that you read my books is a testament to what a kickass therapist you are. I firmly believe that when everyone is born we should be assigned a therapist and I'm so grateful I lost my mind at the perfect time that I got to have you as mine.

To Athena, you crazy bitch: I wouldn't have started writing as a form of therapy if you hadn't driven me insane. Let's not do it again, shall we?

And finally, to the hubs: You are my "Mighty Alpha," first reader, TikTok approver, cliff jump pusher/catcher, favorite encourager, IRL book boyfriend, best friend forever, and the love of my life. You are literally the first person to ever tell me a story I wrote was good enough to send out in the world and you never let me give up on this one even though my confidence was shot to hell. I am so incredibly thankful for you believing in me

100% and encouraging me when it was crazy and not financially sound to do so. You've saved my life and you've changed it for the better. I wouldn't want to spend a moment of it without you. Thank you for making every day an HEA.

Love,

Greer Rivers

ALL ABOUT GREER

Greer Rivers is a former crime fighter in a suit, but now happily leaves that to her characters! A born and raised Carolinian, Greer says "y'all," the occasional "bless your heart" (when necessary), and feels comfortable using legal jargon in everyday life.

She lives in the mountains with her husband/ critique partner/ irl book boyfriend and their three fur babies. She's a sucker for reality TV, New Girl, and scary movies in the daytime. Greer admits she's a messy eater, ruiner of shirts, and does NOT share food or wine.

Greer adores strong, sassy heroines and steamy second chances. She hopes to give readers an escape from the craziness of life and a safe place to feel too much. She'd LOVE to hear from you anytime! Except the morning. She hates mornings.